C0-AZR-641

Search for Love

First of Three Volumes
in the Trilogy

God, a Man, and a Woman

by

R. Edward Wheeler

Lost Coast Press
〰
Fort Bragg, CA

Search for Love
Copyright © 1998 by R. Edward Wheeler

All rights reserved. No portion of this book may be reproduced or transmitted by any means, mechanical or electronic, without written permission from the publisher.

ISBN: 1-882897-25-0

Lost Coast Press
155 Cypress Street
Fort Bragg, CA 95437

Phone: 707-964-9520
Fax: 707-964-7531

www.cypresshouse.com

Cover photo of Jean Harlow
courtesy of Marilyn Monroe
Westin Editions, Ltd.

This work is dedicated
WITH LOVE
To you, the reader, and to Jesus Christ, who gave Himself
for us, that He might deliver us from
this present evil world.

WITH REPENTANCE
Toward my wife, whom I loved too much too soon; to my
sons,
whom I failed as a father, and to their mother,
whose trust I betrayed.

WITH GRATITUDE
To Dwight Hervey Small
Nora Fox / Nancy Cannon
Richard Crutchfield
Therese Howes / Maria Mahoney
and
Arby the Locksmith

WITHOUT WHOSE HELP
This story might have been buried in the dungeon of despair
Without ever being told.

And the Lord God said, It is not good that the man should be alone; I will make him an help meet for him.

And of the rib, which the Lord God had taken from man, made he a woman, and brought her unto the man.

— Genesis 2:18, 22
The Bible

(HAPTER ONE

⇒ It was half past high noon, on the third of October, at the world's most unusual prison. From a desk in my cellblock in the west wing of the prison, fifth level, I was about to carry out, for the last time perhaps, a routine requirement that I had dutifully observed for the preceding 12 years—add some personal sentiments to a birthday card for my wife, Florence.

The sombre setting for this romantic ritual was the Maynard B. Gray prison in Lansing, Michigan, U.S.A. It was a T-shaped three-winged structure, eight stories high, having none of the conventional restraints designed to prevent prisoners from escaping. There were no bars on the windows, no armed guards or searchlights, and the prison was just a five-minute walk from the downtown business district of Michigan's capital city—population, 230,000. In fact, it was a prison only to me. To all the other residents of the city, as well as to out-of-town visitors, the Gray "prison" was just a modern state office building of glass and suntan concrete, housing the Michigan State Highway Department. But after eight years on a dead-end clerical job in the Highway Department's Right of Way Division, I felt a stifling sense of imprisonment about my job, as surely as if I had been surrounded by steel bars.

I brushed the crumbs of a hurried, vending-machine lunch from my desk adjacent to the open doorway leading from the hallway into the Engineering section, and spread out the birthday card for my wife. Perhaps surveying the card again would

1

nudge my depressed state of mind into a creative mood. From behind me came the slap of playing cards on another desk, and the alternating groans or chuckles from four other Highway employees who gathered every lunch hour for pinochle around the desk of Homer Scroobie, portly Right of Way Engineer. But before I could get my mind in gear for the domestic duty confronting me, my mental musing was broken into by the stentorian voice of Caleb Sterne, chief Right of Way Engineer, from behind me.

"Hey, Gar . . ."

I swung around in my swivel chair to face him as he approached from the alcove at the back of the long room where his own desk was located. Decked out in a bow tie, plaid sport coat, and with a topcoat slung over one arm, he was obviously leaving for the day, as he frequently did on Friday afternoon.

". . . where the Hell were you ten minutes ago?" he demanded, stopping by my desk. "There was a long distance call for you. I didn't see you, and none of the guys knew where you were."

I looked up the lean, six-foot frame of the Chief Engineer, my boss, into the square-jawed face, topped by silvery hair, with gold-rimmed glasses perched on a jutting nose that would have befitted a Roman general.

"I had to run downtown and get a birthday cake, Caleb," I explained, pointing to the white, square box on top of the file cabinet near my desk, "my wife's birthday is today. Do you know who it was that called?"

"No. It was some lady. She wouldn't give her name, just said she'd call back later."

The probable identity of the caller flashed through my mind, but I dared not voice my suspicion to Caleb. I turned my eyes away from his curious, probing gaze, lest he see some hint of the sudden flurry of ambivalent emotions that his announcement had stirred up within me.

"Thanks, Caleb."

"That's all right. Wish your wife a happy birthday for me,

Gar," he said, turning away, "and have yourself a good week-end."

But as Caleb turned to step through the open doorway leading into the hallway, he jerked to a stop and threw up his arms protectively to avoid a forceful bodily contact with Hubert Funke, his assistant engineer, who came rushing through the doorway at that moment.

"Hey, watch it, Hubert," Caleb exploded indignantly, as the two faced each other in the open doorway, "one of these days somebody is going to get hurt the way you come through that door."

I sat there a moment, turned toward the doorway as an amused spectator of their dialogue and starkly contrasting dimensions. Caleb was tall and lean; Hubert was short and fat. I was somewhere midway between both of them, in regard to both measurements and age. Caleb was older than my 42 middle-aged years, and Hubert was several years younger.

"Sorry, Caleb," Hubert apologized, "I just wanted to be sure I caught you before you left in case you had any special instructions for the afternoon."

"I'm glad you asked me," said the Chief Engineer, looking down at his chubby assistant, "there is something you can do."

"What's that, Caleb?"

"See that white box on top of the file cabinet by Gar's desk?" he queried, pointing.

"Yeah, what about it?"

"Well, that's got a birthday cake in it for Gar's wife. Just keep an eye on it and make sure none of these chow hounds in here try to get into it."

"That shouldn't be any trouble," said Hubert, confidently. "Was that all you wanted me to . . ."

"One other thing," cut in Caleb, shifting his topcoat to his left arm, so he could point with his right arm to the card players gathered around Homer's desk. "That damn card game is supposed to stop at one o'clock. And don't let these guys goof off in here this afternoon just because I'm gone."

"Don't worry, Caleb, I'll keep 'em humping."

"You better," Caleb responded with mock severity, "or Monday morning your name will be 'mud' instead of 'Funke.' Hell, maybe that would even be an improvement."

With a chuckle of self appreciation at his witticism, Caleb stepped out into the hallway and disappeared from view. But Hubert had no need to be fearful of Caleb's threat, even if it had been serious instead of facetious. For by Monday morning Caleb Sterne, a picture of robust health as he left that day, would be dead.

Hubert stepped on into the Engineering section room and paused by my desk.

"So this is your wife's birthday; right, Gar?"

"Yeah, but I think the cake is safe, Hubert. Don't worry about it."

"Well, I hope you don't make the same mistake I did on my wife's last birthday."

"What happened?"

A mischievous grin spread across Hubert's cherubic face as he began to relate the instructive episode.

"Well, I was the one elected to put the candles on the cake and I accidentally put on three too many. When my wife saw it, if we hadn't had company in the house, I know I would have gotten that cake right smack in the face. And I'll guarantee you, I never heard the last of it; probably never will."

"I'll try to remember that, Hubert," I grinned, in response to his infectious chuckle. "Thanks for the warning."

Hubert passed on to his desk at the rear of the room, adjacent to that of the Chief Engineer, and I turned my attention again to the domestic ritual that had become traditional in the twelve years of my marriage to Florence. In recognition of each other's birthday, as well as those of our three sons, we had always exchanged birthday cards, frequently a present, and always a birthday cake with candles. Then, trying to push from my mind mingled feelings of both anticipation and apprehension about the impending long distance phone call from an unknown caller, I stared at the cover of the comic birthday card I had picked out for my wife earlier that morning from the concession stand in the lobby. The colorful seascape on the cover, showing a half-submerged mermaid, her breasts discreetly hidden by long hair, had obviously been designed to attract the male eye, while the sentiment inside was aimed at a supposed female recipient, whether girl friend or wife.

"There may be lots of fish in the sea . . but you're the only one for me."

As I pondered the blatant hypocrisy in even this humorously worded avowal of love toward my wife, my misgivings were shattered by the shrill ring of the telephone from behind me. With my desk abutting the very front wall of the Engineering section, the conversations, the actions, the sounds, were always behind me. The jangling sound momentarily froze both my mind and my body. Was this the expected long distance summons from an unidentified caller that Caleb had mentioned? I knew it was not a call for Caleb. His personal phone was on his own desk at the rear of the room. The one that had just rung was closer, on the desk of Edgar Harwart, an engineering aide, and was used for incoming personal calls to employees in the section.

"Damn it to Hell!" I heard Edgar explode behind me as he got up from the card game at Homer's desk to step over to the phone on his desk. "Every time I get a good hand, that damn phone rings. Don't people know we stop for lunch around here?"

The insistent ringing stopped as Edgar picked up the phone and spoke in a more softly modulated voice.

"Right of Way Engineering . . . yes, just a minute, please."

Then Edgar called my name.

"Gar, it's for you. Long distance."

With a sudden surge of excitement mingled with some apprehension, I got up and stepped back to Edgar's desk, a short distance behind my desk, and picked up the phone.

"Hello?"

"Is this Mr. Garfield Roby?" asked the female operator.

"Yes."

5

"Just a moment for long distance, sir." Then to the party on the other end, "Go ahead, please."

The honey-soft voice that I heard next, and the intimate greeting, shattered my composure, even though I had rightly guessed who the caller might be.

"Garfield, is that you, darling?"

Pressing the phone receiver hard against my ear in an instinctive attempt to keep the voice at the other end from being heard by listening ears around me, I turned my back on the circle of fellow employees crowded around Homer's desk. I hoped that none of them had seen the sudden flush of embarrassment that I had felt suffuse my face at the intimate salutation.

"Yes, this is Garfield," I replied tersely, choking back the words of endearment that welled up within me, hoping to convey an impression to those around me that this was an impersonal business call.

Conflicting feelings flooded through me. I wanted to speak aloud the cherished name of the woman who had spoken my name in such loving accents, yet I didn't dare. Some of my fellow employees knew that my wife's name was Florence. The very sound of the sensually exciting voice at the other end had filled my heart with a spurting geyser of joy; yet I was also irritated that this call had come to me at the office, in violation of my previously expressed wishes.

"I know you asked me not to call you at work, darling, unless it was an emergency," the silken voice continued, "but I just thought you'd want to know that I'll be taking the early Greyhound bus from Detroit. I'll be arriving in Lansing two hours earlier than I said I would in my last letter. It was so hot and stuffy in my room that I thought I might as well get an early start. It's always more comfortable at the Roosevelt there in Lansing than it is here in Detroit. So if you can get over to see me earlier, we'd have more time together. But if you can't, I'll understand and I'll be looking for you at the regular time. I just thought you'd like to know."

"I'll be over as soon as I can," I replied, as brusquely as if

I were setting up an appointment with a life insurance sales-man, "probably between six and seven."

"Thank you, darling," the melodious voice continued, knowing the reason for my formality of tone and expression. "It's so wonderful to hear your voice again. It's like you're very close to me instead of a hundred miles away. I love you so, and I've missed you so. I thought this week would never come to an end. And I know you can't say anything like that to me right now because there are probably other people near you, aren't there?"

"Yes, that's right."

As I listened, I was thankful for the covering conversation going on among the four card players at Homer's nearby desk.

"That's alright then, sweetheart. I can wait until we're together so you can tell me in person. But come to me as soon as you can. I can hardly wait, I'm so hungry to see you and hold you again."

"I'll be there as soon as I can," I repeated, trying to keep out of my voice the irritation I felt at being put into an emo-tional straitjacket; unable to respond as I wanted, to the woman on the other end of the line; sounding so close, yet a hundred miles distant.

"Then so long for now, my beloved, and God bring us together soon."

"So long. See you later."

I hung up the receiver with a genuine sigh of relief that the frustrating mixture of pain and pleasure was ended. I stepped back to my desk, noting by my watch that I still had ten min-utes left of my lunch hour in which to finish writing out some seemingly sincere but innocuous expressions of a love for my wife, Florence, that no longer existed within me. I sat down at my desk again and pulled open the middle drawer to look for a red felt pen with which to add a festive touch to the greeting card. It might help conceal my lack of real feeling for the occa-sion.

But as I rummaged in the drawer beneath a miscellaneous mixture of office supplies, my fingers felt the hard edge of a plastic tag attached to a key. Momentarily diverted from my original intention by curiosity, I pulled the key out from under a clutter of papers. As I held the key up before my inquiring gaze, recognition and remembrance flooded through me. I had forgotten that I had hidden the key there several months before, but I would never forget the circumstances connected with it. Feeling at once a tug that drew me back to scenes related to the key, yet impelled to finish Florence's birthday card in the few moments left of lunch hour, I slipped the key into my pocket. Later, on coffee break, I could again review the bittersweet scenes associated with it.

After further groping, I found the red felt pen I had been seeking, closed the desk drawer, and again got back to the domestic duty that had already been interrupted twice in the closing minutes of my lunch hour. But as I again tried to focus my thoughts on the birthday card for my wife, my feelings and mental images were drawn irresistibly, like metal filings to a magnet, to the long distance phone call and its implications for that night. And to escape the mental prospect of the conflicting demands that would be imposed upon my time and loyalties that evening, I let my thoughts wander beyond the narrow boundaries of my own constricted life, to a contemplation of current events in the larger world beyond that had been fed into my mind earlier that day in a hasty scanning of the daily newspaper.

The recent news reports underscored the impression in my mind that, in many ways, the year of my wife's thirty-fifth birthday was an auspicious year in the world. It was the year that Lyndon B. Johnson occupied the White House in Washington, in the wake of John F. Kennedy's assassination. Khrushchev still ruled the Kremlin in Moscow, and the Cold War in Vietnam was still hot. Martin Luther King was planning civil rights demonstrations in the South, and George Romney was in his third term as Michigan's first Republican governor in 20 years. Against this turbulent national background, a trivial truth loomed larger in my mental foreground.

This was a festive day for most state employees. It was

"T.G.I.F." day—Thank God it's Friday. I was vaguely aware, also, that for many other Americans across the nation, the third of October that year was a day of national significance. An Indian summer day, with the temperature in the 80s, it was ideal for the final baseball game in the World Series being played in Boston that day between the St. Louis Cardinals and the Boston Red Sox.

But finally, after several minutes of mental wool gathering around the world and back, a glance at my watch, showing only five minutes left of my lunch hour, impelled me to resolutely fix my attention on the yet unmarked birthday card on the desk before me.

"Damn," I muttered under my breath, as I applied the red felt pen to the greeting card, "why did she have to come on Florence's birthday, of all nights?"

With no answer forthcoming to my rhetorical question, I forced my fingers to scrawl a terse comment across the bottom of the card.

"Happy Birthday, Florence, from your ex-boyfriend, Gar."

With that necessary ritual finished, I replaced the greeting card in its envelope, got up and tucked it under the string that enclosed the birthday cake box on top of the file cabinet by my desk. And with lunch hour ended and the card game at Homer's desk breaking up, I turned again, with a sigh of soul suffocation, to the routine and trivial tasks I had learned by rote in my eight years as a lower echelon clerk in the Highway Department.

As I pulled from a mail basket on my desk a sheaf of forms requesting copies of various highway road plan sheets, from other state agencies, property owners, or attorneys, I heard a portable radio on the desk of Edgar Harwart, behind me, being turned on. Evidently, in the absence of Caleb Sterne, the Engineering section was going to be treated to a vicarious participation in the most newsworthy athletic event of the year.

"Turn your radio up a little, Edgar," called Hubert Funke from the back of the long room, "I can't hardly hear it."

"Me neither," piped up Elwood Jassey from the back row of drafting tables.

As Edgar complied, the strident voice of the sportscaster doubtless carried the thoughts of most of my fellow workers away from their tedious tasks to a great sports stadium in Boston.

"Today, under sunny skies, there are 34,000 baseball fans jammed into the stadium at Fenway Park to watch the final game of the World Series between the . . ."

As I tried to block out the sound of the sportscaster's voice and focus my mind on the papers on my desk, my lack of interest in this great national sporting event probably set me apart from many other ball fans across the country as being an un-American American. But somehow, I could not get excited as Cardinal pitcher Bob Gibson stepped to the pitcher's plate that day; partly because of my ever-present sense of vocational imprisonment; and partly because I stood on the verge of the breakup of a family, which would lead me into a traumatic test of dividing my loyalties that very evening.

But in addition to this internal turmoil being added to the sounds of the radio behind me as distracting factors, my eardrums were also abruptly assaulted by verbal static from another source.

My desk abutted a partitioning wall that separated the Engineering section from the Excess Property Unit on the other side. A two-foot gap between the top of the partition and the ceiling made the partial wall a barrier to sight, but not to sound. Over the top of the partition, like a tennis ball bouncing over a net, came ricocheting the strident speech of Wally Woolwimp, black, buck-toothed assistant supervisor of the Excess Property section. His animated account of his recent honeymoon trip to Mexico collided in the air above my head with the staccato shouts of the sportscaster and roar of the crowds at Fenway park coming from the radio, accentuated by exclamations of chagrin or elation from fellow employees in the Engineering section.

Feeling that there were too many distractions, both internal and external, to allow me to concentrate on the paper work on my desk, I decided to turn to one of my alternate routine tasks. Getting a handful of red lead pencils and a ruler from my desk drawer, I got up and stepped over to a spare drafting table near the windows which I used for part of my clerical operations, a job that required only minimal mental effort. Laying down red pencils and ruler on the gently sloping top of the drafting table, I hoisted myself up onto the tall draftsman's chair that resembled a cushioned bar stool.

Spread out across the top of the table was a large road plan sheet such as were made up for every area of federal or state highways on which the Highway Department was working. As part of my job, I had to perform a less than skilled operation that was identical to that done by most kindergarten-age children in their school coloring books. I had to shade in red the needed parcels of land that had already been acquired by the Highway Department; parcels that were in the process of being acquired by court litigation had to be marked with diagonal lines. This visual record keeping enabled engineers and attorneys and property appraisers to determine at a glance how much land had yet to be acquired to complete a particular area of highway construction. But in all the years I had been performing this routine task, I had never felt any elation or satisfaction at doing well, at the age of 42, what I had once done almost as well when a child in kindergarten.

Nevertheless, resolutely turning my mind away from the troubled evening ahead of me, I tried to ignore the first inning excitement of the last game of the World Series, mingled with Wally Woolwimp's animated description of dog racing in Mexico, to play again the role of a vocational kindergartner.

It was more than two hours later that I had worn the sharp points of half a dozen red lead pencils to a blunted roundness. As I was about to get up, not only to sharpen the pencils, but to stretch my muscles as well, a lusty shout of salutation hurtled over the partition in front of my drafting table, penetrating the radio crowd sounds from behind me like a battlefield mortar shell. It exploded against my eardrums with a warning of imminent danger, even though I had not heard my own name mentioned.

"Hi Wally, you old son of a gun you, how are you?"

The detested and familiar voice hailing Wally Woolwimp on the other side of the wall in front of my drafting table was that of a former temporary employee in the Right of Way Division who had left his job in the Highway Department to resume an interrupted college education in preparation for a law career. It was the voice of garrulous Gary Goforth, with the piercing gaze of a prosecuting attorney, the too loud voice, and painfully personal questions, evidently back for a social visit. For weeks after I had graduated from Michigan State University in the spring of that year, he had dogged me with questions whenever he would see me; in the file room where he worked, in the halls, the rest room, the cafeteria, and on the elevators.

"Any job nibbles yet, Garfield?"

Finally, rather than confess to him and other listening ears the dearth of job offers, the one interview failure, and the growing pile of letters of rejection, I had started telling him that I was being deluged with so many good job offers that I couldn't decide which one to accept. Now, I stood before the drafting table, only half hearing the rattling repartee between Gary and Wally, momentarily paralyzed at the prospect of the scene that would surely ensue if Gary should step into the Engineering section to see how the World Series game was progressing. As soon as he saw me, I could anticipate what he would cry out in tones of incredulity, loud enough for everyone else in the room to hear.

"Why, Garfield, old boy, what are you still doing here? Man, I thought you'd be long gone from this place once you got your diploma from M.S.U.!" And after the World Series game was over, I could expect comments and questions from many of my fellow employees, to whom garrulous Gary's blaring announcement would come as gossipy news, heard for the first time. For I had deliberately avoided publicizing my graduation from Michigan State University in the spring of that year, at the age of 42. Gary's noisy newscast of my vocational failure to my fellow employees would be like salt in the wounds of the job rejections I had encountered since graduating.

Seized with a sudden determination to avoid such a painful episode before fellow workers in the Engineering section, with after-effects that might linger for months, I grasped for any legitimate reason I could think of to leave my work area for as long as possible to avoid such a confrontation with noisy, nosy Gary Goforth. I stood up by the drafting table, intending to vacate the premises before Gary could finish his dialogue with Wally, still wafting over the partition that separated us. A glance at my watch provided the legitimate chance I needed to leave the Engineering section for half an hour at least. It was 3:15, time for my afternoon coffee break, which I could adjoin to an immediately improvised errand in another part of the building.

I stepped quickly back to my desk, unnoticed I was sure, by fellow employees whose attention was focused on the ball game if not on their work, and snatched up a rolled Chronoflex plan sheet original from a basket on my desk. One of my routine tasks was to take plan sheet originals to the eighth floor and have ozalid prints made for anyone who requested them, including property owners, appraisers, engineers, and others. Now was a good time to run this errand and at the same time escape the damning disclosure I faced by remaining in the area.

Like a desperate criminal attempting a jail break under the nose of an inattentive guard, I headed briskly for the open doorway leading out of the Engineering section, with the rolled Chronoflex plan sheet in my hand. Stepping out into the hallway, where I could look into the Excess Property section on the other side of the partition, I cast a furtive, sidelong glance toward the desk of Wally Woolwimp, and was relieved to see that garrulous Gary was standing with his back to me, facing Wally's desk. Hurriedly, I stepped over to the stairway exit door and pushed against it, expecting to hear Gary's accusing voice raising an unholy alarm at my obvious escape attempt. But as I pushed through the heavy door, Gary was preoccupied in firing questions at Wally.

"So how do you like married life, you old son of a gun, now that you've been married two weeks?"

"Hey, man, if I had known it was so much fun, I would have gotten married sooner," came Wally's jubilant reply.

Gary's gregarious guffaw was cut off as the stairway door closed behind me, enfolding me in welcome silence. I raced up the stairway, not slowing my pace until I reached the landing on the next floor. Then, thankful that I had made good my escape without being seen by garrulous Gary, I proceeded on up the stairway at a more leisurely pace to the eighth floor.

On the eighth floor, I walked past draftsmen at their tables to a cubicle at the extreme west end of the wing. In the cramped quarters of the small room, several people stood waiting as Darrell Chitty, who had an even more monotonous job than I did, stood in front of the huge Bruning reproduction machine that occupied one-half of the small room. All day long he stood in front of the machine, inhaling ammonia fumes, feeding original road plan tracings in between the rotating cylinders that could make any number of ozalid print copies from the original.

"Six copies when you get to it, Darrell," I said, catching his eye as I laid the rolled up Chronoflex original into the basket for incoming work orders. "I'll be back in about 20 minutes for them."

"Just a minute, Gar," he said, turning away from the machine to a small desk beside him.

I waited as Darrell, one of the few fellow employees who knew something of my struggle to get through college, pulled out a drawer and extracted a magazine. The other workers waiting in the cramped quarters leaned aside as Darrell stepped over to the doorway of his small room and handed me the magazine.

"I thought there might be something in here that might interest you, Gar."

I glanced at the cover of the magazine as he handed it to

me. Across the top in bold, black letters was the title, "Jobs, U.S.A."

"Thanks, Darrell, I'll look it over."

He turned back to the ceaselessly turning cylinders of his machine while I turned and walked down the wide hallway that led to the elevators, the magazine rolled up in one hand.

As I started to pass the commodious office of Nelson Crumroy, Chief Engineer of Bridge and Road Design, a novel addition to the open visitor's lounge area adjacent to his office stopped me in my tracks.

My attention was drawn to a table, waist high, about five feet square, covered over with a transparent plastic dome, like some futuristic city of science fiction. It had not been there on previous trips to the eighth-floor reproduction unit. Stepping closer, I saw that beneath the glass dome was an amazingly realistic scale model of one of the more spectacular interstate interchanges that the Highway Department was currently building as part of the federally financed interstate highway program. Welcoming any novel diversion that would delay my return to my own work area until I was certain garrulous Gary was gone, I examined with interest the table-top display.

On all four sides of the glassed-over interchange were miniature, realistic replicas of houses, complete with doors and windows, in a life-like setting of sidewalks, lawns, trees and side streets. There were factories with smokestacks and schools. The land area was covered with a green carpet imitation of grass, with the swells and rills of a natural landscape. From all four corners, ribbons of concrete, simulating the highway yet to be built, curved and converged toward the focal point of the display—a tri-level interchange arching above the double lanes of an expressway upon which miniature cars of different colors and styles were spaced at irregular intervals as on a real highway.

As I surveyed the marvelous model of highway engineering in wonderment, I sensed a presence beside me at the same time I heard a familiar voice.

"Quite a piece of work, isn't it?"

I looked up into the angular face and diagonal grin of Nelson Crumroy, who had just stepped out of his office. I looked at the man who had interviewed me for my first job in the Highway Department more than eight years before, noting the white, close-cropped hair accentuated by gold-rimmed glasses. Since our first meeting, he had climbed closer to the top in the Highway Department hierarchy while I had remained close to the bottom.

"Is this the way it's supposed to look when it's all finished?" I asked, recognizing the location of the proposed I-475 and M-78 interchange near the city of Flint, Michigan.

"It will if the goddam contractors follow the specifications on the plans," he snorted, "and that's something you can never count on. Why, Hell, just yesterday I had a man in my office from down near White Cloud where we're widening a state trunk line. He'd just gotten back from Florida the day before and found half a dozen trees in his front yard had been cut down. His neighbors told him the Highway Department did it. So he came storming into my office and wanted to know what the Hell the idea was. He said he hadn't given the Highway Department permission to cut down any trees on his property. So I got out the road plans, and sure enough, he was right. The contractor didn't follow the plans and he cut down the trees on the wrong side of the road. So I sent him to the contractor who was doing the job. I told him, 'Hell, we can't afford to pay for somebody else's mistakes. We make enough of our own.'"

"It must have taken somebody a lot of time to make this model up," I ventured, as we stood looking down at the scenic urban panorama.

"I think somebody told me it took several fellows in the Cartographic section something like 1700 man hours of labor from start to finish."

"What's it supposed to be for? I mean, does it have some practical value?"

"It's going to be set up in the city hall over at Flint," he explained. "I guess the idea behind it was that when some of

16

the business firms that are going to have to relocate, and the city fathers see how this interchange is going to actually help business there instead of hindering it, it may cut down on the property we'll have to take by condemnation. Going to court to get property costs money and takes time, and you never know when a judge is going to rule for you or against you. It's kind of a public relations gimmick more than anything else."

Encouraged by the Chief Design Engineer's uncustomary dalliance and willingness to explain things that really had no vital connection with my job as a lower echelon clerk, I felt emboldened to ask another question that had kept popping up in my mind on previous trips past his office.

"May I ask," I said, nodding in the direction of his office, "who the distinguished looking gentleman is in the picture behind your desk? Is that your father, by any chance?"

"Hell, no!" he expostulated, grinning crookedly at being suspected of such filial sentimentality. "That old geezer is Horatio S. Earle, the founder and first commissioner of the Highway Department, starting back in 1905."

He followed the direction of my gaze through the open doorway of his office to the portrait on the wall behind his desk.

"Quite a character," he commented admiringly, "I guess he had a helluva time getting a road building program started in this state. He had to go out and campaign among farmers to get their support for a road building program. I've heard that at one place, after a discussion at the Town Hall, the farmers in one community said to him. 'Mr. Earle, after talking it over, we've decided that we don't need any new roads.' So Earle told them that in a different township on the other side of the state, he asked all the horses and jackasses to vote as to whether they wanted roads built or not. He said, 'All the horses voted "yes," but the jackasses voted "no."'"

With that, Nelson Crumroy turned and stalked away, chuckling to himself, having spared all the time he could in a moment of informal camaraderie with a lowly clerk whom he had inducted into the state bureaucracy nearly a decade before. I continued on in the opposite direction to the elevator that would take me to the basement cafeteria for a coffee break that could delay my return to my work area on the fifth floor for at least another twenty minutes.

As I waited for the elevator, the hum of a motor from somewhere down the hall grew louder, approaching the place where I stood. A moment later, a motorized wheelchair appeared around the corner, driven by a sparse, middle-aged man with unruly hair and dark glasses, whose useless legs were pulled together at the knees in an unnatural conjunction. I immediately recognized Benedict Godwin, an attorney with a whole mind but half a body, who worked in the Attorney General division of the Highway Department.

"Hi, Ben," I greeted cheerily.

He looked up at me with a sickly semblance of a grin.

"Hi, Garfield," he gargled, in a hoarse voice that seemed as if it were forced up through a pipe in his throat with great effort.

He brought the wheel chair to a smooth stop near me just as the elevator doors opened. I stepped quickly onto the elevator and pushed the button that held the doors open while Ben zoomed onto the elevator with such speed that I winced, expecting him to ram the back panel. Instead, he stopped just as his toes touched the back and elevator doors closed.

"Want to push six for me, Gar?" Ben rasped, looking up at me like a sparrow with a broken wing, his head tilted at a peculiar angle.

"Sure, Ben, be glad to."

I pushed the button for the sixth floor and as the elevator started descending, I watched admiringly as Ben swung the wheel chair around so that he was facing the doors, ready to exit without wasting time maneuvering the motorized wheel chair or running the risk of hitting someone if he backed out in reverse gear. As the elevator stopped on the 6th floor, I tried to cover over the pitying concern I felt for Ben's physical infirmity with a facetious warning.

"Ben, I think I should warn you," I said, holding the elevator doors open, "that if you don't slow down in that wheel chair around here, you're going to get a ticket for speeding one of these days, and you might lose your driver's license."

"Thanks, Gar," he replied with a gargling laugh, and disregarding my advice, shot off the elevator like a race car driver at the Indianapolis 500 races.

As the elevator continued its descent toward the basement cafeteria, my thoughts lingered on the pathetic sight I had just witnessed, momentarily pushing from my mind my apprehensions over the prospect of a humiliating encounter with garrulous Gary. Perhaps I was affected more deeply than many of my fellow employees by the sight of Benedict Godwin in his wheel chair because my own mother had been confined to a wheel chair for the preceding twenty-five years, and still was, as a victim of multiple sclerosis.

Then, my pitying speculations about the crippled attorney, afflicted in the same way as my mother, ended as I stepped off the elevator in the basement, and entered the wide promenade that led into the subterranean world of the Gray building cafeteria, the culinary kingdom ruled by Gus the Greek. Here, I could find a place of refuge where I could delay for another twenty minutes my return to my fifth-floor cellblock, where the risk of a public exposure of my academic success but vocational failure awaited me.

Moments later, in the basement cafeteria of the huge office building, I was seated at a table that abutted the west wall of the spacious employee eatery, with fewer than half a dozen other employees scattered around the huge dining area that accommodated two to three hundred people during rush hours. Allowing my pot of tea a moment to cool, I turned my attention to the magazine Darrell Chitty had given me on the eighth floor moments earlier. Picking it up I noted that under the bold title, "Jobs, U.S.A." on the cover, was a smaller announcement that even after all the rejections I had met within the broadcasting and film industries, had the power to kindle my immediate interest. The few words I saw had the power to momentarily revive within me the slowly dying hope that I would ever achieve anything vocationally that was better than what I presently had—the status of a clerk in a great state agency. In a small box in the lower right-hand corner of the cover was the announcement that this particular issue of the weekly magazine contained "a special listing of employment opportunities for persons forty years old and over." That was me!

With suddenly aroused interest I opened the magazine to the index, then to the page numbers listing the actual job opportunities for persons forty years old and older. But as I began to scan the list of jobs being held out to the "40 and over" class, my interest began to evaporate as rapidly as it had been ignited. The kinds of jobs that were available were none that I either wanted or felt qualified to do. There were openings for truck drivers, security guards, gas station attendants, night watchmen, and male nurses at mental institutions. But there was no mention of any positions in the fields of radio, television, or film production in which I had acquired skills through five grueling years of part-time university attendance. There was no hint of a need for a documentary film producer or a radio script writer or an assistant program director at a TV station.

I laid the magazine aside and poured a stream of steaming, amber-colored tea into my cup beside several packs of salted crackers. Could this be the reason that I was still just a lowly clerk in the Highway Department, I pondered, sipping my tea slowly—just because I was past the age of forty in a youth-oriented society? The question suddenly reminded me of the key which I had found hidden away in my desk drawer during lunch hour and had slipped into my pocket. I pulled it out and held it up in front of my eyes, gazing at it broodingly, like a police detective trying to unravel a mystery on the basis of a single piece of material evidence.

Balancing the hard, white plastic identification tag between thumb and forefinger of my right hand, pain swept my eyes. I gazed again at the familiar words in bold, green letters inscribed on one side of the tag.

"Auditorium Hotel, Cleveland, Ohio."

I didn't have to scrutinize the key more closely to see the room number engraved on the hard, shiny surface. I knew it by heart and would never forget it—Room 717. As I turned the plastic tag over in my hand, I reread the brief instructions which I had disregarded.

"To return, drop in mail box. No postage required."

It was obvious that in the past, other guests at the hotel, as well as myself, had forgotten to turn in their room keys when checking out. But perhaps to no other guest who had occupied a room in all the years of the hotel's history, had a hotel room there and the key to it meant as much as this one had meant to me. With what high hopes I had unpacked in that hotel room in Cleveland several months before. Now, the key belonged with the letters of rejection in a file at home which I had received from various job applications in the television and film industries. But this one, the job prospect that was intimately connected with this key, had been special. It had been the job I had wanted more than any of the others; and the one I had probably come the closest to getting, to the point of having been called down for an expense-paid interview.

I had not discovered that I still had the key until I had returned to Lansing after the interview. Then I had clung to it, as the children of Israel had kept the brazen serpent that Moses had made in the wilderness, long after it had served its initial purpose. I could not let go of this tangible evidence of how close I had come to finding the vocational niche in life for which I was ideally suited by temperament, talent, and training. The key I held in my hand had been like the key to a different life; a key that had opened a door of opportunity just wide enough and long enough to let me glimpse a wonderland of fulfillment and achievement beyond. Then, soon afterwards, that door had been shut in my face without a satisfying explanation, and with no prospect that any similar door would ever open for me again.

But like Lot's wife, I could not help looking back for a

moment upon the scenes conjured up by that key; a great and distant city where something I had wanted so much had turned to dust before my eyes.

I laid the key down on a corner of the table by the worthless "Jobs Over 40" magazine, with the same feeling of gentle reverence that I might have laid the silent form of a loved one in a casket, as my mind was drawn back irresistibly to a sequence of photo-flash images and sensations that had been evoked by the sight of the key. I felt again the thrill of anticipation I had first experienced when I had gotten the long distance phone call at work, inviting me to come down to a network television station in Cleveland for an expense-paid interview as a potential associate producer for a weekly documentary series at the station.

There swept over me the impact of the hallowed hour I had spent one Saturday night, alone in Room 717 of the hotel, upon my knees, petitioning God to open the door to a new life for me in that city. Then, in swift succession there flitted through my mind, as I sat there in the sparsely peopled cafeteria, fragments from the all-important interview that had taken place on a Sunday morning at the TV station in downtown Cleveland. Looking back to that decisive episode in my life, I watched the interview unfold again. But this time I was both participant and observer, critically evaluating the questions that had been directed at me by Frank and John, co-producers of the program, and the answers I had given them, for it must have been something I had said that had caused me to lose out as a qualified candidate for the prized position.

Something had been said by me that had neutralized the obviously favorable impression that had been created by my initial letter of application. As Frank had told me in the initial phone call summoning me to the interview, out of fifty applicants from around the country for the position, three had been selected for interviews, and I had been one of the three. As I looked back, a vocational researcher looking for the wrong response that had closed the door of opportunity for me, the preliminary exchanges about the weather, my trip there on the train, were passed over as being inconsequential. The showing of my half hour film comedy, "The High Cost of Education," produced as a student, and my only claim to experience in film production, had evoked laughs and favorable comments from the documentary team. It had been the questions that followed that had tripped me up. In retrospect, only two stood out as having been decisive.

"Since you indicated in your letter of application that you were in military service in World War II, Gar, how come you didn't use your G.I. Bill to get through college instead of working your way through?"

Momentarily immobilized at the totally unexpected question, suddenly fearful that a skeleton in the closet of my personal history from twenty-five years before could have a bearing on my getting the coveted job, I had hesitated to blurt out the truth. For sensing that the truth might alienate them and cancel out the favorable impression I had already made, I had sought to buttress my explanation with a cardinal principle remembered from a public speaking course at the university.

"Whenever you are proposing an unpopular position to a potentially hostile audience, try to identify it, if possible, with some well known and respected figure of history."

One singular example had immediately come to my mind.

"Like Sergeant Alvin York of World War I fame," I had begun, placing myself in illustrious company, "I had some doubts when I was inducted into military service about active involvement in the war. But unlike Sergeant York, I arrived at a different conclusion after weighing the pros and cons of direct participation. He at first had misgivings because of his religious upbringing as to whether he should kill someone in combat. But he changed his mind, resolved his moral scruples against killing, and became famous for his battlefield exploits. I decided that I did not have sufficient justification for killing, and after being denied a transfer to a non-combatant unit by my commanding officer, I refused to bear arms, was sentenced to five years imprisonment and a dishonorable discharge. That disqualified me from any G.I. educational benefits after the war."

Speculating about the possible impact of this long-ago episode from my military experience, I wondered if this could have cost me the job opportunity I had prayed for, and prepared for, for so long. Could my confession have sparked concern that at some later date the station and even the network might have come under criticism by zealous patriots or veterans' groups for harboring a traitor to the country, and a military jailbird, on their payroll? I had to admit that this was a real possibility.

Or perhaps I had lost the job, not in the friendly exchange in the plush offices of the TV station, but later; after the film showing and the disturbing question about my military background, where the interview had been continued in an informal setting over lunch. I remembered the fast ride, ignoring posted speed limits, in John's flashy red sports car, along Cleveland's lakefront expressway, to a fancy restaurant called "Pier W." Situated picturesquely on a peninsula that jutted out into Lake Erie, it provided diners with an exciting view of lake traffic, with steamers passing by, and here and there the white, breeze-billowed triangle of a sailboat. Perhaps it had been there, I reflected sadly, at the fashionable restaurant, with Lake Erie blue and beautiful in the background, while muted music blended with cultured voices, the tinkle of silverware and the lilting sound of an artificial waterfall, in a setting of tropical plants and birds, that I had been disqualified by the disclosure of my personal convictions on one particular subject that were derived from the Bible.

"One of the projects we're looking ahead to in the near future," John had confided, broaching the subject which might have killed my chances of being accepted, "is a documentary film about a home for alcoholic priests just outside of Cleveland."

I remembered having been stunned at the disclosure. I had heard of individual cases of alcoholic priests, but had never guessed that there were a sufficient number to have warranted the setting up of a special treatment center for them. John had then proceeded to advise me of the delicate, diplomatic preparations that had already been made for filming such a documentary.

"You see, Gar, although this place is a private facility, operated by a layman, we still couldn't do it without the Bishop of the diocese knowing about it. If we had gone and asked him for permission, he might not have given it officially. So we didn't ask him. We just informed him politely that this was something we were making plans for since the manager of the facility had already given his consent, and several of the priests there were willing to be interviewed."

"And the Bishop didn't object?" I asked, keeping my utter astonishment in check.

"No; since alcoholism is a disease, the Bishop felt that it was right to make this information available to the public, and to show that priests were not immune to this disease."

As we ate, Frank had volunteered fuller details about the upcoming documentary. While I listened to Frank, I was thinking thoughts which I didn't express. Of course the Bishop would not object to such a presentation if alcoholism were presented as a disease. This could be no more of a reproach to a priest than if he had contracted tuberculosis or cancer. But I knew that the Bible declared plainly that drunkards would not inherit the kingdom of Heaven. Would God keep a man out of heaven, priest or not, for getting a disease? Of course not. Then it was clear to me that according to the Word of God, alcoholism was a sin, not a disease. Would I be required, I had wondered silently, if I were working on this project, to select, to slant, to edit material in a way that would ignore and even deny what God had said on the subject? Was this a price I would have to pay in order to get this job which I wanted so much? I felt that a discreet inquiry was in order.

"What happens," I broke in, "if there is a difference of viewpoint in assembling material for a film, like this one about alcoholic priests?"

"Like what, for instance?" Frank had asked, a friendly glint kindled in his eyes at the prospect of an intellectual joust.

"I mean," I began, choosing my words carefully, "if I were working on this film, and I'm not convinced that alcoholism is a disease, and you are trying to present it in the film as a disease, how do you reconcile or deal with the differences in viewpoint among members of the production team?"

"What viewpoint do you have on the subject?" John had asked.

"Well, the term 'alcoholic,'" I began, "is only a new, nicer sounding label for what the Bible would call a 'drunkard.' And the Bible says that drunkards shall not inherit the kingdom of Heaven. Now I'm sure that God wouldn't keep a man out of Heaven just for contracting a disease, like leprosy, or tuberculosis, or cancer. Therefore, from God's point of view, as found in the Bible, alcoholism is not a disease. That's the viewpoint I take, and I think it would be difficult to reconcile with the disease concept."

In the wake of my reply, Frank and John had exchanged glances of some kind of mutual understanding across the table.

"I don't know," Frank had answered, in a distinctly cool tone of voice and manner, "we've never had a problem like that come up before. I think we could work out some kind of acceptable compromise."

From that time on the conversation had seemed inhibited. And back at the TV station an hour later, Frank had a final word.

"We've got a couple of more people to interview next week, Gar. Some time after that we'll let you know our final decision."

Three weeks later the letter had arrived from Frank, advising me that they had chosen someone for the job who had "more actual experience in the production of documentary films." The explanation for my having been turned down did not ring true to me. They had known, before I or the other applicants were interviewed, who had the most "actual experience." It was something else, I was persuaded, that had lost me the job; something to do with my personal beliefs or history, rather than my lack of professional film experience. Perhaps it had been my dishonorable discharge from military service for a seeming lack of patriotism. Perhaps it had been the Biblically derived opposition I had voiced to the disease concept of alcoholism.

Weary of grappling with the mystery of why my most recent efforts to effect an escape from my vocational prison had failed, I turned my gaze to a contemplation of the therapeutic scene spread out on the wall beside my table. Immediately adjacent to the table where I sat was an extended alcove in the wall that was probably two feet deep by ten feet long; a depression that went from the floor to the ceiling. Starting at table-top level, above cedar wood paneling, there commenced a painted mural of a country landscape. It gave off a Cinerama-like effect of depth because of the extended indentation in the surface of the wall on which it was painted. I took a long swallow of tea and sought escape from my present situation and surroundings by losing myself in the rustic panorama that had been skillfully portrayed by some well-known artist in vivid colors on the wall beside me.

But I did more than passively survey the marvelously realistic mural. I stepped into it, as surely as if I had been endowed with some occult power to actually leave my body sitting there in a chair at the table while I stepped completely out of the world in which that body was confined; out of the world of a cafeteria in the basement of a huge, state office building that had become a vocational prison for me; out of my confined life as an infinitesimal cog in a vast, bureaucratic machine.

I stepped out of that depressing, imprisoning world and set my feet down upon the dirt-covered road which began abruptly at the edge of my table, as though the cafeteria itself had been dropped down in the middle of a quiet countryside, and there was an opening in the wall beside me through which I could step from the closed-in cafeteria into a rural, pastoral setting.

Suddenly transported to a different world, I could feel through the soles of my shoes the rough, uneven surface of the dirt-covered, wheel-rutted country road. A little cloud of dust rose around my feet as I kicked against an unnoticed rise in the road. On the far side of the road I stopped a moment and leaned against the top rail of a split-rail fence, several segments of which guarded the approach to a bridge. The bridge, just ahead of me, crossed a swiftly flowing stream—too small to be called a river, too broad to be described as a creek. The rivulet wound a serpentine way through a landscape of rolling hills ridged with trees; a pastel blending of soft greens, dull browns and yellows, in which the faded red barns and white farmhouses stood out in marked contrast. The rails of the fence on which I leaned were uneven and rough-hewn, smaller at one end than the other, as if made up of scraps for which some neighboring farmer had been able to find no better use. As I surveyed the terrain of the countryside spread out before me, some of the sounds and scents of boyhood, stored away in my memory, were revived to bring life to the vista spread out before me.

From close at hand came the sibilant rush of water as the little rivulet with the energetic thrust of a mountain stream rushed along between the grassy, tree-lined banks on its way to some distant sea. In a tranquil setting of stillness and rest, the stream alone showed signs of life. It seemed strangely out of place in the pastoral setting, thus striking a chord of kinship within my own being, as one who had felt out of place in society, a square peg in a round hole for too long. The seething stream evoked memories of other rivers and streams I had stood beside, burdened at times by the thought that I was standing still in life while the river I stood beside rushed on to some important destination appointed by its Maker.

There had been that frothing, rock-pierced mountain stream in Camp Hale, Colorado in World War II, where I had stood alone many winter nights, even after taps had sounded and the lights in barracks windows had been snuffed out, listening to the rushing of the glacial water hurtling past while I scanned the star-studded heavens, seeking answers to the questions about life and death, good and evil, war and peace, that were besieging my consciousness as the day of overseas embarkment drew closer.

There had been the hours spent beside the ever-changing Red Cedar river, which wound a twisting, turning course across the thousand-acre campus of nearby Michigan State University, three miles to the east of the soaring dome of the state capitol. I remembered the Red Cedar in the summer as a placid home of domesticated ducks and a watery rendezvous for canoeing lovers; in the spring, a flood-swollen giant overspreading its banks; and in the winter, a frigid conveyor of giant cakes of river ice that were smashed to pieces on the rocks of its rapids. It was beside the Red Cedar that I had first tasted the sensual wine of a sexual encounter with a girl who had subsequently gone to Chicago to have an abortion as a result, and who thereafter had passed out of my life. And it was beside the Red Cedar, much later in life as an older student, that I had pensively walked one afternoon, so immersed in a sombre longing for a distant destination of achievement which I had little assurance of reaching, that a campus policeman had approached me to ask if I was alright; thinking, perhaps, that I might be contemplating suicide, as at least one other student had done in a preceding year.

I turned from the melancholy episodes of the past that had been evoked by the rivulet to the more substantial stuff on the bridge which carried the country road across its back. It was a stone-arched bridge, reminiscent of the ancient Romans and their aqueducts that had survived a thousand years and more of use. A knee-high protective guard wall on either side of the road looked as if it had been designed so that weary travelers, such as I, could stop and rest atop the stone balustrade and listen to the music of the swiftly flowing stream beneath. It was a bridge that spoke of a bygone age, when men were not in such a hurry that they could not take time to build a structure that would endure, and that was beautiful as well.

One aspect of the peaceful countryside before me which drew me on, inviting me to walk further into its peaceful depths, was the complete absence of any sign of life. There was no farmer coming down the road with his wagon and team of horses to crowd me off the road while he passed. There was no hired hand working around the barns, or in the plowed fields, to view me with suspicious eyes as a stranger entering a rural community where every neighbor knows the other by sight and by name. There was not even a vigilant Collie dog, guarding some front porch or dozing in the shade of the trees surrounding the farm houses, to bark at me and challenge my advance. There wasn't even a single child to eye me curiously, to call names, to ask unwanted questions as to where I was from and what I was doing there, to push my mind back to the awareness that I was fleeing from my environment where I belonged.

My footsteps made a hollow, thumping sound as I crossed the bridge and followed the winding, narrow country road through the deserted countryside; past plowed fields, the clusters of white farm houses with their surrounding satellites of barns and sheds. I walked unmolested, unnoticed, into the center of this Cineramic scene, a small, white country church with a Colonial spire pointing toward Heaven. As I looked at the church, a possible explanation occurred to me as to the total absence of any signs of life in the countryside through which I had thus far walked. All the inhabitants of this small community were probably gathered together there in the little country church to listen to the preaching of the eternal Word of God to lost men and women.

On the rolling swell of hills behind the church, separate groups of balsam, spruce and fir trees fanned out in a semi-circle, strung out like regiments of soldiers looking down on the scene, as if protecting the inhabitants while they were gathered together in some solemn conclave in which Heaven had an interest.

Then, as it had been with the racing rivulet which I had crossed, the sight of the little country church ahead of me brought the real past crowding into my present moment of fantasy escape. For the thought suddenly occurred to me that perhaps the people who lived in this sprawling, isolated and picturesque little rural farm community might be gathered at the church not for Sunday morning service, but for a Saturday afternoon wedding. The thought came suddenly to my mind as I recognized that the little white church before me was so much, too much, like the very country house of worship in which I had been married . . . a marriage that was now crumbling after twelve years and three children.

It suddenly seemed to me as if it were my marriage that was taking place inside that little church, crowded full with relatives, friends and neighbors. And yet, while I was inside being married, I also stood outside now, witnessing that event as a spectator. Like the instantaneous explosions of a flash camera, scenes from that long-distant event passed before my mind's eye. I saw myself standing before the assembled crowd of guests, much to the astonishment of the minister . . . pointing to a huge painting of Warner Sallman's "Head of Christ" on the wall behind me . . . I heard myself speaking long-forgotten words . . . "Like the wedding at Cana, described in the Gospels, and with all due respect to the beauty of Florence, my bride, it is Christ who is the guest of honor at this ceremony today, for it was He who brought us together to fulfill His purpose in our lives."

Then, I saw myself again, kneeling with Florence, my bride, before the minister while he placed a hand on each of our heads and asked the blessing of God upon our marriage. I watched the slow-moving film superimposed upon the image of the little white country church . . . standing before the assembled guests, cutting the wedding cake and passing out pieces to each one . . . opening the pile of gifts before the inquisitive eyes of all the onlookers . . . then the hand shakes, the embraces, the well wishes in the afternoon sunlight on the porch of the church . . . the embarrassment of trying to drive away and finding that the front bumper of the car had been lifted onto a large rock so that the front wheels spun vainly in

31

the air . . . and then, finally driving off with the tin cans clattering in the road behind us, kicking up a smoke screen of dust on the country road.

Abruptly, the intrusion of a painful segment from my recent past shattered the illusionary effect of a fantasy walk into a painted countryside. I ran back to the reality of the present; back to the hard, gray Formica top of the table by the wall of an almost empty cafeteria in a huge, state office building. I returned to my crackers and lukewarm tea and turned my back on the painful memories that had threatened to surround me like the host of ills released from the mythical box of Pandora in Greek legend.

With a hand that was not steady, I replenished my half-empty tea cup with more hot water from the shiny metal pot. I looked around the cafeteria, but no one had apparently noticed my mystical escape into the world of the rural countryside depicted on the wall beside me, nor my return. I sipped my tea, then glanced at my watch.

I had been gone from my desk only twenty minutes in my determined attempt to avoid a face-to-face encounter with garrulous Gary Goforth; yet it seemed like at least an hour, perhaps because I had relived so much of my life in those few, fleeting moments seated at a table in the cafeteria. I slipped into my pocket the key to a doorway of opportunity that had been closed in my face, picked up the magazine Darrell had lent me and got up to leave. By the time I went back up to the 8th floor, picked up my print order and returned to my desk on the 5th floor, it would be a quarter of four. By that time, nosy, noisy Gary Goforth should be gone from the wing where I worked.

Stepping off the elevator on the fifth floor minutes later with my reproduction order in one hand, I peered down the hallway to see if Gary was still in the area. He was nowhere to be seen or heard. Breathing a sigh of relief, I walked down the hallway to the west end of the wing where I worked and stepped through the open doorway into the Engineering section.

It was obvious, as soon as I stepped through the doorway, that the final World Series game of the season was over. The radio was off. The big, plan-reading table was clear of roosting Highway ball fans from other sections. I cast a furtive glance to the rear of the Engineering room to see if my extended absence or return had been noticed by Hubert Funke. It was evident that he was more interested in the road plans spread out on his desk than in my recent exit and return.

Relieved, I returned to the drafting table where I had been working. As I hoisted myself up onto the drafting stool for a final hour of the childish, kindergarten coloring chore that was part of my job, my eardrums were assaulted by a tale of woe from the lips of corpulent Homer Scroobie. Both he and George Flunker, another engineer, were leaning against the waist-high air-conditioning units by the windows.

"Damn it all anyway," I heard Homer complain to George, "I suppose I'll have to take those two dozen eggs over to that damned, absent-minded Phoebe or they'll be left here over the weekend; then she won't want 'em."

"Who?" George asked.

"Phoebe Philpot, over in Cartographic."

In his spare time, Homer served as middle-man between an enterprising farmer and state employees who liked to buy farm-fresh eggs. Each week, on Friday afternoon, he sold from forty to fifty dozen eggs to employees from other sections who passed in and out of the Engineering section in a steady stream. Along with his baseball and football pools, I wondered how Homer found time for his engineering duties. A moment later he padded out of the room sedately with two cartons of eggs under one arm.

As I tried to concentrate on the menial task I was doing, troubled thoughts kept intruding about the conflicting demands between desire and duty that I would face that evening after I left work. The prospect of the emotional balancing act phone call I had gotten earlier, and the boxed birthday cake on the file cabinet by my desk, became added factors of strain in the context of my sense of vocational imprisonment, newly intensified by the near encounter with Gary Goforth.

But finally, at ten minutes to five, the Engineering crew started leaving for the anticipated delights of the weekend. As my fellow workers straggled out, I laid down my coloring pencil but continued sitting there at the drafting table, looking out the window beside me. Down below, the figures of state employees leaving the huge office building reminded me of ants emerging from an ant hill.

"Want to close all the windows when you leave, Gar?"

The voice of Hubert Funke broke into my sober contemplation of the scene below. I turned my head to see him facing me as he stood in the open doorway.

"Be glad to, Hubert."

"Thanks, Gar. See you Monday; and remember—don't make the same mistake I did on my wife's birthday."

With a wave and a reminiscent chuckle at the episode he had shared with me at lunch time, Hubert disappeared into the hall. I got up, the last employee to leave, and began closing the bottom sections of the bay windows all the way to the back of the long room. Then, back at the front of the room, I donned a light sport coat, stuck the birthday card into my coat pocket, picked up the cake box carefully, and stepped out into the hall.

But after several steps, abruptly remembering something important I had almost forgotten, I wheeled around and stepped back into my work place. I set the cake down on my desk, then reached into my pocket and pulled out the key from a hotel room in Cleveland that had been the object of my fruitless speculations on afternoon coffee break. I didn't want to take a chance on Florence finding it at home and dropping it in a mail box; neither did I want to tell her my reasons for wanting to cling to it. I needed it to help me endure the daily grind of a job I despised. It would help, from time to time, to bring forth the key as a visible, tangible reminder of how close I had come to escaping my vocational prison.

I opened the middle drawer of my desk and, with one last,

lingering look, dropped it into the drawer. Then, as a sudden surge of bitterness swept through me at the golden opportunity that had slipped through my fingers, I slammed the desk drawer shut with violence. The angry "bang" that followed was to me like the iron door of a prison inmate's cell clanging shut for life. Then I picked up the cake box and again headed for the elevators. Getting off on the main floor, Percy Proud, the night watchman, beckoned me over to his desk in the lobby.

"How do you like this, Mr. Roby?" he asked, holding up a pencilled drawing for my inspection.

I leaned down over his desk and surveyed a landscape scene of a medieval castle beside a lake, with forest-covered mountains in the background.

"Hey, that's really good, Percy," I said, with genuine admiration, "I don't know why you're working at this job when you've got talent like that."

A glow of embarrassed pleasure reddened Percy's face at my sincere tribute. I had seen numerous other specimens of his art work—drawings of human faces, full length figures, animals, landscapes—all of a professional calibre. My word of praise obviously provided some needed encouragement.

"Why, thank you, Mr. Roby. I do hope to get into commercial art someday, but I think I need more practice. That's one reason I like this night watchman job. I can sit here and draw almost all night without any interruptions. I'm taking a correspondence course right now that's really good. I think it's going to help me a lot."

"Well, stick with it, Percy, and I'm sure you'll make the grade."

"That's just what I'm going to do," he nodded affirmatively, "even if it did cost me my marriage. I still think it's worth it."

The hint of tragedy behind the friendly facade that Percy had always shown, as well as the fact that I was on the verge of a similar domestic debacle, curbed my impatience to be gone.

"What happened, Percy, if you don't mind my asking?"

"Oh, my wife thought it was a waste of time. She couldn't put up with my putting in so much time drawing, so she divorced me."

"Sorry to hear that, Percy."

"Well, that's life," he shrugged philosophically.

Having given Percy all the support I could as a fellow struggling mortal, I was anxious to move on to the pleasant and unpleasant obligations awaiting me that evening. I held up the cake box as justification for an abrupt departure.

"I'd better get going, Percy. My wife's birthday is tonight."

Percy's face beamed with evident delight at my announcement.

"Well, I'm glad to see that somebody is still happily married. Wish your wife a happy birthday for me, Mr. Roby."

"Thanks, Percy, I'll do that," I called over my shoulder, and headed for the exit.

I carefully maneuvered the cake box through the revolving door and soon thereafter descended the wide, concrete steps of the Gray office building "prison" that led to the street level. Feeling oppressed in spirit by the agenda of demands, both time-wise and emotionally, that I faced that evening, I crossed the street and headed for my car in the nearly empty parking lot. Seconds later, in a six-year-old station wagon, I was driving west toward that complex constellation of human relationships with a wife and three children, designated by society as "home."

CHAPTER 2

⟹ It was less than fifteen minutes after leaving the Gray prison parking lot that I turned right onto "the street of dirty children" in a west side, racially mixed neighborhood. A crowd of nearly a dozen of them broke up a ball game being played in the middle of the street as I reduced my speed. The motley mixture of street urchins parted before my station wagon like sea water being cleft by the advancing prow of a ship. It was an interracial assortment of white, black, and Hispanic children whose home was the streets during the summer months. Their faces registered disgust as I drove through the middle of their improvised ball diamond; most of them obviously unconvinced of my right as a motorist to drive down this public street at this time of day.

At the end of the block, instead of swinging around the corner onto the street where I lived and into our driveway, two houses from the corner, as I usually did, I braked to a stop and parked the car on the adjoining street where the ball game was in progress. Driven by a guilty compulsion to make of Florence's birthday as special an occasion as I could, I was planning to sneak the birthday cake into the house through the back door without her seeing it until after supper.

I got out of the car, lifting the cake box carefully, drawing curious glances from some of the children playing ball. Then, instead of following the sidewalk around the corner to the front of our house, I cut across the back yard of a ramshackle building on the corner; once a neighborhood grocery store, but recently converted into a black church.

I continued on across the adjoining back yard of our next-door neighbor, a Ukranian brick layer who had been taking care of his wife, an invalid with Parkinson's disease, for the last twenty years. As I passed his back porch and a smoldering oil drum incinerator, Steve opened a screen door and stepped out on his porch. Glancing up at him, I saw that he was dressed in his usual attire; undershirt, work pants, soft-soled shoes, and the ever present unlit cigar clenched between his teeth. With a full, ruddy face, and a ring of white hair surrounding his bald pate, he could easily have been mistaken for Soviet Premier Khrushchev.

"Hiya, Gar," he waved, "Whatta you got? You gotta birthday or a wedding anniversary or a something?"

I paused to satisfy his neighborly curiosity, feeling a twinge of pity and admiration for his faithful care of an invalid wife.

"My wife's birthday," I replied, gesturing with the box.

"You gotta good woman, youra wife," he wagged his head approvingly, "damn good woman."

I suspected his favorable appraisal was based on Florence's many good-neighbor gestures toward his invalid wife.

"I agree with you, Steve," I answered over my shoulder as I continued on into my own back yard.

I heard no more from him as I continued on around the back of the two-story frame rented house where we had lived for four years. As I turned the corner to enter the side door, I could hear six-year-old Paul at the piano, doing his daily hour of keyboard practice under his mother's vigilant tutelage.

"No use wasting money on lessons," she had said, "until he gets to the point where I can't help him anymore."

Holding the cake box behind me out of sight, I tried to open the screen door on the side of the house quietly, so as not to attract anyone's attention. Paul, engrossed in the open piano book before him, didn't notice my entrance, but I was seen by his two younger brothers, four-year-old Philip and year-and-a-half-old Korah.

"Daddy!" Philip squealed, rushing toward me.

Paul stopped his playing and looked over at me, echoing Philip's glad cry. Korah, too, dropped his tinker toys, and raced toward me unsteadily on wobbly legs. But from the kitchen, the sounds of pots and pans rattling, and the clatter of dishes was not interrupted, although Florence had undoubtedly heard the announcements from the boys heralding my arrival. In recent months, my daily return home from work had become increasingly less of an occasion for Florence to come to the door and welcome me with open arms. For there had been too many times during the past year when she had been turned away when she had reached out to me. As Philip rushed up and crowded close to me, while Korah clung to my legs, I held the boxed birthday cake behind me, out of danger. But this movement only aroused their attention more.

"What you got, Dad?" Philip asked, wide-eyed with excitement.

Paul, sitting at the piano bench, and Korah, arms wrapped around my knees, looked at me expectantly, eagerly awaiting my word of explanation.

"Sh-h-h," I hissed quietly, putting a finger to my lips and then pointing to the kitchen, attempting to convey the information that this was a surprise for their mother.

With my free hand, I reached down and massaged the top of Philip's thick thatch of brownish hair, then ran my fingers through Korah's blonde locks. Paul, unable to sit still through this exciting conspiracy, slid off the piano bench and, leaning close to me, cupped his mouth with one hand and whispered.

"What is it, Dad?"

I again put my finger to my lips, invoking silence, then gently disengaged myself from the encircling grip of Philip and Korah. I turned away from them, beckoning them to follow me, as I stepped back into the short hallway adjacent to the spinet piano. I stepped past the open stairway leading to the upstairs bedrooms to a closed door that led into a large back room that I used as a study. As I opened the door with my free hand, holding the cake box by its string in the other, Paul and Philip surged close behind me, with Korah coming close behind. As we all crowded into the back room on this exciting, secret adventure, Florence's voice followed us from the kitchen, brusque and imperious.

"Paul! Just because your father comes home, you don't have to quit practicing."

"Just a minute, Mom," Paul called back from beside me, "Dad's got something he wants to show me."

I gave Paul a glance of exasperated rebuke for having risked arousing Florence's curiosity to come and see what I had brought home. But her devotion to housewifely duties overcame her curiosity, if she had any, engrossed as she was in preparations for supper. Relieved, I set the box down on the cluttered top of my desk, then untied the string that held the lid of the cake box shut. As Paul and Philip crowded up to me on either side, Korah grasped the edge of my desk and hung onto it to steady himself in an upright position so that he, too, could see the unfolding of this curiosity-kindling mystery. While the boys watched, as if expecting me to perform some magical fete, I lifted the cake carefully out of the box by its circular, pasteboard base and set it down on the desk close enough to Korah so that he could see it too.

"Gee, is it somebody's birthday?" Paul asked, first to notice the inscription on top of the cake decorated with pink roses.

I nodded affirmatively to Paul. I hadn't had time to have Florence's name inscribed on the cake.

"Is this Mommy's birthday?" Philip whispered incredulously, looking up at me.

As I nodded, I saw Korah lift a hand, intending to stab an exploring finger into the middle of the white frosting. I grabbed his hand just in time.

"No, no, Korah!" I cautioned quietly.

"Doesn't that look good?" Philip intoned. "Are we going to have some too?"

"Certainly," I assured him, "we all are, after supper."

"Paul!" exploded Florence's voice from the kitchen. "Get back to the piano."

"Shoot!" Paul snorted in disgust, but turned and stepped back through the hallway into the living room and resumed practicing.

I closed the door behind him and locked it, and let Philip and Korah watch as I retrieved some birthday candles from a desk drawer and began putting them on the top of the cake. As I carefully spaced five candles in a circle on the cake, a feeling of weariness seeped through me because I was engaged in a ritual which had long ceased to have meaning or value for me. And I couldn't help wondering if the annual observance of her birthday meant anything to Florence either. But it obviously meant something exciting to Korah. As I inserted the fifth and final candle on the cake, he stretched further over the edge of my desk to get a closer look.

"Why did you put just five candles on, Dad?" Philip asked in bewilderment, "Mommy's more than five years old, isn't she?"

"Yes, she certainly is, Philip," I smiled, "each candle stands for seven times. Five times seven is thirty-five; that's how old your mother is. There wouldn't be room enough to put thirty-five candles on."

"Is that how old Mommy is, really?" Philip asked incredulously.

Evidently to him, thirty-five was as astronomical a figure as thirty-five thousand would have been. Suddenly, Korah reached the end of his self control and jabbed one pudgy hand toward the cake, but just as quickly, I reached out and encircled him gently in my arms, pinning his arms against his body. He squirmed and squealed in protest as I picked him up and unlocked the door.

"Let's go back in the living room, Philip."

As Philip stepped out of the room behind me, I turned back, still holding Korah, squirming in my arms, and locked

41

the door again to keep him from going back to finish the unfinished business that was obviously still on his mind. As I stepped back into the living room with Korah, Paul eyed me suspiciously from the piano bench and stopped his playing long enough to whisper an accusing question.

"Did Philip get a piece of that birthday cake?"

I set Korah down on the floor by the piano and bent down to whisper a reassuring answer.

"Nobody will get a piece until after supper, Paul."

As I stood by the piano a moment while Paul searched for the place where he had stopped on the music sheet before him, Korah crawled back to the locked door of the study and pushed vainly against it. When the door did not yield to his pushing, he sat down on the floor, leaning against the door, and looked at me imploringly, emitting a pleading whine which was his wordless way of begging.

The extended silence from the piano was noted by Florence, still busy in the kitchen.

"Paul!" she exclaimed in mounting anger as she stepped to the doorway between the kitchen and the living room, "if you stop your practice again . . ."

Then she saw me.

"Oh, hello, Gar, supper will be on the table in two jerks."

She brushed a strand of brunette, home-permanented hair back from her perspiring forehead. It wasn't an attempt to make herself look more beautiful for her husband. She had given that up as a vain endeavor. She swept the stray lock of hair back out of her way as she might have brushed away a circling fly. Standing in the doorway with hands on her hips, she glared at Paul. She stood there in her typical working clothes—skirt and cotton blouse, anklets and low-heeled shoes; no lipstick, no make-up, no powder or perfume, no silks or satins or feminine frills; just a housewife who was tired from a day of cleaning house, getting meals, disciplining children, and changing diapers.

"Well," she stormed at Paul, "are you going to get on with your practice or do you want me to get a stick?"

Paul scowled at me, as if rebuking me for not protecting him from the tyrant mother who stood in the doorway, then bent his head to the music sheet in front of him. As he soberly picked at the keys, he added a vocal accompaniment tinged with a rebellious undertone.

"Mister frog is full of hops . . . . That's because he hops a lot . . ."

I gave Paul an encouraging pat on the shoulder, then walked over to the sofa and sat down beside Philip to listen to the rest of Paul's piano practice. Korah still sat before the locked study room door, bemoaning the fact that he could not continue his examination of the curious-looking birthday cake. Above the sound of Paul's one-finger piano playing and low-key singing, Korah's whining reached Florence's children-attuned ears in the kitchen.

She stalked into the living room and swept up Korah from his unavailing vigil by the study-room door.

"Are you wet again?" she asked, as if expecting him to answer.

She thrust an exploring hand beneath the waistband of his plastic pants.

"Heck, your pants are alright," she concluded, setting Korah down on the floor by the piano, "I don't know what you're whining about."

"I know what he wants," blurted Philip, trying to be helpful to his mother.

I squeezed his shoulder and gave him a warning look to keep him from giving away the surprise.

"Well, what does he want, if you're so smart?" Florence asked, turning to look at Philip as she stood in the kitchen doorway.

Philip clapped his hand over his mouth in deference to my warning signal.

"It's a secret," he hedged.

"Secret!" she snorted, "he's probably just hungry. Well, he'll just have to wait like everybody else."

As Florence disappeared into the kitchen, I leaned back on

the sofa, put my arm around Philip's shoulders and drew him close to me. I felt burdened by Florence's evident strain over the trivial issues of Paul's stopping his piano practice to greet me; of Korah's understandable begging to see more of the strange looking and appetizing object I had hidden in the back room.

"If she were getting from me the expressions of love that she has hungered for and been denied for months," I thought to myself, "she would be far better equipped to deal with the demands of the children."

While Paul continued laboriously with a sequence of simple melodies about frogs and airplanes and church bells, singing aloud the ones he knew, silent on others, and with Philip content to sit quietly beside me, my thoughts centered upon my deteriorating relationship to Florence. What she wanted and needed from her husband was a sincere embrace, a kiss of sexual passion such as she had known during our honeymoon and the first several years of our marriage. And I felt the futility of trying to supply that need with a decorated birthday cake and a funny greeting card. These gifts were supposed to be an evidence of love, but in reality, I knew they were but a smokescreen designed to hide from her what she had already probably sensed; my lack of genuine love for her. Suddenly, Philip broke into my sombre train of thought.

"Daddy," he announced excitedly, as Paul continued his practice, casting an occasional accusing glance at me for not having rescued him from the ordeal of piano practice, "why don't we go outdoors and play ball?"

"Florence," I called, "have I got time to play ball with Philip before supper?"

"No, you haven't," she scolded from the kitchen, "I'm just about ready to put it on the table now."

"Shoot!" Philip reacted in disgust.

As Philip settled back on the sofa, head bowed in dejection, Paul stopped his playing to cast a triumphant look at his younger brother, happy that Philip could not go outside and play ball with me while he had to stay inside and endure the torture of piano practice. But Philip was not to be put off so easily.

"Can we play ball after supper, then, Dad?"

Philip's face brightened suddenly, like the sun breaking through a storm cloud, at the prospect that his wish might yet be granted. But as he waited expectantly for my reply, a silken-voiced plea from the long distance phone call I had received at the office that afternoon coursed through my mind.

"Come to me as soon as you can."

"Maybe, for a few minutes, Philip," I conceded reluctantly, unable to quash his hopes completely.

Paul whirled around on the piano bench, suddenly in danger of having his younger brother seize some advantage that he was going to be denied.

"If Philip gets to play ball, I do too."

"Yes, you too, Paul," I assured him.

"Goody, goody," he grinned, slapping his hands together in a spasm of delight.

As Paul resumed his practice with renewed vigor, little Korah looked at me reproachfully from the hallway leading to my study. While Florence was putting food and silverware on the dining room table, and my attention was momentarily divided between listening to Paul at the piano and watching Korah, a surge of sibling jealously prompted Philip to make another bid for my undivided attention.

"Daddy," he exploded, jumping up to face me in the excitement of his new bid for my attention, "I got a great idea."

I shrank inwardly at what might be coming, for surely it would be a suggestion that I do something; a new kind of physical exertion for which I had neither the time nor the energy that evening. In addition, I was committed to an appointment that evening that I would have to hide from him behind some plausible excuse. I tried to hide my inner weariness behind a manufactured smile as I looked at Philip.

"What is it, Philip?"

"Why don't you go with us to Gramma's house tomorrow,

45

and then while Mommy is cleaning Gramma's house, you can take us fishing at that lake?"

"Yeah, Dad," Paul echoed exuberantly, whirling around on the piano bench, "that is a great idea. You promised to take us fishing sometime."

"I can't do it tomorrow, boys," I protested weakly, "I've got some overtime work to do at the office."

"Darn it all, anyway!" Paul muttered, turning listlessly back to the piano.

"Shoot!" whined Philip, echoing Paul's one of disgust, turning his back to me and moving away from the sofa.

"Why do you always have to work, anyway?" demanded Paul petulantly, his back to me.

Florence had evidently heard the exchange, for she appeared abruptly in the kitchen doorway, a bowl of mashed potatoes in her hands.

"Your Daddy would just rather be at the office by himself than he would with us," she answered Paul in an accusing tone.

Philip took her explanation at face value as being the whole truth and turned to me, unbelief written on his face, his blue eyes widening in shocked wonder, as if he had just been told that I had sent a million Jews to the gas chambers.

"Daddy, is that true?" he demanded.

"No, it isn't true, Philip," I assured him, anticipating a rebuttal from Florence. It was quick in coming.

"It certainly looks that way to me," she retorted, looking directly at me as she brushed a rebellious strand of hair back out of her eyes with one hand.

Florence whirled away then to carry the dish she was holding into the dining room. Philip, head bowed, crushed in spirit by the devastating accusation against me from his mother, started slowly walking toward the stairway that led to the second-floor bedroom.

"Where are you going, Philip?" I asked.

"To bed," he mumbled, half turning toward me. "I feel sad because you won't take us fishing tomorrow."

46

"Stay down here," I ordered firmly, "supper's almost ready."

Philip stopped, obeying me to the point of halting his progress toward the stairway, but still rebellious to the point that he would not return to where he had been sitting beside me on the sofa. Then, like the sound of a bell at a boxing match, Florence's summons from the dining room brought a temporary resolution of the conflict.

"Gar! Come in here and bring the boys before supper gets cold."

"Coming," I called.

I stepped past the piano to the door of my study where Korah still sat vainly whining for a closer encounter with the birthday cake hidden in my room. As I picked him up, Paul remained sitting at the piano, crushed by the disappointment of not being able to go fishing with me the following day. Philip stood at one end of the sofa, hands folded behind him, head bowed; a miniature of a monk at prayer or sorrowful meditation.

"Paul and Philip," I said softly, standing in the hallway that led to my room, holding Korah, "come here a minute."

Perhaps thinking that I had relented in my refusal to take them fishing the next day, they crowded close around me.

"What do you want?" Paul asked crossly, still doubtful that I had changed my mind.

"Listen," I whispered, bending down toward them, "after supper, I'll bring in the birthday cake for your mother with all the candles lit. Then, after I set it down on the table, we'll all start singing 'Happy birthday' to your mother; okay?"

Philip was easily distracted from the fishing expedition which he had proposed. He squeezed his hands together and suppressed convulsions of delight shook his body at the prospect of the surprise which was going to be sprung on his mother. Paul, however, was adamant in his unwillingness to be diverted from Philip's really "great" idea to my "not-so-great" substitute. Nevertheless, he mumbled a grudging agreement with my proposal.

"Gar!" complained Florence's voice from the dining room. "Are you coming? Supper's going to get cold."

Paul and Philip tagged along behind me as I carried Korah into the dining room that was adjacent to the kitchen. As I deposited Korah gently in his high chair next to Florence, who always sat at the end of the table nearest the kitchen, an argument developed between Paul and Philip as to who would sit at the other end of the table to be closest to me. I snapped the tray in place on Korah's high chair and turned to arbitrate the dissension between his two older brothers.

"Who sat next to me last time?" I asked.

"Paul did," Philip replied promptly.

"No, I didn't; Philip did," Paul rebutted furiously.

"Why don't you tell them both to shut up and sit down?" Florence snapped.

There was only one way I could think of on the spur of the moment that would satisfy Florence's irritated demand for a speedy resolution, and the need of Paul and Philip for an equitable decision from their father.

"Since nobody's sure who sat next to me last time," I proposed, delving into my pocket and drawing out a quarter, "let's flip a coin."

"I'll take heads," Paul announced immediately, always first to express his preference in any situation.

"And I'll take tails," Philip agreed happily.

While Florence looked on in disgust, Korah stared in wonderment at the strange ritual, and Paul and Philip stood close beside me awaiting the outcome. I flipped the quarter into the air, caught it on the palm of my hand, then slapped it down on my wrist.

"It's tails," I announced, lifting my hand from my wrist so both boys could see. "Philip gets to sit next to me tonight."

"That's not fair," Paul muttered as he took a seat across the table from me, "Philip sat beside you last time."

"If the food's cold, it isn't my fault," growled Florence as we were all finally seated around the rectangular dinette table.

Out of deference to Florence's evident mood of exasperation at the delay, I abbreviated the customary giving of thanks for our food to the bare minimum. Then, the succulent supper of meat loaf, mashed potatoes and gravy, mixed vegetables and salad, was interspersed with tidbits of domestic information from Florence. Her widowed mother, Hilda, was having trouble with arthritis in her shoulders. Florence had heard a mouse in the kitchen the night before and we'd have to get some mousetraps. Paul and Philip both had to be back to the dentist soon for a check-up. While Florence's report on domestic developments was being given, Korah entertained himself and whoever was watching him by picking up peas off his plate, one at a time, and dropping them with a small splash into his glass of milk.

In my contribution to the family recital of events of the day, I didn't mention the near encounter with Gary Goforth, nor the reaction his unexpected visit had sparked in me. Neither did I bring up the rediscovery of the almost-forgotten key to the hotel room in Cleveland, Ohio, that I had occupied with such high hopes several months before. Both episodes were too personally painful to bring up as casually dispensed items of supper table trivia. Nor could I disclose to Florence and my sons that day's most distinctive deviation from regular office routine—a long distance phone call which, although they wouldn't hear about it, would affect each of them in the form of robbing them of a major portion of my time, affections, and attention for that special evening of Florence's birthday.

I was the first to finish eating, got up from the table and walked to my back-room study. After lighting with a match the five pink candles on top of the cake, I picked it up carefully, holding it by a heavy circular pasteboard plate on the bottom, and carried it slowly so that the ensuing draft would not blow the candles out. I entered the dining room from behind Florence, so that the boys saw me first with the cake and its circle of burning candles. While little Korah stared in wide-eyed wonder at the spectacle, Paul and Philip began to sing with me, somewhat off key and in only approximate unison.

"Happy birthday to you . . ."

Florence turned around in her chair on the first note, and an expression that was a combination of amusement and disgust spread over her face.

"Happy birthday, dear Mommy . . . may God bless you."

The boys and I finished our singing performance as I set the cake down in the middle of the table. From my inside coat pocket I pulled the envelope with the birthday card in it.

"Special delivery," I said, holding it out to her.

She was not visibly impressed as she took it from my hand, deftly bypassing Korah's outreaching grasp.

"I don't know why you bother with this," she said, as she began to pry open the envelope.

"Just to let you know you're appreciated," I told her sincerely, as I pulled out my chair and sat down again.

"Appreciated, my eye!" she snorted, pulling the card out of the envelope. "If you appreciated me, you'd stay home once in a while instead of running off someplace every chance you get."

The cryptic criticism in her rebuke, and its hidden significance for our marriage, was lost upon Paul and Philip. They were much more interested in the burning candles, as was Korah, as he stared, transfixed by the five pyramids of flame.

"Hey, Dad," demanded Paul, mystified, as Florence read her birthday card, "how come you only put five candles on Mom's birthday cake?"

Florence looked up from the card long enough to supply a caustic answer.

"He probably forgot how old I really am, Paul."

"No, that isn't it, Mom," Philip defended, "there wasn't room enough on top of the cake for all the candles, so Dad let each candle stand for seven years, and five times seven makes thirty-five, and that's how old you really are; right, Dad?"

"That's exactly right, Philip."

"Can I blow out the candles, Dad?" Paul pleaded.

"No, me," Philip protested.

Korah, too, whined for a privilege that he didn't know the

danger of as I pushed the cake further out of his reach. Then I took a knife and cut off one pink rose to plop on the tray in front of him to keep him occupied until the cake was cut.

"Neither one of you blows out the candles," I said firmly. "It's your mother's birthday. She's supposed to blow them out."

A cackling laugh erupted from Florence as she grasped the message of the birthday card. Her laugh seemed partly spontaneous, partly forced.

"Let me see it," Paul begged, and Florence passed it over to his outstretched hand.

"The only fish in the sea, huh?" she asked, regarding me with skepticism written on her face. "That's a good joke."

"Would you like to blow out the candles so I can cut the cake?" I asked, evading the issue of the truth or lack of it in the birthday card sentiment.

Florence drew in a deep breath and, with one strong exhalation, blew out all the candles. Five minutes later, after Paul and Philip had each finished two pieces of cake, and while Florence was still feeding some to Korah, I pushed my chair back from the table.

"Can we play ball now, Dad?" Philip asked excitedly, getting up from the table.

"For a few minutes, Philip," I said, reminding him that our playing time would be brief.

For I was looking forward in that moment, with a rising fever of excitement, not to the backyard ball game with my sons, but to my scheduled encounter that evening with someone who could abundantly supply a need and a hunger that neither my sons nor Florence knew anything about.

"Goody, goody," exclaimed Paul, squeezing his way around the table from the other side.

As I passed Florence on my way to the kitchen, followed by Paul and Philip, I paused by her chair as she maneuvered a forkful of birthday cake into Korah's eagerly opening mouth.

"Happy birthday, Florence."

"Yeah, happy birthday," she echoed, in subdued sarcasm, "it would be happy if I had a husband that loved me."

I paused in the kitchen doorway to attempt a rebuttal.

"Why do you think I went to the trouble and expense of getting you a birthday cake and that card, if I didn't love you?"

"Just to be nice," she retorted, looking up at me accusingly. "Oh, you're very nice, very thoughtful and considerate, but that's not love."

I moved to one side of the kitchen doorway as the boys crowded past me to get to the back yard and the promised ball game. I stood there, knowing what Florence meant. She didn't have to be more specific. She meant the growing dearth of whispered words, "I love you, Florence," which she had once heard from me, but never heard anymore unless she spoke them first and I responded in like vein out of a sense of obligation. She meant the substitution of occasional pecks upon the lips for the prolonged, passionate kisses she had once received. She meant the complete absence of any sexual contacts between us for more than a year, dating from before Korah's birth.

As I stood there dumbly, groping for words, she looked up at me with a fierceness born of a long unsatisfied hunger. Her eyes reached out to me, expressing the longing that she was too proud to put into words; unwilling to implore me, yet silently begging for the expressions of love that had been evoked in her mind by my remarks. My gaze fell beneath her own seeking, demanding, accusing, hungering probe, and I felt moisture beginning to gather at the corners of my eyes at the revelation of her desperate need.

"Why don't you just tell me the truth—that you don't really love me anymore?" she demanded.

"I can't tell you the truth, not yet," I cried silently within myself, averting her gaze. "It would hurt you too much."

"Hurry up, Dad!" Paul's voice came through the open back door, cutting through the emotional tension of the moment like a knife.

In response to Paul's impatient summons, I walked on through the kitchen toward the back door; my failure to speak further probably confirming Florence's suspicion that I didn't really love her anymore.

In the back yard, Paul, holding the bat in one hand and a softball in the other, tossed the ball to me.

"I'll bat first," he announced, delegating me to be pitcher and Philip the lone outfielder.

I looked at Philip, waiting for a protest from him as to who would be first at bat. But he was happily agreeable to the arrangement. Philip was usually willing to be second on our few fun adventures as long as he was assured that his turn was coming, but Paul always had to be first.

He stood expectantly now under the tree near the back fence that enclosed our yard, bat on shoulder, waiting for me to pitch the ball. I gave him an easy, underhand pitch. He swung vigorously and there was a loud "whomp" as the bat connected with the ball, sending it on a high-flying arc that would have been a credit to any major league player. I turned to watch it sail up into the air over the roof of our next door neighbor and landlady, Mrs. Starke. The ball came down on the shingled roof near the peak, began to roll down toward the ground, tumbled into the eaves trough, and stopped.

"Daddy, Daddy, the ball isn't coming down!" cried Philip in obvious distress.

Paul joined Philip and me as we stood looking up at the eaves trough, watching for the ball to bounce out and on down to the ground. It didn't. It was stuck there.

"Well, Dad, we'll just have to get a ladder and get it down," Paul announced matter of factly.

"I'm afraid the only ladder long enough is in Mrs. Starke's garage," I advised Paul, "and she's gone away and the garage is probably locked."

"How do you know she is?" demanded Paul skeptically.

"Because your mother said so at supper."

"Let's go see," Paul pleaded, "maybe it isn't locked."

"Yeah, we can at least go see if it's locked, Dad," chimed in Philip.

"Even if it isn't locked, boys," I objected firmly, "I wouldn't want to borrow her ladder without asking her. That wouldn't be right."

What I said was true, and I believed it, but it wasn't the whole truth. The rest of the truth was that I didn't want to spend the additional time and effort that would be involved in getting the long extension ladder out, retrieving the ball from the eaves trough and then putting the ladder back. For I had an important appointment for that evening that I was anxious to get to, and which I couldn't tell the boys about. Nevertheless, I felt compelled to further justify my selfish choice by giving the boys an added argument to support it.

"I know Mrs. Starke has a lot of valuable tools in her garage, so I'm positive she wouldn't go away and leave it unlocked. I'm just afraid that's all the ball game for tonight."

I placed a sympathetic hand on Paul's drooping shoulder. Then Philip suddenly thought of an equally happy substitution for the unfinished ball game.

"Daddy, would you take us to the park?"

I sighed as I prepared to say "No." Even though I had gone through this several nights a week during the years I had been attending Michigan State University on a part-time basis, it had not grown any easier. Each night as I had rushed off to evening-school classes, there had been this pleading to stay and play . . . go to the park . . . play ball . . . go bike riding . . . play checkers. Then there had been some justification for turning down their requests. My actions then, the expectation of getting a better-paying job when I graduated, had been mostly for their benefit, as well as for my own personal satisfaction in getting into a kind of work I enjoyed. But tonight I had no such good reason for leaving them. It was for no benefit that could accrue to them in the future that I felt compelled to leave them this evening. It was to fulfill a deep and desperate need of my own.

"I've got to go to the office and work a while tonight, Philip," I evaded.

"It's always work, work, work," muttered Paul morosely, and with the bat over his shoulder, turned away to go into the house.

"Come on, Philip," he called over his shoulder, "we can play with our cars."

"Okay, I'm coming," Philip agreed cheerfully, and turned to follow Paul.

"How about a kiss goodbye, Philip?" I asked.

Philip turned back to grant my request. I bent down to receive his kiss on the cheek and gave him one in return.

"G'bye, Dad," he said reluctantly, opening the screen door. "See you later." .

"See you later, Philip."

I walked down the cinder-scattered driveway alongside the house, stepped up on the front porch, opened the screen door and stuck my head inside. Florence was changing Korah's diaper as he lay quietly stretched out on the sofa.

"I'm going to the office for a little overtime," I called to her. "I'll probably be back about ten or a little after."

My "working overtime" on Friday nights had become such a regular practice in the preceding months, or attending some function at the nearby university in which I could claim a legitimate interest, that Florence had come to take my absence on Friday nights as an accepted part of our life together. It had become almost as much a part of our regular routine as getting up on Sunday morning and going to church.

"Stay until midnight if you want to," she answered, as she bent over Korah.

In the harshness of her tone was resignation to the likelihood that even if I did come home earlier to lie down on the bed beside her, she could not expect any overtures of sexual desire from me. Feeling keenly the reproach in her reply, I closed the screen door quietly and walked off the porch. As I walked down to the corner where I had parked the car, I consoled my conscience with the thought that Paul and Philip, engrossed in playing with their racetrack cars upstairs, had probably already forgotten the momentary disappointment of our one-hit ball game.

As I swung around the corner and drove past the house toward the downtown area, Florence came out on the porch with Korah. I waved to her and, although she saw me, she didn't return the wave. Six blocks from home, I stopped in front of a little grocery store which had a public telephone booth on the sidewalk in front of the store. As I opened the folding door on the phone booth, an obvious odor assailed my nostrils. Some drunk had evidently urinated in the booth several days or nights before. I held the door open with one foot to let the fresh air in while I fished in my pocket for change. The number I dialed was a familiar one because I had called it so many times in the preceding months.

"Roosevelt Hotel."

The male voice at the other end was indicative of the decline which had occurred in the status of the Roosevelt. Once there had been a full-time female operator at the switchboard. Now, one man functioned as both desk clerk, switchboard operator and, at times, elevator attendant as well.

"May I speak to Miss Colette Starr, please?

That was the name attached to the sultry voice that had spoken to me on the phone at work. It was not her real name, but a professional alias she had adopted to help ward off over-amorous male customers whom she encountered every night on her job as a taxi-dancer in Detroit. And it was safer than registering at the hotel under her real name, Mrs. Corrine McVey. The next voice I heard was a familiar one, silken soft, throaty, with emphatic sex appeal.

"Hello?"

There was a vibrant expectation in the tone of the voice, so that the single word spoken conveyed much more than a greeting. In the single word was conveyed a heartfelt hope.

"I hope this is the person whose voice I've been longing to hear more than anything else in the world."

"Hello, Corrine," I intoned gently.

My voice, as I spoke to her, contained, perhaps, a semblance of that piety with which a humble priest might begin the incantation of the Mass in some majestic cathedral. As I waited hungrily for more words, a little boy, five or six years of age, bare-footed and dirty faced, approached down the sidewalk. His disconsolate appearance as he trudged toward me made me think that he was probably on his way to the store to get an ice cream bar or candy, bribed by an uncaring parent, perhaps, to get him out from underfoot. Before going into the store he paused in front of the phone booth and looked at me questioningly. Suddenly, guilt caused me to see, peering out from his besmudged face, the probing eyes of my son, Philip, silently asking a question in childish innocence.

"Daddy, if you had to call somebody, why didn't you use the phone at home?"

I let the folding door of the phone booth slide shut, to endure the fetid odor of urine, and turned my gaze away from the little urchin as he passed on into the store.

"Darling, it's so wonderful to hear your voice again, especially knowing you're so close to me."

The warmth, the welcome, and the love in Corrine's voice flowed over me, silencing with a gentle touch the passing pang of conscience that had been evoked by the sight of a boy who had reminded me of Philip, my son. The love longing in her voice lured me further into another world where there were no accusing eyes; no wounds of heart or mind or memory; only happiness and light and beautiful music and the love of a beautiful woman.

"I'm sorry I wasn't able to get away any sooner, Corrine," I apologized, "but I had things to do at home that had to be done."

"I know, darling," she sighed wistfully, "I just hoped that by chance you might be able to come to me sooner. Otherwise, I wouldn't have called you at the office."

"How is it there at the Roosevelt now?" I asked, knowing that there had been no air conditioning in any of the rooms she had occupied there during preceding months.

"It's really quite comfortable. I've got the blinds pulled down, which makes it cooler. I'm in room 727."

Then there was a brief pause, as if Corrine were waiting for me to speak some expected words, followed by an impatient question.

"How long are you going to make me wait, Garfield, precious?"

"Wait for what, my love?"

"For what I want to hear you say," she pleaded.

"I love you, Corrine."

"I love you, Garfield," she returned, with a tenderness and passion that matched my own. "Darling, how soon are you coming to me?"

"That depends on how hungry you are."

"I'm starved . . . for you."

"I mean physical food, sweetheart. Do you want me to pick you up something to eat on the way?"

"That's my thoughtful lover," she replied.

"How about a hamburger, french fries, and a milk shake?"

"Sounds delicious, but not as delicious as you."

"And not as tasty as you, darling," I echoed tenderly.

"Darling, how much longer will it take you to get here if you stop and get me something to eat?"

"About fifteen minutes."

"Then I'll be seeing you in about fifteen minutes. Goody, goody!"

My heart was warmed by her enthusiasm and by the expression carried over from childhood days to express her delight at the expectation of seeing me soon.

"Might be closer to twenty," I warned, "in case there's a line at the take-out window."

"Just get here as soon as you can, my beloved," she begged.

"I will, and the sooner I hang up, the sooner I'll be seeing you."

"You're right, my darling. I love you so, Garfield."

"I love you, my precious Corrine."

I hung up and pushed open the folding door, relieved to get out of the fetid-smelling phone booth and into the fresh, crisp, autumn air. I hurried across the street, got into my car and drove toward the downtown area.

My stop at Kewpee's Hamburger Shop took a little longer than I had anticipated. It was nearly twenty minutes later that I pulled up in front of the Roosevelt Hotel on Seymour Street, a tree-lined, mostly residential street that ran from the State Capitol in the heart of the city, north to the perimeter of the business district. Centrally located, the Roosevelt was situated just one block from the State Capitol building and only three blocks from the Gray building "prison" where I worked. Once one of the leading hotels in Lansing, it had been pushed into the background by new motels that had taken away much of its business. The huge sign atop the hotel, spelling out the name of the hotel, which had once dominated the night-time skyline in blazing lights, had been darkened in an economy move, and was visible only in the daytime. It had declined from being a center of legislative intrigue to a workingman's hotel, catering to a clientele from lower economic and social strata.

Nevertheless, it had ideally suited the desperate needs of Corrine and me for nearly a year. It was close to downtown, easily accessible to me, and saved an exorbitant taxi fare for Corrine to and from the Greyhound bus terminal on the south end of town. And there were no raised eyebrows on the part of the desk clerk at my periodic Friday night and Saturday morning visits, whenever Miss Colette Starr from Detroit checked in at the hotel for an overnight stay.

I got out of the station wagon with the sack containing Corrine's carry-out supper, since the hotel's restaurant had closed in an economy move. Parked across the street from the hotel, as I looked both ways for oncoming traffic before crossing the street, the corner of my eye registered the towering hulk of St. Stephen's Catholic Cathedral occupying a corner diagonally across from the hotel. As I crossed the street, there came to my mind a flashback scene of myself, years before, when I had been working as an apprentice baker in a bakery just a few blocks down the street.

Often, before going to work at six in the morning, I had stolen quietly into the vast, empty basilica, just to kneel in one of the pews and meditate on the figure of the God-man, Jesus Christ, hanging realistically upon a huge cross that must have been fifteen feet high. The nave of the church was curved around the crucifixion scene like a cinerama screen. The entire curved back wall, thirty feet high from the floor of the altar to the ceiling, was an impressive mural painting worthy of da Vinci. Darkly ominous storm clouds behind the three crosses were squeezing out the afternoon sunlight, and streaks of angry red stabbed across the horizon. Several figures were depicted at the foot of the cross, looking upwards for the miracle of deliverance that had not come.

It was a tragic, touching, and artistically impressive spectacle. When I slid into one of the rear pews just to sit for several minutes and study the silent scene, I did not pause to kneel and make the sign of the cross. I had only gone to St. Stephen's because it was conveniently close to the place where I worked then. Besides that, there were no Protestant churches open at that time of morning, and none of them had such a splendid and realistic representation of the crucifixion scene. Strangely, I remembered, as I pushed my way through the heavy double glass doors of the hotel, that of all the times I had gone into the cathedral in the early morning hours just to meditate for a few minutes on the love of God for me, I had never encountered another worshiper, priest, or nun.

The scene from my past was pushed from my mind then as I passed through the lobby of the Roosevelt. In the attractively furnished lounge area, an elderly man and two dowager ladies sat watching the televison screen. Taped music floated gently in the air. Walking to the open elevator, I saw that there was no operator. Evidently, the desk clerk, presently engaged in registering a middle-aged couple, was also operating the elevator. As I waited before the empty elevator, I turned and looked down the corridor that went from the lobby to the back of the hotel. The closed doors with signs above them were indicative of the decline of the Roosevelt. Through the locked glass doors of the Dome Room, once a bustling restaurant crowded with legislators and state workers, I could dimly see various items of furniture piled in disorderly array. Further down the thick-carpeted corridor were other concessions which had been discontinued . . . Cocktail Lounge . . . Barber Shop . . . Shoe Shine.

"Going up, sir?"

I whirled around at the voice behind me to see the desk clerk, benign, bespeckled, and baldheaded but neatly dressed, standing in the open door of the elevator, the incoming guests behind him.

"Yes, thank you."

I crowded onto the elevator into a corner behind several suitcases.

"Seven, please," I said, as the elevator door closed.

On the fifth floor, the couple with their luggage got off, and I proceeded on to the seventh floor, the top floor at the Roosevelt.

"Here we are," the desk clerk announced genially, as he pulled open the door.

"Thank you."

I stepped off the elevator and the heavy doors clanged shut behind me, leaving me alone in a vestibule containing a Coke vending machine that sometimes worked. I looked into the mirror on the opposite wall of the foyer, and ran a comb through my slightly breeze-blown hair. Then I stepped around the corner that led into the long, thickly carpeted hallway. As soon as I did, I stopped in my tracks, arrested by the breathtaking beauty of the scene that met my eyes. At the far end of the hotel corridor, where a window admitted a fast-fading flood of afternoon sunlight, Corrine stood silhouetted. I could recognize her figure, even though I could not clearly see her shadowed face because I was looking into the light around her.

As I began to walk toward her, she came toward me. The

graceful swing of her hips not only aroused me sexually, but touched my artist's appreciation of beauty in any form, whether the riotous colors of autumn leaves, the sounds of a Tchaikovsky symphony, or the movements of a ballet dancer.

"Is it really you, Garfield?" she called softly, in wondering doubt as we drew closer together.

"It's really me, darling."

I set the sack containing her carry-out supper on the floor in the middle of the hallway and opened my arms to her as she approached with outstretched arms. Then she was enfolded in my embrace.

"How long has it been?" she breathed softly in my ear, after a long, passionate, tongue-probing kiss.

"A thousand years," I answered, as I tenderly kissed the delicate, shell-like contour of an ear, hidden behind the waving, golden silk of her hair.

Then I retrieved the sack beside me and, with one arm around her waist, we walked slowly down the corridor in mutually silent rapture, to the last room on the left. I knew the room at once, without looking for the number on the door, by the protective sign Corrine always brought with her to hang over the doorknob: "Do Not Disturb."

In the room, with the door locked, I carefully set down on the dresser Corrine's sack-supper. Then we embraced, with even more fervor than we had in the hallway. With my face buried in the silken fragrance of her golden hair, a soft sigh was squeezed out of me by her firmly encircling arms.

"What's the sigh for, Garfield, darling?" she breathed into my ear.

"That's because I'm home again," I intoned softly.

"And you're my only home in this world, Garfield."

She pulled back her head to look into my eyes and confirm her verbal admission with a visual pledge of emphasis. I bent my head and lifted her lips to mine like a connoisseur about to sip some rare, exotic beverage, too priceless, too scarce, to be gulped down greedily. Her lips had a taste that seemed like a blend of honey, fresh strawberries and essence of soul.

"May I take your coat, darling?" she asked, stepping back, graciously assuming the servant role of a hat-check girl.

I turned my back to her and held my arms akimbo while she slipped the sleeves of the plaid sport coat off my arms, then hung it up in the closet.

"Now this," she said, stepping up to me and beginning to untwine the knot of my necktie.

I looked into her face and watched her movements, fascinated, as she let the tie slip down the crook of her arm, then unbuttoned my top shirt button. I stood there reveling in her attentions designed to make me feel more comfortable.

"Now your shoes," she commanded, after hanging my tie in the closet.

She took my hand and led me over to the upholstered, red leather chair by the window that looked out on the street, affording a full frontal view of St. Stephen's Cathedral on the corner. As I sat down in the chair that was close to the edge of the bed, she laid down across one corner of the bed, her arms and head hanging over one side near my legs, and began to untie my shoes. Leaning forward a little, I ran an admiring hand over the form-fitting red jersey mini-skirted dress, lingering on the delightful twin hills of her buttocks.

"Garfield!" she remonstrated, in a scoldingly playful tone, as she worked at my shoes, "what are you doing?"

"Just paying tribute to the most adorable ass in the world," I answered, and gave her rump a loving pat.

Corrine tore off my remaining shoe impetuously, sat bolt upright, then fell to her knees in front of me and threw her arms around me like a wrestler.

"You're getting me excited," she exuded, and encircled my head, drawing me down to her lips with passionate vigor.

"No more kisses until I shave," I protested, drawing back from her embrace. "I don't want you to get blistered lips from my beard like you did once before."

"But it's such a nice souvenir to take back with me, remembering how they got that way."

"Nope," I insisted, holding her at arms' length. "You eat

your supper while I shave; otherwise, your supper will be getting cold while I'm getting hot."

"You're such a sweet, thoughtful lover," she said, looking at me lovingly.

"If I am," I replied, as she turned to her sack supper on the dresser and I got up, "it's only what's rubbed off on me from you."

As Corrine sat on the edge of the bed and began to partake of the already-not-so-hot food, I stepped into the bathroom to shave. I turned on the hot-water faucet, unbuttoned my shirt and hung it on the wall hook. My toiletries, which Corrine brought with her each time she came, were laid out for me on the glass shelf under the medicine cabinet; a shaving brush in its plastic container, a glass case with razor and blades, toothpaste and toothbrush, deodorant and after-shave lotion.

As I stood before the mirror, my face lathered with soap, and began to shave, Corrine came in quietly and stood behind me. Without the high heels she always wore, I could just see the top of her head in the mirror as she walked up in her stocking feet behind me. Then, a familiar ritual that I had come to cherish. Stepping up close behind me, she placed her arms under my arms and, placing one hand on my chest and one on my stomach, she laid her cheek against my shoulder and held me close to her. I stopped shaving as she stood on tiptoe so that I could just see her eyes in the mirror visible above my shoulder. I stood transfixed in the wonder of this simple gesture, wondering that her love for me was such that she would want to embrace me and be close to me even while I shaved. Then I turned my lathered face back toward her face, nestled against my shoulder. As I did, she stretched up and lifted her lips to mine, in a kiss that left a ring of soap lather around her lips.

"I love you, my Adam, my Prince Charming, sweetheart husband to be," she whispered, our noses almost touching.

"I love you, my Eve, my princess, my everything woman," and stretched to plant a kiss on her nose.

Then she left as quietly as she had entered, to sit on the

edge of the bed from where she could watch me as I finished shaving. Five minutes later, after stanching a cut on my chin with tissue paper, and having applied after-shave lotion to my freshly shaven skin, I stepped back into the bedroom to stand before her as she was finishing the last swallow of her strawberry milk shake.

Then Corrine's outstretched arms drew me down above her on the bed; beckoning me, calling me, wooing me, away from the world I had lately come from; the world of a job that was stunting and stifling; of a home that was a place of unfulfilled needs and hidden tensions and open conflicts; a world of spiritual aspirations that had not been realized; a world of accusing eyes and a troubled conscience. She drew me down into a world that was Corrine, a world of love and peace and fulfillment; of security and warmth, and a wild, delicious, delirious freedom; a world in which the bed of love upon which we embraced became a launching pad that could catapult us together out of the real world in which we lived, with its painful past, its burdensome present, and its uncertain future, into some far corner of the universe where time and its consequences no longer prevailed, to the very beginnings of Eternity, to the very gates of Heaven.

It was hours later, but it seemed like minutes, that the warning buzz of an alarm clock, like a rattlesnake poised to strike, startled me into premature wakefulness. I sat bolt upright on the bed where I had been sleeping, and felt a wave of relief sweep over me as I discovered that I had not slept the night away in Corrine's room at the Roosevelt Hotel. I was on the studio couch in my own living room, a blanket rumpled half on the floor and the rest over me. From upstairs I heard the creak of the bed and a suppressed sigh of unwanted wakefulness from Florence as she got up to shut off the alarm. Then the relief I felt was followed by momentary bewilderment as I realized that I was sleeping downstairs on the studio couch instead of upstairs in bed with Florence.

Slowly, my bafflement gave way to remembrance as the aftermath of my meeting with Corrine at the Roosevelt came surging through my mind. I laid back down on the couch and pulled the blanket over me as the climax of the night before swept over me. I had come home from my clandestine rendezvous with Corrine to slip quietly into a silent, darkened house, there to go first of all to the bathroom and wash away the telltale smells of sexual passion that I had brought home with me from the Roosevelt. Arriving home nearly an hour and a half later than I had told Florence I would be home, I was thankful to find Florence asleep when I had gone upstairs to lie down quietly beside her on the bed.

But she had not been asleep. She had turned over and reached out to me in sudden, lonely hunger, to touch me intimately as she had not attempted to do for months. Lying on the couch, staring up at the ceiling, I relived the agony of that moment that had frozen my body into immobility, unable to tolerate or respond to the touch of Florence, my wife, where Corrine had touched me so tenderly, so lovingly, so passionately, but an hour before. Yet, I had been unable to voice an objection to Florence nor to push her hand away. For in spite of the fact that emotionally, psychologically, her touch seemed obscene, still she had the legal and moral right to touch me in that way. But there had been no need for me to object. Florence had gotten the message of rejection communicated by my suddenly rigid body, and had flung herself out of bed to rush downstairs, there to throw herself down on the couch and bury her face in a pillow to muffle the sobs that might have awakened the boys, all asleep upstairs.

When I had gone downstairs, dumbly knowing there was nothing I could do or say to comfort her, she had rushed back upstairs to get away from me. So I had settled on the couch, to spend the rest of the night there, separated from Florence, my wife, by a gulf of guilt and betrayal and disintegration of love, which I did not have the heart to reveal to her. The recalled experiences of the night before descended upon me like a heavy hand, holding me down, pinning me on my back. But I had to get up. If I laid there and went back to sleep, the unconsciousness that I craved as a way of immediate escape from the memory of Florence's weeping alone in the night might hold me there well past the eight o'clock appointment I had promised Corrine.

As I pushed myself up from the sofa, muscles sore from the cramped position and the lumpy surface of the couch, and swung my feet to the floor, my gaze fell upon the picture on the opposite wall. It was a well-known painting of Christ, seated and surrounded by children, a girl on His lap looking up into His face, with two boys and an older girl at His feet, each bidding for His attention. It was a good thing, I reflected in that moment, that the future was hidden from children. If they knew what lay ahead of them in life, a life which for many began with such enthusiasm and dreams and budding desires . . . if they had any inkling of the struggles, the frustrations and defeats, and the wounds of body, mind and spirit that they would encounter . . . how many would have been frightened into immobility, as I doubtless would have been as a child if I had known what was in store for me in later years.

If I had known at some point in the past, that step by step, the circumstances of my own making were leading me irresistibly to the events of the preceding night . . . the guilty feeling of coming home from a sexual encounter with Corrine at the Roosevelt, to turn away from an outreach for affection from Florence, my wife . . . if I could have heard the sound of her lonely sobbing in the night . . . would I not have refused to go on to such a future? But I had not known, and now, there was no going back to live over again the choices I had made, the sequence of actions that had dissolved the bond of my relationship to Florence, and had cemented the ties of mind and spirit and body that now bound me to Corrine.

I got up in a T-shirt and pajama bottoms, walked into the kitchen and put on a coffee pot of water to heat while I shaved. Before lathering to shave, I looked at myself in the bathroom mirror. It was the image of a father who had left his children the night before to go to a hotel room and indulge in adultery with another man's wife; and a husband who had left his own wife to sob out her desperate hunger for love, alone in the night.

"You lousy bastard!" I hissed at my reflection, suppressing with difficulty the sudden impulse to strike out at the image in the mirror, knowing that it would do no good.

I finished shaving, then stepped out into the kitchen to put coffee in the dripolator and pour in the boiling water. As I returned to the bathroom to finish my ablutions, I heard Florence coming downstairs. I stuck my head through the bathroom door to see her pouring a cup of coffee for herself.

"Good morning, Florence," I said in a voice subdued by the self-condemnation that I felt.

"Good morning, Gar."

Her tone was cool and distant, and she didn't look at me as she turned to get cream out of the refrigerator for her coffee. I closed the bathroom door to finish my bath, recognizing the tone of her voice. It was the hurt tone, the tone of defeat, of resignation, the tight tone of quiet suppression, a tone that told me more of what she was holding back within herself more eloquently than words could have alone. It was a tone that told me she was holding back expressions of hunger and disappointment and chagrin over her inability to understand what had taken place in the husband who had once loved her, who had once embraced and kissed her passionately, who had engaged in sexual relations with her, who had in former times said tenderly and with feeling, and without being prompted, the potent and life-giving words, "I love you."

I opened the bathroom door to elicit some mundane information from Florence.

"Want to use the bathroom?"

"No, thank you."

Her answer from the living room was curt and restrained. I waited a moment to see if there would be an additional comment in response to my attempt to initiate a conversation to drive away the pain-filled silence between us. But there was no further word, so I closed the door again to finish dressing. Five minutes later I emerged, fully dressed. As I stepped to the cupboard to get a coffee cup, a warning bell suddenly sounded in my mind, reminding me of an especially incriminating bit of evidence that I had almost left behind me in the bathroom. Quickly, I stepped back into the bathroom and swept up a crumpled handkerchief I had extracted from the hip pocket of the trousers I had worn the night before, and had forgotten to transfer to the different pair of pants I had donned. Hastily, lest Florence come in and catch me, like a thief in the act of robbery, I plunged the handkerchief into my left hip pocket. I remembered, without looking at it, that there were smears of crimson on it which Florence would be quick to identify as lipstick; a brand of orange that she would never wear. And besides that, she knew that it had been too long since I had kissed her in a way that would leave a lipstick smear upon my lips.

I trembled inwardly as I stepped back out of the bathroom. It was a dangerous souvenir I had brought home. Corrine did not always remind me to wipe my lips when I left her, and I might have overlooked it myself, had there not been a full-length mirror in the alcove by the elevator at the hotel. Fortunately, I had spotted the incriminating evidence on my lips as I had waited for the elevator and had wiped it away on my handkerchief; then had brought it home, almost to leave it where Florence could find it.

I poured myself a cup of coffee with hands that were not steady. Coffee cup in hand, I walked into the living room and sat down on the circular, brown leather hassock facing the large picture window. Diagonally across from me in an overstuffed chair, Florence sat sipping her coffee. I didn't dare look at her directly, shrinking from eye contact, but out of the corner of my eye I caught an impression of utter dejection. With her plain green cotton housecoat pulled tight around her, and her hair disheveled, her eyes were red and swollen from the crying of the night before.

"You're going to Charlotte today, aren't you?" I asked.

I looked out the window rather than at Florence, noting that the leaves were turning gold on the maple tree in Mrs.

Starke's front yard. It was Florence's usual practice to go every other weekend to visit her widowed mother who lived in the small town eighteen miles west of Lansing, and help her clean the huge farmhouse since the crippling effects of arthritis had in the past several years grown more pronounced.

"I don't know whether I should go or not with these red eyes. Mom will know something's wrong, and she'll ask me about it."

I sipped my coffee and looked out the window as the weight of this additional burden which I had put upon my wife pressed down on me. Across the street a boy on a bicycle rode down the sidewalk, throwing rolled-up morning papers on the porches of his customers. For a moment I envied the simple, carefree life which I imagined he led.

"The hard part is," Florence continued, as if meditating aloud instead of speaking to me, "I don't know what's wrong myself, so I don't know what to tell Mom."

"Maybe it's just old age creeping upon me," I suggested, studiously avoiding Florence's probing gaze as I manufactured a lie designed to hide the truth. "The experts say that after a man passes forty, his sexual desires begin to decline."

The blatant falseness of my statement sickened me, but to Florence, it held out immediate hope.

"Do you really think that's the trouble?" she asked, desperately sincere, eager to clutch at some explanation for my diminution of sexual interest in her other than the one which struck her as being most logical—that I no longer loved her.

"It may be," I answered, assuming an attitude of deep thought and arresting the coffee cup halfway to my lips. "Human beings are complex creatures, hard to understand."

"You can say that again," she agreed, "especially you."

I finished my coffee and stood up.

"You don't know then whether you'll be going out to your mother's or not?"

"I suppose I'll have to," she replied reluctantly, toying with her empty cup. "Mom can't clean that house alone. Her arthritis is so bad she can't hardly lift her hands above her

70

shoulders. If Mom asks me what's wrong, I'll just tell her what you said, that you're getting too old to be interested in loving me anymore."

"I didn't say I didn't love you any more," I countered, knowing that if I didn't protest, she would interpret my silence as agreement with her interpretation.

I sensed that her comment was an oblique attempt to get me to say that I did still love her, spawned by an unvoiced hunger to have me come over to her, and by embracing and kissing her, to reassure her with such actions that there was still some of the romantic ardor within me which she had tasted on our long-ago honeymoon. But while I could deceive her with words, I didn't have the stomach to carry out the lie in deeds. I could not force myself to walk over to her and pretend a feeling which I did not have. Then, like a prosecuting attorney interrogating a witness, she brought forth further damning evidence in support of her suspicion about me.

"Maybe you haven't said that you don't love me anymore in so many words, but you haven't said that you did love me for a long time either, unless I said it first."

I tried to escape by diverting her away from our particular situation into a generalized discussion, where I could hide behind generalities and abstractions in a game of words where I would hold an advantage.

"Do you know what love is?" I asked, looking at her. "There's no use using the word unless you know what it means."

"I don't have to know what it means," she retorted fiercely, as I stood by the hassock, empty cup in hand. "I only know I married you because I loved you, and I thought you loved me."

"The basic ingredient of love," I evaded, "is good will toward another, and I certainly have that for you. I want the best there is in life for you. I want you to be happy."

"Shit!" she spat, getting up from her chair. "If you cared anything about my happiness, you'd stay home once in a while instead of being gone every night, God only knows where."

We stood in the living room facing each other while upstairs the three sons who had been born of our marriage slept on. There was a physical distance between us of ten feet, but in the conditions that had created that physical separation there was a perhaps impassable gulf between us, too broad to be jumped across, too deep to be crossed by climbing down one side and up the other. I stood there in dumb helplessness as Florence stormed out into the kitchen, throwing her coffee cup into the sink with a clatter that would have broken it had it not been plastic, and slammed the bathroom door shut behind her. I stood there a moment, alone in the center of the living room, inwardly shattered by her display of righteous wrath, feeling also that her harsh judgment of me was not just. I had to admit to myself that as she viewed my outward behavior, and as I saw it myself, my actions seemed to say that I cared not an iota for her happiness. But if she knew, as God knew, and as I had experienced, the grief and self-reproach and self-loathing in my heart over the unhappiness I had brought to her, she would perhaps have tempered her angry indictment with forgiving mercy.

As I returned my coffee cup to the kitchen sink and turned to leave the house, Florence came out of the bathroom. I stood there helplessly as she pulled dirty clothes out of the hamper and began to sort them into several different piles on the floor in preparation for the weekly wash.

"What time do you want to leave for Charlotte?" I asked, compelled to arrange the mechanics of a daily schedule even while our relationship was disintegrating.

"The usual time," she replied curtly, head bent to her task, not looking up at me as she spoke.

"Eleven o'clock?"

"Yeah, I could have the washing done by then if the kids don't give me too much trouble."

There was added rebuke in her words. I could lighten her burden by staying home and keeping the boys occupied while she did the washing. But I had promised Corrine . . .

"I'll be home to have breakfast with the boys about 10:30, then."

"Scrambled eggs?" she asked, reaching down to the bottom of the clothes hamper.

"My favorite food," I projected with imitation enthusiasm.

"I'll have them ready," she promised grimly, as she picked up the empty hamper and carried it back into the bathroom, stepping carefully between the piles of dirty clothes on the floor.

There was no affectionate exchange of farewell words as I opened the front door to leave for the office, as Florence believed. There was only the familiar Saturday morning sound of water running from the kitchen sink spigot through a rubber hose and into the round metal tub of the white, old-fashioned washing machine.

As I backed the car out of the drive and drove toward downtown for a brief morning rendezvous with Corrine before she returned to Detroit, I was not driven by the same exuberant hunger that had sent me flying to her the night before. My erotic ardor was diminished somewhat; perhaps, because it had been fed in a passionate session of sexual communion the night before, yet leaving the inevitable aftermath of guilt feelings. But I was further depressed by the realization that I would have to keep locked within myself the deeply disturbing confrontation with Florence the night before and that morning. I would have to manufacture a smile and endearing expressions of love for Corrine while hiding from her the knowledge that my heart was heavy at the remembrance of Florence's red and tear-swollen eyes, resulting from my rejection of her the night before.

I would have to make an effort to hold back this truth from Corrine even as I had been holding back the truth from Florence. Suddenly, I felt like an actor, going from one theatrical performance to another, cast in the role of a deceiver in two separate dramas, and abhorring such a role in both cases. Yet, in both cases it was consideration for another that compelled me to continue playing a part that was personally repugnant to me. It was consideration for Florence, to postpone the havoc that I knew the truth would bring to her that had kept me from blurting it out sooner to ease my own conscience. It was also love for Corrine that would keep my lips from distressing her with a report of what had happened last night and this morning between Florence and me. I would keep the truth from Corrine, that is, if I could keep her from sensing somehow the grief that was hidden away from her sight, deep within me.

As I detoured from my route to the Roosevelt to stop at a restaurant and pick up a carry-out breakfast for Corrine, I lifted a silent but anguished cry heavenward.

"O God, how much longer will this deception have to go on?"

It was a question Corrine had addressed to me many times in the past few months, and one she would probably ask again before I kissed her goodbye at the Roosevelt. But there was one comforting thought regarding this question that I could claim for myself, and that I could finally share with Corrine. In the past few weeks, I had been unable to give Corrine an answer to that troubling question. But this morning, if she asked me that question again, I would have at least the beginning of an answer to give to her.

(HAPTER 3

⇒ The massive bell that was mounted in the battlement-like tower of St. Stephen's Cathedral clanged out its solemn and ponderous message of accusation against penitent Catholics to come to church and confess their sins and be forgiven. Close to the downtown area, it had to compete with the busy sounds of morning traffic, seeking the attention of men more concerned about laying up treasures on earth than being reconciled to the God of Heaven. But from the front room on the seventh floor of the Roosevelt Hotel, across the street from St. Stephen's, where I stood looking out the window, it was impossible to shut out the sound. It had interrupted the reading aloud I had been doing at Corrine's request as she reclined on the bed behind me, munching on the carry-out breakfast I had brought for her.

"CLANG-g-g!"

The volume and resonance of the sound caused the very window in front of me to rattle from the vibrations. Ten blocks to the west, busy with the weekly washing, Florence probably could not hear the sound above the combined noise emanating from the washing machine and the television set. Even if she had heard, I mused, it probably would not have interrupted her grim devotion to duty.

"Aren't you going to read anymore, sweetheart?" Corrine's voice asked plaintively from behind me.

In my right hand I held a book which I had given to

Corrine as a gift several months before and from which I had been reading aloud before the sound of the cathedral bell across the street had begun to pour into the room. It contained an edited collection of quotations, poems, and excerpts that had been written on the subject of love between man and woman. As I had read fragments of what a particular woman's love had meant to such great men as Victor Hugo, Alexander Hamilton, Beethoven, and even Napoleon Bonaparte, I had been impressed anew with what a powerful influence a woman's love could be in the life of a man, great or obscure.

"Let's wait until the church bell stops," I suggested, without turning from the window.

My proposal met with no protest from Corrine. The sounds she made, breaking up pieces of food and masticating food, was interspersed at regular intervals with the mournful "clang" of the giant bell. It was not the usual "ding-dong" church bell sound, in which a bell is pulled so that the clapper inside strikes first one side of the bell, then falls against the other side. It was pulled in such a way that the clapper struck only one side of the bell with a single, reverberating "clang." Then there was a mathematically precise interval of silence, of about fifteen seconds' duration, followed by another "clang."

As I stood looking out the window, listening to the bell and gazing idly at the medieval hulk of the great church where pigeons wheeled about the bell tower, the words from the book I had been reading recurred in my mind.

"O never, never take the priceless gift of love for granted! Hold it close, its magic touch will make each hour enchanted!"

There had indeed been enchantment with Corrine, here in this room, last night. This morning, some of the enchantment was gone. It had been banished from my mind in the aftermath of Florence's uncomforted crying in the night. And it seemed to have been driven from the room this morning, as Adam and Eve had been expelled from the Garden of Eden, by the ponderous pounding of the giant bell across the street.

"Guilty-y-y" it seemed to clang, "guilty-y-y!"

Between bites of food, Corrine was able to inject a running flow of comments and questions into the fifteen-second intervals between the "guilty" clangs of the bell.

"I hope you slept as well as I did, sweetheart."

The words spewed up out of her like a geyser, pushed up from some deep, vibrant deposit of contentment which had been implanted within her the night before.

"Yes," I lied, "I slept alright."

"Good!" she sighed, "we always seem to sleep better after we've had our love fulfillment, don't we?"

"At least I do," she added, using the pause in which I hesitated to answer for a comment that contained both a question and a subtle rebuke.

"Yes, darling, I guess we do."

"You guess?" she queried, in a tone of hurt surprise. "Aren't you certain, darling?"

"Yes, I'm certain, sweetheart."

The tone of my voice was evidently not convincing enough for Corrine.

"Darling, turn around and look at me," she pleaded.

I turned and looked into her eyes that reflected the troubled question in her mind. I was aware at the same time, in my area of peripheral vision, that she was a sexually enticing sight in the transparent black negligee that revealed more than it concealed.

"Now, tell me, darling," she demanded plaintively, "is something wrong?"

"No," I shrugged, "why do you ask?"

"Because you sounded so sad when you were reading, and you look so weary. Did you really sleep well last night?"

In the hidden recesses of my mind I could still hear the sounds of Florence's muffled sobbing in the night. But of what avail to tell Corrine of it? I questioned myself silently. She would only feel hurt by the disclosure that I could be affected by any woman's tears except her own.

"Yes," I repeated the lie, shifting my gaze to look at the autumn scene on the wall above her head, "I slept alright."

Corrine suddenly thought of a practical test to apply to me to check the truthfulness of my answer.

"Darling," she pouted, "I've only had one kiss from you this morning."

I laid down the book on the window sill and walked over to the bed. I picked up the breakfast tray from off her lap and set it down carefully on the bed beside her, then swept her into my embrace. I kissed her hard upon her upturned mouth, at once attracted by her soft, perfumed femininity and at the same time repelled by a sudden impulse of moral nausea that arose within me. It kept me from plunging my tongue into her mouth in a kiss of sexual arousal.

"GUILTY-y-y!" Clanged the bell, reinforcing the surge of self-loathing that had flooded through me.

"My darling's so smooth this morning," Corrine murmured, rubbing her forehead against my cheek.

"Did you miss me, darling?" she asked, looking up into my eyes hopefully.

"Yes, I missed you, and I love you and adore you."

I spoke the words I knew she wanted to hear, then tried to gently disengage myself from her encircling arms.

"Now why don't you finish your breakfast?"

"One more kiss first," she begged.

I leaned toward her and pressed my lips against her own in repetition of the kiss I had just given her, and like the first one I had given her when I had stepped into the room an hour before.

"Why don't you kiss me the way you did last night?" she reproached gently.

I sighed, caught in an emotional vise. I could never explain to Corrine that what I had been through with Florence had put a damper upon my sexual ardor for her, Corrine. And to avoid having to explain, I tried to hide the truth behind of facade of playacting. I embraced her again and pressed my lips to hers, this time pushing my tongue in between her hungrily parted lips, rolling my tongue against hers, and then against the insides of her mouth.

"That's more like it!" she gasped as I drew back. "U-m-m, you get me excited. Do I get you excited?"

"Certainly you do; now finish your breakfast."

Getting up from the bed, I walked back to the window, suddenly aware that the huge bell across the street had finally ceased its slow, doleful clanging. I picked up the book from the window sill, sat down facing Corrine and opened it at random to continue reading to Corrine while she finished her scrambled eggs, toast and tea. As I read aloud the never-before encountered opening lines of "The Woman Who Understands" by Everard Jack Appleton, the lines seemed suddenly reminiscent of the circumstances under which I had first met Corrine. For that reason, perhaps, my voice contained something of my own spontaneous reaction of pathos and feeling as I read the words for the first time.

> As the tide went out she found him
> Lashed to a spar of Despair,
> The wreck of his ship around him—
> The wreck of his dreams in the air;
> Found him, and loved him, and gathered
> The soul of him close to her heart—
> The soul that had sailed an uncharted sea,
> The soul that had sought to win and be free—
> The soul of which she was part!
> And there in the dusk, she cried to the man,
> "Win your battle—you can, you can!"
>
> Somewhere she waits to make you win, your soul
> In her firm, white hands—
> Somewhere, the gods have made for you,
> The woman who understands!

Corrine broke into my reading. "Am I the woman you're reading about, Garfield? Am I the woman who understands you better than any other woman ever has?"

"Of course, darling," I replied, glancing across the room at her.

My affirmative answer was given without thought or reflection, almost as an automatic reflex, knowing it was the answer she needed to hear.

"Then there's just one change we'd have to make in those lines to make them really fit you and me," she continued. "I'm the woman God has made for you, not the gods. We both know there's only one true God."

"You're right, darling."

As I bent my gaze to the remaining stanzas of the poem, the quick answer I had given to Corrine's question continued to revolve in my mind, deterring me from continued reading aloud. There was no doubt in my mind, I reflected, that Corrine was indeed the woman who understood in a wonderful way my needs and desires in the areas of sexual love. But would she also understand the grief I felt over the unhappy encounters with Florence last night and this morning? Could she understand and sympathetically accept the feelings of guilt and self-recrimination that pointed accusing fingers at me? The anguished memory of that scene, called forth by the very question Corrine had innocently asked, suddenly killed my taste for the book in my hands. I closed it, set it back on the windowsill behind me, then stood up and turned to face the window again, my back to Corrine. My action provoked an immediate response from her.

"There is something wrong, isn't there, Garfield?"

"Maybe," I conceded, weary of holding back the truth.

"Why don't you tell me?" she pleaded. "We shouldn't keep things from each other."

I replied factually, without feeling, as I watched the pigeons roosting upon the battlements of St. Stephen's medieval towers.

"Florence wanted some affection last night."

"Did you give her any?" Corrine asked in a tight voice which told me that her insides were being squeezed together in an agony of suspense.

"No," I answered flatly, objectively, with my back still turned to her. "She just cried. I slept downstairs on the couch while she stayed upstairs."

"Darling, turn around and look at me," Corrine pleaded.

I complied with her request but continued standing where I was by the window, the length of the room separating us.

"I know it's hard on you, darling," she sympathized, balancing the half-emptied cup of tea on her lap, "but don't forget how I feel. Don't forget how I felt last night when you left me to sleep in a bed with another woman, when it's me that you love."

"I know."

Before her sobering gaze I dropped my eyes to study the design of the carpet; white flowers, now faded to a dull gray upon a background of drab crimson.

"So that's why you're so depressed this morning?"

"Partly," I acknowledged, looking up at her.

"Is something else wrong?"

"Yes, but there's no use talking about it," I replied with a feeling of hopelessness probably evident in my voice, as I turned and looked out the window again.

In the vast, semi-darkened, candle-flickered interior of St. Stephen's Cathedral across the street, the eyes of my mind pierced the concealing walls and I saw the figure of Jesus Christ upon the cross above the altar. Imagination touched that immobile, lifeless figure of bronze and changed it to a living form of flesh and blood, twisting, turning from the pain of nail-pierced hands and feet, the cruel crown of thorns, the dried blood caked in the corners of the eyes, the parched lips, the shameful indignity of hanging nearly stark naked before a crowd of caviling strangers and taunting enemies, writhing from the pain of being pinioned to the rough wooden cross by iron spikes. I thought of the act of adultery that had been committed in this very room the night before and of how that very act was one of the sins for which the Son of God had writhed in torment upon that cross . . . to save me from the eternal penalty of that single act of sin, as if there had been or would be no others; the punishment of everlasting separation from the presence of God and all the promised bliss that could be found only in His presence. In the love-fevered actions that had taken place in this room last night, I had pounded the nails deeper into the palms of his hands; I had pressed down the jagged crown of thorns deeper into his head.

"Garfield, please turn around and talk to me," Corrine pleaded again.

I turned back to meet her hurt, inquiring gaze.

"What do you mean by saying there's no use talking about it? No use talking about what?"

Then fear, the fear that was ever crouched within her, ready to spring to life at the slightest provocation, seized her again.

"Do you mean that you want to go back to her, that you're going to leave me? Is that what you're trying to say, Garfield?"

"No, Corrine," I sighed, sensing her anguish at such a prospect, "that's not what I'm trying to say at all."

"Then tell me what it is," she pleaded.

She set aside the breakfast tray, a few crusts of toast left, her tea unfinished, and stared at me with a stricken expression, apprehensive about what I was going to say.

"Some time ago," I began, gazing steadfastly into her eyes from across the room, "you complained that I no longer wrote such long love letters to you as I used to do when we first came back together after being apart five years. It's because the joy and peace I used to feel in pouring out my heart to you has been slowly dying away. I feel that I'm dying spiritually because of a grievous sin in my life that I don't seem to have the power to overcome. That's what's wrong."

Corrine's eyes registered pain and perplexity. She gripped the bed sheet into a sudden, frenzied knot as she thought she grasped the import of my words.

"Have you been going to sexy movies behind my back again, or reading those filthy magazines and books like you used to do before we met?"

I suppressed a groan of weariness at her spiritual short-sightedness that could see bygone evils afar off, but could not see the evil occurring under her very nose in the present, in her life and mine.

"No, Corrine, that's not what's wrong. Do you mind if I read you a verse from the Bible to explain what I'm talking about?"

"Of course not, darling. You know I always enjoy having you do that. We should probably do it more when we're together, but it seems like our time together is always so short."

I stepped over to the small nightstand beside the bed, pulled open a drawer and extracted a Gideon Bible. I sat down beside Corrine on the edge of the bed and opened the Bible to the Old Testament book of Leviticus.

"Here's a verse in the 20th chapter of Leviticus, the 10th verse," I said, raising my eyes to hers, "that explains what's been bothering me lately."

I proceeded to read the verse aloud to her.

"And the man that committeth adultery with another man's wife, even he that committeth adultery with his neighbor's wife, the adulterer and the adulteress shall surely be put to death."

I closed the Bible, replaced it in the nightstand drawer, and looked at Corrine, whose troubled expression had grown more apprehensive under the impact of the harsh words of condemnation I had read.

"Even though I've stopped talking about our sex relationship as adultery as I once did, Corrine," I said solemnly, looking deep into her eyes, "I still believe it's wrong. Regardless of how wonderful an experience it seems to us, the verse I read shows what God thought of it in Old Testament times, and still does. And because of our continuing disobedience to His word in this area, I'm beginning to doubt that God will ever use my life for anything. That is what's been bothering me the most."

"Are you blaming me for what happened last night?" she queried.

Her lower lip trembled as she hovered precariously on the edge of tears, where any hint of criticism on my part pushed her. Then, defensively, she added, "You wanted it as much as I did."

"There's never been any question about my wanting you

sexually as much as you have wanted me," I acknowledged, "but I still never thought it was right."

"But you've said yourself that our sexual relationship was good, and even beautiful, because we love each other. I've heard you say it, and you've written it to me in letters."

I bent toward her and took her nervously twisting hands in mine. I gazed into her eyes, my face inches from hers, trying to convey the love which I felt, to soften the seeming harshness of the words I felt compelled to speak.

"What I have said, my beloved, I still say. There is a sense in which our sexual relationship has been good and beautiful because we love each other, and because God intended love and sex to go together. Inwardly, emotionally, psychologically, in regard to our feelings for each other, our sexual relationship has been all that I've said."

"Then how can you call it something evil," she implored, "a sin, something that's bringing you death instead of life?"

"Because," I explained gently, "the Word of God does not take account of inner feelings, whether a man and a woman love each other or not. Adultery is based solely on the outward physical act, not on the inward feelings. Therefore, even though our sexual relationship may be good and beautiful in our eyes, in the sight of God it is sinful. It is still adultery, a violation of the Seventh Commandment."

I stopped talking and drew Corrine into my arms, unable to explain to her this strange dichotomy in my experience, how that inwardly, this relationship to her, including sex, was the most beautiful thing I had ever known; and yet, judged outwardly as the language of Scripture judged, and as God and other Christians would judge, it was ugly; not beautiful. It was adultery. It was sin.

"I love you, Corrine," I whispered into the ear that was close to my mouth, screened over lightly by several wisps of golden hair.

She pulled back out of my arms a moment to look into my face, her eyes shining, while drops of moisture glistened in the corners of her emerald green eyes.

"That's what I've been wanting to hear since you got here, darling, just 'I love you, I love you.'"

She came back into my embrace, holding me close, and I let one hand wander lovingly down the smooth curve of her back, the silken fabric of her negligee failing to conceal the delicate bumps of her spinal column. I inhaled deeply of the perfumed fragrance of her hair and rubbed my cheek against her ear. But closeness to her, I realized in that moment of intimacy, was not just a matter of physical proximity. It was also a spiritual matter. And because I wanted to be close to her completely, spiritually as well as physically, it was necessary to talk, to communicate what I believed was involved in our relationship to God that affected our relationship to each other. I pulled away from her and looked into her eyes.

"Darling, I want you to understand what I believe God says in His Word about our relationship."

"I know," she assented softly, and a little sadly, seeing that I was going to continue with the unpleasant subject that had brought her to the verge of tears.

"Sweetheart," I began gently, "do you remember the place in the New Testament where they dragged a woman before Jesus and were ready to stone her for adultery?"

"Yes."

"Do you remember what Jesus said to her?"

"Go and sin no more," she answered meekly.

"That's right," I concurred, "but what I want you to see is that there was no consideration given by the Lord as to how this woman felt about the man with whom she had been caught in a sexual involvement, and nothing was said about how the man might have felt about her. Maybe they loved each other as much as we do, but Jesus based his judgment wholly on the outward, bodily act that had evidently been seen by witnesses. Regardless of how they may have loved each other, He still called it adultery. That's the only way God could have given a commandment against adultery, based on the outward physical actions because no man could tell what is in the heart of a man and a woman for each other. So regardless of how much we love each other, still our sexual relationship in the sight of God is adultery, and it's sin, and God cannot go contrary to His written word. He cannot approve in our lives what He condemns in His word."

Corrine bent her head dejectedly, anticipating the end to which my line of reasoning was leading.

"But it's wrong to try to put sex out of our life when we love each other," she protested. "We need this expression of love, seeing you just once a week, coming to you after being handled by other men and propositioned to go to bed with them. No, Garfield, my darling, the wrong is in your living under another roof with another woman that you don't love, when you should be married to me. Is it right to go on lying to the woman you're living with, lying to the whole world by letting the world believe you love her and you sleep with her and have sex with her, because they see you going in and out of the same house together? Is it right to go on living a lie, Garfield?"

There was desperation in her tone, and her lower lip was trembling.

"No, it isn't right, Corrine," I conceded, my head bent to avoid her accusing stare.

"Then when are you going to do what I have been pleading with you to do for months?" she demanded desperately. "When are you going to leave that household and put an end to this deception?"

"I've told you, darling," I said, raising my head to look into her eyes, "that I can't just go to Florence and ask for a divorce. When I married her, it was a contract 'until death do us part.' I have no right to break that agreement unless she is willing to break it too. The most I can do is to tell her what has happened in my relationship to you. Then, if she decides she wants to terminate our marriage because I can no longer live up to the terms, she has a right to do so. If she wants to continue with the marriage, then I guess you and I would just have to separate, even though I don't think it would work, and I'd have to tell her that."

Corrine was revived somewhat by my admission. She

reached up and put one hand on each side of my face, lifting my head until I was looking directly into her eyes.

"But when are you going to tell her about us, Garfield? When? And why haven't you told her long before now?"

"Because I know what it's going to do to her," I answered.

I had to look away from Corrine's steadfast gaze, trying to keep a tremor out of my voice that swept through my frame as I contemplated the prospect of telling Florence the truth.

"It will be like putting a knife in her back."

"Do you care more about hurting her than you do about hurting me?"

"There's a difference," I protested, putting one hand down on the bed beside the outline of her blanket-covered feet. "My relationship to you is one of love; my tie to her is one of moral obligation."

"Then which comes first," she persisted, "your love for me or your moral obligation to her?"

"In the sight of God, my moral obligation to her should come first, but I'm not able to live up to it. I tried for five years while we were separated; there's no use trying any longer."

"Then when are you going to tell her?"

Corrine's question was less a request for information than it was an appeal to act.

"I'm going to start this afternoon," I told her, divulging to her for the first time the course I had decided upon.

"Darling!"

Her cry was a mixture of startled unbelief and a sudden delirium of joy. I looked away from the shining jubilation on her face. My pain was equal to her burst of gladness. It was I who was about to strike the match to the dynamite that would blow another person's life to pieces. It was I who was to be the agent of destruction, not Corrine. She would only learn secondhand from a distance the consequences of the explosion. But I would be there on the scene. I would hear the cries of pain, the blazing indictment of my betrayal. Corrine threw her arms around my neck while my own arms hung limply by my side. The same announcement which had brought new life and hope to her, only overwhelmed me with darkness and depression.

"Why didn't you tell me?" she burst out, moving back from me, her hands on my shoulders and her eyes now shining with joy. "I know, you wanted to save the good news for last, you darling, you!"

She took my face in her hands and leaned forward and pressed her lips against mine, forcing my lips open with her tongue and moving her tongue around and back and forth in the moist cavity of my mouth. In that moment, I would rather she had urged me to fall on my knees beside the bed, to pray for the one who would soon feel the sharp point of the assassin's knife pressed into her heart, with what tragic results I could not foresee. Corrine had misunderstood my words.

"Let me explain, beloved," I said, as she drew back from me, her face flushed with happiness.

Her sudden exuberance was subdued as she took in the sobering expression which must have been etched upon my face as I contemplated what lay ahead of me in the course to which I had committed myself.

"Sweetheart, I didn't mean that I was going to actually tell Florence about us this afternoon."

Abruptly, the luminous look of happiness on Corrine's face vanished, to be replaced by a sudden show of bewilderment.

"Darling, I have to look ahead," I began to explain. "When Florence does learn about this, it's going to be like a bombshell. She'll be so emotionally wrought up that she won't know what she's doing. It will be impossible to discuss what to do in a calm, rational manner as to what will be best for the children and for all of us. For that reason, I want to have available, before I tell her, the opinion of one or two experts, marriage counselors, for example, so that she can listen to them and know what they think. I think that's important because she probably won't listen to a word I'll say after she knows the truth.

"Who do you mean by experts?" she asked, suddenly suspicious of this strange, new twist which my conversation had taken.

"Someone whose opinion in the matter she'll respect. I'm thinking of a minister who's had a lot of experience in marriage counseling."

"Who?"

"It's someone you probably never heard of; his name is Geoffrey Golden. He's a pastor in California."

"How in the world can he be of any help if he's in California?"

"By mailing tapes back and forth. I'm going to send him a tape telling him about the situation, and then he'll send one back; more than one if necessary."

"How did you ever get acquainted with him?"

I got up and walked over to the chair by the window and picked up the brown leather briefcase I had brought with me in anticipation of the question which Corrine had asked. From the briefcase I pulled out a book and returned to the bed and handed it to Corrine.

"I got acquainted with him through reading this book."

I sat down on the edge of the bed beside Corrine as she started to thumb through the book which bore the title on the jacket, Manual for Modern Marriage.

"I have another book by the same author," I continued, "which said that he was a pastor in California. So I wrote him a letter, not knowing if he still lived in California, or if he was even alive yet."

"What church is he a pastor of?" Corrine asked suspiciously, looking up from her perusal of chapter headings.

"It's called the Pentecost Covenant Church in Redwood City, California."

To meet the look of skepticism on Corrine's face about inviting a total stranger into our lives to arbitrate our future, I suggested a practical test in support of my decision.

"Why don't you let me read you something from the introduction," I suggested, reaching for the book.

She handed it back to me, and I took it over to the chair by the window, extracting my reading glasses from my inside coat pocket as I sat down. I opened the book to the opening chapter where a particular passage had impressed itself upon my mind, and read aloud to Corrine.

"The pathology of marriage must be a serious concern in the face of mounting divorce statistics. Marriage counseling centers and pastors are sounding an urgent alarm. And the more appalling picture still is of those countless numbers who have not divorced, but are living a lie, whose . . ."

"Darling, that's just what I said to you a few minutes ago," Corrine broke in, "in almost my exact words. You're living a lie, Garfield, and it isn't right."

"I know it isn't right, my love," I conceded. "That's why I'm trying to do something about it. Just let me finish this paragraph."

I backed up to the beginning of the sentence that Corrine had interrupted and continued reading.

"And the more appalling picture still is of those countless numbers who have not divorced, but are living a lie, whose marriage is only an empty shell, a grotesque caricature of the real thing. Disillusioned and apathetic, a seeming majority do little to remedy the situation. Indeed, few seem to know where to turn for help."

I closed the book and laid it down on the nearby end table.

"Now would you like to hear the letter I wrote to Pastor Golden, and his answer?"

"When did you hear from him, darling?"

"Just this week."

I reached into my inside coat pocket and pulled out two letters, both in long, business-size envelopes.

"And you wanted to wait until today to tell me about it in person instead of telling me on the phone?"

"I was afraid there would have been too much explaining," I answered, "and you might have misunderstood, and long distance calls cost money."

"You're right, darling. I understand, and I'm just so glad you're finally doing something about it."

I unfolded a carbon copy of the letter I had written to Pastor Golden from the office several weeks before and began to read it aloud.

"Dear Pastor Golden . . ."

"Darling," Corrine interrupted.

I looked over at her inquiringly.

"I can't decide," she murmured as she gazed at me adoringly, "whether my darling looks handsomer with glasses or without them. They make you look so dignified and mature; like a college professor."

"Thank you, darling."

I pushed the gray plastic frames back on my nose to the position from which they had a tendency to slip and continued reading.

"In your excellent book, *Manual for Modern Marriage,* you write of countless numbers whose marriage is only 'an empty shell.' I find myself in this class, although the woman to whom I am married is not aware that I feel this way. I am, however, without her knowledge, trying to remedy the situation and am turning to you for help."

I paused and looked across the room at Corrine to see if my letter was holding her interest. She was leaning back against the headboard of the bed, regarding me intently, one bare leg swinging idly over the side of the bed.

"Want to hear more?" I asked.

"Certainly, darling," she replied with obvious enthusiasm, "I want to hear all of it."

I continued reading.

"One of the problems people often face, and one seldom dealt with in the church, is that a person may sometimes be caught in the crossfire between two clashing commandments from the Bible, and may not have grounds for determining which commandment should be kept and which one should be broken. In my case, there is a commandment to love the woman I am married to even as Christ loves the church. This would mean that I should willingly die for her, inwardly as well as outwardly. It means that I should set aside my personal needs and feelings, suppress them, ignore them, crucify them, die to them, as much as I can. But there is also the counsel to 'speak the truth to one another.' In the 51st Psalm, David cries to God, 'thou desirest truth in the inward parts.' But the truth can hurt. It can sometimes hurt terribly, cruelly, even when it is spoken in love, leaving wounds that may never heal, leaving scars upon the personality for life.

"So my dilemma is this. Should I follow the command to love the woman to whom I am married, and keep silent about my real feelings to avoid hurting her, or should I tell her the truth? Should I tell her that I married her, not out of love, although I used these words at the time, but as a means to an end, of stabilizing my life, so I thought, so I could be of greater usefulness to God? This insight, of course, has come to me only through the twelve years we have been married. I didn't know myself fully at the time, nor my real, underlying motive in getting married. Shall I also tell my wife the cruel and cutting truth, that for the last seven years of our twelve years of marriage, I have loved another woman—who she doesn't know exists—and still do?"

I paused, my throat dry from reading.

"Excuse me while I get a drink of water, sweetheart."

"I'll excuse you if you'll stop and give me a kiss on the way," she answered, as I put the letters down with my glasses on top of them.

I stepped to the bedside and bent down as she reached up to encircle my neck in a loving embrace.

"My lover," she whispered, her eyes shining, as she continued holding me around the neck, "here I've been having nightmares that you never really intended to marry me, and you've been working hard on it already without my knowing it."

I gently disengaged her hands from around my neck and held them in mine as I stood beside the bed, looking down at her.

"Darling," I chided gently, "I can't say that I'm definitely going to marry you. All that I can do is try to be honest with Florence. What happens after that is in the hands of God."

I looked deeply into her eyes for a moment, trying to emphasize the seriousness and the significance of my statement.

"I know," she breathed pensively.

I stood there looking down at her, and watched the bluebird of happiness that had started to spread its wings in anticipated flight fold them again and huddle down in its hidden nest within her heart. It was not yet time to fly. I lingered beside her a moment, holding her hands tightly, wanting to speak some word of comfort that would assure her that one day we would indeed be married. But I could not. I did not dare attempt to violently wrest the outcome of the matter out of the hands of God in an attempt to resolve it according to my own desires or Corrine's needs.

I released her hands then and stepped into the bathroom. After taking a long drink, I filled a glass to take back with me, then returned to the chair by the window where I had been sitting. I replaced my glasses and resumed reading from my letter to the California marriage counselor.

"I realize that it is not the function of a marriage counselor to give out the right answers, but only to help clarify the issues so that people can arrive at their own answers. But in order to understand the issues, the counselor must be informed of all that's involved, including the history of the situation. In this case, there's a problem of distance. If you are still located in California, it would prove too costly to drop in for a once-a-week counseling session. Therefore, I have wondered if the same results could be achieved by sending you a tape describing the situation, and then yourself sending a tape back with any pertinent questions or comments.

"You may wonder," I continued reading, "why I do not approach the pastor of the church where Florence, my wife, and I regularly attend. The answer is that he has impressed me as being unapproachable because he is so busy. Shall I send you the first tape, attempting to provide you with a history of my marital situation as it has developed?"

I folded the carbon copy of my letter to Pastor Golden, laid it down on the table beside me, then picked up the single type-written sheet which had been sent to me in reply. Before proceeding to read it, I looked over at Corrine, who was regarding me soberly.

"Would you like to hear his answer?"

"Of course, darling," she replied, "but can't you come and sit beside me on the bed? You seem so far away over there. I can turn on this lamp over the bed if you need it."

I got up and walked over to the bed while she reached up and switched on the lamp attached to the wall just above her head. It splashed a soft, yellow spotlight over her, highlighting the golden waves of her hair and lightly accentuating the straight Grecian line of her nose and her high cheekbones, adding a lustrous shine to her invitingly crimsoned lips. I sat down on the bed beside her, gave her a quick kiss, and unfolded the letter from the pastor-author-counselor in California.

"Dear Mister Roby," I read aloud. "Yes, I'm very much in California, my native state, and have just reread your letter with interest and concern. I feel that your suggestion is an excellent one that you send me a tape giving me the history of your situation so that I can try to share some personal evaluation with you. I have done this on previous occasions and find it very convenient to use a tape for reply, and certainly this means that I can convey my thoughts to you in an easy, efficient way without, perhaps, a lengthy, dictated letter through my secretary. So for now, let me say that I will keep your letter in my active file and wait for the tape that will give me a detailed insight into the developing situation, particularly over the past seven years. Cordially yours, Geoffrey H. Golden."

I folded the letter, laid it down in my lap, and looked at Corrine for her response.

"I hope he understands our situation," she sighed, with some air of misgiving.

Then, abruptly, a new and fearful possibility occurred to her, and panic lighted up her green eyes as they darted about my face.

"What if he says that you ought to leave me and stay with her?"

"I'd have to tell him," I assured her quickly, "that I think that would be foolish advice because I already tried it for five years and it didn't work, so why try it again?"

Corrine looked at me in bewilderment.

"But since you know that's what he might say, I don't know why you want to bother to talk with him at all, if you don't intend to follow his advice."

"Like I already told you, darling," I repeated, "I'm doing this primarily for Florence's benefit; not mine. When she learns about this, she won't be able to think straight. It will help her to have someone standing by whose opinion she can trust, who will be able to give her some counsel as to what she ought to do. But regardless of what any expert may say, I'm sure that she won't want to stay married to me once she knows that I love you, and have loved you for the past seven years."

"Are you sure, Garfield? Do you know her that well?"

"I'm fairly certain that's how she'll react but I can't be positive. She might decide that it would be better for the children if we stayed married, but I'm doubtful."

"Why do you say that, darling?"

Anxiety was etched in deep lines upon Corrine's face, and shadows of apprehension darkened her eyes, as she realized that our future was dependent, not upon my decision alone, but upon whatever Florence might decide, with the possibility of her being influenced in some unforeseeable way by the interference of God.

"Florence would know," I tried to reassure her, "that the atmosphere in the home would be too unpleasant. That in itself wouldn't be good for the children or for her. I'm sure she'll want me to get out of the house once she knows the truth. As to whether she'll want to go through with a divorce or not, I can't be certain. We'll just have to leave that in God's hands, to work out what will be best for all of us; for you, for me, for Florence and the children."

"Yes," she capitulated, "you're right, darling. And now I've got a confession to make."

"What is it?"

"It's about our sexual relationship. It's bothered me as much as it has you, but until now I've been afraid that each time I see you might be the last time; that you'd leave me and go back to her."

"I can never go back to her in a sexual way, darling, even if it turns out to be God's will to stay married to her."

The relief Corrine felt at my admission broke through upon her face in a smile.

"Thank you, darling, for saying that. Now that I know that because you're actually doing something about separating from the household, I'm willing to try even harder to get back to being virgins, the way we were when we first met seven years ago; remember?"

"Yes, I remember, beloved."

I nuzzled my nose against the silken warmth of her cheek, my burden of guilt in this area of our relationship somewhat lifted by her impetuous resolution.

"But let me be practical for a moment, darling," I counseled. "If we're going to really carry this out, we have to agree as to a stopping point in our caressing. There is a point of no return, you know. If you get me too excited like you did last night, it's too late to stop, then afterwards my conscience begins to work on me."

"Let's do what you suggested once before," she proposed, brightening at the prospect of victory. "No more taking off our clothes when we're together."

"That would help," I agreed, then glanced at my watch.

"It's a quarter of ten, sweetheart. I've got to be going pretty quick."

"If you'll get the things on top of the dresser and out of the bathroom and put them in the suitcase, I'll start getting dressed now."

"Don't you want to stay here and rest a while longer?" I asked, thrusting the letter from Pastor Golden into my coat pocket and getting up. "It's still a couple of hours before your bus leaves for Detroit."

"No, darling, it's too lonesome here after you go."

Her voice was tinged with melancholy as if I were already gone.

I bent to brush her lips with mine sympathetically, then turned away to help her pack. I set the feminine, pastel blue overnight case on the chair by the window and began to pick up the collection of little items she had brought along to make my visit seem more like I was coming to a familiar home rather than just to a hotel room. As Corrine sat on the edge of the bed in bra and panties, fastening black sheer nylons to her garter belt, I paused a moment to drink in the exotic sight of her.

"Do you know one way I can tell that my feeling for you is love and not lust?" I asked.

"How?"

My question had sufficiently provoked her interest that she paused in dressing, one garter clasp held in her right hand still unfastened while the fingers of her left hand held the edge of her nylon stocking pinched together.

"When a man only likes to watch a woman undress, that's usually lust," I proposed. "But when a man gets just as excited watching her dress as undress, that's love. And I don't know which I enjoy most—watching you take your clothes off or put them on."

"I love you for that, darling," she smiled.

Corrine continued dressing while I finished putting things into her suitcase. Fifteen minutes later, having skirted the downtown shopping district to reduce the chance of being seen with Corrine, I pulled into a parking space at the rear of the Greyhound bus terminal at the south end of the business district. Leaving the engine running, I retrieved Corrine's suitcase from the back seat and walked with her to a somewhat secluded alcove near the rear entrance. The glass in the double doors had been covered with plywood to stave off break-ins, but also providing a somewhat semi-private nook. I set the suitcase down and we reached for each other with a hunger that we both knew would not be slaked again for another week or two. Then I stepped back from the long, passionate parting kiss for a last, all-inclusive look at her gold and green loveliness.

"I love you, darling," I said tenderly, and with a new intensity born of her recently expressed resolution to help keep our sexual desires within boundaries prescribed by conscience and the approval of God. "I'll be seeing you."

"And I'll be seeing you, my beloved, in my dreams until I'm in your arms again. Don't forget to write, and call me when you can."

"I will," I promised.

I waved to Corrine and turned to leave, aware of the danger of lingering in a public place where I might be recognized by someone. I got into the car and pulled out just ahead of a bus that was turning into the wide asphalt drive that circled the terminal. Corrine, standing by her suitcase near the back entrance, waved again as I drove away, down an alley that led onto a side street.

It was approaching eleven o'clock when I pulled into the driveway at home. I looked quickly into the rear-view mirror to be sure that Corrine had erased all the lipstick traces, then wiped my lips with the back of my hand to be doubly sure. As I stepped through the front door, at least one person was glad to see me.

"Daddy!" Philip yelled out happily, and ran to me from where he had been sprawled out on the living room floor in front of the TV set.

Philip grabbed me around the legs in a bear hug as Paul remained seated on the floor, cross-legged, too engrossed in the magical exploits of Superman to get excited about my arrival.

"Hi, Dad," he called, and turned his attention back to the TV set.

"Sorry I'm late," I apologized to Florence, who appeared in the kitchen doorway, disconsolate and disheveled from grappling with the weekly wash while attending the needs of three energetic boys.

"I let the boys go ahead and eat to save time. Do you want yours on the table now?"

"That's what I've been looking forward to all morning. You make the best scrambled eggs in town."

I sat down at the dinette table as Philip sidled up onto a chair beside me to share my brief giving of thanks.

"No more for you, Philip," Florence scolded, when I had finished, as she put a plate of scrambled eggs in front of me.

A moment later, as she returned with buttered toast and coffee, Paul rushed in from the living room to make good use of a brief intermission for commercials.

"Dad," he cried excitedly, standing by the table, "can you go with us to Grandma's today and take us fishing?"

I sighed inwardly at the need to fight over again an emotional battle which I had been through with the boys the night before.

"Paul," I said firmly, looking at him, "I told you last night I've got to work overtime at the office today."

"See, Philip," he said to his younger brother, sitting submissively beside me, "I told you Dad wouldn't change his mind." Dejectedly, he turned away to go back to the TV set.

"Paul," I called to his retreating back.

He stopped in his tracks to hear what I had to say.

"If it's any help to you, I can assure you that I'd enjoy going fishing with you and Philip much more than I will doing what I have to do at the office today."

Paul, evidently unconvinced, made no reply but returned to his place in front of the TV set. Sitting quietly beside me at the table, Philip had evidently taken my statement at face value as being the truth.

"I know why you have to work at the office so much, Dad," he ventured as I continued eating.

He looked at me with wide eyes and a knowing grin, excited at being able to display some mystic knowledge of his father's strange behavior.

"Why," I asked, eying him, with a forkful of scrambled eggs on the way to my mouth.

"So you'll have enough money to take us to a drive-in for hamburgers and french fries and Cokes."

Philip had remembered the essence of a simple lecture on economics that I had given to Paul and him several weeks before; that if they were to have enjoyable experiences like eating out or going for rides at carnivals or an occasional movie, then Daddy would have to work to earn the money.

"You're right, Philip," I praised him, "I'm glad you remembered what I told you."

With my pleasure at his having taken to heart what I had said earlier in trying to convey to the boys the elementary truth that money doesn't grow on trees, was mixed an element of anguish because I had to hold back from Philip an accompanying explanation of the fact that there were expenses which I couldn't tell him about; helping Corrine with bus fare each time she came to Lansing, hotel rooms, sometimes taxi fares, occasional gifts of flowers or candy, and greeting cards. Neither could I tell him the whole truth that on many of the occasions I had said that I had to work overtime at the office, I had no intention of going there. Today it was true. I was indeed going to the office, and I was going to work overtime; but not the kind of work I did on my job during the week, and not a kind of work for which I would be reimbursed by the state.

"Paul," Florence called from the kitchen as I finished my breakfast, "will you go upstairs and get Korah?"

There was only silence from the living room where Paul sat engrossed in a television program. From the kitchen came the rustling sound of empty egg cartons being put into a paper sack in which Florence would bring back five or six dozen farm-fresh eggs from the country. Finally, Paul responded to his mother's request.

"Wait till this cartoon's over."

"You turn that TV set off this minute and get upstairs and get your brother," blazed Florence from the kitchen, "or I'll be in there with the strap."

"Get moving, Paul," I called sternly, "Or I'll be in there with a strap before your mother."

Philip looked at me, eyebrows raised in suspense, as Paul's outraged "Darn it!" came from the living room, followed by his angry stomping up the stairs to the second-floor bedroom. Finished with breakfast, I pushed back my chair and walked out to the kitchen, hoping to relieve Florence's agitated state of mind.

"I'll take these out to the car," I said, picking up the bulky sack of empty egg cartons.

"You don't need to bother," she snapped. "I can do it myself."

It was her way of reacting to my diminishing displays of affection, especially in the area of sexual ardor, in the past few months. She no longer asked me to help her with anything around the house, and seldom accepted my help when freely offered. But in spite of her protest, I carried the empty egg cartons out to the station wagon, and there, opening the back door, made room for the usual necessary equipment that Florence took along on the weekly trips. Then I made two more trips into the house and back to the station wagon; one for a gallon of milk and a diaper bag, and another for the stroller which folded up and laid flat on the bed of the station wagon.

Then, in the bustling confusion of everyone getting ready for the weekly trip to Charlotte, I waited anxiously for a chance to put something else in the back end of the station wagon without being observed. Finally, my chance came. Philip was upstairs looking for a lost shoe; Paul was again on his belly on the living room floor, held captive by a TV cartoon, and Korah was in the bathroom, having the breakfast washed from his face by his mother. Quietly and quickly, unnoticed by Paul, I retrieved the heavy, portable tape recorder from the living room, walked briskly with it out to the driveway, and lifted it carefully into the space I had reserved beside the folded stroller, as far from the back seat as I could get it. Then I covered it with a blanket that was always kept in the back end in case one of the boys wanted to make a bed there on their weekly excursions.

Looking ahead to removing the tape recorder from the back end of the station wagon when we got downtown where I expected to get out, I shrank from the necessity of telling the lie I had manufactured to conceal the use I expected to make of it, an intended use known only to Corrine and an unknown pastor in California.

The station wagon loaded at last, with Paul and Korah in the back seat and Philip sitting between Florence and me in front, I backed the station wagon out of the drive and drove east toward downtown Lansing. Ten minutes later, on a wide, busy, downtown thoroughfare, I pulled into a parking area in front of the picturesque State Capitol.

"I'll get out here," I said, turning to Florence as I shut off the engine and pulled keys out of the ignition.

"What are you taking the keys out for?" she asked.

Florence slid across the seat, squeezing behind Philip to take my place behind the wheel as I got out.

"I've got something to get out of the back end," I said, as I closed the door, staving off as long as I could the additional questions that would follow as soon as she and the boys saw what it was I had hidden in the back.

I stepped quickly back to the rear of the station wagon, unlocked the door, swung it open, and lifted down the heavy tape recorder, aware as I did of the watching eyes of Paul and Korah from the back seat. Returning to the driver's side of the car to hand the keys back to Florence, she saw what I was carrying.

"What in the world are you going to do with the tape recorder?"

"Yeah, Dad," echoed Paul accusingly from the back seat, "I thought you said you were going to work at the office."

Standing close to the car, out of the traffic lane as cars zoomed past, and feeling the weight of the tape recorder, I delivered the lie I had prepared in answer to the questions I had anticipated.

"When I get tired of my regular work at the office," I said, alternating my glances between Florence and Paul, "just for a break I'm going to practice doing some commercials. In case a job offer as an announcer comes through from some radio station, I don't want to be too rusty."

Florence eyed me skeptically.

"You really think something might still turn up?"

"You never can tell," I replied with counterfeit optimism.

"Hey, Dad," Paul asked, as Florence started the engine, "how come you're getting out here if you're going to work at the office?"

The Gray office building, where I worked, was three blocks to the west on the other side of the Capitol building that loomed in the background, overshadowing the downtown business district.

I was glad to answer that question at least with a measure of truth.

"I've got to stop at the bank first before I go to the office, Paul."

"I'll bet you're going to be taking some money out, not putting any in," Florence speculated in a tone of rebuke.

She was right, but I couldn't justify my action. I had expenses which I couldn't tell her about.

"How about a goodbye kiss for your Dad?" I said to the boys, ignoring Florence's veiled probe about my financial affairs.

Philip, the most eager to respond to my request, leaned over behind Florence as she bent forward against the steering wheel and gave me an exuberant peck on the cheek. Then, stepping to the back window which Paul had rolled down, I stuck my head through the window to see Paul sitting with bent head and dejected expression, while on the opposite side of the wide seat, Korah sat regarding me with wide-eyed, happy expectations.

"Got a kiss for your Dad, Paul?" I asked.

"No," he objected crossly, glancing up at me accusingly, "I'm mad because you won't take us fishing at Gramma's like you promised."

"Why don't you stop bugging your Dad, Paul," Florence rebuked angrily. "He told you he's got more important things to do."

I sighed, too pressed for time to go over the same argument with Paul that I had been through the night before, and a few minutes earlier at home.

"Korah," I said, looking across at him, "have you got a goodbye kiss for Daddy?"

Responding immediately to my invitation, he crowded over against Paul and leaned toward me. I kissed him on the cheek, then stood up for a final word to Florence, who had waited with obvious impatience while I went through the familiar farewell ritual with my sons.

"Have a good trip," I said to Florence, who neither offered nor expected a parting kiss.

I stepped behind the station wagon and up onto the curb as Florence pulled the station wagon out into the flow of southbound traffic. Standing on the sidewalk with the tape recorder, I returned the farewell waves of Philip and Korah through the rear window and watched until their bobbing heads became dwindling spheres. Watching the car out of sight, I lifted up a silent appeal to God for His protecting mercy to surround my sons and the woman who was still my wife in the eyes of God and society.

It was a spontaneous prayer, prompted, perhaps, by an apprehensive shiver of guilt at the prospect that something might happen to them on the way to or from Charlotte just because I wasn't going along to drive the car as I usually did. But I had work to do that couldn't be postponed. Surely, I reasoned, as I stood there a moment, oblivious of the traffic sounds and reflecting on my situation, since God favors honesty and truth, and since I am taking steps to end the deception in my marriage, He will watch over my family in my absence.

Standing at the pedestrian crosswalk, waiting for the traffic light to change so I could cross and make a stop at the bank, I glanced at my watch. It was 11:15. Corrine was already on her way back to Detroit on a Greyhound bus, back to another night as a taxi-dancer at the Hollywood Ballroom on Woodward Avenue; back to another night of being held in the arms of other men; pawed, propositioned, offered money to go to bed with them, while Florence and my three sons were on their way to the little town of Charlotte. Inwardly, I was torn in two directions—between the love that followed Corrine, and the moral obligation as a husband and father that followed Florence and the children.

Crossing the street finally, I was more than ever aware of the weight of the heavy tape recorder that kept me off balance. If Florence but knew, I reflected sadly, all there was to know about this tape recorder that had been used lately to encourage Paul in his piano practice; if she but knew that my original reason for buying it six long years before had been the mad dream of telling the world about my love for Corrine and her love for me. And if she had but an inkling of the use to which that tape recorder was going to be put today, in the deserted seclusion of the great empty office building where I worked during the week; if she but knew all that was in my heart, that was going to be poured out on that tape for the ears of a total stranger in far-away California; yes, if she but knew, she would feel the very ground trembling beneath her feet and splitting apart as if torn by a devastating earthquake. But she didn't know. Not yet. Inevitably, she would have to know. Soon, perhaps. And as I looked ahead to the dawn of that approaching day, walking down the sidewalk with the tape recorder to the bank, I trembled inwardly at the thought of the havoc it was going to wreak in other lives. It would be Doomsday for a family, a home, a marriage; my home, my family, my marriage.

I hurried on to the bank at the end of the block and completed the necessary task of bolstering my depleted cash reserves. Then, back to the sidewalk in the warmth of an Indian Summer Saturday in early October, I recrossed the wide shopper-plied street down which my wife and three sons had driven a few minutes before. They could never have guessed that I was on my way to the vast, dreary emptiness of the Gray office building to prepare a charge of dynamite that would shake their lives to the very foundations.

Moments later, winded from my three-block walk in the near noontime heat with the heavy tape recorder, I stepped off the elevator on the fifth floor of the Gray office building "prison." There was a marked difference to forcibly remind me that this was not a regular working day. There were no signs of life. Today, the whole building was like a vast tomb, darkened and devoid of life except for me. The similarity to a mausoleum was appropriate. I had come here in the role of a marital archeologist, to dig among the ruins of the past for relics that would help me to explain to someone else how my present marital impasse had come to be built up; layer upon layer. My own footsteps echoed my progress down the hallway to the far end of the west wing where the Right of Way Engineering section was located.

Stepping through the open doorway of the deserted Engineering section, I plunked down the heavy tape recorder by my desk. In the huge, empty room that seemed now like a deserted battlefield, with the skinny elbows of drafting table lamps sticking up in the air at odd angles, I opened several windows to let some fresh air drive out the stuffiness. Then I returned to the front of the room, hung up coat and necktie on the rack by my desk, and began to assemble the equipment I would need to embark upon an expedition into the past; there to review the scenes of my deteriorating marriage to Florence and my initial meeting with Corrine.

From beneath a spare drafting table by the window at the front of the long room where I sometimes worked, I stooped down above a black metal G.I. footlocker. It was sufficiently hidden there to avoid curious questions from my fellow workers. With a small key on my keyring, I unlocked it and raised the lid. First, I removed a small, table-model radio which had lightened some of the long, lonely hours I had actually done overtime work through the years of getting a college degree. I took the radio to my desk, plugged it in, and turned the dial to my favorite good-music station. As the haunting beauty of a Percy Faith rendering of "Autumn Leaves" chased away some of the dreary atmosphere that accumulates in a great, empty office building on a weekend, I continued assembling the rest of the equipment I would need.

I lugged the tape recorder from beside my own desk back to the last row of drafting tables and set it down on the clean top of Elwood Jassey's table. I didn't dare use my own desk adjacent to the doorway leading into the hall lest someone walk by and hear some damaging disclosure about my marital situation. From Elwood's table I would have a clear view of the rest of the room in case anyone else walked in unexpectedly. Even though it was only a remote possibility that anyone else would show up, I didn't want to take a chance on having my crumbling marriage become a subject of office gossip by having some damning phrase or sentence picked up by unauthorized ears and passed on to others.

Returning to the open footlocker, I bent down and passed over its most priceless contents—several stacks of bulky letters, all addressed to me in Corrine's flourishing handwriting, which I had received at a post office box, unknown to Florence, in preceding months. They provided painful proof of my infidelity to Florence; too precious to me, and too dangerous to her, to risk keeping in some secret place at home. My hands brushed reverently over the love letters, to pull out a seven-inch reel of recording tape I had purchased the week before, besides a microphone and microphone table stand. Then I rummaged carefully beneath the letters to extract one other item I needed; a gilt-framed photograph of Corrine.

I carried these essential items to the back of the room where the tape recorder was set up. Then, quickly, I spliced leader tape onto the seven-inch reel of recording tape that would allow me three hours of recording time on one side, if I needed that much, connected the microphone and threaded the tape onto the recorder. I set up the photo of Corrine in its delicate wrought-gold frame on one corner of the table to give me strength and inspiration as I recorded the story of the beginning and blossoming of my hidden love for her.

Then, surveying the items spread out on the table before me to be sure I had everything I needed, I remembered to get other essential items.

I walked back to the coat rack near my desk in the front of

the room and dug from an inside coat pocket the letter from Pastor Geoffrey Golden in California, that I had read to Corrine earlier that morning at the Roosevelt. With the letter in my hand, I got a coffee cup from my desk drawer and filled it with water from the hallway fountain, in case my throat got dry while talking at length into the microphone.

As I stepped back through the doorway into the Engineering section, the music emanating from the radio on my desk was interrupted for a public service announcement which caught my attention.

"The future of America depends upon the education of its youth," the male voice asserted authoritatively. "A college education is the key to success . . ."

I paused by my desk, waiting for the rest of the announcement.

". . . To help young people get a college education," the announcer continued in a pleading tone, "send a contribution today to 'Dollars for Scholars,' Box 419, Newberry, Connecticut."

"Yeah, I'll send you a contribution—a lump on the head, you big, fat liar," I muttered aloud, as I set the cup of water down on the desk and savagely switched off the radio.

As I returned to Elwood's drafting table in the back of the room, with a cup of water in one hand and Pastor Golden's letter in the other, I felt within me a surge of indignation at the radio announcement. It made me feel like sending a heated letter of protest to the Federal Communications Commission in Washington, D.C. for allowing such misleading propaganda to be sent over the airwaves, which made it appear that the acquisition of a college degree was almost a certain guarantee of a better job and a better income. But then I wondered, was it reasonable to use my own experience as a measuring stick of what the average college graduate might expect? After all, it suddenly struck me forcibly, most young people could expect to graduate from college at a far younger age than 42, as I had. As I set the cup of water and the letter down on Elwood's drafting table, my angry impulse to send the FCC a bitter broadside of protest was quashed as quickly as it had erupted.

I hoisted myself up onto the bar-stool-type drafting chair to begin recording. But first, I turned my gaze for a needed nudge of inspiration, to the color photo of Corrine which she had given me some months before. I looked into the green, gold-flecked eyes, enhanced with eye shadow. Her half-closed eyes suggested the rapture of sexual bliss. Her head was tilted back and her lips slightly parted, a "come hither" expression of erotic invitation. I remembered her telling me how some of her male admirers at the Hollywood Ballroom had started calling her the "Marilyn Monroe of the Hollywood," due to the striking similarity in face and form. I noted again the term of endearment scrawled across the lower corner of the photo, in the elaborate scroll that bespoke Corrine's artistic talent and temperament, "Eternally yours, Corrine."

Then, reluctant to begin the work of destruction that lay before me, I turned my attention to the letter from Dr. Geoffrey Golden spread out on the table before me. I took a drink of water, then reached out and switched on the tape recorder. With elbows leaning against the edge of the drafting table, I began to speak into the microphone on the upright mike stand before me as the reels of tape began turning slowly.

"Dear Pastor Golden. In my first letter to you, written several weeks ago, I confessed that I have been married for twelve years, and that the last seven years of that time I have secretly loved another woman other than my wife, Florence. Since I will be referring often to that other woman, you should know her first name at least. It is . . . Corrine.

"In your gracious reply to my letter, you asked me to begin this history of my marriage dating from the time of my first meeting with Corrine, seven years ago. But as I have thought about it, I have believed that the starting point should be a little farther back than that. As an instructor in a course on marriage at Michigan State University said, 'Our preparation for marriage begins in infancy.' Nevertheless, for the sake of brevity I will begin much closer than that to the point you suggested, and then if you have questions about developments prior to that time, I will attempt to answer them as they arise.

"I think that it may be helpful to begin at a point several months prior to my meeting with Corrine for this reason. As a marriage ·counselor, one of the possible solutions that will doubtless occur to you first is that of healing the breach that has developed between Florence, my wife, and myself. Therefore, I think it would be wise to start at the point where I first began to turn away from Florence. For I did not turn away from Florence because of meeting Corrine. The opening wedge of alienation from Florence came first. If it had not, I might never have met Corrine. So let me begin with an attempt to answer this question: Why did I begin to turn away from Florence after five years of marriage? Or did she turn away from me first?"

I stopped speaking and shut off the tape recorder. The slowly turning reels came to a stop as I paused and sifted through the events of the past, dating to a time seven years earlier, prior to my first meeting with Corrine, when my marriage to Florence had begun its slow but certain disintegration. Looking back, one dramatic event stood out, towering like a mountain peak above the rest. It had been called forth in that moment, perhaps, because the turning reels of the tape recorder had brought to mind the wheels of the automobile in which Florence and I had almost had a near fatal accident one night on our way home from work in Lansing to our home in Charlotte, a small town eighteen miles southwest of Lansing. The almost fatal accident, I recalled, had been brought on by an angry, totally unexpected announcement from Florence that was to have a shattering effect upon the foundations of our marriage.

With this starting point firmly fixed in my mind, I reached out and turned on the tape recorder again. I began speaking into the microphone the fateful words that would soon be entering into the ears of a total stranger, even though a concerned one, in far-away California.

CHAPTER 4

⇒ It was Florence's disclosure, seven years ago," I began speaking into the microphone, "of the anticipated arrival in our home of an uninvited guest for a stay of indefinite duration, that began the disintegration of the ties that had held us together as husband and wife through five preceding years of marriage. Her unexpected announcement was destined to set in motion a sequence of events that caused me to turn away from Florence, or impelled her to turn away from me; the necessary prelude to my turning to another woman, named . . . Corrine. It was in the spring of Lansing's Centennial year, its 100th year of existence as a city, that Florence dropped the verbal bombshell that marked the beginning of the end of our marriage. . ."

In February of that historic year, city officials and civic-minded citizens had begun preparing for a series of Centennial events that was to reach its climax in the following month of June with an antique car parade; a historical pageant of Lansing's past, to be performed in an outdoor stadium with a cast of 1,500 residents; and was to culminate with the inevitable beauty queen contest to choose a representative "Miss Lansing." And in prominent places throughout the downtown area, on lamp posts, buildings, and trash cans, posters boasted the Centennial slogan of Michigan's capital city, "Proud of the Past, and Confident of the Future."

An unconcerned awareness of these impending civic

events was in the back of my mind as I pushed through the busily spinning revolving doors of the Gray office building "prison" at five minutes after five on what was to be a fateful day for the future of my marriage to Florence. It was a Thursday afternoon in the first week of May that year. It was a day, weatherwise, that was typical of Michigan's abrupt seasonal changes. It was prematurely warm, more like summer than spring, with a temperature near eighty. The air-conditioning system in the huge, eight-story office building prison had not yet been activated for the summer. It was a relief, therefore, to me and to many others, to step out of the stuffy building into the May sunshine, where the air was fresh and a slight breeze welcomed the feverish mass exodus of office workers from the building.

With a sport coat draped over one arm and my shirt sleeves rolled up, I was jostled along, like a chip on the sea, by the flood of other state workers. Already, the year I had worked in the Highway Department had begun to pall on me. At first, returning with Florence to my home town of Lansing, after a spiritual shipwreck in Chicago, where an inability to resist the strip-tease bars and burlesque theatres on State Street had persuaded me to abandon preparations to enter the ministry, I had seized upon the clerical job in the Highway Department with the same thankfulness that Robinson Crusoe felt after being cast upon an island following a stormy shipwreck. But like the shipwrecked mariner of Daniel Defoe's sea adventure, after gaining an initial familiarity with this vocational island on which I had been cast up by circumstances, I had begun to long to escape to a kind of work with larger opportunities to develop and use innate abilities. The routine round of repetitious tasks that I had learned by rote were much like the movements of a man working on the assembly line of an automobile factory.

As I walked along in the crowd of state employees, on the wide cement concourse that led to a flight of steps going down to street level, here and there in the crowd a familiar face and greeting would mark someone I knew as they hurried along. It was emotional fatigue, perhaps, more than physical tiredness that slowed my steps more than others around me; the kind of weariness that comes from having abilities and interests that are locked within, unused, untapped in one's daily work.

Five minutes later, in a seven-year-old Plymouth with 50,000 miles on it that we had bought from Florence's mother for three hundred dollars, I nosed into the slow-moving stream of traffic, clogged with the exodus of hundreds of state workers, to pick up Florence. This particular day, that was to mark the beginning of the end of my marriage to Florence, we had driven to work alone instead of with the car pool of three other riders whom we usually rode with as an economy measure. As a husband and wife team, both working for the state, we worked only seven blocks apart, separated by the width of the Grand River, which cut downtown Lansing in half. With Florence working as a typist in the Commerce Department, the corner where we had agreed to meet was midway between the Gray building prison and the Commerce Building.

Near the busy intersection where I was supposed to pick up Florence, I had to wait for a traffic light. Just around the corner where I had to turn, I saw her standing by the curb, waiting for me. She wasn't looking in the direction from which she knew I could be coming, but was gazing upward; either at the sky or at the pigeons that wheeled around the apex of the Masonic Temple across the street from where she stood.

Waiting for the light to change, with Florence oblivious of my proximity, I studied the woman who was my wife; the woman to whom I had said, "I love you" so passionately five years before, at the time of our marriage. And it occurred to me as a new insight, in that brief moment of observation and reflection, that whatever Florence's initial attraction for me had been, it had not been primarily sex appeal. Or perhaps, I speculated, she had looked more sexy then; had taken more pains with her dress and appearance. Her once luxuriant, chestnut hair, which had been shoulder length when I met her, was now bobbed to a masculine-looking brevity for maximum comfort during the coming summer months. Her shoulders were bent slightly forward, part of her habitual posture, whether standing or walking; as if in her teen years her enlarging breasts had been a source of embarrassment to her, and she had begun to hunch her shoulders forward in an effort to hide them.

I noted that her clothes that day, as every workday, were working-girl simple—no frills, a short-sleeved green blouse open at the neck, a straight brown skirt, and low-heeled shoes. I knew that when she got into the car there would be no per-fumed scent reaching out to me from her to awaken the well-springs of erotic desire. Florence did not bother with such aphrodisiacs on working days; only on special occasions.

As I pulled over to the curb and approached the spot where she stood, she changed the direction of her gaze from a skyward contemplation to a grave study of the sidewalk at her feet, obviously absorbed in deep concentration. Not until I stopped the car immediately in front of her did she look up and see me. Before I could lean over and open the door for her, she had wrenched it open.

"Hello, Gar."

The greeting was delivered in a matter-of-fact, impersonal tone as she flounced down on the seat, avoiding my gaze, and slammed the door shut.

"Hello, Flo."

Using the abbreviation of her name, as she did with mine, had become habitual after five years of marriage. I could gath-er from the grim expression on her face that something was wrong, but knew from previous experience that it was better to wait for her to tell me when and if she wanted to, rather than trying to dig out of her what it was that might be bother-ing her. For the following twenty minutes, as I pulled out into the burgeoning stream of five o'clock southbound traffic, I had enough to do to maneuver the car and keep from getting a fender bent or hitting pedestrians who, after the light had changed, dashed across the street in their homeward rush.

Finally, with city traffic behind, on the highway that would take us eighteen miles to the small town of Charlotte, since Florence still hadn't uttered a word about what was bothering her, I switched on the radio in an attempt to divert her attention from whatever it was that had obviously upset her. The announcer's voice on the five o'clock news came into the car; dividing, but not dispersing, the heavy silence that hung between us.

"In Washington, D.C., four Asian church leaders testified before the House Un-American Activities Committee on the efforts of Chinese communists to stamp out Christianity. The church leaders told of how aged Christians, 60 years old and older, are put into what are called Happy Homes. There they are given shots which they are led to believe are for better health. Within two weeks they die. Another witness spelled out in detail one of the atrocities devised by the Chinese Reds. 'They stop the noses of people,' he said, 'and pour water in their mouths. Every time a person breathes, he swallows water, his stomach swells up, and then they stand on it.'"

I switched the radio off suddenly, nauseated, incredulous that such barbaric treatment of human being should be committed by other human beings; actions that seemed to offer indisputable evidence of the Biblical doctrine of the depravity of human nature.

"Want to hear any more of the news?" I asked, as a wedge to break into the shell of silence with which Florence had surrounded herself.

"Suit yourself," she retorted coldly, not looking at me.

I drove on in silence, seeking to hold down my rising temper over her curt incivility by reaching out into the uncorrupted beauty of nature; the blue sky, the fleecy white clouds, the cool greens of meadows and trees, as I tried to wash out my system with the visual beauty of the countryside, the ugliness that had been contained in the news report, as well as Florence's increasingly irritating aloofness. Finally, I ran out of patience.

"Is something wrong?" I finally asked, turning my head for a brief glance at her rigid profile.

"Yes, something's wrong!" she blazed, glaring at me as if I were at fault.

There was such fury in her face and in her tone that my attention was momentarily diverted too long from the road ahead of me. Abruptly, the wildly blaring horn of an oncoming car caused me to intuitively sense, rather than see, that I had allowed the car to edge over the white centerline of the two-lane pavement into the lane of oncoming traffic. Instinctively, too quick to think, as my eyes jerked back to the road, I savagely wrenched the steering wheel to the right. At the same time, as I came abreast of the oncoming car in the other lane, the other driver also swerved to the left. Only the swift and simultaneous actions on the part of both of us had averted a head-on collision. At the speed we were both traveling, that could have been a fatal encounter for all the occupants of both cars.

"Thank God for getting us through that!" I exclaimed, relieved but shaken, and keeping my eyes on the road ahead, "we could have been killed."

"I wouldn't mind if we had been," Florence replied angrily.

I risked an astonished, darting glance at her, seemingly unruffled by the near accident her outburst had caused.

"For God's sake, tell me what's wrong!" I demanded, giving vent to the rising anger I was beginning to feel. "I know you didn't lose your job because you're too good a worker. So what's eating you?"

"I'm pregnant, damn it!"

I would have been more shocked at her announcement, perhaps, had it not been for the fact that her attitude since getting into the car had prepared me to expect some real disaster. The news, when it finally came out of her, was a relief. But before I had a chance to admit that, she continued, elaborating on her terse announcement.

"I expected it when I missed my period," she continued, "but I wanted to be sure, so I went in for an examination today. Damn it all, anyway! Why did this have to happen, just when we were getting caught up on our bills?"

"I can tell you why it happened," I answered silently to myself.

The birth control pill had not yet appeared on the market. Couples who were not yet ready to have children had only the various mechanical contraceptives or reliance on the "rhythm" method of birth control. We had relied on a combination of condoms and the rhythm method during our five years of marriage. But for the first time, one forgotten night several weeks before, one of us had been too tired or too unconcerned to take into account whether it was really a "safe" night for sexual contact. A prolonged period of success in preventing conception had made us both careless. But I tried to think only of some words that would help to lighten Florence's depressed state of mind.

"Well," I began cautiously, taking the tack that misery loves company, "you're not alone. Sooner or later it happens to almost every couple that gets married."

And then the real, hidden reason for her agitated state of mind erupted in a Vesuvian geyser of indignation.

"Most people can afford to have a baby," she charged fiercely, "but here we are, we've been married five years, and we haven't even got a home to live in yet."

"What do you mean, we haven't got a home to live in?" I rebutted with a mixture of astonishment and irritated defensiveness. "Moving in with your mother was your idea, not mine. I just went along with it to help her out. Any time you want to move back into our house in town, we'll do it. I'll just tell the tenants they'll have to move out."

Florence had already looked farther ahead than I had, and reminded me of an imminent change in our financial situation which I had not yet considered.

"You know you couldn't keep up the payments on the house by yourself, and when I'm laid off on maternity leave all the expenses are going to come out of your paycheck. Don't forget that!"

I drove on in silence, looking for a loophole in Florence's analysis of our economic situation that might let in some sunlight of hope onto the bleak landscape. With Florence and I both getting regular payroll checks from the state, there had been no problem keeping up with payments since the time we had bought the rambling seven-room house in Charlotte a year before. And we had only rented the house to tenants and moved into the big farmhouse with Florence's mother, not out of economic necessity, but out of Florence's concern for her mother. She had felt uneasy about having Hilda, her mother, living alone in the country after Brady, Florence's unmarried older brother, had left the farm to go to California for a high-paying job with Lockheed Aircraft. It had been with a measure of unexpressed reluctance that I had given up our own home in town to move into the farmhouse with Florence's mother, but I had done so out of deference to Florence's commendable concern for her widowed mother. Now, with the news of Florence's pregnancy, it appeared to have been a providential arrangement.

"Maybe it will be a good thing to be with your mother when you have the baby," I ventured.

"What do you mean by that?" she demanded, as indignantly as if I had suggested an abortion.

"I mean, she's been through it before. She knows what having a baby is all about. It ought to be a big help to have her around."

"No woman wants to have her first baby in her mother's house . . ." she began, and broke off there.

I cast a furtive, sidelong glance at her and saw her biting her lower lip in the attempt to keep from crying.

Her remark was a shocking revelation to me. I would have pressed her for an explanation of this dumbfounding disclosure if she had not been on the verge of tears. Perhaps, I mused silently as I drove on, in spite of Florence's outward show of concern for her mother, there was some hidden dissonance between her mother and herself, springing from childhood contacts in the areas of sex or childbirth. I didn't know. Perhaps I never would. But without knowing the reasons for feeling as she did, I could sympathize with her position. She did not want to have her first baby in her mother's home, but she would have to because we could not afford to move back in our house and stay there on my paycheck alone. She was trapped in an unhappy situation and, at the moment, I knew of no way to help her get out.

We drove on in silence, each of us preoccupied with our separate reactions to the fact of her pregnancy. I kept within myself the hurt I felt in Florence's implied doubts about my ability to provide for both of us and a baby. And the part that hurt me the most was the likelihood that it was true.

With no further communication between us, we drove the remaining ten miles to the small town of Charlotte. As we approached the outskirts, a huge billboard that marked the city limits suddenly acquired new significance for me. "A Nice Place to Live," proclaimed the sign. Below it, in figures large enough to indicate a certain measure of pride, the most recent population count of the city—9,543. I wondered if the birth of the child Florence was expecting would be of sufficient importance to the city fathers to have a sign painter alter the population count, increasing the total by one. I was doubtful.

As I stopped at the main intersection of downtown Charlotte for a traffic light, Florence sat beside me in grim silence. I scanned the familiar main-street scenes of the small town where Florence had been born on a farm and had grown up as a girl. Charlotte, county seat of Eaton County, boasted nine churches, five taverns, four restaurants, two drug stores, the County fairgrounds, and one theatre that closed in summer, plus a sprinkling of gas stations, a post office, and mercantile stores.

"Yes, this is Charlotte," I mused silently, as the traffic began to move again. "This is the place where our first child, unplanned for, unprepared for, even after five years of marriage, is slated to be born; to arrive as an uninvited guest in the old farmhouse that we are sharing with Florence's mother."

Minutes later, in a scenic countryside, when I turned off the blacktop highway five miles west of town, into the drive that led to the huge, old-fashioned, two-story, white-frame farmhouse, Florence was out of the car and on her way to the house before I could roll up the car windows for the night. I

119

finished with this protective ritual in case of rain that night, in time to see Florence dashing up the steps of the side porch and into the kitchen. Thinking it would be good to give Florence a private time to break the news of her pregnancy to her mother, I stood a moment, leaning against the car, inhaling the fresh, clean, clover-scented air.

Looking up, I scanned the springtime sky where clear, translucent blue showed through the strung-out, sun-crimsoned clouds as I drank in peace from the tranquil countryside. Then, as I surveyed the surrounding terrain of the Berlincourt farm with a greater absorption than I ever had before, perhaps, including the first time I had come here to meet Florence's family more than five years before, I noted details I had overlooked before. I perceived a certain air of seclusion about the towering, two-story farmhouse; the aura which always seems to surround a home that is set in solitary grandeur upon a hill. It struck me anew that this rolling, eighty-acre farm, where Florence had been born and where she had grown up, was ideally located. It was close enough to the small town of Charlotte so as not to be isolated from the comforts and conveniences of city life, yet far enough away to provide the quiet evenings where the stillness was like a blank music scroll on which Nature's talented musicians, the crickets, frogs, birds, and squirrels, could write new and exciting variations on an old, familiar theme each evening.

But then, after surveying all that I could see and remember of the physical configurations of the Berlincourt farm, I pushed myself away from my leaning position against the car. With the edge dulled on my appetite for supper by Florence's angry announcement, I walked slowly across the lawn in front of the house beneath the overspreading branches of mighty and ancient oak trees. As I did, Shep, the black-and-white collie spaniel owned by Brady, came bounding around the corner of the house. He greeted me, not with the warning bark reserved for strangers, but with the vigorous wig-wagging of his feather-fringed tail. I stooped as he came up to me and bent down to gently massage the top of his head. His brown canine eyes looked up into mine in that mystic bond of empathy which can exist only between a human being and a dumb animal. It must have been a generous provision of a gracious God, I mused, when He had planned the creation of all living things.

Then I walked, with Shep trailing along beside me, to the far edge of the spacious lawn, bounded by the dirt driveway on the west side of the house. I sat down on the grass, leaning against the trunk of a sturdy oak, to look westward and soak in the therapeutic warmth of the setting sun. Inside the big farmhouse, I speculated, Florence was probably pouring out her dammed-up feelings of apprehension about the birth of the expected baby. Shep crouched down beside me on the grass, and I laid my hand upon his neck, idly running my fingers through his matted hair while I scanned the countryside. And it occurred to me in that reflective moment that there had been negative influences exerted upon Florence in this setting of idyllic splendor, which she had shared with me in separated fragments through the five years we had been married. It was here, I recalled, on this beautiful, sprawling farm, that Florence had received some unintended sex instruction by her parents, stemming from a typical farm-life episode that she had not forgotten; the lingering influence of which had first been manifested on our honeymoon.

I could still remember her telling me how, as a girl, she had one day ran out to the huge barn with the excitement of a natural, childish curiosity, to witness the expected birth of a calf. But she had been scolded by her parents and sent back to the house; not allowed to witness the event; as if she had done something wrong in even wanting to find out about it. She had arrived at the inevitable, child-like conclusion, not put into words by her parents, that the mechanics which produced babies, whether animal or human, were something secretive, shameful in a way; not to be discussed or observed by young girls.

This attitude toward sex, which she had been saddled with as a child growing up on a farm, had come out on our wedding night. The sexual relationship was to be carried out in the dark, not even in the subdued light of a bedroom. It was to be gotten over with as quickly as possible with no preliminary foreplay; no exploring of erotic stimulation or response. This negative input from her farm childhood inheritance had been a poor preparation for marriage. It had put an emotional straitjacket upon me in my sexual overtures toward Florence.

Then, sitting there under the sheltering oak, the long fingers of the setting sun caressing my face with warmth, and with Shep's recumbent form pressed against my leg, I suddenly thought it strange that either Florence or I should have been so perturbed about the arrival of a baby after five years of marriage. Most married couples, I reflected, would have been disturbed that it had not happened much sooner. And I became aware of something new that had not entered my thinking during the five years we had been married. Whatever there may have been within me of needs or expectations, which I had lumped together in the words "I love you" to Florence, I had not married her with the expectation of becoming a father to a child uppermost in my mind. Neither had I married her with any conscious awareness that she would be expecting of me, as a husband, to provide a secure home and a dependable income sufficient to care not only for ourselves but for one or more children as well. On the contrary, from the beginning of our marriage, there had been deliberate precautions taken, in the use of contraceptives, which I had initiated, not to have children.

And I wondered, for the first time, if, while I had been groping for my vocational niche in society, Florence had kept her own instinctive desire for a home and children tightly locked within herself, as she had patiently stood beside me, pouring a large share of her own earnings into several years of education and training that had apparently come to nothing; money and self-denial and effort just poured down the drain. As I dwelt on Florence's patient attendance upon my fruitless vocational groping during the five years of our marriage, out of gratitude to her, I felt a desire welling up within me to become what she perhaps had secretly hoped I would become—a breadwinner capable of providing an adequate home and income for herself and a family.

Suddenly, I felt Shep's body stiffen beneath my encircling arm, and a restrained growl of excitement rumbled in his chest. He evidently had seen some specimen of wildlife in the nearby field that had escaped my attention. Then he was gone, racing furiously down the dirt road that led to the barn, in pursuit of a rabbit, perhaps, or a cat that had strayed from a neighboring farm. I got up to go into the house, sweeping the pastoral prospect of open fields beyond the barn with a final, encircling inspection. The panoramic view poured over me a cascade of unforgettable impressions and sensations. There had been balmy spring weekend afternoons, spent walking through the forest on the back of the farm, entranced by the remarkable profusion of spring wild flowers, pointed out and identified by Florence. There had been hot summer afternoons spent picking wild blackberries that had wound up in one of Hilda's golden-crusted, mouthwatering pies. And there had been evening hours, spent leaning against one of the majestic oak trees in the front yard, as I had just been doing, watching the stars grow bright in the darkening sky; sometimes with Florence beside me, sometimes alone, reviewing bittersweet memories of the days in Chicago when I had been fired with the vision of entering the ministry as my life work.

As I followed the dirt driveway to the back of the house, thinking to enter the kitchen from the side door on the west side of the house, Florence's mother stepped out on the enclosed porch, a blue plaid apron stretched across her ample girth.

"Garfield!" she exclaimed, standing on the porch as I drew near, "where have you been? I looked for you out in the front yard but I didn't see you anywhere."

"I was sitting behind a tree with Shep, just resting. I thought Florence might be having a talk with you and might like a little privacy. That's why I didn't come in the house sooner."

Behind her delicately gold-rimmed glasses, Hilda Berlincourt's finely lined eyebrows were pinched together in bewilderment, a facial reaction that Florence had inherited from her mother. Several strands of grandmotherly white hair, unloosed in her busy preparations for supper, had strayed from the silvery, encircling braid that heralded the approach to her seventieth birthday.

"Why she wasn't talking to me, Garfield," Hilda exclaimed in astonishment. "Why, mercy, she just said 'hello' to me as she went through the kitchen, and went right upstairs to your bedroom. I haven't heard a peep out of her since. I thought maybe you and she had a little disagreement and I was just waiting for one or the other of you to show up."

I was as much surprised at the report of Florence's action as her mother obviously was to have witnessed it.

"You mean, she didn't even tell you she's . . ."

"She didn't tell me anything," Hilda spouted. "What in the world is wrong with her? Or maybe it's none of my business."

"Florence is going to have a baby," I announced simply, standing on the step below Hilda and looking up at her as I spoke.

The emotional turmoil I had been through over Florence's reaction to her pregnancy, and my own reservations about the possible effect which the baby might have on my own unresolved vocational groping kept back that exuberance, that spontaneous delight with which most new fathers announce the expected birth of a child. Hilda didn't notice.

"Why, Garfield," she gasped in evident delight, "that's wonderful news. That's nothing to run upstairs and mope about. What kind of a daughter have I got, anyway?"

We climbed the cracked concrete steps of the side porch together and I held open the door leading into the kitchen for Hilda.

"I guess Florence is worried that we won't be able to keep all our bills paid when she has to quit work to have the baby," I told Hilda, stepping into the kitchen behind her.

The savory aroma of wieners and saur kraut, fried potatoes and homemade biscuits, mingled in the atmosphere, revived somewhat my emotion-enervated appetite.

"Let me speak to that daughter of mine, Garfield!"

Hilda stalked off to the stairway door that led to the upstairs bedroom.

I walked on into the front room parlor and sat down at the spinet piano. It was one of the cherished household items that Florence had brought into our marriage. As my admiration was evoked at the sight of the magnificent instrument, I remembered Florence telling me proudly how she had paid nearly two thousand dollars for it out of her own wages. As I stroked on the keys the melody of a once popular song, the remembered lyrics expressed the wistful longings that I felt at that moment.

"Somewhere, over the rainbow . . . . Skies are blue. And the dreams, that you dare to dream, really do come true."

A few moments later I heard the stairway door open, then softly close again, followed by the slow, heavy footsteps of Florence's mother padding her way into the front room. I stopped playing and turned around on the piano bench as she sat down on the sofa across the room from me.

"Florence will be alright, Garfield," Hilda assured me with a maternal smile. "Don't you worry about it. We'll all get along just fine."

I turned back to the piano, switching to some familiar hymns as Hilda returned quietly to the kitchen. I was thankful that Hilda had not sought to probe my ambiguous feelings about becoming a father. But neither Hilda's reassuring words, nor the anesthesia of comforting music could chase away from my mind the pain that still burned there following Florence's implied doubts that, as a breadwinner, I could not make the grade in providing for a wife and a child.

And the following morning, having a cup of coffee at the kitchen table, I learned of one very practical reason as to why Florence might not want to have the baby in her mother's house, whatever other obscure psychological reservations she might have had. Florence came downstairs and, after a tense greeting to me, poured herself a cup of coffee. After one swallow, she set the cup down on the sink unfinished, as one of the first unpleasant physical results of pregnancy, "morning sickness," swept over her.

"Oh," she gasped, as the swallow of coffee produced a violent reaction, "I feel like I'm going to vomit."

She clutched her stomach as if to hold back the coming eruption.

"Is mom in the bathroom?" she gasped.

"I'm afraid she is," I answered, jumping up from the table. "Hold it until I get a pail."

But Florence couldn't wait. I stopped in the middle of the kitchen, watching helplessly, as she ran to the kitchen door, flung it open with such violence that it banged against the kitchen table, and catapulted down the steps to halt a few feet from the house by the gnarled apple tree. Her back was turned to me and I watched her through the kitchen window in mute compassion as she bent over, gripping her abdomen, making retching sounds which I could hear through the open door. Then her sudden attack of nausea was aggravated by the abrupt appearance of Shep, who had been summoned by the slam of the kitchen screen door. He came up to Florence and stood looking up at her, wagging his tail in dumb sympathy over her obvious distress. Her immediate reaction was understandable.

"Get away from me, you damn dog!" she shouted, straightening up and aiming a kick at the poor animal.

He disappeared around the corner of the house, tail between his legs, as Florence came back into the kitchen.

"It was only phlegm," Florence said, as she came back into the kitchen, gasping from the exertion and the abdominal spasm, "but I sure felt like I was going to heave."

I sat back down at the kitchen table silently as she poured her remaining coffee into the sink.

"I guess I won't be drinking any more coffee until this is over," she said as she passed by me to go to the bathroom.

"You can just thank God you're not a woman. A man gets off pretty easy."

I sat at the table alone, my coffee suddenly rendered tasteless by Florence's caustically intoned criticism; prompted, no doubt, by her new awareness that a man had to experience none of the physical discomforts of having a child.

But there were psychological pains for a man suddenly propelled into the unexpected responsibilities of fatherhood that Florence knew nothing about. And on our car-pool ride to Lansing that morning, I said nothing to our fellow riders about the bombshell announcement which Florence had made to me the day before which had almost resulted in a fatal automobile accident. I decided to leave to Florence the time, place, and wording in sharing this information with our fellow pool riders.

So I sat silently beside her on the back seat of the roomy station wagon owned by one of our pool riders, while the conversation flowed back and forth between the other occupants of the car. I heard their words bouncing back and forth around me but didn't really listen or respond to them. My thoughts were preoccupied with Florence's plight. I thought of her being unexpectedly pushed into the uncomfortable experience of an unsought pregnancy, with the double handicap of doubts about my ability to provide for a family, and trapped in a house where she would rather not be living while bearing her first child. And there was little I could do, I realized soberly, to alleviate her physical and mental distress unless I could somehow get a better-paying job to bolster my meager income as a lower-level clerk in the Highway Department. But I silently resolved, as we traversed the familiar eighteen miles between Charlotte and Lansing, to explore that remote possibility on my lunch hour that very day.

My concern to reduce Florence's economic anxiety about the coming baby was to propel me into conflict with a powerful agency of state government; a conflict that was to shake the foundations of our marriage. It began innocently with an indication that Providence was smiling upon my well-intentioned effort. Under Civil Service rule, entry into a better-paying job depended upon passing an examination, just as in high school or in college.

So on my lunch hour that day, I walked three blocks to the state office building housing the Civil Service Commission. Among the announcements of imminent examinations to be given was one that generated a sudden spurt of hope within me, for a Social Worker 1-A position which would pay $100.00 more per month than I was then earning. For I was pleasantly surprised to read that my two years at Michigan State University was acceptable in place of actual paid experience in the field. When I stepped into the Civil Service personnel office, the response of the receptionist was like a smile of approval from God.

"Just fill this card out and we'll mail it to you when the examination date is established," she instructed, handing me the card, then adding, "You got here just in time."

"What do you mean?" I asked, puzzled by her cryptic comment.

"The closing date to take that exam is today at five o'clock, and that's an exam that's only given every two or three years."

That night, in the spacious kitchen of the Berlincourt farmhouse in Charlotte, when I shared my buoyant expectation of a better-paying job with Florence, as we sat at the supper table with her mother, she was skeptical about the outcome.

"Do you really think you've got a chance?" she asked doubtfully, the question springing from my preceding five unsuccessful years of vocational groping.

"I wouldn't bother with it if I didn't think so," I retorted sharply, stung by her lack of confidence in me.

I hid the hurt which I felt at her skepticism, but took it with me to the examination for Social Worker 1-A, in the mammoth cafeteria of a Lansing High School. Before stepping through the main entrance of the school, I paused to drink in some needed words of encouragement and challenge that were engraved in concrete above the massive double doors.

"To each is given a book of rules . . . . A shapeless mass and a bag of tools . . . . And each must fashion, 'ere life has flown . . . . A stumbling block, or a stepping stone."

"Lord, let this examination be a stepping stone to a better life for Florence and me," I prayed as I entered.

Two weeks later, when the mail brought a report that I had passed the written examination, I was more confident than ever that the Lord was making a way, both for my vocational interest in helping people who needed help and for Florence's economic fears. There only remained one more hurdle to surmount before being qualified for the better-paying job—an oral interview, which I thought would be a cinch to pass. Two men interviewed me; one from the Social Service Department, where I expected to be working soon, and one from Civil Service, in an informal question-and-answer session lasting twenty minutes.

I was stunned a week later, as was Florence, to be informed that I had failed the oral interview and therefore would not qualify for the Social Worker 1-A job. The next day I went to the Civil Service offices and asked to see exactly what had been written down about me by the two-man oral interview board. A Civil Service hearings examiner sat across his desk from me as I reviewed what had been written about me that had resulted in a failing score by a narrow margin of five points. As I read, I held in check the simmering indignation at the caricature that had been written about me.

"Would it do any good to discuss these ratings with anyone with a view to having them changed?" I asked, "or are they irrevocable and final?"

"Final," he pronounced, with the assumed authority of a Supreme Court judge, "unless you want to request a hearing to have the findings of the oral interview board reviewed."

"I certainly do want to request a hearing," I responded emphatically.

"That's your privilege," he shrugged, "although I might as well warn you that hearing boards hardly ever reverse the judgment of an oral interview board. You really haven't got much of a chance of getting the results of your examination changed."

As I sat facing him in stunned silence at his prediction that the course I had chosen could only culminate in defeat, he continued sucking on his pipe; he regarded me as if I were some strange new species of insect being looked at under a microscope for the first time by a disinterested scientist. A pinpoint light of hostility also seemed to have been kindled in his eyes, as if he had been personally affronted that I should have intimated that there might be something wrong with the ratings I had been given. The picture of gloomy foreboding on Florence's face and the cry of an unborn baby nudged me into continuing on a course that was probably futile.

"I'd still like to try it," I replied firmly.

For only I knew how much blatant falsehood and misrepresentations there were in the appraisal of me by the two-man oral interview board.

"Then the thing to do," he responded sardonically, inhaling on his pipe, then laying it down on an ashtray, "is to write a letter to the Civil Service Commission requesting a hearing. They'll set up a date for the hearing and notify you of it by mail."

That night at the supper table with Florence and Hilda, I shared the report of my intention to request a hearing in the hope of overturning the erroneous judgments of the oral interview board. Hilda's response was positive and spontaneously exuberant.

"Good for you, Garfield!" she exclaimed, "maybe you can knock some sense into their heads."

Florence's reaction was just the opposite; entirely negative.

"Why don't you forget about it instead of going to all that trouble? That's one job you're never going to get."

After supper, in spite of Florence's gloom-and-doom prediction, I retired to the upstairs bedroom and, on my ancient but sturdy typewriter, requested a hearing by the Michigan Civil Service Commission. As I reviewed again the critical evaluation of the oral interview board, it became increasingly obvious to me that some of the criticisms for which they had given me a failing score were totally ridiculous; some were blatantly untrue; some were misleading in the way they were phrased. Their criticism that I had not "reported" any specific vocational objective in life did not mean that I didn't have one.

For there still pulsed at the core of my being—beneath layers of disappointment and frustration—the compulsion to communicate to the world around me the astounding discovery I had made in the military prison during World War II; that Jesus Christ was not a dead figure of history, but wonderfully alive in the present hour; that He could and would transform the life that was opened to receive Him as Lord and Savior; that the Bible was indeed the living Word of the living God, containing the truth about man's past, his present, and his future. Although I had judged myself unworthy to proclaim these truths from behind a pulpit, still, it was the underlying, if hidden, goal of my life to find some other ways to communicate those discoveries to the world around me.

A week later, I received a reply to my request for a hearing. It was couched in the legal language of impending conflict: "Garfield A. Roby versus the Michigan Civil Service Commission." It hinted at a battle between unequal protagonists; a solitary individual pitted against the intimidating might of a powerfully entrenched agency of state government. The notice informed me that on Thursday afternoon, the 21st of August, the second floor of the Lewis Cass building in Lansing was to be the scene of the head-on collision between myself, a poor man trying to support his family and heal his wounded self-esteem, and the agency of state government entrusted with weeding out the fit from the unfit; in a governmental application of Darwinian theory, the survival of the fittest.

But even with so much to gain and nothing to lose by the scheduled encounter, it was a contest which I might well have avoided had I not been pushed into it by the pressures that were being generated by the expanding new life in Florence's belly; the unnamed, unknown, and uninvited guest whose arrival in our home could be neither denied nor delayed.

On that fateful day that was to have a devastating chain reaction effect upon my marriage, I sat in the second-floor hallway of the Cass office building, just outside a hearings room of the Civil Service Commission. I had spent the fifteen minutes prior to the showdown discussing the case with Rudy Sylvester, a half-blind epileptic whom I had asked to appear as a witness of some of my unpaid social work in the community. Several years before, I had spent time every week going to the Michigan School for the Blind, reading to Rudy and other blind students their required class work to ensure and expedite their progress toward graduation.

Abruptly, our dialogue was interrupted as a Civil Service receptionist appeared before us.

"They're ready for you now, Mr. Roby. Is this gentleman a witness for you?"

"Yes," I responded, "this is Rudy Sylvester."

"Will both of you just follow me, please?"

She waited a moment as I gathered up my arsenal of documentary weapons from the chair beside me, then led us down the hallway a short distance to a closed door with a frosted glass panel labeled Conference Room A. She opened the door and Rudy and I followed her into the huge, rectangular conference room, brightly illuminated by the brilliant August sunlight which poured through the windows along the west side of the room.

Then I saw the enemy, like the Philistine army which David faced, strung out across one end of the large room; five men and one woman; seated in plush, high-backed chairs fit for a monarch. They were securely fortified behind a long, mahogany table. From the mammoth conference table at which the six people were sitting, a shorter table had been set up abutting it, so that the smaller table jutted out from the center section of the longer one like a short dock extending out into a lake from the shoreline. On each side of the shorter table was positioned a folding chair facing in the direction of the long conference table.

"You gentlemen can sit here at this table," smiled the receptionist, indicating the two chairs flanking the smaller table.

I thanked her, and as Rudy and I sat down, she turned and left the room, closing the door behind her. Since our arrival had not been announced by the receptionist, none of the hearing-board members appeared to have noticed that Rudy and I were there. They all seemed busily engaged, perhaps making notes or talking about the results of a preceding hearing, or the merits of the one about to begin. I took advantage of their momentary inattention to set up the portable table easel between Rudy and myself, then positioned on it, in the sequence I planned to use them, the four poster boards containing the major points of the attack I had planned on the oral interview findings. From a briefcase, I withdrew pertinent letters of recommendation qualifying me for the social worker position, and arranged them in a pile in the order in which I expected to use them.

Having done that, the six members of the hearing board still appeared to be unaware or unconcerned about the presence of Rudy and me. It gave me a moment of calm before the storm in which to study the enemy whom I would be facing in an eyeball-to-eyeball confrontation. What I saw and what I remembered from the preliminary steps leading to this imminent encounter was not encouraging. I remembered the warning of the Civil Service hearings official who had shown me the outrageously misleading criticisms of the oral interview board.

"A hearing review board hardly ever reverses the findings of an oral interview board."

This meant that the six people assembled before me were there not primarily as an independent, fact-finding body dedicated to discovering the truth about my qualifications for the job. They were there mainly as defenders of the status quo; to uphold the judgment of the oral interview board, whether true or false. And their demeanor and appearance, as my eyes swept down their ranks in a cursory scrutiny, only reinforced this suspicion.

At the far end of the long conference table on my right, a sixtyish, sourpuss woman with frizzled brown hair and fire-engine lipstick, whom I took to be the secretary for the proceedings, was squirting her glasses with a purse-size tube of cleaning solvent in preparation for the coming conflict. Of the two men who sat next to her, talking in low undertones, one had a long, sallow-skinned face with a shock of unruly hair and a Groucho Marx mustache, while the other had a moon-round face and a pate as bald as a bowling ball. Next to them, in a central position suggesting a position of leadership, sat a heavy-set, middle-aged man whose appearance struck me most forcibly of all six because of his resemblance to Hollywood actor Edward G. Robinson as he had portrayed a gangland mobster named "Little Caesar." His black hair was combed back in an oily slick, his eyebrows were thick and bushy, and his lips were clamped down on an unlit cigar in a cruel, tight line. At the moment, he was industriously applying a handkerchief to some real or imaginary stain on his suit-coat lapel.

Just beyond Little Caesar, eying the table in front of him, sat a youthful, junior executive type with a summer crew cut and sporting a red bow tie. Like an out-of-place drummer from a rock-and-roll band, he was nervously beating a pencil against a pad of paper before him. And next to him, at the extreme left end of the long table, was a gray-haired professorial type with goatee, leaning back in his swivel chair as he sucked placidly on a pipe and stared out the window.

Finally, after several moments during which Rudy and I had been completely ignored, Little Caesar finished his coat-lapel dry-cleaning operation and looked up at Rudy and me with the cold, clinical gaze that might have been accorded two strange species of insects. But instead of acknowledging our presence with either a nod of the head or a word of greeting, he looked down the table at the spinsterly woman whose cleaned bifocals were now sedately in place on her nose.

"I guess we're ready now, Mrs. Fussler," he announced, confirming my suspicion that he was the chairman of the hearing panel.

At Little Caesar's announcement, the two men who had been talking in low undertones became silent. The paunchy, professorial type who had been looking out the window, laid his pipe down in an ash tray and sat up straight in his chair. The frustrated, crew-cut pencil drummer laid his pencil down beside the note pad in front of him. All six pairs of eyes were suddenly focused on Rudy and me. Except for the secretary, whose gaze seemed neutral, all eyes showed hostility, as if they resented having been called away from more important pursuits, such as golfing or fishing, to spend a hot, humid summer afternoon in a stuffy conference room. Then the secretary, peering through her bifocals at the paper on the table before her, read aloud.

"This is Mr. Garfield Roby and Mr. Rudy Sylvester, who's appearing as a witness for Mr. Roby."

"Which one is Mr. Roby?" broke in Little Caesar, regarding Rudy and me with an icy stare of interrogation.

"I am," I responded.

"You're the one who requested this hearing?"

There was an undertone of intimidation in the tone of his voice, whether intended or not.

"Yes, sir."

"Alright," he nodded authoritatively to the secretary at the end of the table, "go ahead, Mrs. Fussler."

"Mr. Roby," she continued, after nervously clearing her throat, "has requested a hearing to review the oral interview for the Social Worker 1-A examination which he took on July 27th. The passing score for the oral interview was 28. Mr. Roby was given a total score of 23."

As the secretary proceeded to read off the fallacious and malicious criticisms which the two-man oral interview board had raised against me, the five men who sat strung out along the long conference table exhibited the same sort of bored unconcern that is often seen in legislative chambers when some senator or representative is filibustering to prevent passage of a bill. Obviously unimpressed by what they were hearing, their glances wandered here and there; at the ceiling, out the window, at papers on the table in front of them, but not at Rudy or me. Finally, she was finished.

"Just relax now, Mr. Roby," said Little Caesar, the leader, as his movie counterpart might have said to a gangster rival before mowing him down with a machine gun, "these hearings are very informal. If you can point out any place where there was discrimination against you, go ahead."

The rasping, belligerent tone of his voice contained, not a concerned invitation to bring forth hitherto hidden evidence that might tip the scales in my favor but, rather, the same kind of arrogant challenge that the Philistine giant Goliath had hurled at David. His tone and attitude were daring me to pit my puny strength and my pitiful weapons of paper and truth against the bureaucratic giant called the Michigan Civil Service Commission. I hesitated in launching the vigorous attack I had planned, feeling overwhelmed by the hostile atmosphere and by being outnumbered six to one, with the additional might of a vast state bureaucracy standing behind the six who faced me across the conference table. Then, in my moment of need, the ancient words of David to Goliath swept through my mind, mixed with phrases of my own making.

"Thou comest to me with a sword, and with a spear, and with a shield, but I come to thee in the name of the Lord of hosts . . . to win the respect of my wife as a provider, and to find vocational fulfillment for myself."

With the encouragement from scripture that I needed to begin, I pointed to the first of four poster boards I had leaned against the table easel, one on top of the other. The figures were calculated to emphasize the narrow margin by which I had been given a failing score.

"You will note on this card . . ." I began.

"I don't think there's any need to waste time going over the percentages on your score," broke in the crew-cut junior executive with the red bow tie, fiddling impatiently with his pencil, "we've already heard those."

I paused in my presentation and looked at Little Caesar, directly in front of me, for either approval or rejection of this interruption. He rolled the unlit cigar from one side of his mouth to the other.

"I agree. No need to go over the same ground twice."

It was to be the first of a series of needling interruptions which would throw into confused disarray the logical sequence in which I had planned to present my systematic attack on the criticisms of the oral interview board. I swallowed my objections and turned the first poster card face down on the table in front of the easel, revealing the next one behind it. It was the card on which I had set down, in ascending order of importance, the four criticisms that had been leveled against me in abbreviated form as "No goal"; "No interest"; No Background"; and "Dislikes Women." But before I could follow through on my plan to take up evidence refuting these four objections, one at a time, I was again interrupted; this time by "Moon Man," the round-faced, baldheaded panelist who evidently possessed a caustic sense of humor.

"Dislikes women?" he asked in simulated shock, as if he hadn't heard the criticism at all in the reading by the secretary, "what would happen to the human race if all men felt that way?"

As he asked the totally irrelevant question in a mocking tone of voice, he looked not at me, but down the table at the elderly secretary, who responded with an answering grimace of rebuke at his flippant attitude. Little Caesar removed the cigar from his mouth long enough to look down the table at the heckler and remonstrate with him for the wrong reason.

"My God, Winfield, let's not get into a question like that or we'll be here all afternoon trying to answer it, and I want to get in eighteen holes of golf when this is over."

Snickers erupted from several of the men as the chairman replaced the cigar in his mouth and looked at me accusingly as if I were the cause of this devious delay.

"Go ahead Mr. Roby."

"These are the four criticisms which the oral interview board made," I continued, trying to shake off the rattling effect of the practical punster, "And I'd like to take them one by one and present evidence to show that these criticisms were either wholly false or misleading in the way they were worded."

But again, before I could proceed, Little Caesar plucked the cigar from his mouth and interrupted in a patronizing, pontifical tone.

"I suggest, Mr. Roby, that in the interest of saving time, we get down to the really important criticism of no background in social work. If that's settled, maybe we can forget the rest."

"If I read the examination announcement correctly, sir," I responded, looking the chairman directly in the eye, "that objection should never even have been raised by the oral interview board, and shouldn't be brought up here. The examination announcement stated that two years of college, with courses in the social sciences, would qualify a person for the job in the place of paid experience in the field. And I have a letter here from a Social Science professor at Michigan State University that. . ."

"What you read on the examination announcement, Mr. Roby," rebutted the goateed, pipe-smoking, professorial-type panel member, "only qualified you to take the examination. It didn't qualify you for the job. And the representative from the Social Service Department who was a member of the oral interview board evidently decided that you weren't qualified."

"Have you had any background of social work, Mr. Roby?" pursued Little Caesar, rolling his cigar from one side of his mouth to the other.

Feeling obligated to defer to the chairman's right of leadership in conducting the hearing, I reached out and laid down on the table another poster board which would be completely bypassed. In spite of the fact that I believed this criticism was not warranted according to the wording of the examination announcement, I had come prepared to demolish it. The third poster card, now in view, was labeled with the oral interview board's objection of "No Background." In rebuttal to this alleged deficiency, I had listed several pertinent examples of education and experience.

Under "Experience" was listed some five city, county, and state agencies for which I had done volunteer social work, including the Eaton County Jail in Charlotte. But again, even before I could begin to clarify and explain the abbreviated terms on the display board, I was interrupted by another heckling question from the crew-cut pencil drummer.

"Jail work!" he expostulated, "what does that mean?"

Growing increasingly perturbed at not being allowed to present the supporting evidence as I had prepared it in orderly sequence, I reached over the pile of letters beside me and fumbled through them until I found the right one.

"This is what it means," I answered testily, holding up the letter in front of me. "This is a letter from Elwin Swift, sheriff of Eaton County where I live and, with your permission, I'd like to read several pertinent excerpts from it."

I didn't wait for approval or dissent from the chairman. I proceeded to read aloud.

"This letter is being written in recognition of the service which has been rendered by Mr. Garfield Roby, a resident of Charlotte, and presently employed in the Michigan State Highway Department in Lansing. For more than a year, Mr. Roby has assumed responsibility for maintaining a religious service every Sunday at the Eaton County jail in Charlotte for the benefit of inmates. In addition to coming to jail every Sunday, he has invested a good deal of time in calling on inmates after their release from jail, to encourage them and offer help."

"Pardon me, Mr. Roby," the chairman broke in, "but I don't see how this has any bearing on your qualifications for the social worker position."

"If you'll allow me to read one more paragraph," I shot back with some show of the irritation I was beginning to feel, "perhaps you'll see that it does."

I could feel Rudy's eyes on me in empathetic helplessness at the way the hearing was going. I read on, speeding my pace.

"As to the value of these services," I continued reading, "it is a matter of record that at least one man whom Mr. Roby contacted through these services, who had previously been committed to the Eaton County jail a number of times for drunkenness, has not been apprehended for any such offense in nearly a year, dating from the time that a significant change took place in his thinking and attitude as a result of Mr. Roby's counseling. The change in this one individual's life has resulted in a real savings in terms of dollars and cents for the County. For this, and other reasons, I can commend Mr. Roby for his work here, and testify as to its value in the field of significant social work."

I looked up at the members of the board as I laid the letter back down on the table, to find expressions of boredom and disinterest on their faces. It was apparent that to most of them, what I had read seemed totally irrelevant and unimportant.

"It's very nice, Mr. Roby," Little Caesar observed in a paternalistic tone of voice, wagging his cigar in the air for emphasis, "that you felt inclined to help these men in this way. But I fail to see where this in any way qualifies you for the position you applied for, and I fail to see where it points up any evidence of discrimination by the oral interview board."

It was evident that the sheriff's reference to "a real savings in terms of dollars and cents" had not impressed him or other members of the review board.

"It all depends on your concept of social work," I countered testily, glaring at the chairman with some of the indignation that was beginning to boil in me. "Perhaps it's just as much social work to be able to do something to help people from going on welfare as it is to dole out money to them after they get on relief. If you can do something for a man whose family has been on welfare because he's been in and out of jail so much, so that the man becomes a self-supporting respectable member of the community, I call that social work. Maybe you don't."

Then, before there was any response from any member of the panel to what I had said, another member of the panel who hadn't spoken up yet—the sallow-skinned undertaker type with unruly hair and a Groucho Marx mustache, sitting next to Little Caesar—snarled another question at me, like a denizen of a wolf pack attacking a wounded deer.

"Let's not spend the whole afternoon belaboring one point," he growled, "I've got other things to do today besides this hearing. Let's move on to some of these other things. What have you got against women, Mr. Roby? I'd like to know what you have to say about that."

His accusing stare, his tone of voice, and his way of phrasing the question was so violently opposed to the impartiality and objectivity I had expected from the hearing, that I was momentarily stunned into speechlessness. It was like a judge in a courtroom directing a question to an accused prisoner even before the evidence had been examined.

"We know you committed the crime. Now tell us why you did it."

"It should be obvious," I replied sarcastically, "that I don't dislike women, or dislike working with women, because I married one."

"They must have gotten the impression from something you said," pursued the chairman, stabbing his cigar at me, "that you didn't like working with women."

I began to relate the context of personal experience out of which I had asked a question which the oral interview board had grossly misinterpreted.

"When I was a boy, during the depression, my family had to seek help from the Social Services Department. So whenever a case worker came to the house to review our financial situation, it was always a woman; never a man. That's where I got the idea that maybe this was exclusively a woman's job. Then, more recently, I have visited my wife's office in the Commerce Department. There I saw nearly an acre of desks, all occupied by women, with not a single man in sight. Supposing that a similar situation might prevail in the Social

Services Department, I asked if the Social Worker 1-A position for which I was applying was primarily a woman's job. When the oral interview board asked why I was asking that question, I answered that "I wouldn't want to be the only man surrounded by 10,000 women."

Hilda' self-disparaging agreement with my expressed concern echoed in the back of my mind, divested now of its humor. "Who would want to be surrounded by a bunch of cackling hens all day?"

"That was the remark that got you in trouble," interjected the pipe-smoking professorial type in a smug tone of psychiatric omniscience.

Little Caesar looked down the table at his colleague and nodded in agreement. But there was no concern expressed, either by the chairman or any member of the panel, to dig deeper for factual evidence as to whether such a use of figurative language constituted evidence that I disliked working with women at all. And because of the evident lack of concern on the part of any of them to determine the truth or falsity of this charge by the oral board, I felt it was useless to reach for any of the four letters in the pile beside me from four women employees with whom I had worked, all commending me for a friendly, helpful, and cooperative working relationship. I felt that the hearing was over, and it had not even really begun. Little Caesar vocalized my feeling.

"I think we've covered all that's necessary to be brought out at this hearing, Mrs. Fussler," he announced, cigar in hand.

Like a boxer in the ring, groggy from head and body blows but with enough presence of mind to realize that the referee was signaling the end of the fight, I began gathering up my mostly unused poster boards, my unread letters of recommendation, and dismantling the portable easel. As I did, I could feel Rudy's eyes on me, staring at me in pained perplexity because he had not been called upon to say what he could in my defense. But I was so convinced, at that point, that there was no real concern on the part of the hearing panel about getting at the truth, that I felt it would be a waste of time to request or demand that Rudy be allowed to speak on my behalf. The thought crossed my mind that a minimum show of courtesy, at least, if not a concern for the truth, should have prompted the chairman or some member of the hearing panel to have called on Rudy for his testimony after he had gone to the trouble to get there. But no one made a move to reopen the hearing which Little Caesar had indicated was now closed.

"Let's go, Rudy," I said, getting up and gathering my impotent arsenal of documents, less than twenty minutes after we had entered the room.

He pushed himself up from his chair clumsily, looking at me with a bewildered expression. As he walked around the end of the table, he bumped into his own chair which I had pushed back a little, trying to be helpful. Then I started for the door, Rudy with his white cane lumbering behind me like a trained circus bear. I was leaving the hearing feeling like a man who had made an undignified and unsuccessful attempt to catch a greased pig at a picnic. With all the real, hard, tangible evidence which I had brought with me, including Rudy, to disprove the fallacious findings of the oral interview board, the truth about my qualifications for the job had not been brought out.

Then, in a desperate, last-minute effort to pull the disjointed segments of the hearing into a concrete conclusion, if only to relay to Florence and others, I stopped abruptly just before reaching the door and turned to face the hearing panel. There was suddenly a comic climax to the tragic travesty of a search for truth as Rudy, not expecting my sudden stop, could not react swiftly enough, and bumped into me, knocking me and the metal legs of the easel against the door with a resounding clatter.

"Oh, excuse me, Gar, I'm awfully sorry," Rudy apologized, his face red with embarrassment.

"That's alright, Rudy," I assured him, then directed a partial remark to the hearing board members.

"If possible, gentlemen," I called, loud enough to bring to a sudden cessation the talking and rattling of papers that had followed our movement toward the door, "I'd like to take with me from this hearing something constructive so that this will not prove to have been a total waste of your time and mine."

All eyes were directed toward Rudy and me as we stood by the door, the hearing board members obviously surprised at this anticlimactic twist to the hearing which they had regarded as finished. The secretary at the end of the table looked perplexed, not knowing whether she should add my post-hearing remarks to the official transcript of the hearing.

"In the event I should want to apply for this position again," I said, "what would you recommend that I do so as to increase my chances of achieving a passing score on the oral interview part of the examination?"

In truth, I had no such intention or inclination. The blatantly unfair appraisal by one of the oral board interviewers, who was an employee in the Department of Social Services, had soured me on the whole department. But I couched my request in those terms, thinking it might improve my chance of getting some kind of concrete and meaningful response from the hearing panel. It was not Little Caesar, the chairman, who was first to respond to my question, but the crew-cut junior executive with the red bow tie.

"I'd say you just need to do a better job of selling yourself to the oral interview board."

"There was nothing in the examination announcement," I countered, "which suggested that as a prerequisite to getting a passing score on the oral interview. I assumed the interviewers knew what they wanted to find out about my background and so I limited myself to responding to their questions about me and asking some about the job."

"Selling yourself is an implied requirement, Mr. Roby," Little Caesar broke in with an expansive wave of his unlit cigar. "Success is always a matter of salesmanship, no matter what field you're trying to get into."

The other members of the hearing panel nodded their heads or murmured their agreement. But feeling the need to carry away a more specific definition of what they meant by "selling myself," I posed a hypothetical situation.

"Then would you gentlemen say that to increase my chances of passing the oral interview, should I apply for the job again, that it might be helpful to get some experience in selling something, like vacuum cleaners, or used cars, or real estate?"

"Wouldn't do you any harm," shrugged the chairman, "and it might do you a lot of good."

"And has it occurred to any of you that if I had the interest and the aptitude to become a successful salesman in some other field, that I wouldn't even have bothered to apply for this job?"

"That's your choice, Mr. Roby, It's a free country."

"And what about my use of figurative language?" I asked, still incredulous that my innocent but vividly worded question had been twisted into a gross falsehood which I hadn't succeeded in dispelling.

"Stay away from figurative language," the chairman responded. "Just state the facts as simply as you can without any flowery language."

"So you'd say," I attempted to summarize their inane advice, "that if I should ever apply for this position again, that I should try harder to sell myself to the oral interview board and avoid figurative speech."

"As simple as that," agreed Little Caesar, still clinging to his cigar like a baby to its bottle.

"Thank you, gentlemen," I grimaced.

The scorn I felt must have been evident in my tone of voice as I opened the conference room door.

"You'll hear from us, Mr. Roby," the chairman called as I went out the door, Rudy close behind me.

"I know what I'll hear from you," I muttered cynically. As I walked down the hallway with Rudy toward the elevators, Florence's negative prediction about my chances of getting the job echoed in my mind like the melancholy music of a funeral dirge.

"That's one job you're never going to get."

At that moment, still smarting from the unfair hearing fiasco I had just fought my way through, I was inclined to agree with her. Two weeks later, my depressed doubts and Florence's pessimistic prediction were confirmed in a letter from Civil Service.

As Florence and I arrived at the farm from our jobs in Lansing one night and stepped through the front door, Mother Berlincourt, aware of the importance of the expected results of the hearing, called out from the kitchen.

"Garfield, there's a letter for you from Civil Service on the TV set."

Standing by the door, I reached over and picked up the envelope and opened it. Florence stood close beside me, still cherishing some faint hope, in spite of the gloomy prediction I had made as to the results, that the hearing board might vindicate me instead of the two-man oral interview board. I unfolded the single sheet of typewritten information as Florence looked over my shoulder, sweeping over details already familiar to me. Listed by name were the five members of the hearing panel, plus the secretary, Rudy Sylvester, and myself. At least they had mentioned Rudy even though they hadn't called on him. Then I came to the part I was really looking for near the bottom of the page, designated in bold print as "FINDINGS."

Mother Berlincourt, sensing the significance of the letter, had padded into the living room to quietly stand by Florence, looking on.

"Here's the verdict," I read aloud. "The Hearing Board could find no evidence of manifest unfairness or discrimination in the oral interview part of the Social Worker 1-A examination administered to Garfield A. Roby. The Hearing Board affirms the result of the examination."

"That means . . .?" Florence began.

"That means," I broke in, "that in the opinion of the Michigan Civil Service Commission, the oral interview board was right in everything they said about me and, therefore, I do not qualify as a Social Worker 1-A now or . . . ever, probably."

I laid the execution notice of Florence's hope down on the television set and walked into the front parlor to sit down on the sofa. Even though I had anticipated the verdict which I had just read, it surprised me with the impact that it had, like a stout blow to the stomach. But I had been warned that this would probably be the outcome. I remembered the words of the Civil Service spokesman when I had first gone to review the ratings the oral interview board had given me.

"A hearing board hardly ever reverses the findings of an oral interview board."

But I had presumptuously proceeded anyway, ignoring the warning; partly because it had seemed a mockery of justice for a bellicose bureaucrat to predict the outcome of a hearing even before it was held; and partly also because I was confident that my case would prove to be an exception to the general rule.

Florence, picking up the paper I had laid down on the TV set, followed me into the living room and sat down beside me on the sofa, studying the page full of statistics, while Hilda stood in the archway between living room and dining room, hands on hips, not knowing what to say.

"All I can say," Florence finally exploded fiercely, throwing the offending sheet of paper down on the sofa between us, "is that these people must have rocks in their heads."

Some of her indignation doubtless sprang from the disappointment she felt at being cheated out of the increased income which my confident predictions had led her to expect would soon be in our hands.

"How ridiculous can you get?" she went on, "saying that you weren't interested in the position, when you went to all that trouble to get it!"

"Can I see that paper, Garfield?" Hilda asked, stepping over toward me and holding out her hand.

I picked up the sheet of paper from the sofa and handed it to her. She turned and settled into the rocking chair across from the sofa to study it, like a private detective, seeking clues that might have been overlooked that might unravel this mystery. Florence sat beside me in glum silence while her mother examined the pertinent information on the Civil Service notice of official and final rejection.

"It looks to me, Garfield," judged Hilda, after several minutes of intense concentration, "that it's what you might call a 'bum rap.'"

Then an odor hinting of impending disaster assailed her nostrils from the kitchen.

"Oh mercy! I'll bet those fried potatoes are burning!"

She pushed herself up out of the rocking chair, dropping the letter on the chair, and rushed out to the kitchen.

"They're not burned, but they're certainly a crispy brown," she called from the kitchen. "Come and get 'em while they're hot."

At the supper table, after Hilda's homespun prayer, Florence kept her eyes focused mostly on her plate. The old gloom that had first enveloped her upon the discovery of her pregnancy settled back around her like an aura of imminent disaster. Fortunately, through those few painful moments at the table, enough things had happened in Hilda's life recently to enable her to maintain a running stream of conversation with no help from me and very little from Florence. With no appetite for either food or company, I did not linger at the table for seconds.

I walked into the front room, as far from the kitchen as I could get, like a dog running off to some remote corner to be alone and lick its wounds after being bested in a dog fight. Sitting there alone, the sight of the letter of rejection from the Civil Service Commission, on the rocking chair where Hilda had dropped it, brought a painful analogy to my mind. Just as Hilda had dropped the letter to rush to the kitchen, so had I been dropped as quickly, and with far less concern, by the Civil Service Commission. They had indeed conformed to the letter of state law by granting the hearing I had requested to review the findings of the oral interview board. But the spirit and intent which had originally framed the law—to discover the truth—had been totally missing. The truth about my qualifications for the job I had applied for remained hidden within me and the few who had known about it while the errors in judgement, the falsehoods fabricated about me, were now on public display in the files of the Civil Service Commission.

Suddenly, I felt an impulse to leave the premises before the activity in the kitchen was finished; before silence would return in which this little domestic disaster could be further questioned and speculated about. The pain was too sharp, too deep. I didn't want to talk about it any more with either Florence or her mother. I grabbed my lightweight summer suit coat and headed for the kitchen where Florence and her mother were just finishing the kitchen cleanup. My position, jointly shared with Florence of Young People's Sponsor at the Gilead Baptist Church in Charlotte, suddenly offered a legitimate excuse for getting away from the house for a while, to be alone.

"Flo," I said pausing by the kitchen door, "I think I'll run into town for a little while and see Dave Brown. I've got some things to work out with him for the next Young People's meeting."

Dave was the youthful, unmarried assistant on many of the activities and excursions we had planned for the young people in the past. Midweek conferences had become a regular part of our church activity agenda.

"Tell him 'Hi' for me," Florence responded listlessly.

There was no enthusiasm in her voice, nor did she turn away from the kitchen sink to look at me when she spoke.

"Okay," I replied to her back, "I'll be back in an hour or two."

Hilda gave me a parting smile from the kitchen range but didn't speak, probably sensing my need to be alone for a while. I returned the smile and pushed through the screen door on the side porch. Her smile had been spontaneous, showing her feelings. Mine had been manufactured, intended to conceal rather than reveal how I really felt.

When I backed the car out of the drive onto the smooth blacktop highway and headed east toward Charlotte, it was not with any intention of seeking out Dave Brown. There was no need for any conference with him. I drove through downtown Charlotte to the north end of town and turned left onto a two-lane concrete highway that led to the small town of Eaton Rapids, ten miles southwest of Charlotte. I had no desire to be seen by a friend or acquaintance in Charlotte and asked the inevitable question, "How's everything going?" For my answer, if brutally honest, would have to be that "everything's going wrong."

And I was not mentally or psychologically prepared to answer the questions that might follow, as to why the birth of our first child, after five years of marriage, had become an occasion for depression rather than rejoicing; and why, at the age of 35, I was a failure rather than a success, in the eyes of both my wife and myself.

(HAPTER 5

⇒ In the quaint, small town of Eaton Rapids, twenty minutes after leaving Charlotte behind, I drove down the wide main street lined with shops, stores, and restaurants toward a quiet place of refuge that I had frequented before in times of turmoil. In the center of town, I turned off Main Street onto a side street that led to a unique island park, set in the midst of the wide, tree-lined Grand River, which twisted and turned its way through the heart of the rural town. I parked the car and walked across a bridge that connected the island to the street and made my way down a short flight of steps to the summer-greened surface of the tree-shaded island. I passed by the picnic area and the octagon-shaped band shell where concerts were held, and walked to the northernmost point of the island that was less than half a mile long and a quarter of a mile wide. There, I sat down on the thick, newly mown grass and leaned against the slightly angled trunk of a giant elm tree.

Momentarily projected back into similar boyhood scenes beside a picturesque, wooded creek near my home, I picked up a handful of pebbles near the base of the tree trunk and began throwing them idly, one by one, into the smooth surface of the gently flowing river. The place where I sat came to a tapered point just beyond my stretched-out legs, like the bow of a ship.

Watching the placid flow of the water coming toward me, it was easy to imagine myself on a ship, traveling to far-away places with strange sounding names; away from the emotional crisis I faced; the fear of financial capsize that was gnawing at Florence; away from the painful memory of having been rejected by the two men on the oral interview board who had been only smiles, with an outward show of friendliness when I had talked with them, while in their minds they had been thinking disparaging thoughts about me which they hadn't disclosed; away from the recollection of the hearing farce, which had only been salt in the wound of rejection previously inflicted by the two-man oral board.

Sunset turned to early twilight as I sat and listened to the final evensong of robins and sparrows, broken into at irregular intervals by the scolding chatter of a fox squirrel. On the larger area of the island that was behind me, I could hear fragments of low-toned conversations and bits of laughter as couples strolled hand in hand around the perimeter of the island. From the far end of the island, the sound of children playing floated past me. And in the sky Heaven's lamps were turned on as the night sky darkened, bringing to my mind words from one of the Psalms.

"When I consider thy heavens, the work of thy fingers, the moon and the stars, which thou has ordained . . . . What is man that thou art mindful of him, and the son of man, that thou visitest him?"

Sitting there alone, my wounded spirit drank in the balm of Nature, as Nature's God intended; the whisper of a summer breeze causing the leaves on the branches above me to sing softly and sibilantly, the rising moon in the east, the muffled sound of traffic on the main street of Eaton Rapids, a block and a river away.

But inevitably my thoughts returned from a contemplation of the peaceful scenes and sounds of Nature around me to the situation from which I had sought temporary escape by running from the big farmhouse. I had been weighed in the balances of Florence's mind and been found wanting in the roles of breadwinner, provider, and potential father. And I wanted to be a success in these roles, if for no greater reason than that she expected me to be; the rightful expectation, perhaps, of any woman marrying any man.

Yet, along with this newly born desire to live up to Florence's hope of me as an adequate provider for a family, there was something else within me; a difficult-to-analyze feeling which lingered as an uneasy aftermath of Florence's announcement of her pregnancy. It was a feeling like that of a cage door being shut upon something within me that had not yet spread its wings, depriving me of the needed freedom to continue my vocational groping; disappointed at having abandoned the ministry; and unable to accept my role as a clerk in a large state agency as the highest work of which I was capable. I felt that somehow, this part of me that was still seeking the life work for which I was fitted needed to be free of the obligatory duties of parenthood in order to find and fulfill its God-intended destiny.

As I left the island refuge nearly two hours later, to return home to Charlotte, a new possibility occurred to me as a way of coping with the financial crisis that the birth of our first child might entail; a way that might compensate for the social worker position I had lost. If I couldn't get a better-paying job with the state, perhaps I could find a second part-time job to supplement my regular income.

Encouraged by this newly generated hope, I stopped at a drug store in the small town's main street to get the daily newspaper published in Lansing.

Then, in a restaurant, in the five-block downtown area of the town, over a cup of coffee, I pored over the "help wanted" columns in the classified ad section. Ten minutes of scrutinizing the small print of several columns of ads produced only one hopeful possibility for which I might be qualified. Taxi drivers, both full and part-time, were needed by the Courteous Cab Company in Lansing; one of the two major taxi competitors in the capital city. Desperately impelled to waste no time in alleviating Florence's financial fears, as well as apply a healing balm to my self-esteem which had been sharply wounded with the announcement of her pregnancy, I called the cab company, even though it was after business hours. As I expected, I was told that I would have to call back on Monday and speak with the manager.

Back home that night, I didn't tell Florence where I had really gone instead of seeing Dave Brown. Neither did I mention my plan to investigate the possibility of getting a part-time job as a taxi driver. I didn't want to give her any more false hopes that might be shattered. I would wait until I knew that I had the job before telling her about it.

The following Monday I left work two hours early for an appointment with Jim Garvey, cab company manager, so that I would not have to tell Florence about it. In the cab company office, several blocks from downtown Lansing, Jim Garvey's steel-grey eyes darted from my application to my eyes. His questions and answers came terse and fast, the result of long hours spent as a dispatcher, answering calls and giving radio instructions to cab drivers.

"How's your driving record, Garfield?"

"I haven't had a ticket for anything except parking over-time in ten years."

"Do you have a chauffeur's license?"

"No. What do I have to do to get one?"

"No problem there, Garfield, as long as you already have a valid driver's license and a good driving record. Just go down to the city clerk's office and fill out an application. It will cost you six dollars and they'll need a recent photo of you. It takes about a week to process."

"What's the salary?"

"All our drivers work on a commission basis, Garfield. You keep sixty percent of everything you take in, and the company gets forty percent. You pay for whatever gas you use. You also keep one hundred percent of whatever tips you get."

It sounded at first hearing like the company was making an exorbitant profit while the drivers did most of the work, but I was in no position to wheedle. The baby was on the way and there were no other jobs available.

"What would the hours be?"

"You'd have to work at least three nights a week. Right now what I need is a driver to work Monday, Wednesday and Friday nights. You'd have to work six hours on Monday and Wednesday, which would be from 6:00 p.m., when our night shift starts, to midnight. Drivers who work on Friday night are expected to work until the bars close at 2:00 a.m. Does that sound like something you'd be interested in?"

Only the mention of working Wednesday night sounded a warning bell in my mind as being a source of possible conflict with the unyielding pastor of Gilead Baptist Church in Charlotte, where Florence and I attended.

"Would it be possible to work one night other than Wednesday?"

The youthful manager eyed me cooly from behind his desk, as if I was a vagrant asking for a handout, and his voice conveyed a sudden sense of irritation.

"Look, Mr. Roby, this isn't a social club where you can just drop in whenever you feel like it. I'm running a business. If you don't want to work on those nights, I've got a lot of other applications to check out. Frankly, I picked you over some of the younger guys who applied because I thought that being a little older, you'd be more mature and dependable. Maybe after you've been with us for a while it might be possible to trade nights with one of the other drivers. But for right now, it's a case of working the nights I mentioned. Take it or leave it."

I sat silently, weighing the possible consequences of my choice, while Jim Garvey sat behind his desk staring at me as if trying to penetrate my skull and see my thought processes.

"I'll take it," I said. "When do I start?"

"As soon as you get your chauffeur's license."

I looked at my watch. It was 4:15. If I hurried, I could get to Woolworth's downtown, get a "take your own" photo for fifty cents, and get to the City Hall and still catch my car pool ride at 5:15.

"Maybe I can still get down to the City Hall before it closes and get my application in today," I said, standing up.

"Been nice talking with you, Garfield," said Jim Garvey, getting up and extending his hand. "I look forward to having you work for us."

Forty minutes later, in the city clerk's office on the third floor of the city hall, I finished filling out the brief application for a chauffeur's license and handed it to the clerk along with my six-dollar fee and photo. The Lansing City Council, which had to approve all such applications, was to meet that night.

"With luck," the clerk assured me, "you should have your license by the end of this week."

"If I get the license and the cab-driving job," I thought silently, walking out of the office, "it won't be a matter of luck. It will be a matter of the intervention of Heaven on my behalf."

Two nights later, on Wednesday evening, at the Gilead Baptist Church in Charlotte, I was to face a heated rebuttal that God would endorse the part-time taxi-driving job. I had resolutely determined to say nothing to Florence about the pending part-time job until the last hurdle was cleared and I had the chauffeur's license in my hands. It was a providential development, I thought, as I left the Berlincourt farm for the Wednesday night meeting at church, that Florence had not felt like going with me. That way I could seek an opportunity to speak to the pastor privately, which I wouldn't have had if Florence had accompanied me.

I was five minutes late when I pulled into a parking slot in front of the church that was located a block off the main street and a stone's throw from the County jail and courthouse in the center of town. It was a utilitarian structure, one story high, with white siding, a refurbished stone front and plate glass doors. There were no stained-glass windows; only plain household glass on the inside covered with plain brown drapes.

To become members of Gilead Baptist Church, Florence and I had been required to give verbal testimony to the pastor and the deacons that we had both undergone the experience described in the New Testament as "conversion" or the "new birth." It was firmly held by the leadership of the church that requirements for admission into the local, visible church should be no less than the requirements for being admitted into Heaven. And Jesus Christ had warned specifically that "Except ye be converted, and become as little children, ye shall not enter into the kingdom of Heaven."

Calvin Savage, the youthful pastor of the church, no older than myself, strongly emphasized the Scriptural concept of the "priesthood of all believers," and all members were regularly exhorted to become "soul winners." The majority of the residents of Charlotte, the state of Michigan, the nation, and the world, were lifted up as objects of prayerful concern, and as being on the road to eternal destruction unless they were reached with the Gospel message and became converted, born-again, Bible-believing Christians. Florence and I had gravitated to this particular church when we had moved from Chicago to Charlotte; not because it was Baptist, but because it was a church which held to the Word of God in preaching and in practice.

The twelve to fifteen people, the average prayer meeting attendance, who sat clustered together in the center section of pews near the front of the church, were singing a familiar hymn as I walked down the carpeted aisle from the back of the church. Leading the singing with a strident, baritone voice, and waving his arms with the gusto of a military commander exhorting his troops to charge into battle, was the pastor, Calvin Savage.

Even on this extremely hot, humid August evening, he had not abandoned a green necktie that went well with the dark brown business suit he wore. He glanced at me as I came down the aisle, giving me the visual rebuke I had anticipated for being late. I slid into one of the folding, theatre type, hard-backed and hard bottomed chairs behind Deacon Ed McCoy. His head hid me from the accusing eyes of the pastor.

Calvin Savage was two years older than myself, dark haired, of athletic build, who looked at the world through horn-rimmed glasses and walked with a limp in his right leg from a World War II wound. He pulled no punches in his preaching or personal counseling. If the Bible said that a man who had not been converted was on his way to an eternal, burning Hell, he proclaimed it, whether in the pulpit or on the street. Several members who had left the church since he had become pastor had charged that he was alienating more people than he was winning by his brusque manner and blunt speech.

Uncertain of the page number in the hymn book from which the congregation was singing, I sat and listened.

"Blessed assurance . . . Jesus is mine. Oh, what a foretaste of glory divine. Heir of salvation, purchase of God . . . . Born of His Spirit, washed in His blood."

The hymn finished, I bowed my head in concert with the others as the pastor invited the congregation to join with him in invoking God to take note of what was transpiring in the little one-story building off the main street of a small town in the Midwest U.S.A. His prayers were always generously sprinkled with Biblical quotations or allusions. He began with a borrowed petition from David in one of the Psalms . . . "Search me, O God, and know my heart, and see if there be any wicked way in me." He brought forth a quotation from the first epistle of Peter, reminding God of His promise that "the eyes of the Lord are over the righteous and His ears are open unto their prayer." He prayed for those who were too ill to attend church that night, and for those who were too unconcerned to come. And finally, he asked God to speak to those who were gathered there that evening through the portion of Scripture that he was going to read.

"Now, turn with me, if you will," he announced, "to First Timothy, chapter four, verse one."

I opened my own Bible to the place specified while the rustle of turning pages whispered around me.

"That's a sound I love to hear," commended the pastor, "God's people turning the pages of their Bibles. It's something you don't hear in a lot of churches nowadays."

Then he read aloud the passage in question.

"Now the Spirit speaketh expressly that in the latter times some shall depart from the faith, giving heed to seducing spirits, and doctrines of demons . . . . Speaking lies in hypocrisy; having their conscience seared with a hot iron."

He lifted his eyes from the open Bible on the portable lectern before him and looked at his small congregation soberly.

"Brethern," he began, "I'd like to speak for a few minutes tonight on the subject of 'Departing from the Faith.' The Word of God says that in the latter times; that is, in the days just preceding Christ's return to earth, some shall depart from the faith. This same truth is found in Second Thessalonians, chapter five, where Paul declares that the day of Christ's return will not come 'except there be a falling away first.' And brethren, and sisters, to live by faith means a daily warfare. There's no standing still. If we are not contending for the faith once delivered to the saints, we are in danger of departing from it."

His following words of exhortation fell heavily upon me as he proceeded to flail at the congregation with his words, like a man applying a heavy stick to an obdurate donkey that was not pulling a loaded wagon as fast as possible. His tone and temper would have better fitted the locker room of a great athletic stadium where a dispirited football team needed such words to turn an attitude of anticipated defeat into confidence that victory was attainable. It would have seemed more appropriate to the sales manager of a large business, trying to whip up greater zeal on the part of a group of lethargic salesmen gathered before him. It would have qualified him to lead a platoon of soldiers into a hopeless combat situation.

But for me and for how many others I couldn't tell, his words caused me to withdraw into myself in weariness of spirit. I didn't need any more demands laid upon me. I needed something to help lift the weight I already carried. I didn't need to have my obvious failings pointed out and belittled; I needed encouragement and strengthening to cope with the demands of economic survival. But finally, at the close of the twenty-minute exhortation to go out into the highway and byways, to buttonhole every stranger and witness to them as the surest way to avoid defecting from the faith, he got around to the main business of the midweek meeting.

"Now before we go to prayer, do we have any special requests that ought to be remembered?"

There followed the vocal expressions of the usual impersonal requests having little or nothing to do with the hidden needs of the individuals gathered there; as if they had no particular needs, no problems, no frustrations, no pressures pushing them toward courses of action dictated not by strength but by weakness; not by wisdom but by passion; not with a clear mind but with one beclouded by worry or self-abnegation or lack of confidence.

"We should remember Mrs. Abercrombie," quavered an aged female voice from somewhere in front of me. "She's in the hospital with a broken hip."

"Yes," assented the pastor, "let's pray for her."

"We should pray for the service next Sunday," volunteered Deacon McCoy in front of me, "that souls will be saved."

"I'll say 'Amen' to that, brother," the pastor agreed emphatically. "Any more requests?"

After a few more requests of a general nature, the small congregation was divided up; the men to go to the small room on the left of the pulpit; the young people to the corresponding room on the right side; with the women and children remaining in the auditorium. And while there were smiles and greetings and handshakes exchanged among the half-dozen men who entered the little room with the pastor, to get on our knees and talk to God, we left twenty minutes later knowing little or nothing more about each other's personal needs than when we entered.

I came with my own particular burden, as each of the others probably did, and left with it, unlightened by having shared it with other men who were spiritual "brothers" by virtue of having gone through that same experience of conversion, spiritual new birth, that I had gone through. And after the prayer meeting was concluded in the main auditorium with a final hymn and benediction by the pastor, I waited behind until everyone else had left.

I approached the pastor at the rear of the church as he was waving farewell to the last family. Quick to note any symptoms of spiritual decline in his flock, he asked a leading question as he extended his hand to me.

"Where's your wife tonight, brother?"

"She didn't feel up to coming."

"Brother Roby, that's the time we need to be in prayer the most," he rebuked. "In Matthew 18:1, it says that Jesus spake a parable unto them to this end, that man ought always to pray, and not to faint."

"But when a woman's going to have a baby," I defended instinctively, "she's got an extra load to carry around."

"You mean she's . . ." he began, a little flabbergasted.

"She sure is."

"Well, congratulations, brother," he apologized, "why didn't you say so sooner? Why didn't you announce it at prayer meeting tonight? I know the rest of the folks would have been glad to hear about it."

"I don't think Florence would appreciate any unnecessary publicity as long as it can be avoided."

"Brother, that's something you can't keep secret very long," he laughed, completely missing or ignoring the possibility that there might be some underlying problem in my hint of Florence's reluctance to advertise the impending event.

"That's why I may not be attending prayer meeting for a while," I added.

The smile vanished from his face, his mouth settled into a grim line, and his eyes narrowed, like a boxer who has just received an unexpected blow from his protagonist.

"What's that got to do with not coming to prayer meeting, brother?"

There was suppressed hostility in his tone, as if I had announced that I was going to start attending a Moslem mosque on Wednesday nights, or inaugurate a practice of visiting all the taverns in town on that night.

"I've applied for a part-time job to keep up with expenses when Florence has to quit work. I'll be driving a taxi in Lansing three nights a week. One of the nights will be Wednesday."

"Brother," he warned in a sombre tone, "I don't know what your circumstances are, but I'm sure you're making a mistake. When a Christian stops coming to prayer meeting, you can count on it, his spiritual life is going to decline."

"I'm only trying to show a little consideration for my wife," I protested, "that's the only reason I'm going to do it. She's afraid we'll be snowed under with bills when she quits to have the baby, and she's probably right."

"Brother Roby," he said, in a more conciliatory tone and putting a hand on my shoulder, "I know how you feel. I know what it is to have bills, too. But God knows about that, and He's made provision for our needs if we'll just meet the conditions He lays down."

"Such as?"

"Jesus said, 'Seek ye first the kingdom of God and his righteousness, and all these things shall be added unto you.'"

The pastor let his hand fall from my shoulder and paused to let the verse of Scripture exert its full impact upon my thinking. Then he proceeded to add a word of personal testimony.

"Brother, I've lived by this verse since I've been in the ministry, and my family has never gone hungry yet."

As I stood there silently on the top landing of the short flight of steps leading to the outer doors, the pastor regarding me intently, two separate reactions to his statement emerged in my mind. I thought of what Florence's reaction would be to my quoting this verse of Scripture to her to allay her financial fears. I could almost visualize her facial reaction and her interpretation of the verse. She would interpret my following the course the pastor was recommending as an attempt to evade my responsibility as breadwinner, shifting onto God the job that I should take care of myself. And at the same time I was aware of a weak link in the pastor's application of Scripture to my particular case. He was equating the injunction to seek first the kingdom of God with regular attendance at the midweek church service.

"Is there anything in the Bible," I ventured tentatively, "that says I am supposed to be in church every Wednesday night from 7:30 to 8:30?"

"Let me read you a verse in Hebrews," he answered, opening his Bible. "Here it is, brother, in Hebrews 10:24. I'll read it to you. 'And let us consider one another to provoke one another unto love and to good works . . . not forsaking the assembling of ourselves together as the manner of some is, but exhorting one another, and so much the more as ye see the day approaching.'"

"But it says nothing about how often we are to assemble together," I pointed out, "whether once a week or once a month. Nor does it say what day we are to assemble."

"Brother Roby," he countered, sounding exasperated at what impressed him as an irrelevant objection, "the logical time to assemble with other Christians is when they're gathered together in the church. That's on Sunday morning, Sunday evening, and Wednesday night. And I can testify from my own experience, Gar, that I need the mid-week prayer meeting. It's the most important service of the week for me."

I knew the futility of discussing the matter further with him. Even if I attempted to explain the whole situation to him, including Florence's morbid fear of financial capsize, he would remain convinced that he was right and I was wrong.

"Well, it's not certain that I'll get the job yet," I admitted, trying to end our talk on a friendly note instead of a mood of hostile confrontation. "I'm still waiting on a chauffeur's license to come through. And knowing how you feel, I guess it wouldn't do any good to ask you to pray that I'll get the license."

An impish grin spread over the pastor's face as he suddenly grasped the possibility of spiritual sabotage to thwart a course of action on my part which seemed to him to be more the enticement of the Devil than the leading of the Lord. His suddenly smug expression conveyed to me the impression that he might start praying that I would not get the needed chauffeur's license.

"No, brother Roby," he conceded soberly, "I couldn't pray for something which I'm convinced is contrary to God's will for you, and in direct opposition to the Word of God."

"Well, pray for Florence and me," I said, trying to muster a smile to hide my agitated state of mind as I turned to leave, "even if we aren't here on Wednesday nights for a while."

I started down the steps toward the outer doors of the church.

"Just one more thing I'd like to say before you go, Brother Roby," his voice pursued.

I paused on the bottom step and looked back up at him.

"You have a responsibility as Young People's Sponsor. Young people will be influenced by your example. And I don't feel that it's setting a good example to be consistently absent from prayer meeting, as you're evidently planning on doing."

"Do you think I ought to resign?"

"That's up to you, Gar. But I don't think any elected officer of the church should be a regular absentee at prayer meeting. I'd think about it before making a decision if I were you, and pray about it."

"Thank you, Pastor," I said over my shoulder as I turned for a final wave of the hand.

His face and eyes registered no smile, but a blend of sober concern and a questioning outreach, as if he were trying to analyze my spiritual state and my true motive for the course of action I had proposed. I wondered in that final moment if he were thinking of me as part of a literal fulfillment of the Bible prophecy which he had preached about that evening, of some who would "depart from the faith." This may have been the disturbing possibility that crossed his mind as I pushed through the double glass doors and stepped out into the humid summer evening.

And at home, Florence had a question for me when I stepped into the big farmhouse to find her sitting in the living room with her mother, who was doing some sewing.

"Did you tell everybody I'm pregnant?"

"Only the pastor," I said, dropping into an easy chair in one corner.

"Why did you have to tell him?" she groaned.

"He wanted to know where you were, and so . . . "

"Why didn't you tell him it was none of his damn business?" Florence flared.

"Why, Florence!" Hilda remonstrated, mildly indignant as she looked up from her sewing, "he was just concerned about you. What's wrong with that?"

I heard the rest of the conversation as I got up and walked to the kitchen for a glass of iced tea.

"He's too nosey," I heard Florence spout, repeating a criticism I had frequently heard her level against Pastor Savage. "He goes around sticking his nose in other people's business too much."

I returned to the living room with my iced tea and sat down in the old, high-backed rocking chair.

Then the coming baby and Florence's agitation over the publicity campaign about it that had been launched in the church that evening was forgotten for the moment as Florence and her mother discussed a fruit-and-vegetable canning undertaking that was to be launched before the summer was over.

As I sat in the rocking chair sipping my iced tea, I heard their voices but didn't listen to what they were saying. Instead, the disembodied face of Pastor Calvin Savage came back to my mind as his parting words at the church filtered through my mind again.

"I think you're making a mistake, brother. When a Christian stops attending prayer meeting, you can be sure his spiritual life is going to decline."

And the next day, in the light of the pastor's warning, a strange thing happened. As Florence and I got out of our car pool ride from Lansing, into our own car parked in downtown Charlotte, to drive the five miles out to the farm, the engine began emitting a knocking sound. I pulled over to the side of the road, got out and raised the hood. Florence got out to look, too. Neither of us could see anything that was wrong.

Back in the car, Florence proposed a tentative diagnosis.

"Probably the tappets need adjusting, or maybe we've got a worn-out piston."

Florence knew more about automobile engines than I did from watching her brother, Brady, work on them through the years he had grown up with her on the farm.

"Want to stop at a garage in town?" I asked, as we pulled away from the curb.

"Heck, no!" she emphatically rejected the idea, "they'd stick us with a bill for twenty-five or thirty dollars and might not even fix it right at that. We'll leave it. Maybe Frank and Faye will come over this weekend and he can look at it. He might be able to tell what's wrong with it, at least, even if he can't fix it."

I felt a sudden impulse to tell Florence about the part-time taxi-driving job that would bolster our income. But then, remembering Florence's disappointment when I didn't get the social worker position, I determined to keep silent until it was a certainty. And that would not be the case until I held a chauffeur's license in my hand. But as we drove the five miles from Charlotte to the Berlincourt farm, the knock in the engine sounded like a death rattle to me.

"I suppose the car will start to fall apart now, along with everything else," Florence predicted gloomily, her face averted from me. "I sure wish Brady hadn't gone to California; he could fix it, whatever it is that's wrong, and it wouldn't cost a lot of money, either."

Her remark, although it may not have been her intention, had the effect of comparing me with her brother, Brady; and in the comparison, at least as an auto mechanic, I came off second best. When we finally pulled into the dirt driveway at the Berlincourt farm, it was with relief that I shut off the engine and the motor knocking that was a reproach to my mechanical incompetence and, at the same time, a reminder of Brady's superiority in this area.

As I followed Florence to the house, I wondered if the sudden development of engine trouble was a rebuke from the Lord; a heavenly confirmation of Pastor Savage's warning for having decided to give up attending prayer meeting to take on the part-time taxi-driving job. Was it a warning, I wondered, that He would cancel out the financial gains of the part-time job by swallowing it up in things like car repairs? If He could remove the lynch pins from the chariot wheels of the Egyptians as they pursued the fleeing Israelites into the Red Sea, surely He could introduce engine trouble into a second-hand Plymouth that was seven years old and had fifty thousand miles on it.

"Brady!"

I heard Florence's squeal of delight from behind her as she opened the screen door and stepped into the dining room. And when I stepped through the doorway behind her, I, too, saw her brother, Brady, who was supposed to be in California, sprawled out in his favorite leather upholstered chair. He was dressed in denims and sweat-soaked T-shirt, his heavy-duty, dirt-caked work shoes stretched out carelessly on the leather Ottoman in front of him. Hilda sat in the rocking chair by the dining room table facing Brady.

"Hi, Boots," he grinned at his sister, using the nickname that was part of their childhood heritage.

From behind Florence, I returned Brady's greeting to me. She stood just inside the front door, arms akimbo, staring at her brother with undisguised delight. Florence voiced the question that was running through my own mind.

"What are you doing here?"

Shep, the farm collie, ambled over to me, tail wagging, to nuzzle my hand with his cold nose in a silent greeting as I stood behind Florence waiting for Brady's answer.

"Just came back for a couple days of plowing to keep the farm in the Soil Bank."

"Oh!"

I relaxed somewhat at Brady's answer and bent down to return Shep's welcome with a massage of his ears. As I fondled

167

Shep, Florence stepped over to the dining room table, drew out a chair and sat down close to her mother.

"You'll be going back to California, then?"

Looking over at Florence, I noted the animated expression of interest on her face as she queried her brother. He was the first person who had been able to draw her out of the shell into which she had retreated since the discovery that she was pregnant.

"Yeah, I'll be going back," Brady answered, a cigarette dangling from his mouth. "I've gotta' be back to work out there at eight o-clock Monday morning."

Then Brady turned his attention to me as I dropped into a chair by the TV set and Shep wandered back to sit at Brady's feet.

"Hey, Gar. I hear you got congratulations coming. I sure was surprised when Ma told me about it."

Brady beamed with sincere happiness. It meant not only that I was going to be a father, but that he was also going to be an uncle to the child that would be born.

"Yea, congratulations," Florence muttered, with an abrupt reversion to her gloomy state of mind. "If I'd had my way it never would have happened—not until we were better situated, anyway."

"Why, Florence Roby," Hilda exclaimed in amazement tingled with indignation, "what a thing to say!"

"What's the matter, Boots?" Brady asked, sitting up in his chair and taking the cigarette out of his mouth while a shocked expression sobered his features. "I should think you'd be happy . . . or maybe I'm sticking my nose in where I shouldn't."

"Maybe so," Florence concurred, then changed the subject abruptly. "Say, Brady, would you mind taking a listen to the Plymouth engine? I think the tappets need adjusting. It just started knocking on the way home tonight."

"Sure, be glad to."

Brady continued sitting upright in his chair, a dark question in his eyes as he tried to fathom the reason for his sister's obvious distaste at being an expectant mother.

"That can just wait until after supper," Hilda announced authoritatively, getting up. "It's all ready to put on the table. We were just waiting for you and Garfield to get here."

"I'm not hungry," Florence announced, getting up. "I think I'll go upstairs and lie down a while." She walked to the stairway that led to the second-floor bedrooms and opened the door.

"Brady, let me know when you're ready to look at the car."

Hilda looked on in open-mouthed surprise as Florence closed the door behind her and went upstairs. She stood in the open archway between dining room and kitchen, near the chair where Brady sat.

"My!" she exclaimed, eyeing me sympathetically, "if I haven't raised some queer children."

"I don't know about that," Brady rebutted as he tugged at Shep's ears, "I always figured I was pretty normal."

"Yes, Brady," his mother agreed, "you certainly are. I'm glad I've got at least one child who isn't peculiar."

With that, Hilda bustled into the kitchen to finish putting supper on the table, leaving me alone in the huge dining room with Brady and Shep. As we sat there waiting for supper, I knew Brady was probably wondering what was going on in his sister's mind that she should seem depressed rather than elated at the prospect of having a baby after five years of marriage.

"I think Florence is afraid the bills will pile up when she quits work to have the baby," I told Brady.

He seemed greatly relieved at the disclosure. He slid back down into a relaxed position in the chair, and his ruggedly handsome features softened from the stern lines into which they had been drawn at Florence's expressed distaste over becoming a mother. To Brady, this seemed like a trifling matter to be upset about.

"If that's all it is," he said, letting one arm fall over the edge of the chair to massage Shep's neck, "there's nothing to worry about. She always was a worry-wart about money, anyway."

"I don't think you ought to talk about your sister that way, Brady," Hilda called from the kitchen. "She just likes to be able to keep her bills paid when they're supposed to be, and I think that's a good way to be. It would be nice if more people felt that way."

"Yeah, but she carries it too far," Brady protested.

After supper Florence came downstairs at Brady's call, and the three of us went out to have Brady listen to the engine knock that had developed on the way home that night. With the hood raised and engine idling, Brady listened, probed, pulled wires, and made some adjustments with a wrench and screwdriver while I held the flashlight for him in the gathering dusk. In five minutes of skilled manipulations, Brady had silenced the ominous-sounding knock. Then Florence and I waited in the front yard while Brady backed the Plymouth out onto the blacktop road and test drove it a mile down the road.

"It sure is nice to have a brother who knows something about cars," Florence said, as we watched the tail lights of the Plymouth recede in the distance. "I wish Brady had decided to stay here on the farm instead of going to California, so he'd be around in case we need his help."

I was silent, feeling the sting of the comparison between Brady's competence and my own incompetence in the area of car repairs. Five minutes later, the headlights of the Plymouth swept over the yard as Brady pulled into the driveway, the former engine knock still conspicuously silent.

"I don't think the engine will give you any more trouble, Boots," predicted Brady, stepping toward us as he lit a cigarette.

As we walked back to the house, with Florence and I both expressing our appreciation to Brady, he countered with an unexpected proposal to me.

"Say, Gar, I wonder if you'd mind giving me a hand tomorrow. On the ground I've been plowing for the Soil Bank, there's a lot of big stones I've got to pick up before I can drag the ground for planting. If you could come along and pick up the stones and throw them into a wagon, I wouldn't have to jump down off the tractor every time I come to one. It would save me a lot of time."

After having saved us a probable car-repair bill of from fifty to seventy-five dollars, I couldn't refuse.

"Sure, Brady, be glad to help you all I can."

The next morning, as we sat at the kitchen table finishing a typical "farmer's" breakfast, Florence reminded her mother that she would be driving into town in a little while to get some chloroform; that meant death for five unsuspecting kittens she had found in the barn the previous week.

"You mean to tell me you're actually going to chloroform those poor little things?" Brady asked, pushing back his chair and getting up.

He looked at Florence, scraping the last of the pancake batter out of the bowl onto the griddle. I couldn't tell whether his seeming shock was real or simulated, calculated to simply tease his sister.

"To save Mom twenty bucks, certainly I would!" Florence shot back.

"What do you mean, save twenty bucks?" queried Brady, in real astonishment, evidently ignorant of this aspect of the surplus kitten problem.

"That's what the Humane Society would charge you to put them away if they came and got them—four dollars for each kitten."

"Wow, I didn't know that," Brady confessed, reflecting the surprise I had shown when I had first heard that from Florence.

"And I'm not going to have anybody dump them off in somebody's front yard the way some people would," Florence continued. "They're our problem."

"I'll tell you what I'd do with those kittens," Brady proposed, blowing a cloud of cigarette smoke toward the ceiling, "I'd take them out in a field and put a twenty-two slug through each one of 'em."

I got up to leave the room, violently repelled by Brady's callousness in suggesting that he could perform such a barbaric act with no compunction whatever. As I left the kitchen, I heard Hilda's anguished reply.

"Oh, mercy, Brady. I think I like Florence's idea a lot better. If it has to be done, I'd rather have it done her way. It doesn't seem so cruel. But I'm glad you can do it, Florence, because I don't think I could."

"Neither could I," I thought to myself, as I passed beyond earshot of their continuing conversation.

And with the solution to that familiar farm problem resolved by the time I returned to the kitchen, Brady was eager to get going on another typical farm challenge—picking up rocks out of a field to be plowed. Dressed in denims and blue work shirt, I looked as much a farmer as Brady. But there the resemblance ended. After a fast, stomach-shaking ride over the rutted, bumpy lane, standing on the plow hitch of the tractor and clinging to the iron saddle seat where Brady sat, he drove out onto the field where the hay wagon was parked on which we could load the rocks and stones that were to be picked up. After hitching the hay wagon to the tractor, the work began.

Brady would drive a little ways, pulling the heavy hay wagon, then stop and I would jump down, pick up two or three large stones, then throw them onto the floor of the wagon with a rattle and crash. After four hours of jumping down, bending over, and throwing rocks onto the wagon— some that required Brady's help to lift—I was ready to quit for the day. But then Florence appeared with some sandwiches and coffee for a brief field lunch. After two hours more, Brady called a welcome announcement.

"Gar, I'd better go back to the barn and get some more gas. I'm getting pretty low. You might as well go along too. I think you've done about all you can to help me. From now on it's just a matter of pulling the drag and seeing how much ground I can cover by the time it gets dark."

I climbed up to my standing position on the plow hitch, grasping the iron seat with both hands, and Brady put the tractor into high gear. We went careening across the field and up the hill, the cleats in the massive rear tires throwing chunks of dirt behind like the waves left in the wake of a paddlewheel steamer. As we came up behind the barn, we encountered a grisly sight. Florence was shoveling dirt into a large hole which she had dug behind the barn, and which evidently contained the bodies of the five chloroformed kittens. I felt a twinge of nausea at the sight, as if I had witnessed the murder and surreptitious burial of human beings. Brady stopped the tractor near Florence long enough to call a question to her.

"Get rid of the cats?"

"Yes," she said, pausing a moment to lean on the shovel.

"You know what your name's going to be from now on, don't you? Boots, the cat killer."

There was cruelty in Brady's humor, although he may not have intended it, akin to that which had caused him to find delight in pulling the tail of the poor three-legged feline mother the night before, and who would now be searching the barn in vain for her five missing kittens.

"Somebody had to do it," Florence shouted fiercely, and I read a rebuke to myself in her tone, as if I could have volunteered to do the unpleasant duty. "Anyway," she added defensively, "it wasn't as bad as shooting them."

"It's all the same to me," Brady retorted, above the noise of the tractor engine.

I jumped down from the tractor.

"I'll walk from here, Brady," I said.

He put the tractor into gear and raced away around the barn and out of sight. I stepped over to where Florence was patting the ground with the shovel, then scraping leaves and twigs over the spot, perhaps in a determined effort to hide the grave and its contents from the mother cat.

"Don't you think it was better than shooting them?" Florence demanded as I approached.

"Yes, I think so," I said, "although I wouldn't have had the guts to do what you did."

"Somebody had to do it," she repeated testily. "That's stupid to pay a Humane Society twenty dollars for doing the same thing, and that's what they'd do. Gas isn't much different than using chloroform."

With one hand grasping the shovel, Florence stooped down to retrieve the nearly empty chloroform bottle from the ground.

"I'll carry the shovel," I offered, stretching out my hand for it.

"It's not that heavy," she protested in her characteristic spirit of independence; then relenting, "but if you insist."

She handed the shovel to me and we walked around the barn toward the house.

"It was nice of you to offer to help Brady today, Gar. I'm sure he appreciated it."

"It was the least I could do for his fixing the car. Maybe he saved us a forty- or fifty-dollar repair bill."

"Brady's a nice guy," she acknowledged admiringly as we walked, "even if he is a little sarcastic sometimes. He'll make some woman a darned good husband."

As I walked up the grassy knoll behind the house, Florence beside me, I wondered if I detected a note of wistfulness, almost envy, in her reference to her brother. I wondered if she was thinking how nice it might be to have a husband who, like Brady, could fix a car; could earn enough money to take care of a wife and child and still have plenty left over for extras like a new car, new clothes, vacations; a husband who would be satisfied for life in one trade, with no vocational groping or jumping from one job to another like a jackrabbit. In all these areas, I had to admit that Brady was better qualified than myself to fulfill the obligations of husband and father; even if he did smoke and drink a little beer and spout sarcastic, even sadistic remarks at times; even if he didn't ever read the Bible or go to church or pray or speak or live as if there were a God.

I turned for a final wave to Brady as he spun the tractor away from the barn and headed back for the field that we had de-stoned. At the house, Florence and Hilda started getting ready to pay a visit to Florence's bachelor uncle, Irving, who lived in a house trailer by a lake ten miles distant. I declined out of sheer physical weariness Florence's lukewarm invitation to accompany them, unswayed by her mother's enthusiastic endorsement of the idea.

"I need to rest a while," I demurred.

"I should think you would want to rest, Garfield," Hilda sympathized as Florence preceded her out the door. "For someone who isn't used to doing farm work, you've put in a pretty good day."

"I don't know if I ever will get used to it, either," I returned, leaning against the archway between the kitchen and the dining room.

Hilda paused in the doorway before stepping outside to share a final bit of folklore from her background on the farm.

"It's like Florence's father used to tell Brady, 'Son, it's hard work to work hard.'"

The screen door closed on Hilda's parting peal of laughter, accentuating the silence that now flowed through the big, empty farmhouse. I glanced at my watch showing three o'clock. Too fatigued to take a shower, although I felt the need of one, I climbed the steps to our second-floor bedroom in time to see Florence back her mother's maroon Chevy coupe out of the driveway. I watched a moment as the car went west on the blacktop highway that ran in front of the house, then laid down and stretched out my aching muscles on the big double bed. A shaft of afternoon sunlight coming through the west window of the immense bedroom warmly touched my hand that lay outstretched to the edge of the bed.

My closing thoughts before sleep overtook me included a depressing comparison between Brady and myself. He had started the day two hours before I had even gotten up, and was still driving his bone-shaking iron horse furiously across the back fields of the farm like a Roman charioteer, racing with the sun to finish his course before darkness fell, while I lay on a bed, completely worn out, a wobbly weakling by comparison. Then the sweet unconsciousness of exhausted sleep overtook me.

"Gar! Hey, Gar! Wake up!"

Brady's voice penetrated my sleep-drugged mind at the same time I felt my leg being shaken by a hand. I opened my eyes and was immediately disoriented by the change in my surroundings. I had closed my eyes with bright sunlight streaming through the windows. Now the room was dark except for the artificial light that poured into the room through the open door that led out into the hall stairway where a single electric bulb illuminated the stairs. I made out the form of Brady standing near the foot of the bed, looking down at me.

"Sorry to wake you up, Gar," he apologized, as I swing my fee to the floor and sat up on the edge of the bed.

"What time is it?" I asked.

"Twenty minutes to eight."

I had slept nearly five hours. I must have been worn out.

"Is Florence back yet?" I asked, as the circumstances that had surrounded me when I first lay down came back to me.

"No," Brady answered, leaning against the footboard of the bed, "they probably won't be back for another hour yet if they went to see Uncle Ervie. He's quite a talker. Once you get him started you can't shut him off. Ma's probably doing his washing, too. If she didn't go over and do it for him once in a while, I think he'd wear the same clothes all hear round."

Then Brady broached the reason for having disturbed me.

"Why, I wouldn't have woke you up, Gar, except I got a little problem maybe you can help me with."

"What's the problem, Brady?" I asked, surprised in my still groggy state of mind that there would be any situation in which Brady would need to call on me for help.

It had always been the other way around. It was Brady who had always been the capable one, who could handle any situation that arose without calling on anyone else for help, least of all me, his brother-in-law. I flipped on a lamp by the bed and Brady pulled up a chair from the corner of the room.

"It looks like I kind of overstayed my visit," he began. "I've been calling the airport to see what connections I could make to get back to California in time to go to work Monday morning. And the problem is, that unless I can get to Chicago by five o-clock tomorrow afternoon, I won't be able to make a connection that will get me there in time. The problem is in getting to Chicago. There's no planes tomorrow, no train that would get me there on time, and I'd sure hate to ride a Greyhound bus. Even if I did get there on a bus, I'm not sure I could get from the bus station to the airport through that downtown traffic. The airport's a heck of a ways from downtown. So I was wondering what you'd think of driving me down to Chicago tomorrow."

"That's about a four-hour drive down there and four hours getting back," I speculated. "If we got an early start there wouldn't be any problem."

"I wouldn't want you and Boots to miss church," Brady protested.

"That's alright, Brady," I brushed aside his objection, "I don't mind and I'm sure Florence won't mind."

Then I thought of Florence's probable reaction to the economic aspects of the trip, the cost of gas and the wear on the car. It would put an additional five hundred miles on the car by the time I got back. Brady guessed the thought behind my silence.

"I'll be glad to buy the gas for the trip if that's what you're thinking about," he broke in, "and if you don't want to put that many miles on your car, we could probably take Ma's. She wouldn't mind."

Brady's suggestion showed a lack of consideration for his mother that Florence had frequently charged him with; that he could so casually make plans for using his mother's car for such a long trip without even consulting her about it first. But his personal relationship to his mother was part of his own life over which I had no jurisdiction.

"I'll be glad to drive you there, Brady," I said, "but as to which car we take, let's see what Florence and your mother think about it."

With that preliminary preparation agreed upon, Brady went back downstairs, leaving me sitting sleep-drugged on the edge of the bed. It was ironic, I thought, as I sat there on the side of the bed, trying to think my tired muscles into mov-

177

ing, that this twist of circumstances should be taking me back to Chicago; back to the very scenes of defeat that I had left more than a year before; back to the place where I had abandoned preparations to enter the ministry, for reasons still hidden from Florence, from Pastor Calvin Savage, and from the members of Gilead Baptist Church who had elected me to be a leader of the young people in the church.

It was two hours later, nearing ten o'clock, when Florence and her mother finally returned home to find me finishing a snack in the kitchen. Brady was gone, having borrowed our car to visit friends before returning to California on Sunday. Hilda, tired from her strenuous afternoon, retired to her bedroom almost immediately, leaving Florence and me alone. I waited until we were in our upstairs bedroom getting ready for bed before broaching the plans I had made for the following day.

"Why did he stay so long?" Florence groaned, when I told her the reason for Brady's request to drive him to Chicago. "That'll put five hundred miles on the car by the time you get back."

Sitting on the edge of the big double bed in cotton pajamas and bathrobe, she spurned with contempt the suggestion I relayed to her from Brady, that Hilda's car be used for the trip.

"I didn't think I should turn him down," I countered, defending the agreement I had made to drive Brady to Chicago. "After all the times he worked on our car and wouldn't take any money for it."

Florence mumbled a begrudging agreement before I turned out the lights, offered a brief prayer by our bedside, and we got into bed. I lay there in the dark beside Florence, my back turned to her, feeling let down at her failure to show any pleasure over my having offered to help her brother out of a minor crisis.

"What time do you think you'll get back?" she asked.

"If I skip church," I replied, "we could leave about eight o'clock in the morning. Since it's about a four-hour drive, we should be there by one in the afternoon, and I'd probably get back about five or six."

"That's a lot of driving," she murmured drowsily. "You're going to be tired when you get back. I hope you weren't expecting me to go along."

"I wouldn't think it would be wise, in your condition," I conceded. "That's why I didn't ask you."

"In my condition is right," she answered, her back still turned to me. "I'm just glad we'll be skipping church tomorrow. Pastor Savage will probably have to announce to the whole congregation that I'm pregnant."

"He probably will," I agreed.

In the following moments of silence, while Florence seemed to be drifting off to sleep, I lay awake beside her and stared through the nearby window into the black, star-studded sky. As I thought of the morrow and the trip to Chicago with Brady, a host of accusing memories that had their birthplace in that great city came crowding around me from the surrounding darkness, like the ghosts of Christmas past that haunted Scrooge in Dickens' Christmas Carol. Then physical fatigue from the hard day's work I had done helping Brady pushed the troubling images from my mind as I slept the sleep of sheer physical weariness.

In the morning, even though Brady had overslept as a result of getting home so late the night before, we still could not suspend the final farewell ritual of eating our way through one of Hilda's fabulous farm-style breakfasts, with bacon and eggs, fried potatoes, toast and homemade preserves, pancakes, orange juice and lots of coffee. Afterwards, comfortably stuffed, I sat in the living room waiting for Brady to finish packing his belongings as Florence cleaned up the kitchen and Hilda got ready for church.

The church that Hilda attended, in spite of allegedly adhering to the Bible, was as different from Gilead Baptist Church, where Florence and I were members, as night from day. It was a small, non-denominational country church, a one-room, white-frame structure with a picturesque bell tower. The elderly, white-haired part-time pastor, who worked as a clerk in a hardware store during the week, did not, like Pastor Savage, paint disturbing and vivid word pictures for his small congregation of sinners in the hands of an angry God, and did not give any embarrassing exhortations for his listeners to come forward and receive Christ as a personal Savior. Pastor Savage would have called him a false prophet, preaching smooth things unto the people out of the deceitfulness of his own heart.

As Hilda stood in front of the living room wall mirror pinning a gold-flowered broach on her dress, a final touch before leaving for her church, she remembered something she had forgotten to tell me the day before.

"Garfield," she called, turning from the mirror, "did you find your mail yesterday?"

"No. I didn't see anything on the TV set where you usually leave it, so I didn't know there was any."

"I'm sorry, Gar," Florence apologized, hearing her mother's question as she came from the kitchen, "it's my fault." She walked over to the buffet by the dining room table and pulled out a small envelope hidden behind a napkin holder. She brought it into the living room where I sat on the sofa and held it out to me. I held back any indication of the sudden hope that spurted up within me as I reached out for the small business-type missive.

"I was dusting the TV set," Florence explained, "and just stuck it over there. You were out in the field with Brady, and I forgot all about it."

The small, square envelope had the name of the Lansing City Clerk's office in the upper left-hand corner. As I looked at it I knew it could only contain one thing—my chauffeur's license! But immediately, another disturbing possibility put a straitjacket upon my inclination to jump up and give a victory shout. Perhaps it contained a notice that my application for a chauffeur's license had been turned down for some reason as far-fetched and ridiculous as those for which I had been denied the social worker job. Florence stood before me, curious, waiting for me to open it. As the hope of success and the fear of failure struggled within me, preventing me from opening the letter, Brady walked into the living room.

"I guess I'm all packed, Gar, so whenever you're ready to take off, we can get started."

Brady's announcement brought a providential way of escape from an unpleasant situation. If the letter from the city clerk contained another disappointment like the letter from Civil Service about the social worker job, I didn't feel up to facing it in the presence of Florence, her mother, and Brady. Brady's entry had triggered my mind to remember something I had almost forgotten.

"Wow!" I exclaimed, feigning chagrin and thrusting the letter into my inside coat pocket, "I just remembered I haven't told Pastor Savage yet that I won't be there for Young People's meeting tonight. Even if I get back in time, I'll be too bushed. I'd better run into town and tell him about it."

I looked at my watch in a state of simulated agitation.

"I can still catch him at home before he leaves for church if I leave right now," I said, hurrying toward the door. "Brady, I'll be back in about twenty minutes and then we can take off."

"Take your time, Gar. I'll be ready when you get back."

"Aren't you going to let me see what's in that letter, Gar?" Florence demanded, her suspicion aroused that I was trying to hide something from her.

"I'll open it when I get back," I promised, as I opened the door and started to leave.

But like a bloodhound with the scent of a criminal action in its nostrils, Florence was not satisfied.

"Why can't you just call him on the phone?" she demanded, following me to the door.

"I've got to talk to him in person," I threw back over my shoulder hastily, and shut the door behind me, cutting off further discussion.

I walked quickly to the car, backed it out onto the blacktop surface of the road and was on my way to downtown Charlotte. A mile down the road, safely out of sight of the Berlincourt farm, I pulled over to the shoulder of the road and stopped. With the engine idling, I reached into my inside coat pocket and pulled out the small, white window envelope from the city clerk's office. As carefully as if there were a check for a million dollars inside, which I didn't want to risk mutilating, I pulled up the flap of the envelope with mingled emotions of hope and apprehension. Would it be another rejection, or would my efforts be crowned with success this time? The answer, as I carefully extracted the contents of the envelope, was like a look into a mirror. There was my own smiling face looking up at me from the coveted prize of a chauffeur's license, bearing the approving signature of a member of the Lansing City Council. I looked heavenward as if there were an open sky above me instead of the upholstered roof of a vintage Plymouth sedan.

"Thank you, Lord," I breathed aloud, as certain as I could be that only the intervention of Heaven in my behalf had secured this privilege for me.

I sat there a moment longer, staring at the license in mingled gratitude and unbelief. To me, it was as good as money in the bank—additional revenues that would change Florence's gloomy financial fears to happy expectations. Then I replaced the cherished symbol of my enhanced ability as a breadwinner in its envelope and put it back in my pocket. Then I drove on into Charlotte and stopped at a restaurant to call Pastor Savage. Elated as I felt over my new economic advantage, I didn't feel up to a face-to-face confrontation with the pastor over what I had to tell him. I could indeed have called him from the farm. I had only wanted to get away from the house long enough to discover in complete privacy what the envelope from the city clerk contained.

The telephone at the pastor's home was answered promptly by his wife, who asked me to wait while she summoned her husband to the phone. His voice, when he answered a moment later, was expectant.

"Good morning, Gar, and praise the Lord. I hope you're calling to tell me some good news about what we talked about Wednesday night."

"Well, it's good news to me," I responded, "but it may seem like bad news to you. My chauffeur's license arrived yesterday, so I will be following through on that taxi-driving job. But the reason I'm calling you this morning is to tell you that Florence and I won't be in church this morning, and I won't be there for Young People's meeting tonight. I've got to drive my brother-in-law to Chicago so he can catch a plane for California and get back to his job on time Monday morning."

The pastor's voice was heavily tinged with an undertone of impending disaster.

"Brother Roby, I've thought about it and prayed about it since you told me that Wednesday night, and I'm more convinced than ever that in taking a job that will keep you away from the church consistently on Wednesday nights, you're making a big mistake."

"How can it be a mistake?" I rebutted, with a show of irritation. "The Bible says, 'He that provideth not for his own household is worse than an infidel, and hath denied the faith.' And that's all I'm trying to do—provide for my wife and for the addition that's coming."

"That's true, brother," he countered, "but God's will has to be done according to His word, and being absent from the house of God consistently when the door are open can't be with His approval."

"I'm sorry, Pastor, but I don't see any other way out. It will probably only be until after the baby is born and Florence can go back to work."

Exasperation at my evident obstinacy was creeping into the pastor's voice.

"Gar, I haven't got time to talk any more about this now; I've got to get down to the church. But I just want to say one more thing. If you're going to go this route, I really think you owe it to the church to turn in your resignation as Young People's sponsor. Have you talked that over with your wife to see how she feels about it?"

"No, but I'm going to as soon as I finish talking to you."

"Well, maybe you'll change your mind about taking the

job after you talk to your wife, Brother Roby. I'll be praying about you and your wife. Have a good trip to Chicago, and we'll talk about it later."

I hung up and left the restaurant, my buoyant resolve to follow through on the taxi-driving job not the least diminished by the pastor's dire warning. As I drove back to the Berlincourt farm, the stern opposition which the pastor had expressed toward the part-time job was washed from my mind by the anticipated glow of happiness and pride on Florence's face when I told her the good news. Back at the farm minutes later, I could hear Florence playing the spinet piano in the living room as I walked up the grassy slope to the house. As I stepped into the big living room, she stopped playing and turned on the piano bench to face me as I sat down on the sofa across the room from her. Hilda had evidently left for church and Brady was somewhere else in the house.

"Well, did you see the pastor?" Florence asked.

"I talked with him and everything's settled for tonight. But he suggested that I talk over something with you before I make a final decision."

"What's that?"

"Would you mind if we resigned as Young People's sponsors, if it would mean a substantial increase in my income?"

"Of course not. I won't be able to get out and gallivant around with those teenagers any more now that I'm pregnant. But what's that got to do with your income?"

Like an African Zulu warrior handing a lion skin to his mate as proof of his manhood, I pulled the envelope from the city clerk out of my inside pocket, stepped across the room and handed it to her.

"I was wondering if you were just trying to get out of showing me this," she said, opening it up and pulling out the license.

"A chauffeur's license? What's this all about?"

"To make up for losing the social worker job," I announced, with as much quiet authority as Moses must have exuded when he came down from Mount Sinai with the Ten Commandments. "The Lord has provided something that may bring us more money than that job would have. I'm going to start driving a taxi in Lansing, probably next week."

There was sudden panic in Florence's voice and on her face as she stared across the room at me, the chauffeur's license gripped in her hand.

"Do you mean to tell me you're going to quit . . ."

"No," I cut in quickly, grasping her misunderstanding, "I'm not going to quit my job in the Highway Department. I'll be driving a taxi part time in addition to that; three nights a week. It will make up as much, if not more, than what I would have earned if I had gotten the social worker job."

Then I sat there waiting expectantly, almost hungrily, for the accolade of praise, for the overflow of sudden happiness from Florence. But there was only silence and a sober expression on her face.

"What hours will you be driving a taxi?" she asked finally. And there was a hint of desperation in her voice.

I looked at her across the room, but her head was turned away from me as she stared out the window. The chauffeur's license was gripped in her right hand like a telegram containing a death announcement. It was evident that I had failed again in my effort to change Florence's gloomy state of mind to one of happiness, in spite of the burden of extra hours of labor I was willing to assume.

"In order to work at all," I answered mechanically, my enthusiasm suddenly drained, "I have to work at least three nights a week; two of them from six until midnight and the third from six until two in the morning."

"Is that why you want to resign as Young People's Sponsor?" she asked quietly.

"No. I'm resigning because one of the nights I'll be driving will be Wednesday, and Pastor Savage felt that if I was going to be missing prayer meeting every Wednesday, that I shouldn't hold down that office and set a bad example for the young people in the church."

"What right has he got to ask you to resign?" she blazed. "You were elected to that job by the whole church. They should decide whether you should resign or not; not him. He makes me sick, anyway; always sticking his big nose in where it doesn't belong."

"Even if he hadn't asked me to resign," I answered wearily, "I probably would have anyway. It would be too much with the part-time job. I wouldn't have the time or ambition to plan any special programs."

There was a long silence while I savored the bitterness of Florence's total lack of enthusiasm for my effort in securing a part-time job to keep our budget balanced.

"I thought you'd appreciate it," I finally said defensively.

"Appreciate it!" she snorted indignantly, "have you forgotten I'm going to have a baby?"

"No, I didn't forget it," I retorted heatedly, standing to my feet. "Why do you think I applied for the job in the first place? So you wouldn't have to worry about our not being able to keep the bills paid."

"But I'd rather have you around in case I need you."

There were tears in the quaver of her voice, if not in her eyes, as she anticipated some mishap during her pregnancy.

"What if I should have a miscarriage, and you're twenty miles away in Lansing where I can't reach you, God only knows where?"

"In an emergency your mother can always drive you to the hospital," I countered. "She's going to be around."

"That's not her job. It's yours!" she shot back furiously. "I'm not going to unload any more of my responsibilities on Mom the way Faye and Betsy and Brady have done."

I walked over to the living room window that looked out on the spacious lawn with its majestic oak trees, trying to still the emotional turmoil within me by contemplating the serene scenes of nature. Then, in agitated, rapid-fire delivery, Florence brought forth arguments that seemed to shoot full of holes my expectation that the part-time taxi-driving job would really bring in more money.

"This would mean," she charged, "that on the three nights you drive a cab, you'd have to drive our car to work so you could get back home. Since our car wouldn't be used in the car pool, I'd have to pay for my ride home on the nights you work. There will be gas and depreciation on our car. You'll have to get your supper at a restaurant three nights a week. So you'll probably wind up no further ahead than you would be if you just stuck to your job in the Highway Department."

I remained standing by the window with my back to Florence, feeling the impact of her argument against the part-time job, with no facts or figures available with which to offer a rebuttal. Her analysis could have been right, but her way of pointing it out to me, in a tone of withering scorn, was wrong. It left me feeling that I was a bigger failure than ever as a provider; that all I had done was to make arrangements to pour more than twenty hours of labor a week down the drain for nothing. I suddenly felt too thwarted, too frustrated in my sincere desire to please her, to be able to defend my position with vigor and objectivity. My inability to respond was given a reprieve as Brady walked into the living room from the kitchen.

"Hope I'm not butting in where I don't belong," he apologized, sensing the tension in the atmosphere between Florence and me.

"Not at all, Brady," I responded, turning to face him and hiding my desolate feelings with a synthetic smile.

"Why, I just came in to ask a favor of you, Gar," Brady, whose station wagon was in California, continued. "If you don't mind waiting a little bit to get on the road, I'd like to borrow your car if I could to run a little errand. It won't take but a few minutes."

"Sure, Brady," I responded, stepping over to him and handing him the car keys, "take all the time you need."

"I just remembered," he explained, taking the keys, "that I told Burt Clark, a farmer friend of mine who lives down the road a couple of miles, that I'd help him make out the papers to get his farm in the Soil Bank. Those things have to be turned in pretty quick or he won't be eligible. It shouldn't take more than half an hour."

Florence, who had sat on the piano bench, a dispirited bystander to the exchange between Brady and me, called out to him as he turned to leave.

"Brady, do you want me to make some hamburgers to take with you?"

"I don't think so, Boots," he replied, turning back to face her, "that breakfast Ma fed us ought to last me all the way to California, but maybe Gar would."

Florence's contemptuous reaction to the part-time taxi-driving job had killed my interest in food and in almost anything else.

"I don't think so, Florence."

"Suit yourself," Florence shrugged, obviously offended, as Brady continued on out the front door. "I was just trying to save you from spending money in a restaurant on the way there and back."

Feeling an obligation to spare Florence tormenting visions of myself squandering money on lavish meals at fancy restaurants as I traveled to Chicago and back, I gave a grudging consent to her proposal.

"If you want to make a couple of cheese sandwiches and fill a thermos bottle with coffee," I compromised, "I'll take them along."

Florence jumped up to hurry to the kitchen and prepare the take-along lunch as Brady went out the door to drive down the road on a good-neighbor errand, leaving me alone in the large front room. I stepped over to the piano bench and picked up the chauffeur's license and torn envelope where Florence had dropped them in disgust. The smile on the likeness of my own face that looked up at me from the license no longer evoked an answering grin of triumph on my own face. It seemed now like an impish smirk of mockery that was in agreement with Florence's withering scorn.

Yet, like a mariner in a stormy sea, surrounded by the wreckage of his ship of hopes, I clung to the angrily discarded license, never guessing in that moment of domestic desolation that the chauffeur's license and the job opportunity it could secure for me were to become a catalyst, a connecting bridge that would eventually lead to my meeting with another woman who was destined to usurp Florence's place of preeminence in my life.

Feeling dejected and rejected, I reinserted the license back in its envelope and thrust it into my inside coat pocket. Perhaps, I speculated, I could prove Florence's dire predictions about the part-time job to be wrong; that I would indeed be able to bolster our soon-to-be-depleted financial reserves. At least it held out the prospect of some support for my badly battered self-esteem.

On my way to the upstairs bedroom to get some extra rest, I called to Florence in the kitchen.

"Let me know when Brady gets back."

Welcoming a few minutes of being alone in which the sting of Florence's caustic criticisms could abate before starting on the long trip with Brady, I wearily climbed the steps to the second-floor bedroom and stretched out on the bed. The half hour that Brady had expected to be gone turned into two hours before I heard our car turn back into the drive, followed by Florence's shouted announcement up the stairway.

"Gar! Brady's back."

Downstairs a moment later, I found Brady, with his blue canvas airline bag, ready to go. He was apologetic as he explained how his neighbor had sought his help with a minor mechanical problem on his tractor, which Brady had remedied.

"I'll wait for you in the car, Gar," he said, then called a final farewell to Florence in the kitchen.

"So long, Boots. If I don't see you again before the baby arrives, good luck!"

"Thanks, Brady, I'll let you know how it comes out."

Five minutes later, with Brady waiting in the car, Florence handed me a paper sack containing an ample lunch and a thermos full of coffee. In my hurt reaction over the attitude she

189

had displayed toward the part-time taxi-driving job, I felt no inclination to reach out and embrace her before leaving. Neither did Florence evidently feel any such tender impulse.

"I hope you don't have any trouble with the car," she said cooly, in a detached tone as I turned to go.

Standing there by the door in the living room, only a few feet apart, because she seemed more concerned about the car than about me, I felt as if the distance between us was greater than the two hundred and fifty miles that lay between Charlotte and Chicago. As I walked down the gentle slope of the shade-dappled lawn to the car, the contempt which Florence had expressed toward the part-time taxi-driving job was like salt in the wound of rejection I had received from the Civil Service Commission.

As I backed the car out of the drive, Florence stepped out onto the porch to wave farewell, but I felt that it was more for Brady than for myself. And driving eastward toward Charlotte, on the first lap of the long journey, I felt that there was nothing in my relationship to Florence to draw me back home to her, eagerly, willingly. Only moral obligation. Her attitude, since the time she had informed me of her pregnancy, had ceased to be one of praise, warmth, and confidence. Instead, she had communicated to me, increasingly, a disdain that was darkened by a tinge of despair over my supposed lack of ability to pilot our domestic ship through the stormy straits of parenthood without suffering financial shipwreck.

Neither in the preceding weeks nor in that parting moment, had she given me adequate expressions of confidence and love that might have fortified me against the inducements to infidelity, whether vicarious or real, that abounded in a great metropolis like Chicago. It was a dangerously vulnerable state of mind for a middle-aged and frustrated married man alone in a strange city far from home, as I would be after leaving Brady at O'Hare International Airport in Chicago in a few short hours.

CHAPTER 6

⟹ The biggest and busiest commercial airport in the world is O'Hare International Airport, twenty-two miles northwest of downtown Chicago. From its acres of concrete runways, there is a plane landing or taking off every minute of every hour, around the clock, with more than 2,000 aircraft movements in and out of the airport on some days.

At five minutes past five, on the Sunday afternoon I had driven Florence's brother there to catch his plane to California, I stood in the midst of a small group of other spectators, behind the protective barrier of cyclone fence, to watch Brady's plane take off. Leaning against the shoulder-high railing of the sturdy fence, I watched as the giant hundred-passenger jetliner taxied to the far end of the runway and circled around for the takeoff. Had there been debris of any kind on the runway, it would have been sent spinning into a violent whirlwind as the blast from the jet engines pushed the plane down the runway at a swiftly accelerating speed. From a hundred yards away, the rising crescendo of the supersonic engines was like the angry scream of some gargantuan, prehistoric bird, determined to defy the laws of gravity which pressed it down to the earth. Then, happening so fast that the precise point where it occurred was lost in the blur of movement, the mammoth aircraft was no longer on the ground but in the air.

As the plane climbed into the sky on a gently ascending

and invisible slope, it conveyed the confidence of a skyborne Hercules, assured of victory. I was on that plane also, in imagination, caught up in the excitement and adventure of a flight to distant scenes and never-before visited cities. Then, as the plane that was carrying Brady to California grew smaller in the sky, my vicarious involvement in the takeoff evaporated like the rapidly disappearing vapor trail left behind by the giant, manmade skybird. The hard substance of the fence against which I leaned registered on my mind again. I was still on the ground, and the ancient words of David, the sweet psalmist of Israel, filtered through my mind, tinged with a subtle envy of my own making.

"Oh, that I had wings like a dove, then would I hasten and fly away from the windy storm and tempest."

Then the dispatcher's voice boomed over the PA system, above the scream of incoming and outgoing planes.

"Flight forty-six for Las Vegas now loading at Gate Number Five."

Spectators who had stood around me for a final wave to friends or relatives drifted away, leaving me standing there by the fence alone. I continued standing there, a solitary human island of silent immobility in the sea of sound and color and movement that was the world's greatest airport, unaware of my surroundings, witnessing instead scenes and voices that had followed me from the events of recent days. As I stood there, the spectral shapes and voices that had followed me from Charlotte and Lansing were joined by others; evoked, no doubt, by my proximity to the place of their birth, the teeming city of Chicago, near at hand. They were faces and happenings resurrected from the time beginning more than four years before, when I had come to Chicago, shortly after marrying Florence, with the high aspiration of preparing for the ministry as my life work.

In one of the scenes that was conjured up before my inner gaze, I was walking again with Florence down the wide, cement beachfront walk along Lakeshore Drive on Chicago's near north side. It was a Sunday morning and, as we often had done on our way to historic Moody Church, we distributed Gospel tracts to the early Sunday morning swimmers and sunbathers along the lakeshore. I saw us pause before an elderly couple sitting on a bench, to offer them a tract, only to stand there sympathetically but helplessly as a paroxysm of violent coughing shook the man's emaciated frame, almost bending him double. But when it had subsided he had gasped out an apology and graciously reached for the tract I had held out.

In the months following that episode, as Paul had seen a vision of a man in Macedonia calling out to him for help, so had I continued to be troubled by the vision of the elderly, consumptive man, still sitting there by the lakeside, waiting for another spasm of coughing that might be his last; waiting, perhaps, for me to return and speak the words I had not spoken that morning; to finish a work of intercessory prayer and witnessing that might have affected his eternal destiny.

Time and distance had not effaced the details of that scene; they had only altered the role of the unidentified man. Then, he had been a silent suppliant for my help. Now, he appeared in my mind as the ghostly image of Samuel, the prophet, evoked from the grave at the bidding of King Saul, by the witch of Endor. And as the fearful likeness of the deceased Samuel had materialized to condemn Saul and pronounce judgment upon him, so too the old man of my past now appeared as my judge, to accuse me of having abandoned him and thousands of others like him in that great city, who, like the inhabitants of Nineveh to whom Jonah was sent, spiritually "knew not their right hand from their left." So, to the unpleasant awareness that as a breadwinner and provider I had failed Florence in the five years of our marriage, was added in that moment the more bitter remembrance that I had failed God in the task to which I had believed He had called me.

In failing Him, I had failed also, countless multitudes in that great city of Chicago, of whom the spectral memory of the elderly couple by the lakeshore were representative. I had possessed the light, but I had left them in darkness. I had possessed the key to eternal life, but had forsaken them in the valley of the shadow of death, without hope. And all because in my own personal life, I had failed to gain control over one of the powerful drives that God had implanted in man at the time of Creation, an elemental urge that on too many occasions I had obeyed rather than commanded. For I had finally concluded that it would be folly to hope for a public ministry that was a success while my private life was a failure in this area.

Suddenly, as I stood there by the fence at O'Hare Field in Chicago, minutes after Brady's plane had disappeared in the sky, I wanted to fly also; to escape from the whole ghostly swarm of memories that had come crowding around me; memories of scenes of defeat that had led to my abandoning preparations to enter the ministry, and the whole procession of unhappy events that had begun with Florence's announcement of her pregnancy: a series of events, each of which had found me lacking in some important requirement, whether the findings were true and I had to acknowledge it, or whether they were false and I could do nothing to obliterate them, such as the findings of the oral interview board and the farcical Civil Service hearing that had followed.

As I watched a giant passenger plane like the one Brady had boarded a few moments before takeoff, there was within me no resurgence of that moment of envy I had felt. For I realized that the kind of flight which a plane—or a train, or a ship, even to the farthest corner of the world—could provide was no guarantee of escape from the condemning host of recollections that had trooped around me, to stand pointing at me with accusing fingers and staring at me with condemning eyes. For I knew that the mind can keep on working, regardless of a change of locale, recapitulating the experiences one desires to forget, upon the hidden inner screen of the imagination. The only way to escape such tormenting visions for a while was to displace them with other real scenes that had such a powerful pull and capacity to generate intense excitement, that they could hypnotize the mind by their toxic pull, and hold the imagination focused upon them, blotting out for a while all previous memories. At such times, driven by a compulsive need to forget the past or escape the present or postpone the future, some men turn to alcohol or drugs. Temperament and habit suggested a different form of escape to me.

From the files of my mind, where mental films of all the varied experiences of my life had been stored, many of them forgotten until needed, a vivid picture was recreated that had been stored there several years before and forgotten until this moment of need. It was one of the few holiday visits to Charlotte that Florence and I had made while living in Chicago. En route, the Greyhound bus on which we were riding late at night passed through the outskirts of what had appeared to be an Arabian Nights harem built up into a city, not far from Chicago. Florence had been asleep on the seat beside me while I was awake, watching the night scenes slip past. What I had seen had shocked me as if I had stumbled upon a modern-day Sodom or Gomorrah, where the paramount pursuit of the inhabitants was the unrestrained stimulation and satisfaction of sexual appetites. The blatantly brazen, life-size posters I had seen along the main street of the town came back to me in all of their seductive and suggestive color; posters and enlarged photos of scantily clad women that had adorned the bars and burlesque theatres and night clubs for several blocks on both sides of the main street. In such a place as this, I thought, I could find the stimulants that could induce a momentary forgetfulness of the failures and disappointments of the recent past, as well as the gloomy prospects for the immediate future.

I turned away from the fence that enclosed the runways of the world's greatest airport and hurried through the pedestrian-congested length of the terminal on my way to the airport parking lot. As I pushed through the swinging glass door that led to the parking lot, I saw people in front of me who were also leaving the terminal, being handed leaflets by a middle-aged man wearing a sport coat and baggy pants and white shoes that needed cleaning. He looked like a former pugilist, with a pug nose, cauliflower ear, and a bulldog jaw. Probably a union man protesting against one of the airlines, I thought, as I approached. As I came abreast of him, he thrust one of the leaflets at me.

"Have a Gospel tract, sir," he invited respectfully, as I took it from his hand out of instinctive courtesy.

I almost stopped dead in my tracks as I stared at him in open-mouthed astonishment, so unexpected was the kind of literature he had given me. It was identical to the kind of tracts I had once passed out to passing pedestrians on busy Chicago street corners, as a student at Moody Bible Institute several years before. But things had changed since then, and I had changed.

I thrust the cheaply printed folder into my coat pocket and hurried on. The interrupting incident was pushed from my mind as soon as I reached my car, got in, and pulled a road map from the glove box. Spreading it out over the steering wheel, I quickly located the destination I had in mind, about twenty miles southeast of Chicago. In my distraught frame of mind, I could think of no better launching site for a temporary escape from reality than the sex-saturated main street of Calumet City, Illinois.

As I drove out of the airport parking lot and nosed into the Sunday afternoon southbound traffic, I drove like the Biblical Jehu in his chariot. Few things can impel a man to irresponsible speed in a recklessly driven automobile like the prospect of finding a place where he can escape, for a while, a host of disturbing memories. The traffic lights I passed through, the cars I passed, the turns I made, were executed as learned habits, without conscious awareness of danger in the way I drove, unrestrained by the risk of a fatal accident. My mind was miles ahead of me, at my destination, a place of temporary escape, and my body was only speeding to catch up with it.

It was just getting dark when I drove into Calumet City on State Line Avenue, the unique main street that at the same time separated two cities and two states—Calumet City,

Illinois, and Hammond, Indiana. The street was just as I had remembered it, ablaze with lighted marquees advertising female entertainment. I pulled over to the curb and parked alongside the first cabaret I came to, the Gorgeous Girlie Show Bar. As I mounted a short flight of steps off the sidewalk to enter the bar, boasting "Live Entertainment," two men, shabbily dressed, standing nearby on the curb, looked me over as if they were immigration officers sizing up a foreign visitor. As I reached the top step, one of the men spoke to me.

"Better not go in there," he called, in a tone that warned of imminent danger of some kind.

My hand was arrested in midflight toward the brass doorknob. I was as startled by the unexpected words spoken by a total stranger, as if they had come directly from God, in a demonstration of divine ventriloquism, using the man's lips to speak and dissuade me from opening the door.

"Why not?" I asked, pausing on the top step, my heart stilled by the warning.

"After the girls in there con you into buying 'em drinks, they'll make you go off in your pants. Then you'll have to pay a cleaning bill besides," came the stranger's reply, as they were both seized with spasms of obscene cackling.

The crude remark produced a mixed emotional reaction within me. I was repulsed by such coarse language from a total stranger, called out on a public street corner. But at the same time, there was something in the words that pointed to the Devil as the probable instigator, rather than God. For they had the effect of inciting my desire to enter, rather than quenching it. But as I pulled the brass doorknob of the solid wooden door, which contained no window that would afford an outsider a glimpse of what was within, another message was relayed to me silently, unheard by the men standing on the sidewalk. Its mode and message bore more surely the stamp of Divine origin. It was a half-remembered verse of Scripture that came rustling through the corridor of my mind like a single leaf blown before the wind. There was a sigh and a lamentation inherent in the words; they were words, not of entreaty, but of excommunication; they were words that denoted the sadness of the righteous over the departure of the reprobate.

"The dog is turned to his own vomit again, and the sow that was washed, to her wallowing in the mire."

Then I yanked open the door and stepped from the lighted street into the semi-darkness of the interior. The door closed of its own accord behind me, shutting out the vulgar cackling on the street corner and the whispered warning I had ignored and the host of unhappy memories that had pursued me from Charlotte to Chicago and from the airport to Calumet City.

I stood there just inside the door for a moment; partly to give my eyes time to adjust to the darkness, partly hypnotized by what I saw and heard and felt. Behind the bar, which extended in a half circle out from the back wall, out into the center of the semi-darkened room, was a circular stage at shoulder level to the patrons who sat at the bar. On the stage, spotlighted in a circle of soft, pink light from the ceiling, was a shapely redhead, displaying the kind of "live entertainment" promised in neon lights outside to prospective customers. Six people sat strung out around the circular bar; two men and a woman at the far left and, near the center section, three sailors dressed in summer whites.

Between the scantily clad girl on the stage and the customers at the bar was an aisle wide enough to accommodate the bartender as he traversed the length of the curving bar on periodic trips to keep his customers plied with liquid refreshments. The aisle at the same time doubtless served as a separating moat of protection for the girl on the stage, putting her beyond the reach of men whose inhibitions had been loosened by liquor.

The girl on the stage, whose upswept hairdo gleamed golden red in the pink glow of the overhead light, was dressed to reveal more than to conceal. A pale green, transparent baby doll gown, beneath which she wore no bra, enhanced the translucent flesh of her full breasts that needed no artificial

198

means of support. There was a stretch of bare, quivering belly exposed between the hem of the baby doll gown and the elastic band of bikini panties that clung to her rounded hips. Her bare, well-shaped legs, spread wide apart, curved down to ankles that were elevated by red, high-heeled patent leather pumps. The Oriental music that flowed around her from a concealed source backstage filled the semi-darkened room with its slow, sensuous beat, and might have been much like that to which Salome had danced, to wring from a lust-inflamed king Herod the head of John the Baptist.

Abruptly, I could sense that I was not just a watcher; I was also being watched—by the bartender. The girls who were paid to disrobe on the spotlighted stage were not being provided as a public service to sex-hungry men, but only as an inducement to get them to come in and buy alcoholic beverages.

"Plenty of seats at the bar, Mac," he grimaced, leaning on the shiny, mahogany counter and waving toward the half-dozen empty bar stools at the right end of the bar.

The three sailors, held captive by the sensuous movements of the half-nude girl on the stage, paid no attention to me, oblivious of the bartender's pointed remark. As I moved out of the semi-gloom by the door, toward the empty stool closest to the wall at the far right end of the bar, my own eyes returned to the seductive movements of the stripper on the stage as she began to remove the baby doll gown that covered her torso, to the accompaniment of cheers from the sailors. And then the bartender was in front of me to demand the expected payment for the sexual stimulation I had already gotten in my several moments of voyeuristic viewing.

"What'll it be, buddy?"

The harsh contrast between the woman's form and the bartender's face was like the difference between being caressed by a kiss and clobbered with a club. In the pink light, she looked soft as silk; in the gloom at the periphery of the circle of light in which the woman postured, he looked hard and ruthless, capable of any brutality, as if his job as a bartender was only a front for more sinister pursuits. I looked at him only long enough to give an order that marked me as a stranger in the place; the name of a beer that was familiar to me only because of the advertisements I had seen along the highway en route from the airport.

"Give me a bottle of Schlitz," I said, my gaze returning to the stripper.

"All we got is Blatz," he countered, in a tone that dared me to insist on my original choice.

"Okay, make it Blatz."

A moment later, he set a tall, foaming glass of beer on the bar in front of me. Then, lifting the tall, cold glass of unfamiliar, salty-tasting liquid to my lips, I sat, like the three sailors, mesmerized by an act that was probably more sexually enticing than that which had held King David spellbound on a rooftop in Jerusalem centuries before, as he had watched another man's wife bathing on the rooftop below him. Here, in Calumet City, Illinois, the basic act of disrobing by a woman had been refined to an art; with the addition of music, a skilled blending of light and shadows that hid the wrinkles and accentuated the curves, with clothes that were designed to show more than they hid, to be taken off rather than put on.

The appetite which held me captive to the spectacle of a half-naked woman performing an obscene dance upon a stage before total strangers was something dark and basic in the sexual makeup which I shared with most males of the species, past and present. It was that perverted instinct which had led to the birth and perpetuation of the world's oldest profession, prostitution, and had given rise to some of its modern handmaidens—the strip tease, and pornography in magazines, books, and films. It was an appetite for intense sensation, without any of the snags, the delays, the conflicts, the demands, involved in the personal relationships between lovers or between husbands and wives. It provided a form of escape from life, a floodtide of excitement, stimulating the senses, blocking out thought and memory, focusing all of life, past, present and future, into a single, exhilarating experience of sensory stimulation.

In the center of the stage, stripped of the baby doll gown, clad only in the bikini brief panties and high heels, the woman matched the final flurry of drum beats with a climax of pelvic undulations. Then her movements ceased simultaneously with the music and she paused, breathless, legs spread apart, breasts heaving, and her body glistening with perspiration.

I clapped as loudly as the sailors, as she turned to leave the stage, a final ovation that was continued as the nearly nude redhead who had just left the stage was followed by a brunette, fully clothed in a shimmering black floor-length evening gown, with rhinestone-glittered shoes and fuchsia elbow-length gloves. As she began a hip-swinging perambulation around the circumference of the stage, I pulled a handkerchief from my hip pocket to wipe the passion-generated perspiration from my forehead, then took a sip of the beer which had set on the counter untouched for the last moments of the preceding stripper's performance. Appreciating the coolness, if not the flavor of the beer, and anticipating a repetition of the sensation that had flooded through me seconds before of being lifted out of myself on the floodtide of sexual desire, I felt a hand softly laid on my left shoulder.

I turned my head to look into the face of the woman who had been standing at the other end of the bar with two men when I had come in. In the daylight her face might have looked hard and drawn with middle-age weariness. But in the semi-gloom of the bar, and with cleverly applied makeup, there was a suggestion of youthfulness about her. The red jersey dress into which her buxom figure had been poured set off the flaxen hair. The dress was cut too low in front and too high at the hemline for street wear. The perfume she wore reached out and enveloped me like a pleasant anesthesia before she put an arm around my shoulders and, standing beside me, pressed her body close against mine.

"How about buying me a drink, honey?" she pleaded.

"Sure," I responded, inebriated by the atmosphere of sexuality in the place.

"You're sweet," she purred, pressing closer to me and running a hand up and down my back. "What's your name, honey?"

"Garfield," I said, stopping short as I was about to give my last name also, suddenly aware that there might be unpleasant repercussions back home if it were ever known that I had been in such a place.

"Garfield; that's an unusual name," she mused, looking into my face and eyes intently for any tell-tale signs of duplicity. "Mine's Kim."

She encircled my neck with one hand and drew my face down to hers for a moist, tongue-probing kiss. Then she drew the empty bar stool beside her closer to the one I sat on and hoisted herself up onto it. By then, the ever-present bartender was in front of us.

"The usual for me, Joe."

The bartender moved away swiftly and was back by the time I had pulled my wallet from my hip pocket, to place a thimble-sized glass of liquid on the counter in front of Kim.

"That'll be two bucks," he said.

By the time I had laid the money on the counter, Kim had downed the thimble full of "the usual" which the bartender had brought to her.

"You ever been here before, Garfield?" Kim asked, pressing her leg against mine.

"First time."

"You must be from out of town. Chicago?"

"Lansing, Michigan," I said, rotating my half-empty glass of beer in one hand and flicking a glance at the brunette on the stage as she started to unzip the black evening gown.

Kim probably noticed my glance and sized me up as a man who had come into the place, drawn more by the lure of live entertainment than by an appetite for alcohol. And her seemingly innocent question had elicited other important information from me. I was not a native of the town or region who would be likely to return again soon. I was just a tourist, passing through, with the likelihood that I might never be back. She reached out and turned my face to hers with an encircling hand and pulled my head toward her own.

"Give me another kiss, honey," she begged.

As she pulled back, after the long, salivary kiss that had probably left a streak of crimson lipstick around my mouth, my eyes, motivated by that erotic instinct which causes a man to inspect the parts of a woman's body that have sex arousal value, slipped down to the shadowed cleavage between her pushed-out breasts. And I was startled to see something that I would never have expected to see in such a place. Swinging free, in the few inches of space between her ample bosom and my chest, suspended from a delicate gold chain that hung around her neck, was the historic emblem of Christianity, a cross. It shone dully in the light that spilled over the edge of the bar from the overhead spotlight that encircled the stripper on the stage, who stood there undulating her hips in time with the music.

Kim released her hand abruptly from the back of my neck and drew back, intuitively guessing what I had seen that had enveloped me in a moment of silent amazement.

"Wondering about this?" she asked, reaching down and lifting the golden cross from the shadowed recess between her half-exposed breasts.

The cross shone more brightly as she lifted it above the level of the bar counter and more light fell upon it.

The prospect of a word of explanation that could unlock this mystery I had encountered drew my attention completely away from the woman on the stage who was about to discard another item of clothing.

"It might surprise you," said Kim, with an enigmatic smile that was both defensive and disarming, "but I go to Mass every Sunday I can. Last week I even went to Confession. First time in years. It really made me feel good, you know, like taking a bath on the inside."

With that brief glimpse into her hidden personal life, she let the cross fall back in place and extracted a pack of cigarettes and a lighter from a small purse on the bar in front of her. She lit up, inhaled, and blew a cloud of smoke toward the ceiling while I watched, temporarily at a loss for words.

"Contrary to what most of the fellows think who come in here," she continued meditatively, "there's more to life than just getting laid."

"I agree," I said, turning my eyes back to the girl on the stage, at once erotically stimulated by Kim's uninhibited language and intellectually startled by her honesty.

But I was not there seeking truth. I was searching for a temporary escape from some of the accumulated psychological pressures and frustrations and defeats of recent months. And so, while I answered the flaxen-haired bar girl sitting beside me, I was responding on a different level to the visual message being projected by the stripper on the stage, who was now down to bra and panties and black mesh nylons.

"It's true," I finally responded, self-consciously refraining from the frank expression for sexual intercourse which she had used, "it isn't everything, but it's quite important."

Perhaps my remark jarred her back into a temporarily forgotten awareness of her occupational role there. She was there to induce me to spend as much money as possible, not just to be a sociable conversationalist, exchanging views on life with whoever came through the door.

"Hell, yes, it's important," she grinned, grinding out her cigarette in the ash tray. "I enjoy a good lay, I'll admit it. But it has to be with the right guy, not just any Tom, Dick, or Harry."

Then, encircling my waist with one arm, she sought my lips again. Her tongue forced my lips open and plunged into my mouth at the same time that her right hand slipped down onto my lap and then between my legs, with the deftness of one long practiced in performing such intimate handling of strangers. She discovered the reaction that had been produced, partly by the erotic displays of the strippers on the stage, and partly by her own unrestrained caressing and kissing.

"Christ, honey! You've got a real hard on," she exclaimed.

My mind registered shock at the almost blasphemous

incongruity of coupling that sacred name with a vulgar reference to the male sex organ, but my aroused desires stifled the offense which I ought to have felt more deeply and expressed vocally.

"Got any ideas as to what I should do about it?" I asked, looking into her eyes.

"Did you ever have it French kissed?" she asked.

As she squeezed gently with her right hand, a sly grin spread across her face, evoking memories of a Mother Goose story about a wolf inviting a pig to go to market with him.

"No, I never did," I answered, excited at the prospect of learning about this erotic enticement.

"If you've got five dollars, we can go in the back room and I'll show you how it's done," she purred.

Then, to reassure me that she was willing to do this only because she liked me so much, she added that "the five dollars is just for the use of the room."

I reached into my wallet, opened it away from her gaze so she could not see how much I had. When I had come into the Show Bar nearly an hour before, I had nine dollars and a little change to get home on. Since arriving there I had spent three dollars; one for my own beer, and two for Kim's drink. I had six dollars left. Unhesitatingly, I pulled out the five, returned my wallet to my hip pocket and handed the five to Kim.

"Come with me, honey," she smiled, and got off the bar stool as she tucked the five-dollar bill down into the front of her dress, between her breasts.

I followed her around the end of the bar. She paused a moment to lean over the bar and whisper something to the bartender, then led me to an alcove covered with curtains at the rear of the barroom. She pulled back the curtain and invited me to step inside. It was hardly more than a large-sized closet with a wooden bench along one side, long enough to accommodate two people.

"Unzip your pants and sit down, honey," she urged.

But before I could comply, the curtain was pulled back by

someone on the outside. A waitress stepped half way into the curtained closet, carrying a tray and a small glass of liquor.

"It's mouthwash, honey," Kim explained pleadingly, "we have to use it. Just costs two bucks. You can afford that, can't you?"

I pulled out my wallet and opened it for her inspection.

"Is that all you've got, honey?" she asked, dismayed, as she saw the one remaining dollar bill.

"That's all."

Kim spoke to the other bar girl with the tray of mouthwash, in what I immediately recognized as a language fad that had been popular when I was a high school student, a garbled form of English called "pig Latin." It had been so long since I had indulged in this childish grammar game that I didn't catch what she said. But the girl with the glass of "mouthwash" disappeared behind the curtain.

"I'm awfully sorry, honey," said Kim, sounding genuinely sympathetic, "if I had known that's all you had I wouldn't have brought you back here. But rules are rules, you know. If I break 'em I'll be out of a job."

I believed her, partly because she was a talented actress, and sounded and looked so sincere. I believed her also because my mental powers of discernment were doubtless dulled by the appetite which had been aroused within me, both by the dance exhibitions I had witnessed, and by her fondling at the bar. These had stimulated a need for the release of that primitive, orgasmic flood within me, held back, dammed up, pushing for release against the distended member of my body that her probing hands had teased into tautness. My mind clouded by sexual hunger, I saw only what I wanted to see; the release of that physical tension which had been built up within me since I had entered the bar.

"I'm afraid we'll have to go, honey," Kim said, facing me. "I'm not supposed to stay back here with a customer for more than five minutes."

I stood facing her, then put my arms around her waist and looked into her eyes. Then I spoke words that were spawned by the molten lava of sexual desire that was welling up within me, seeking release.

They were words that were compounded of the urge to escape from the memories of failure that had sent me bolting from O'Hare Field several hours before. They were words that were inflamed with the erotic displays of sight and touch to which I had been exposed since stepping into the dim, passion-heated interior of the Show Bar. They were words that had been spoken in ignorance and passion by men since time immemorial; words that had led too many times to disillusionment, divorce or despair. They were words that had frequently been both the root and the fruit of a double deception; their true nature hidden from the man who spoke them, and their consequences hidden from the woman who believed them. They were words that I had even spoken, in a far different setting, to the woman I married.

"I love you, Kim," I said, totally unaware of the incongruity of addressing such words to a virtual stranger.

"You can't love me, sweetheart," she protested gently, and with a gleam of what might have been pity in her eyes, "you don't even know me."

"I know that I want you to spend the night with me," I countered feverishly. "Will you?"

"Where, honey?"

"I'll get a room at a hotel," I blurted, my mind too clouded with desire to remember that I had only one dollar left in my wallet.

"Sure, honey," she answered, running her hands down the lapels of my coat, "I'll stay with you, but I don't get out of work until one o'clock in the morning."

"That's okay. Shall I pick you up then?"

"Sure, honey," she smiled patronizingly. "Come back about one o'clock. But we'd better go now, or I'll be in trouble with the boss."

Kim pushed aside the curtain and I followed her out of the alcove. Two more men had come into the place and were sitting at the bar, watching the brunette stripper who was nearing the climax of her near-nude dance. Beside me, Kim reached for my hand, squeezed it, and leaned close to whisper in my ear.

"I'd like to sit with you some more, honey, but I'll have to go and talk to some of the other customers for a while."

"I understand," I said, "business is business. I'll see you about one."

"Okay, honey," she smiled.

Perhaps it was only because of the shadow cast by the stripper on the stage that Kim's final smile seemed more like a smirk. As I left the bar, she approached one of the two new men who had come in, to ply her trade of getting a man to buy her drinks.

Ten minutes after leaving the gorgeous Girlie Show Bar, I drove into a gas station. The attendant who came out was youthful and friendly.

"What'll it be?" he grinned through the open window that I had rolled down.

"Depends on whether we can make a deal or not."

"What kind of a deal?"

"I've still got about two hundred and fifty miles to drive to Lansing, Michigan, and I'm almost broke. I was wondering if you'd let me have a tankful of gas and ten dollars cash, and take my wrist watch as security."

I slipped the watch off my wrist and handed it to him, immediately encouraged by the fact that he was interested enough to at least take the watch and scrutinize it.

"When I get back to Lansing," I explained as he looked at the watch, "I'll mail you back the money, and you can mail the watch back to me."

He held the watch to his ear.

"It's an eighty-five-dollar watch," I said, trying to push him into an affirmative decision.

"I know a Benrus is a good watch," he conceded, then asked to see my driver's license.

I handed him my driver's license. He looked at it a moment and grinned.

"I don't think I can lose too much on a deal like this," he said. "Even if you don't pay me, I ought to be able to get twenty-five dollars out of this watch."

Five minutes later, I pulled out of the gas station with a clean windshield, a tankful of gas, and ten dollars cash in my pocket. Several blocks from the service station, I pulled over to stop at a diner to get a bite to eat and to make a long distance phone call which I couldn't have made in the hearing of the attendant at the gas station. The phone call to Florence, claiming a broken fan belt which would require an overnight stay until I could get it replaced, was a bone thrown to the watchdog of conscience, to keep it from growling and disturbing my planned night of erotic forgetfulness with Kim. And after a penny-pinching lunch, I prepared to leave the diner and look for a hotel room and a night of revelry with the flaxen-haired stripper at the Gorgeous Girlie Show Bar.

"Do you know of a reasonable hotel around her?" I asked the matronly, gray-haired woman who took my money.

She directed me to a cheap, workingman's hotel five blocks away. I found the hotel to be old, but clean and quiet, and got a room for seven-fifty for Mr. and Mrs. John Smith.

"My wife will be in later," I told the elderly male desk clerk. "Oh, and by the way, could you let me know when it's twelve o'clock? I have to go out and get my wife, and I lost my watch earlier this evening."

"Yes, there's a phone in the room. I'll call you then."

I took the elevator to the fourth-floor room with double bed and bath. After a shower, I stretched out on the big, comfortable bed for two and a half hours of half-sleep fantasy, whetting my appetite for the night ahead by remembering the lascivious movements of the strippers I had seen in the Gorgeous Girlie Show Bar earlier, and visualizing again the erotic endowments of Kim in her tight, red dress.

At midnight, summoned to full wakefulness by the desk clerk, I got up, dressed, and walked out of the hotel lobby at 12:30. I still had half an hour before I was to pick up Kim at the Show bar, which was only five minutes away by car.

Pondering what to do in that half hour of waiting, I saw an advertising slogan of a local florist shop in the hotel lobby, "Say It With Flowers." Both my temperament and erotic expectations seized on the idea as one calculated to reinforce the evidently favorable impression I had already made on Kim. But where could I hope to find any flowers in Calumet City at such an hour, and at a price I could afford? I was certain there wouldn't be any florist shops open at such an hour. Even so, piqued with the idea, I got into my car and began to cruise the streets, looking for flowers; any kind, any place.

After what I guessed to be nearly twenty minutes of aimless driving, I was about ready to abandon my search when I saw something in the dark shadow of a house on the right side of the street just ahead. As I drew closer, I could see that it was indeed what I had first suspected—a border of flowers on someone's private lawn, growing close to the house. I stopped beside the house, noting that everyone in the house had either retired or was gone away, for the house was in darkness. Sitting there in the car, close to the curb, with the engine idling, I looked up and down the street which was devoid of cars and pedestrians. Although the side of the house where the flowers were growing was in shadows, from the nearby street intersection, a street lamp spilled enough illumination over the area so that I could readily be seen by anyone who happened to pass by and witness what I planned to do.

Then, quickly, furtively, I slipped out of the car, leaving the engine running, and stepped quietly across the sidewalk and onto the shadowed strip of lawn that bordered the sidewalk. A dew-moistened fragrance arose from the thickly clustered blossoms growing close to the house. I bent down and swiftly snatched a handful of the fragrant flowers, then hurriedly returned to the car, expecting at any moment to hear the sound of an outraged shout from an awakened occupant of the house, or the blast of a shotgun, aimed at a suspected burglar. But the only sounds punctuating the midnight stillness of the empty street were those I made; my heavy breathing, and the car door being opened and closed, quickly and quietly. Then, with the handful of stolen flowers on the seat beside me, I drove away, holding my breath until I was safely back on the well-lighted main street of Calumet City, without having heard the warning siren of a pursuing police car behind me.

I parked on the street near an all-night diner that was just a block from the Gorgeous Girlie Show Bar, to put a necessary finishing touch on the illegal transaction I had just committed in the name of love.

"What will you have, sir?" smiled the friendly, middle-aged waitress, as I sat down at the long lunch counter, along with several other customers.

"That depends on how much time I've got," I replied, looking down the length of the diner but seeing no clock on the wall. "Can you tell me what time it is?"

"Five minutes to one," she said, glancing at her wrist watch.

I ordered a cop of coffee and then, from the obliging waitress, borrowed a piece of paper, a pencil and a rubber band. She handed them to me with a knowing grin, obviously suspecting that a man who appeared off the street at one o'clock in the morning with a handful of flowers must be on a romantic mission. Between swallows of coffee, I inscribed a brief message to go along with the flowers.

"To Kim, the prettiest girl in Calumet City, from Garfield, with love."

I rolled the paper into a funnel shape, inserted the flowers in it, and twisted the rubber band around the middle of the bouquet. Then, sensing that it must be one o'clock, and not wanting to be late in picking up Kim, I left my half-finished cup of coffee, paid my check and hurried out, the primitively wrapped bouquet in my hand.

Had I still possessed a shred of sober objectivity in my thinking processes, I would have been able to grasp the utter absurdity and shame of my position as I walked down the brightly lit main street of a sex-saturated sin city, and would have been ridiculed into abandoning the venture at that moment. There I was, a middle-aged youth leader in the church, married for five years to a woman who was then pregnant with my first child, on my way at one o'clock in the morning, with a bouquet of stolen flowers, to a lust-born date with a honky-tonk stripper who wore a golden cross around her neck. But I couldn't see myself as I was, or as others who knew me would have seen me. For mentally mesmerized by the lurid, lustful anticipation of spending the night with Kim, my reason was as beclouded as that of any man under the influence of alcohol.

In the Gorgeous Girlie Show Bar at one o'clock, I sat down at the bar and laid the bouquet of flowers on the polished counter top. There were more men in the bar than there had been on my first visit earlier in the evening. I looked around for Kim, but she was not in sight. Probably backstage, changing into street clothes to go out with me, I thought. The stripper on the stage at the moment was the redhead with the upswept hairdo who had been on the stage when I had first came in. Then the bartender was in front of me.

"What'll it be?" he asked.

This time I knew the right answer to his question.

"Blatz."

A moment later, he set a foaming glass of the brew on the counter in front of me and swept up my dollar. I had scarcely lifted the glass to my mouth when I felt a hand on my shoulder. I turned, expecting to see Kim. But it wasn't her. It was the brunette who had been performing on the stage during the time I had sat at the bar talking with Kim earlier.

"Hi, honey," she pouted, duplicating Kim's approach, both in wording and honeyed voice, "how about buying me a drink?"

"Sorry," I smiled, "I'm just here to pick up Kim."

"You're too late, sweetheart," she replied. "Kim left with her boy friend about half an hour ago."

The stunned disbelief which I felt must have shown on my face.

"Honest, hon," she repeated emphatically, "I saw her go out myself about half an hour ago. Why would I lie to you?"

"She told me to pick her up here at one o'clock."

"Kim's like that," the brunette explained with seeming sympathy, and shrugging her shoulders as if mystified. "She'll make a date with one guy, then go out with somebody else. She's sort of unpredictable; you know what I mean?"

Only at that moment did it occur to me that I had been taken; that Kim's promise had been made just to get rid of me; that she had not intended to be around when I returned. And the reported "boy friend" might have been some stranger who had come in after I did, who had struck her fancy more than I had, or someone with more money in his wallet than she knew I had—just one dollar when I had left earlier. I slid off the stool and started toward the door.

"Thanks for being honest," I said over my shoulder to the brunette bar girl.

"Hey, what about your flowers?" she called as I reached the door. "Want me to give them to Kim?"

I paused at the door before opening it and turned back to see her inhaling their night-dewed fragrance. Probably real flowers were seldom seen in the honky-tonk bars of Calumet City.

"Give them to anybody who appreciates flowers," I said.

"Gee, thanks, mister," she called after me, as I stepped out and closed the door behind me.

On the street, in front of the Gorgeous Girlie Show Bar, in the greenish glare of the overhead light, the street suddenly seemed dirtier than it had when I first arrived. And I felt dirty; and empty. I stood there a moment deliberating what to do next. The hotel room would seem lonely and drab and uninviting after having envisioned being there with Kim. I looked into my wallet and saw that I had three dollars left, plus some change, from the ten that the gas station attendant had loaned me. I could spend a dollar and the change I had and still have two dollars for breakfast in the morning before starting the long drive to Lansing.

I walked down the street, eyeing the posters outside the striptease bars, all of which were still open. At several of the places I passed, a male attendant stood on the sidewalk by the door, like a circus sideshow barker, trying to induce the mostly male pedestrians to come inside.

"No cover charge! Continuous show! Best show in town! Beautiful girls!"

They all sang the same song in an effort to get more business, somewhat slack in recent days because of a steel strike then in progress. I paused in front of the Torrid Tropicana Strip Cabaret, partly because there was no uniformed huckster in front trying to urge me inside. Impelled by a need to fill the emptiness I felt with noise, movement, and the presence of other people, I stepped inside. This cabaret was much roomier than the Gorgeous Girlie Show Bar, but the basic commodities were the same—sexual and alcoholic stimulation.

Just inside the door and stretching back about a third of the way along the wall on one side was a long bar with stools. Beyond the bar jutting out into the center of the room was the stage where the strippers performed. Fanning out from the stage in all directions were tables for customers, only half a dozen of them occupied at the moment by single males and couples. At the bar, perched on stools like vultures waiting for males like myself to come in, were several bar girls who intermixed their stripping with attempts to coax male customers into buying them drinks. I sat down at a table next to the stage and ordered a beer from the miniskirted waitress who came to the table promptly. It was only several minutes later that one of the bar-girl strippers, a platinum blonde, approached me with a honeyed plea to buy her a drink. I gave her a blunt rundown of my financial situation.

"Sorry, but I've got just enough money to buy one bottle of beer for myself."

The exotically painted face that had seemed reasonably attractive when illuminated with a smile suddenly puckered into a sour expression. There was disdain and disbelief in her eyes as she mentally wrote me off as a tightwad rather than what I really was, a poor man on the very doorstep of destitution.

"Well, don't spend all your money in one place, Buster," she sneered sarcastically, and stalked away in a hip-swinging exodus from the vicinity of my table.

As I watched her walk away from my table indignantly, the impression of her disdainfully puckered face as she had spoken to me triggered a bizarre trick of memory superimposure in my mind. For some strange reason, that fleeting expression of disgust on her face brought to my mind the spinsterly prune face of a film comedienne of my boyhood moviegoing days, with a name as funny as her screen antics, Zazu Pitts. As I continued sitting there, unruffled by the bar girl's understandable show of irritation at my inability to spend money on her for drinks, I sipped my glass of beer slowly and meditatively to make it last as long as possible because I couldn't afford another one.

Idly watching while one stripper after another came on stage and disrobed to the beat of sensuous music, I wasn't really seeing the action or being aroused by what I was looking at. I was too preoccupied, thinking about my past, my present, and my uncertain future, as I groped for some formula that would enable me to achieve success of some kind in a life that thus far had been only a series of failures. I let my thoughts wander where they would and, surprisingly, they were drawn to the long-forgotten film comedienne, Zazu Pitts, whose name and image had been evoked in my mind by the swift change of expression on the face of the bar girl who had just left my table.

The film comedienne's name, held in my conscious mind, was like a magnet drawing metal filings to itself. It drew from the forgotten files of memory, along with the dimly remembered features of the spinsterly screen star, a scrap of information about her personal life that I had read somewhere years before. Abruptly, I straightened up in my chair, suddenly completely oblivious of the erotic undulations of the stripper almost at my elbow, as I stared into the darkness at the far end of the half-empty cabaret and saw a vital correspondence between the life of a film celebrity of another day and my own failure-frustrated life.

An invading insight about myself, such as sometimes overtakes people in an hour of desperation, like a flash of lightening illuminating an entire countryside, seemed to reveal vital connecting links between a long-forgotten fact about a bygone film star, my own failure-flayed life and the newly acquired chauffeur's license in my inside coat pocket. These separate elements were suddenly joined together in a golden, gleaming continuum that was like a road leading into a Promised Land of the success that had long eluded me. But at that moment, standing startled on the brink of an amazing discovery about myself, my stream of thought was broken into as a sensually endowed bar-girl stripper in a tight-fitting dress of silvery, metallic material, and coal black hair, stepped up to my table, apparently undaunted by having seen one of her cohorts unsuccessfully solicit me for drinks only moments earlier.

"Hi," she said, her crimson lips parting in a friendly smile and her mascara-laden eyelashes winking as she pulled out a chair opposite me, "like some company?"

As I looked up at her, preparing to give her a rundown of my financial situation that would doubtless turn her away, I noted that she had on enough jewelry to have done credit to a member of royalty or to a movie star. She had rings on her fingers, bracelets around her wrists, and dangling, crystal earrings that shimmered in the subdued ceiling light that fell over the table. I was not stirred by the scintillating sexuality she projected as an essential part of her job there. My interest in sexual excitement as a way of temporary escape from my problems had been completely extinguished by the trickery which had been practiced on me at the Gorgeous Girlie Show Bar up the street. But I was eager to find listening and sympathetic ears into which I could pour my newfound knowledge about myself and the direction for future success to which it pointed. But I assumed that she had approached my table, like her turned-away predecessor, not to listen to me talk, but to get me to spend money on her, which I didn't have to spend.

"I'm sorry," I said, as she sat down, reluctant to see her smile turn into a grimace, "but I . . ."

"I know what you're going to say," she interrupted, with a smile instead of a pout, as she placed a small, jeweled hand purse on the table in front of her. "I heard what you said to Dorothy a few minutes ago. That's not why I stopped by. I wouldn't even think of asking a guy who's down to his last dollar to buy me a drink. My name's Roseanne; they call me Rose around here. What's your name?"

"Garfield."

At that moment, like a distant vulture spotting its prey, the waitress who had brought me a bottle of beer when I first came in, swooped down on us. She was a middle-aged, peroxide blonde without the necessary looks or shape to double as a stripper.

"What'll it be, Rose?" she asked, looking at the blackhaired stripper sitting across from me, "your usual?"

"Not this time, Jennifer. Just bring me a ginger ale, and put it on my account. I'm paying for it."

The waitress stared at her, dumbfounded.

"How do you expect to make any money in this joint that way?" she demanded incredulously, "buying your own drinks?"

"Look, Jennifer," the stripper snapped, peevishly snapping shut the purse from which she had extracted cigarettes and a jeweled cigarette holder, "I've been sitting on that damn bar stool for three hours waiting for business to come in. I'm about due for a little relaxation."

Obviously miffed at having her advice spurned, the waitress turned her attention to me.

"How about you, sir?" she asked, noting that my glass of beer was two-thirds gone, "can I bring you another drink?"

"No, thank you," I replied, picking up the tall glass and swirling around the golden liquid that filled the bottom two inches of the glass, "I've had my quota for tonight."

217

With a look of disdain like that of Dorothy, the bar girl who had approached me earlier and left with a sarcastic remark, she turned away to get a ginger ale for my companion. As Roseanne artfully inserted a cigarette in her jeweled cigarette holder, such as I hadn't seen since the movies of long ago, I felt momentarily tongue tied, my mind still mesmerized by the prospect that I had stumbled upon a key to finding the success that had thus far eluded me in life, just before Roseanne had broken into my stream of thought about Zazu Pitts.

Across the table, Roseanne, lighting up her cigarette, exhaled a stream of smoke ceilingward and, holding up the jeweled cigarette holder for my inspection, offered a word of explanation.

"I don't use this when I'm alone," she explained, "it's just part of the femme fatale mystique I try to project on the job. The fellows who come in here are likely to buy more drinks for me if they think I'm a high-class broad."

I exchanged an understanding grin, impressed that she was sharing with me one of the necessary tricks of her trade for making a living by not only stripping, but hustling drinks from the mostly male customers who came in.

"I really just stopped by to apologize for Dorothy and the smart-ass crack she made when she left your table," continued Roseanne, tapping the ash from the end of her cigarette. "She's kind of down because she's behind on her car payments. She's got a kid in the hospital, and business has really been bad the last couple of weeks since the steel strike started. A lot of the guys who come in here work in the steel mills, and when they don't have any money to spare after they pay their rent and grocery bills, they just don't come in. But I guess you know how that is. You been hit hard by the steel strike, too, I guess, hunh?"

"No, I don't live around here. I live in Lansing, Michigan, which is about 250 miles from here. I just brought my brother-in-law to O'Hare airport so he could catch a plane for California. I was on my way back home and just stopped off here for a little . . . well, uh, entertainment, you might say."

"I see," smiled Roseanne somewhat condescendingly, "I gather you're more interested in the broads than the booze."

"You might say that," I agreed lamely, suddenly feeling embarrassed at the remembrance of the lust-fed fiasco I had been through an hour earlier at the Gorgeous Girlie Show Bar up the street.

"What line of work are you in up in Lansing, Garfield?" she asked, eyeing me appraisingly as she inhaled deeply of her cigarette.

"Just a clerk in the Highway Department there," I admitted apologetically, "but I might be getting into something different. It's just something I thought of since I came in here. As a matter of fact, your friend Dorothy kind of brought it into my mind."

Her accented eyebrows arched in surprise, Roseanne ejected a stream of smoke through her pursed lips as she stared at me in bewilderment.

"I must have missed part of what she said. I didn't hear her say anything except that nasty crack about not spending all your money in one place."

"It wasn't something she said," I explained, "it was the way she looked when she said it."

"The way she looked?"

"Yeah, for some strange reason, the sour expression on her face when she spoke reminded me of a prune-faced film comedienne I used to see in the movies when I was a boy. Her name was Zazu Pitts. She's been long gone from the movie world; probably before your time, right?"

"I can't say I recall the name," admitted the stripper, after pausing to ransack her memory, "but what's she got to do with you?"

Before I could reply, the waitress was back at our table. Setting down the ginger ale Roseanne had ordered in front of her, she added a warning in a confidentially lowered tone of voice.

"If I were you, Rose," she cautioned, bending down over the stripper so her voice wouldn't carry beyond the area of our table, "I wouldn't spend too much time with a customer who isn't buying any drinks. I don't think the boss will like it. And with business the way it's been lately, it wouldn't take much to push Jason into giving you your walking papers from this place."

"Thanks, Jennifer," said the stripper, eyeing the waitress with an expression of resentment for her unwanted counsel, "but don't worry about me. I can take care of myself, and I'll talk with anyone I want to."

"Maybe I'd better move on," I proposed, pushing back my chair as the waitress walked away. "I wouldn't want you to get in trouble on my account."

"Sit still," urged Roseanne, "I can handle the boss. We've had differences before. He knows how hard it is to find gals with the shape to be strippers, who are willing to con the creeps and sex perverts who come in here into buying them drinks. I'm not putting you in that class, understand. It isn't often I get a chance to talk with a real gentleman. So relax. I'd really like to hear what else you were going to say about this Zazu . . ."

"Pitts," I supplied, as she groped for the last name.

"Yeah, I'd really like to know what she could have to do with your deciding to change your line of work just since you came in this place."

Reassured of her sincere interest and that she was not in danger of losing her job over me, I pushed my chair back up to the table. Evidently intrigued by what I was going to say, Roseanne snuffed out her cigarette and returned her jeweled cigarette holder to her purse.

"Like I was saying about this Zazu Pitts," I resumed, as Roseanne, arms folded on the table in front of her, regarded me intently, "after Dorothy walked away from my table, I started thinking about this old-time move comedienne. For some strange reason, I remembered something that had happened in her life that I had read about years ago. It was after she had achieved a modest success as a funny girl on the stage. She became obsessed with a desire to become a straight, dra-

God, a Man, and a Woman

matic actress. She begged for a chance to do a dramatic role, and got what she asked for. But in her first straight dramatic role, everything she said on the stage, even though it was dead serious, came out sounding so funny that the audiences roared with laughter. Her first dramatic role was a success as far as box office sales were concerned, but a terrible personal failure in realizing her ambition to become a dramatic actress. So she gave up on the hope of ever becoming a dramatic star and settled for playing funny roles for which she had a natural talent. So as a comedienne, she went on to be a great success, in films as well as on stage."

"So what does this have to do," asked Roseanne, looking baffled, "with getting into a different kind of work from the job you've got now, which I presume you don't like any more than I like being a drink-hustling stripper in this crummy joint?"

"It came to me," I explained pensively, looking into the gloom at the far perimeters of the cabaret, "as I was thinking about that episode from the life of Zazu Pitts, that maybe the reason I haven't achieved the success I want in a vocation is because I haven't gotten into a kind of work where I can make use of a natural aptitude I have, instead of fighting against it."

"What kind of work is that?" asked Roseanne, genuinely curious.

I paused before answering, as a veritable Niagara of remembered impressions from the past poured through my mind. It was a panorama of scenes that made up my sexual history, beginning in the pre-adolescent years when the emerging spark of sexual attraction within me had been fanned into flame by the furtive inspections of girlie magazines in the local drug store. In swift succession, there flowed through my mind humiliating episodes from the following years when I had fought a hidden battle to suppress or sublimate this aroused sexual proclivity within myself. It was because I had lost the battle too many times in this area of my life that I had felt compelled to abandon preparations for the ministry as my life work; a major decision for which the sub-

terranean motivation had been concealed from Florence, my
wife; from the Dean of students, faculty members and fellow
students at Moody Bible Institute in Chicago; and subsequently hidden also from the pastor, deacons and members of
Gilead Baptist Church in Charlotte, Michigan, who had elected me to be, of all things, a youth leader. So I had left Moody
and Chicago in moral and spiritual defeat. Now, a little more
than a year after leaving Moody and preparations for the ministry, I was back in the midst of scenes much like those I had
formerly frequented in downtown Chicago.

It was in such seductive settings, I silently soliloquized,
that I had been waylaid, like Samson in the Old Testament,
and shorn of my spiritual strength and purity by the painted
Delilah's of the strip-tease bars, the burlesque theatres, and the
adult movie arcades. Calumet City, where I sat across from a
painted princess of the Tropicana Strip Cabaret, reviewing my
past and planning my future, was a realistic replica of the sordid scenes I had fled on State Street in Chicago; more brazen
in its display of female flesh on the outside, and more daring
in its obscene exhibitions inside; due, perhaps, to the proximity to the Indiana state line, just outside the doors, a legal and
easily accessible refuge of escape in case of an unlikely raid by
police.

"So why keep fighting a losing battle?" I silently asked
myself, as Roseanne, gazing at me intently, sat patiently waiting for a word of explanation to her curiosity-prompted query.

"This is your natural environment," I mused silently, seeking to crystallize a host of remembered experiences into an
abbreviated statement of insight and intention that I could
share with the woman who sat across from me, "the business
of marketing sexual stimulation and satisfaction to lust-hungry
men. This is where you should find a place for yourself. This is
where you can finally achieve success because you have an
absorbing passion of long years standing in the subject, and
you've got creativity and imagination, the prerequisites of success in any field."

"Well," Roseanne finally broke into my stream of thoughts

apologetically, "if I'm getting too nosey with my questions, just say so, and I'll leave."

"It's not that," I assured her, meeting her intent gaze, "it's just that there's so much to say that it's difficult to put into words."

I paused, sobered and saddened by the irresistible conclusion I had been persuaded to adopt, then plunged into the attempted explanation which she had patiently waited to hear from me.

"You'd like to know," I began somberly, "what line of work I think I should get into that I have a natural aptitude for, which I've been resisting for a long time the same way that Zazu Pitts once resisted her natural flair for comedy, which resulted in failure for her. I was just thinking before you sat down, that after all my failures in life, perhaps I could achieve success in a business something like this."

I waved my hand in a circle to take in the darkened, empty far perimeters of the strip cabaret, ending by pointing toward the stripper on the nearby stage who was in the initial stage of disrobing to the beat of sensuous music.

"The business of selling sexual services to lust-hungry men, like the ones who come in here," I continued. "For years, I've tried to resist being pulled in this direction. I gave up preparations for the ministry as my life work because of my failure to overcome this inclination. They say that water seeks its own level, and when I was preparing for the ministry in Chicago several years ago, something in my makeup just drew me irresistibly to the strip-tease bars on State Street in downtown Chicago, much like this one, and to the burlesque theatres and the adult movies. So instead of fighting this inclination any longer, I have decided to yield to it and let it carry me where it will. Maybe it will be like a tide carrying a ship to a distant port where it can unload its cargo and make a fabulous profit and, in the process, bring me the success I've been seeking so long."

Roseanne gazed at me intently, toying with her glass of ginger ale, appearing both amused and amazed at the chain of reasoning which had been triggered in my mind by a simple, fleeting facial expression on the part of one of her fellow bargirl strippers.

"You mean you're thinking of opening a place like this back in Lansing?"

"No, that's not exactly what I had in mind."

I hesitated before proceeding, thinking that my companion, who had been reasonably friendly and interested in my life up to this point, might suddenly change her attitude and get up and leave when I told her of the change in occupation I had been contemplating.

"I was thinking of a sideline that wouldn't require so much capital to get started, and would probably bring in a bigger income in less time than a place like this."

"What could that be?" Roseanne asked, appearing intrigued by my cryptic comment.

For answer, I reached into my inside coat pocket and pulled out the envelope from the city clerk's office in Lansing that I had gotten before leaving for Chicago. I pulled the license out of the envelope and held it up for her inquiring gaze.

"A chauffeur's license?" she asked, looking baffled. "How do you figure that's going to make you more money with less outlay than by opening up a place like this?"

"I'm going to start driving a cab part time in addition to my regular job," I explained, "when I get back to Lansing."

"I think you're kidding yourself if you think you're going to make a bundle that way," she retorted quickly. "Some of the guys who drive cabs in this town come in here and they aren't rolling in dough, let me tell you. Some of 'em are just making enough to make ends meet; especially the ones with a family."

"I'm thinking of something else besides just picking up cab fares when I'm driving the cab," I added. "It was something that came to me after Dorothy walked away from my table. I remembered something that was on the chauffeur's license application that I wondered about at the time. It was a promise not to use the vehicle I would be driving for 'immoral purposes.' And it just came to me while I was sitting here thinking, what the City Council must have had in mind when they included that pledge in the application. They probably realized that in any big city, the connecting link between out-of-town male visitors and prostitutes is the taxi driver."

"That's different," agreed Roseanne, seeming not to be offended by my salacious scheme. "I'm sure you could make some money that way as long as the vice squad doesn't catch up with you. Some of the girls here are into that. One I know makes a hundred bucks every time she goes out with a guy. I've even been propositioned a few times myself. But I've been leery about getting involved. I've heard too many stories in this town about weirdos who beat up girls if they don't do everything they're told to do, and sometimes the jerks don't even pay off like they promised. One girl from one of the other bars got killed here by some nut she went out with about a year ago. So I've never really been tempted to get into that, even though it does pay more money for less work than hustling drinks and stripping."

"I'd never let any woman who worked for me be physically abused like that," I countered spontaneously. "I'd screen the customers and weed out the sickos, and maybe even have a bodyguard on hand so if the woman working for me was in danger, she could blow a whistle or holler and get help on the spot. And since the woman would be doing the dirtiest part of the deal, I'd see that she got the biggest share of the profits."

"There might be a chance of getting into some big money in a city the size of Chicago or Detroit," Roseanne observed thoughtfully, "but is Lansing big enough to make a go of it?"

"Maybe not if I just relied on conventions and out-of-town visitors, but just three miles from Lansing is a wide-open market, Michigan State University, with thousands of students. There must be at least five or ten thousand hungry males among those students who would be interested in buying the product I'd be selling. So once business got going, I could quit driving a cab part time and maybe my job with the state as well, and develop this into a full-time business enterprise."

"There might be a potential market there," Roseanne nodded approvingly.

Then, still feeling the sting of having been sexually swindled at the Gorgeous Girlie Show Bar down the street, I added an emphatic pledge.

"And when I do get into the business of selling solid sexual satisfaction to hungry males, you can be sure of one thing. I'll see that they get their erotic dollar's worth. I won't trick them out of their money by promising satisfaction that won't be produced after they've shelled out their money."

In response to what I thought must have sounded like a shocking change of vocational direction to the bar-girl stripper who sat regarding me soberly, and with an expression that seemed to sympathize with my struggle to achieve success, she voiced a concern that up to that time had not entered my mind.

"You said you came down here to bring your brother-in-law to O'Hare airport. That means you're married, but not too happily, I gather; right?"

"Right on both counts," I conceded, reluctantly.

"Were you planning on telling your wife about this new business sideline you're going to get into?"

"No way," I replied, toying with my nearly empty beer glass and visualizing the explosion of moral outrage on Florence's part if she were told. "She'd tell me to get out of the house and probably start a divorce."

"If she's like that, and she ever found out what business you were into, you could expect a divorce then. Are you ready for that?"

"If that's what it takes to achieve success," I pledged grimly.

Then, grasping what was hidden from Roseanne; the bizarre contradiction between this proposed business venture and my position as a professing Christian and lay leader in the church, I added a bitterly voiced commentary on my plan for a form of vocational success that might supplant my previous failures in life in this area.

"Maybe," I mused, gazing into the physical darkness at the outer edges of the cabaret, and the spiritual darkness that was gathering over my projected future, "I'll achieve the dubious distinction of becoming the world's first Christian prince of prostitution."

"Hey, Rose!"

Like an unexpected gun shot, we were both startled by a harsh, masculine voice at our elbows. We both looked up to see a stocky, short, baldheaded man in sport clothes staring down at us, one pudgy hand resting authoritatively on the edge of our table.

"I'm not paying you," he continued to my companion, disclosing his identity as her boss, "to sit and socialize with customers who don't buy drinks for the girls."

"I just sat down here for a few minutes, Jason," she retorted defensively, looking up at him, "to give my butt a break from sitting on that bar stool waiting for business to come in."

"Maybe if you'd get outside on the sidewalk," he rebutted angrily, "and wiggle your ass a little instead of sitting on it so much, we'd have more business coming into this place."

I sat there, a dumb spectator of the bitter employee-employer altercation, unable to think of anything to say in defense of the stripper who had befriended me. But Roseanne didn't need my defense.

"Listen, Jason," she replied heatedly, looking up at him, "when it comes to wiggling my ass for a living, I'll do it up on that stage, but I'll be damned if I'll do it out on the sidewalk for you or anyone else."

Unruffled, as if accustomed to such spats with the women who worked for him, he glanced toward the front door momentarily, then continued, lowering his voice.

"Well, listen to me, Rose baby. There's a guy who just came in, sitting at a table by the door. You get your ass back there and sweet talk him into buying something more than a bottle of beer for himself, or you'll be back in the kitchen washing dishes instead of sitting out here like a movie queen."

"I get the message, Jason," she said coldly, getting up and picking up her hand purse from the table.

Angrily, she whirled away from my table and began walking in the direction of the potential new customer that Jason had pointed out. Then, seeming little mollified by Roseanne's grudging obedience to his command, he directed his still-simmering hostility toward me.

"As for you, buddy, you've about used up your parking time here for one bottle of beer. If you aren't going to buy any more drinks for yourself or the girls, go somewhere else."

I felt that I had no grounds for rebuttal. His criticism, from the standpoint of a businessman seeking a profit from his business enterprise, was justified. I had probably been there for over an hour, dawdling over one glass of beer, ignoring for the most part the live entertainment on the stage by my table, as I had groped for a formula for success in my own life, and had indeed found one through the unwitting assistance of one of his bar-girl strippers.

"I was just leaving," I said, getting up, meeting his hostile stare.

The belligerent bouncer boss turned away as I started to thread my way between the mostly empty tables on my way to the door. As I saw Roseanne sitting at a table with the man Jason had directed her to, she beckoned and called my name.

"Hey, Garfield, come here a minute."

I walked over to her table and she introduced me to her customer, a grubby-looking middle-aged man in work clothes named Bufford, whom she had evidently talked into buying her several drinks, since there were several empty, thimble-sized glasses on the table in front of her.

"I just wanted to give you my phone number, Garfield," she said, handing me a small card. "In case you're down this way again, give me a call. If I'm not working, maybe we can go out for the evening someplace, away from this crummy joint. And when you get your new business set up in Lansing, give me a call. If business doesn't pick up pretty soon, they'll be locking the doors on this place, and I'll be looking for another job. I might even be willing to go to work for you if the setup's right and the pay is decent."

"Thanks, Roseanne," I said, touched by the concern of a total stranger for my future, and shoved her card into my pocket. "I'll remember that. Been nice talking to you."

With a farewell wave of the hand to Roseanne and her male companion, I turned away and stepped through the swinging doors of the Torrid Tropicana Strip Cabaret. On the sidewalk, just outside the door, I lifted my right hand to look at my watch, to be momentarily shocked by the forgotten fact that I no longer had a watch. It was several blocks away, in the custody of a gas-station attendant who had unknowingly financed a proposed night of revelry with a bar-girl stripper who instead had stood me up, sentencing me to spend the night alone in a lonely hotel room.

I walked a block down the mostly deserted street, past other strip joints and X-rated theatres still open for business, to the little diner where, more than an hour before, I had written a note of sex-sotted endearment to Kim that she would probably never read. But even if she did, I reflected bitterly, it would only be to laugh at the sucker who had taken her "come-on" seriously. When I stepped inside the diner, I was relieved to see that the waitress from whom I had borrowed writing materials earlier had been replaced by a matronly, gray-haired grandmother. From her, I ordered all that my rapidly dwindling resources could afford—a bowl of chili and a glass of milk, which would leave me a dollar for a skimpy breakfast.

Strung out along the counter of the all-night eatery, several other men sat hunched over their post-midnight meals of hamburgers and black coffee. They all had the haggard expressions of men who had sought escape from their problems in a round of visual and liquid stimulants available on the street outside. But finally, like myself, perhaps weary in body, impoverished financially, they had come back to the reality facing them in the drab light of the fast-approaching dawn. As I sat at the counter, taking long swallows of milk between spoonsful of the hot, highly seasoned chili, I was thankful that someone stepped over to the juke box at the rear of the diner and inserted some coins.

The country music that came billowing through the diner drove away the weary silence that was punctuated listlessly by tired voices. It helped to chase away my awareness of the feelings of frustration and emptiness that had piled up within me as a result of the long evening, completely devoid of any real satisfaction. Since fleeing O'Hare Field earlier in the day, I had found in Calumet City a few fleeting moments of escape on the wild floodtide of sexual excitement. But I was now reaping the mental and psychological hangover; the spent fury of having been tricked and cheated; the thwarted feeling of having a basic hunger aroused to fever pitch, then left unslaked.

It was like the experience of a thirst-crazed desert wanderer, dashing forward to a suddenly spied fountain of life-giving water, only to stoop down and lift dry sand to his lips.

As I sat at the lunch counter, alternately chilled by the cold milk and warmed by the steaming chili, with my inner emptiness pushed to the periphery of my awareness by the invading music, I thought of something that Kim, the fickle, flaxen-haired stripper, had said to me in the curtained, closet-like back room at the Gorgeous Girlie Show Bar, the evil effects of which had not been completely washed out of my system by the few preceding moments of truly meaningful communication with Roseanne in the Torrid Tropicana Strip Cabaret.

In the heat of lust, unable to grasp the possibility that I had been tricked into parting with five dollars for a promise of sexual gratification that had not been delivered, driven by the compulsion to release the seething life-force that had been generated within me, I had spoken some words to her, spontaneously, without any thought of their purely chemical origin or the bizarre setting in which they had been uttered.

"I love you, Kim."

Her answer came back to me with an inflection of pity that I had missed at the time.

"You can't love me, sweetheart. You don't even know me."

As I thought of the brief exchange, it suddenly struck me as a new idea that there could be a vital connection between knowing a woman and loving her. It occurred to me that had I been more keenly aware of my emotions and completely honest in expressing them, I might have worded the nature of her attraction for me differently. And I realized, in clear-minded retrospect, that the pathetic episode of gathering up a handful of stolen flowers to carry to Kim had only been a personality peculiarity on my part. It said nothing about the nature of the inner force which had prompted that foolish gesture. Both a gift of flowers and forcible rape, I reflected, could spring from the same elemental male urge to copulate.

Then my mind was drawn irresistibly to a long backward look, to my first meeting with Florence. Had I meant something more when I had first spoken those three words, "I love you," to Florence before our marriage, than when I had spoken them to Kim? Whatever the difference in kind or degree, it was obvious to me, in looking back, that I had hardly known Florence any better than the sex-arousing bar girl who had objected that I couldn't love her because I didn't even know her. If Florence had not objected the first time I used those words, perhaps it was only because she was not as well acquainted with the sexual nature of men as Kim had evidently become in her work as a bar girl.

But Kim, the honky-tonk bar girl and stripper, had left me with more than a disturbing question about the nature of the attraction that had led to my marriage with Florence. She had also sparked in my mind a resolution that, in the unsavory business I had decided to launch when I returned to Lansing of selling sexual services to hungry males, I would not treat a customer the way I had been treated—induced to spend money for promised satisfaction which would not be provided. If I was going to be a successful whoremaster, I would be an honest one. I would see that the customer got all that was promised to him. There would be a label on the package of sexual satisfaction that he was buying, and the package would contain all that the label advertised. I would see that the customer got his erotic dollar's worth, a guideline for my envisioned business that I had fiercely voiced to Roseanne in the Torrid Tropicana.

Then, my austere, early-morning snack finished, I left the diner to walk down the street to my car. As I again passed the Gorgeous Girlie Show Bar, still open for the kind of "sucker" business I had given them earlier, it evoked a new flood of disgust and anger within me at having been sexually swindled there. I had forgotten that I had disregarded two warnings that had been given me before entering the place; one from sinful men, and the other from a holy God.

Entering the lobby of the hotel at two-thirty in the morning, I was relieved to see a different desk clerk on duty. There would be no need to explain why "Mrs. Smith" was not coming in with me. And up in my room, as I removed change and keys from my coat pockets, I pulled out two disparate items that were to be prophetic of my future. One was the card containing Roseanne the stripper's phone number, which I tucked into a hidden compartment of my wallet for possible future reference. The other was a crumpled Gospel tract I had been given earlier in the day when I was leaving O'Hare airport after Brady's plane had taken off.

Unfolding the crumpled tract that I had thrust into my pocket angrily at the time, my curiosity was aroused by the cover picture. It was an illustration of a locomotive engine racing down a train track with a string of cars in its wake and an engineer visible in the window of the cab. I read the opening words beneath the arresting illustration.

"Like the engineer of a fast express train, who doesn't know that a bridge on the track ahead of him has been washed out, you too may be on your way to destruction without knowing it."

That was enough for me. Angrily, I wadded up the tract and threw it into the wastebasket. Then I undressed and piled into bed, alone instead of in the company of a seductive woman, and immediately fell into the sleep of sheer physical and emotional exhaustion.

Back in Lansing, Michigan by noon the next day, Monday, after four strenuous hours of fast and furious driving, I called Florence at her job from the lobby of the Gray building. She had called my boss earlier that morning to explain that I was stranded overnight in Chicago with car trouble and wouldn't be in until noon. My answers to her questions were a mixture of fabrication and fact. I told her that I had hocked my watch—not in the hope of spending the night in a hotel room with a honky-tonk stripper, but in order to get the broken fan belt replaced. And then, the new business venture which I had conceived in the Torrid Tropicana Strip Cabaret, in Calumet City, met its first show of resistance from Florence; at least the part of the scheme that Florence knew about—the part-time taxi-driving job.

"You'll be picking me up to go home tonight, won't you?" she asked.

"I was planning on starting the new job tonight."

"You mean you're still serious about that taxi-driving deal?" she exploded, as if she had thought the long drive to and from Chicago would have pushed it out of my mind.

"Yes, I'm still serious about it."

Now I had an even stronger motive, however disreputable, for taking on the job.

"So that means you haven't changed your mind about resigning as Young People's leader at the church?"

"I haven't changed my mind, and I doubt if Pastor Savage has changed his," I answered, reminding her that it was the pastor, not myself, who had originally introduced the idea of my resigning.

"It's the stupidest thing I ever heard of," Florence snorted, repeating a phrase she had previously coined to express her disgust when I had first broached it to her before leaving for Chicago.

I ignored the contempt in her tone and tried to think rationally of the need to make arrangements for Florence to get home to Charlotte from work that night.

"You'll be able to get a ride home in the car pool, won't you?"

"I suppose so," came her disgruntled reply.

But there was another little transportation problem that would arise on each of the three nights I planned to drive a cab. Getting to Charlotte in the car pool would be no problem, but the five miles from downtown Charlotte to her mother's farm would be. She couldn't, and wouldn't, ask members of the car pool to drive her that far out of their way to get her home.

"Can you call your mother when you get to Charlotte, and have her come and get you?"

"Don't worry about me," she snapped, displaying her fiercely independent spirit, "I can take care of myself."

"I'll be home about . . ."

Bang! The receiver on the other end was either dropped or thrown into its cradle on the desk in her office, cutting off my sentence in the middle. I replaced the receiver on the pay phone slowly and sat there in the phone booth, wrapped in sad, silent meditation. Had she but pleaded with me, even at this late stage, to abandon the part-time job, I might well have capitulated. Had she shed one tear of entreaty, I would not have been able to resist her. But it was not in Florence's make-up to beg anyone for anything, not even her husband. Her scathing indictment of the part-time cab driving job had only hardened my resolve to continue on the course I had charted.

But that night, at five o'clock quitting time, the cumulative effects of having been up half the night before in the honky-tonk hideouts of Calumet City, and the long drive to Lansing that morning, had wearied me to the point of calling Jim Garvey, the youthful manager of Courteous Cab, and suggesting a compromise plan for the evening. I proposed my coming over for a briefing session, to have him show me all I needed to know, then I would start driving on Wednesday night of that week. He accepted my proposal.

It was after six o'clock, after the night shift drivers had all checked out, that I sat beside Jim Garvey in one of the cabs behind the big service garage while he instructed me in the elemental operations of driving a cab. He had no inkling, of course, that since he had first interviewed me a week before, that the job had become for me a potential means of implementing a private sideline business of my own which would prove to be much more lucrative than the meager wages I would earn as a driver. It was even possible, I speculated, that in time, my income from the private sideline I expected to launch might even exceed his salary as manager of the cab company.

"That's about it," he concluded, after an instruction period that had lasted about forty minutes. "Any questions?"

"Just one. When's payday?"

"Every Friday," he grinned knowingly. "We hold back one week's pay on new drivers in case of damage to a cab that isn't covered by insurance. If nothing happens while you're driving for us, you get it when you quit. Of course, whatever tips you get go into your own pocket each night you drive."

Back in Charlotte by eight o'clock, I did not relish facing Florence as I walked up the sloping lawn of the Berlincourt farm. I anticipated more of the smoldering hostility that she had expressed on the phone at work. As I drew near to the house, I could see Florence and her mother moving about in the kitchen, evidently finishing up the supper dishes. As I entered the dining room door, Florence craned her neck from the kitchen to see who it was.

"What are you doing home this early?" she asked, in a tone of mingled surprise and sarcasm. "I thought you were going to be driving a taxicab until midnight."

"I was too tired to start tonight," I told her, sinking into the gentle embrace of the rocking chair just inside the door. "I'm going to start Wednesday night instead."

Florence turned back to the dishes in the kitchen sink without any further comment as Hilda came to stand in the archway between kitchen and dining room, hands on hips, a soiled apron wrinkled around her expansive midriff.

"My, I should think you would be tired, Garfield," she exclaimed. "Would you like some supper? I wasn't expecting you, but there's enough left over to make a plateful."

"I'll get him something, Mom," Florence intervened.

I knew Florence's offer was not made because she would find a special delight in preparing my supper. It was prompted by her dutiful determination not to unload upon her mother any task that she deemed to be her own, such as feeding her husband. As I sat there, idly watching Florence go through the motions of warming my supper, while Hilda busied herself with odds and ends of the kitchen cleanup, it was almost like watching a waitress in a restaurant who was a total stranger. It was not that Florence's basic underlying attitude toward me had changed. I could understand that her expressed belligerence toward the part-time job had sprung from fear for herself; fear that something might go wrong during her pregnancy, and I would not be on hand to help. Deep down, beneath the surface layer of aloofness and hostility, she doubtless felt the same toward me as when we had married.

But at the invisible fork in the vocational road which had opened up before me in my own mind, in the Tropicana Cabaret in Calumet City, I had started down a road which, unknown to her, was leading me, step by step, farther away from her. The instruction session I had been through earlier that evening for the cab-driving job was one step. And the following day, during my lunch hour at work, a brisk fifteen-minute walk from the Gray building to the State Library was a trip that carried me a step farther down the road that was leading me away from Florence and away from the God whose call to the ministry I had abandoned.

At the library, I picked out several books that I thought might be of help in launching the new business enterprise for which the cab-driving job would be a springboard. One was a documentary study entitled, *The History of Prostitution*. There was one by Kinsey on the sexual life of women, which I thought might prove useful in motivating and training women to work for me. And in the hope of learning something from someone who had been successful in the business I was planning to launch, I checked out an autobiography entitled, *A House is Not a Home*, by the famous call-house madam of a previous generation, Polly Adler. I was probably the only incipient whoremonger who had ever sought to establish himself in the profession by getting books on the subject from the public library.

On Wednesday, in furtherance of my perfidious plan, I dropped two letters in the mail at the post office, just two blocks from the Gray building. Both derived from my newly conceived scheme to achieve success. One was to Pastor Calvin Savage and the deacons at Gilead Baptist Church, in which I announced the resignation of Florence and myself as Young People's leaders. The other letter, containing a check for twenty dollars, was mailed to a gas station manager in Calumet City, Illinois, dispatched with the hope that the attendant who had given me a tankful of gas and a ten-dollar loan would return by mail the wrist watch that I had left with him as security. And that night, after finishing my eight hours in the Highway Department, as Florence was riding home with the car pool riders, I drove to my new part-time job. In Lansing, a city of 230,000, I had to spend much valuable time that first night on the job getting directions out of a street directory and a map of the city. But one of the trips I made pointed up the potential for the business venture I was preparing to establish.

It was nearing nine o'clock, and the dispatcher instructed me to go to one of Lansing's largest downtown hotels. There, three men piled into the back seat.

"Take us to the Red Rail, driver," one of them said.

Fortunately, the Red Rail, although I had never been inside it, was sufficiently notorious in Lansing that I knew its location on the north outskirts of the city. The three men, who were probably attending a convention at the hotel, had been drinking. The laughter, the ribald jokes, flowed around me like water around a floating duck as I tried to keep my attention on traffic and keep one ear open to the two-way radio. As I stopped for a traffic light, a segment of the continuous flow of talk from behind me invaded my mind.

"Charlie Adams was telling me . . . you both know

Charlie," came a slurred voice from the back seat, "he was telling me how he was standing in this gas station waiting for a fill-up, and these two guys were there, and one said to the other one, 'Hey, Mac, what do you say we go out tonight and get a strange piece.' And the other guy said to him, 'Hell, man, if I got a piece at home, it would be strange!'"

There was a volcanic eruption of hooting from the back seat, mingled with the sound of hands being slapped on backs and legs. Then, as the light turned green and I depressed the gas pedal for a brisk takeoff, the talkative one addressed a question to me.

"Hey, driver, they tell me the Red Rail is a good place to pick up a broad; is that right?"

"I don't know," I answered, turning my head back toward the rear seat, "I've never been there myself."

"What the Hell kind of a cab driver are you?" demanded the volatile one belligerently. "You're supposed to know where the action is. That's where cabbies get their big tips, steering guys like us from out of town to the right places."

"I'm kind of new at this business," I defended. Then, seeing a potential beginning for the sideline I was preparing to start, "but maybe the next time you come to town I can be more helpful. Ask for Garfield Roby at Courtesy Cab."

"Well, damn, I hope so," he replied. "You sure haven't been much help tonight, except you got us to the Red Rail, and that's where we wanted to go."

Then we were at our destination—the rambling, one-story ranch-type bar that advertised liquor and dancing, in neon lights. The three men piled out, adding a two-dollar tip to the three-dollar fare. I drove away from the Red Rail with a jubilant assurance that there was a ready market for the kind of service I was planning to start selling from the front seat of the cab I drove; sexual satisfaction to lust-hungry men. It only remained to find the woman, the first to begin with, who would be willing to sell the access rights to her body; and the place where the buying and selling could be carried out, away from the prying eyes of the police.

(HAPTER 7

⇒ On that long Friday night of that first week I started driving a cab part time, from six o'clock in the evening until two o'clock Saturday morning, I used the sometimes lengthy lulls between trips to do research on the hidden business venture I was determined to launch. I began scanning one of the books on the history of prostitution I had checked out of the pubic library.

From the preface to the scholarly, well-documented volume, I learned that one of the chief reasons many married men frequented prostitutes was to seek the kind of sexual stimulation that most were afraid to request from their wives, such as oral stimulation. The discovery immediately suggested to my mind the need for a training course for the women I would employ; to teach them all the erotic refinements that could be employed to satisfy a man's sexual desires and fantasies, barring masochism, torture, violence. I would train them to be experts in pleasing a man sexually; giving them the kind of instruction that any prospective bride should have but seldom got because there were no provisions made for such a curriculum, either at home or college and, of course, not in the church.

It was two thirty in the morning by the time I turned in my earnings and log trip sheets for the night and started the long, lonely, eighteen-mile drive to Charlotte. The Berlincourt farmhouse was in total darkness when I drove into the gravel drive more than half an hour later. When I crawled into bed beside Florence a few minutes later, she had only one thing to say, in a sleep-muddled, irritated voice.

"What time is it, anyway?"

"A quarter after three," I whispered.

"A fine time for a married man to be getting home," she complained bitterly.

As I laid there in the dark beside Florence, her back turned to me, her complaint had no power to soften the plan that had further hardened in my mind as a result of the research I had done earlier that night. It was a solitary venture I had embarked upon; an attempt to convert my preceding failures in life into success, by the only way that temperament and circumstances seemed to have left open to me. After a few moments of silence, with no move on the part of either of us to exchange a goodnight kiss or embrace, I heard the labored breathing that indicated she was falling asleep again. And before I fell asleep, there was no silent prayer sent Heavenward that night.

It was not until the following Saturday evening, after having slept until one o'clock in the afternoon, and as sunset turned to dusk, that an oppressive cloud of guilt settled down over my mind at the course I had conceived on the trip to Chicago, and had begun to implement. I was sitting at the kitchen table alone, sipping coffee, while Florence and her mother were quietly doing some mending in the living room. In idly thumbing through a religious magazine, I had come across a poem that had arrested my attention. My eyes ran over the disturbing words of the first stanza again, as the magazine was spread out on the table before me. It was entitled, "His Plan For Me," by Martha Snell Nicholson.

> When I stand at the judgment seat of Christ
> And He shows me His plan for me,
> The plan of my life, as I might have been
> Had he had His way, and I see . . .

I stopped there and looked out the window, where a

warm, Indian summer wind of early October whipped and flounced the washing that Florence and her mother had hung out on the lines to dry earlier that day. I looked beyond to the distant fields and the drifting, white cloud clusters that scudded across the darkening sky. I was thinking that the judgment seat of Christ, and my appearance there, in shame and sorrow, was in the indefinite future. There was a closer, almost equally disturbing judgment awaiting me on the morrow—the boring stare and rigidly accusing "John the Baptist" visage of Pastor Calvin Savage.

As he looked at me, his eyes would ask questions about my inner spiritual condition, from which I inwardly shrank at the very prospect, as a mole attempting to burrow underground to escape the light. I could not bring out into the light of the pastor's scrutiny, that fork in the road that had materialized in my own mind, in a dimly lit, drum-shaken strip-tease bar in Calumet City a week before. Nor could I speak of the distance I had already traveled down that road; that low and loathsome road that might lead me to a dubious kind of success in life. I shrank inwardly at the very thought of the eye-to-eye encounter with Pastor Savage, which I saw no way of avoiding.

To meet his ferreting, accusing gaze, to sit for two hours through his teaching and preaching ministry, would be sheer mental torture. I was certain that I could not hide what was growing within me from his ruthlessly stripping gaze. I was certain that he would be able to detect a sense of restraint in my attitude and speech that would provoke a suspicion on his part that there was growing within me, a bent of mind, a premeditated course of action, that required the concealing mantle of darkness rather than of light for its successful fruition. And I would doubtless walk away from such an encounter, feeling, and probably looking as guilty as indeed I was, if the facts were known to him, as to what I had done and was preparing to do.

But I could see no way out. I could think of no excuse for missing church that would stand up to Florence's questioning. Although I had resigned as Young People's leader, with

Florence's concurrence, this was no reason for not continuing to attend there. We were still members of the church. Florence was the pivot on which the painful issue hinged. If it were not for having to explain to Florence my reasons for not wanting to attend church there on the following day, the painful encounter with Pastor Savage could be avoided. Then, as I sat there, as if drawn by some telepathic awareness that I had been thinking of her, Florence came walking out into the kitchen and drew a glass of water from the kitchen sink. Then, leaning against the sink and facing me, she spoke in a tone that intimated that the "cold war" attitude she had first taken toward the part-time cab-driving job might be thawing. Perhaps the rebellion she had felt at first and bluntly expressed was melting down into resignation.

"Did you make a lot of money last night?" she asked.

"About twelve dollars," I told her, "plus three seventy-five in tips."

"So how much of that do you get?"

"All of the tip money, plus sixty percent of the twelve dollars I took in. But the first week's pay is held until I quit, in case of an accident that isn't covered by insurance."

"Let's see," she began calculating, "sixty percent of twelve dollars would be seven twenty, plus three seventy-five in tips. That would be ten ninety-five, about eleven dollars for the eight hours you put in."

"That's about right," I concurred.

"Boy!" she exclaimed in disgust, "that's a little over a dollar an hour."

"When I get to know the streets better, I'll make more," I countered. "I won't have to waste time looking them up in a directory."

"I still don't think you're going to make any money after you consider all the expenses," she persisted, reverting to her original stance, "but I'm not going to say any more about it. Find out for yourself."

Then she turned to a more painful subject, the one I had been thinking about before she came into the kitchen.

"So that means you're not going back to being the Young People's leader at the church?"

"Pastor Savage said it would be a bad example for the young people," I reminded her, "as long as I'm holding down a job that makes it necessary to miss church every Wednesday night. So that rules out my holding the position unless Pastor Savage changes his mind, and I doubt very much if he will."

While Florence stood by the sink regarding me intently, I looked out the window, thinking that I had even stronger reasons now for resigning from the position as leader for the young people. I could not visualize myself going through the hypocritical posturing of being an officer in the church, especially as a leader for young people, while pursuing the hidden course I had embarked upon.

"Since you won't have to be there on Sunday, then," Florence broke into my thoughts, "would you mind going to some other church for a change tomorrow?"

It was an effort to keep from turning to face Florence and show the pleasure and astonished relief I suddenly felt at her wholly unexpected proposal. Before I could give my enthusiastic endorsement, she continued with her own reasons for wanting to attend a different church.

"I think it would be a nice change to hear somebody besides Pastor Savage for once. Besides that, I wouldn't have to see that snotty Shirley Forrest sassing her mother in the church, then marching up to the front of the church to play the piano. That burns me up."

"I think it would be alright," I answered quietly, risking a casual glance in her direction. "How about going to the Angel Road Bible Church?"

"Any special reason for wanting to go to that one?"

"I know the pastor, Reverend Lazarus Loverly. He helps out at the county jail service once a month."

"Is he good?" Florence asked.

"Well," I began hesitantly, groping for a precise appraisal, "he's not anything like Pastor Savage. He's . . ."

243

"That's good enough for me," Florence broke in, needing no further word of commendation. "Anyone who isn't like Pastor Savage would be a relief."

With that issue settled, Florence whirled away to rejoin her mother in the living room, leaving me sitting in the kitchen, greatly relieved that I would be spared the encounter I had dreaded, of seeing Pastor Savage, face to face, eyeball to eyeball. And on the following Sunday morning, Florence and I drove toward Charlotte, as we had been doing every Sunday morning for the preceding year, but instead of going into town where the Gilead Baptist Church was located, I turned right at the west limits of the city onto the two-lane state trunk line that led southwest to Battle Creek. Five miles and ten minutes later, after a pleasant drive through the autumn-hued countryside, I turned off onto Angel Road, where we could see just ahead the old-fashioned, red-brick country church with the bell tower. The Angel Road Bible Church, "the brick church with the Bible message," was affiliated with the Independent Fundamental Churches of America.

We drove into the crowded church parking lot a few minutes before the eleven o'clock service was scheduled to start. Florence, with characteristic independence, was out of the car, even with the increasing difficulty of rapid bodily movements in the fifth month of her pregnancy, before I could get around to her side to open the door. At the front door of the church, we were greeted by a pleasantly shocked Reverend Lazarus Loverly, who knew that we were members of the Gilead Baptist Church.

"Brother Roby!" he exclaimed with genuine pleasure, "glad to see you here this morning. I wasn't expecting to see you till this afternoon at jail service. Is this your wife?"

"Yes, this is Florence. Florence, Reverend Loverly."

After a handshake came the inevitable observation that was now easily discernible to the most casual observer.

"I see you're expecting, Mrs. Roby. Your husband didn't tell me."

"I only see you once a month at the jail service, Reverend

Loverly," I defended, "and we don't have much time to talk then."

"You're right," he conceded affably.

My remark triggered a proposal from him.

"Say, Brother Roby, if it's alright, I'd like to bring along one of the men from my church to the jail service to give a testimony, and his son, too, if it would be alright. He's a Marine, home on furlough; just been saved a year. He accepted the Lord at one of Dr. Charles Fuller's Old Fashioned Gospel Hour broadcasts out in Pasadena, California."

"Be glad to have them both," I assured him, suddenly aware that this might make it easier for me to bow out of my long-established participation in the weekly jail service.

During the preceding week, as I had continued to lay the groundwork for the business venture I had conceived in Calumet City, Illinois, I had experienced a sharp decline in my former interest and zeal in helping out with the weekly Sunday afternoon service at the County jail. Because of my religious background, having been converted while in a military prison in World War II, Pastor Savage had put me in charge of the jail service.

"That's at three o'clock, isn't it?" the pastor had asked.

"Right; I'll see you at the jail at three."

Then we walked on into the nearly filled church and found an empty pew on the right side near the front. The interior was more spacious and ornate than the Gilead Baptist Church. The high, vaulted roof, with varnished wooden supporting beams visible, gave an impression of vastness reminiscent of the great cathedrals of Europe. Around us, as the organist softly played familiar hymns to induce an atmosphere of quiet prior to the beginning of the morning service, neighbors and church members, who hadn't seen each other for a week, held low-keyed conversations about almost everything except the basic reason for which they were supposed to be in church.

Eventually the service started, following the customary

agenda in a fundamentalist church—the congregational singing, the inevitable announcements, the collection, the reading of Scripture, and the pastor's opening prayer. Then, following a familiar hymn by the choir, "Rock of Ages," Reverend Loverly got up to preach.

Reverend Lazarus Loverly, no taller than myself, with beak-like nose, black hair, and well-padded face and frame, whose relaxed features fell more easily into a smile than a frown, was as different from Pastor Calvin Savage in temperament and preaching style as a violent thunderstorm is different than an April shower. Calvin Savage always seemed driven to emphasize the wrath of a holy God against sinners, while Lazarus Loverly gave prominence in his preaching, with fervency and conviction, to the love of God for sinful men.

Calvin Savage, like a spiritual prosecuting attorney, a throwback to the Inquisitions of the Middle Ages, seemed compelled to ferret out sin in a man's life and bring him face to face with it. Reverend Lazarus Loverly was gripped by no such obsession. If he spoke of the wrath of God, and of Hell, as indeed he had to do in order to declare the whole counsel of God, it was with heartbreak in his voice, and often with tears in his eyes.

Reverend Loverly left it to the Holy Spirit to convict men of sin and to do the necessary work of bringing them to confession and repentance. He was not the meddler in men's personal lives that Florence had often accused Pastor Savage of being.

I sat on the pew beside Florence while the alternating words of earnest entreaty, or gentle rebuke from the pulpit flowed around me as water swirls around a rock jutting up out of the midst of a smoothly flowing river. The words that I heard, even from the Scriptures, rubbed against me but did not touch me inwardly. There was no softening of the hard purpose that had crystallized in my mind a week before in a strip-tease cabaret in Calumet City. And at the close of the service, we again shook hands with a smiling Reverend Loverly at the front door of the church, after having gone through the ritual of exchanging names and handshakes with several people who had recognized us as being first-time visitors, and had urged us to return.

On the way home Florence expressed her reaction to the new church and the new pastor.

"This is the first time I've enjoyed being in church for a long time," she confessed, as we drove homeward. "I sure wish we could start going there regularly instead of going back to Gilead Baptist."

Florence's unexpected proposal suited the downstream course I was secretly following. It would spare me the painful exposure to Pastor Savage's penetrating gaze and probing questions about my obviously declining spiritual health. It would enable me to avoid embarrassing inquiries from members of the Gilead Baptist Church as to why Florence and I had resigned our position as leaders in the Young Peoples group, as well as fending off useless urgings on the part of other members to return to the job.

"Maybe we can continue going to Angel Road Church," I conceded, trying to sound casual. "It is kind of restful for a change."

"You can say that again," Florence echoed vigorously.

And that afternoon, at twenty minutes to three, I sat alone in our car near the red brick county jail in downtown Charlotte, awaiting the arrival of Reverend Loverly and his two companions for the regular Sunday jail service for inmates. In spite of the sharp drop of interest I had felt in regard to the jail service, I did not feel as free to stop my involvement in it as I had done in regard to the Young People's sponsor in response to Pastor Savage's stern recommendation. I was reluctant to upset the delicate rapport that had been established with the sheriff and the officers at the jail. Maintenance of the Sunday service for inmates had been granted to Gilead Baptist Church because Pastor Savage had been the only pastor in the city who had cared enough about the eternal destiny of the inmates to have sought and secured permission for the weekly services. While Pastor Savage had consented to my recommendation that other pastors of outlying evangelical churches be invited to participate, there was always someone from Gilead Baptist Church, usually myself, as an official liaison contact with the police officers.

As I sat in the car waiting, I hoped that Dave Brown, the youthful, hard-working assistant young people's leader, would show up for the service as he usually did. If he did, I could relinquish the liaison role to him and excuse myself from participation. The search for a slimy kind of success that I had started out upon had quenched my desire to exhort inmates of the county jail to turn their lives over to Jesus Christ. I felt as if my spiritual authority as an ambassador of Heaven had been suspended; whether temporarily or permanently, I could not tell.

It was with relief that I saw the familiar figure of Dave Brown, with his wavy blonde hair, infectious grin, and loud plaid sports coat, approaching my car at about the same time that Reverend Loverly, in his station wagon and two men with him, pulled up alongside my car. As I got out of the car to go through the heavy-hearted formality of meeting the two strangers Reverend Loverly had brought with him, I was glad that the pastor was already acquainted with Dave Brown from previous jail services. It would not be quite as bad as leaving the pastor in the custody of a total stranger.

On the sidewalk by the county jail, in the warm autumn sunshine, and within sight of the iron-barred windows of the two-story, red brick jail, we all came together. Interspersed with the exchange of greetings was a joking dialogue between Reverend Loverly and Dave Brown about Reverend Loverly's facetiously expressed intention of stealing me away from Gilead Baptist Church to join his church. It was not the time nor the place, I decided, to follow up with what would have been a bombshell announcement to both of them; that Florence and I had already decided to shift our regular church attendance to the "brick church with the Bible message," where Reverend Loverly was the pastor.

The introduction of the young Marine corporal, twenty-four years old, and dressed in summer uniform, brought a spasm of mental pain which I hid behind a smile. He had the bright eyes, the flushed face from inner happiness that I, too, had experienced and revealed years before in military service as a newborn Christian. It was something of that same glow, in greater degree, that the Israelites had seen upon the face of Moses when he came down from the craggy heights of Mount Sinai, after forty days and nights in solitary communion with God, bringing down the stone tablets on which God had written the Ten Commandments with a finger of fire.

"What communion hath light with darkness?" I thought silently, in momentary anguish as I shook the young Marine corporal's hand, "or what concord hath Christ with Belial?" I felt suddenly and deeply excluded from fellowship in this little company of Christian soldiers; not by any mood of ostracism on their part toward me, but simply because they were walking in the light, and I had turned away in search for an elusive something called "success" in devious paths of darkness. As the size of the group that had gathered there on the sidewalk made a sudden impression on my mind, it opened an easy way of escape for me to avoid going into the jail service.

"Dave," I said, turning to the zealous young man with whom I had prayed and labored over the young people's activities in Gilead Baptist Church, "I just remembered something the sheriff said. He said he would rather we would limit our group to four people, and there's five of us here. So I think I'll leave you in charge of the operation and go home and get some rest. I need it with this part-time taxi-driving job I've taken on to help with expenses when the baby arrives."

There were expressions of consternation and regret on the part of Reverend Loverly and Dave, but there was no arguing with a rule that had been laid down by the sheriff. So, after a brief time of prayer, standing there in a circle on the sidewalk with heads bowed, the four men walked toward the jail while I got back into my car to return to the Berlincourt farm.

Florence, doing some ironing in the kitchen, was shocked at my early return until I explained my very legitimate-sounding reason for not having gone into the jail service with the others.

"I hope you won't give up the jail service if we quit going to Gilead Baptist," she said, as I turned on the burner under the coffee pot, "or could Pastor Savage nudge you out of that, too?"

"He could, I suppose, but I don't think he will."

But even as I spoke the words, I was thinking ahead to some legitimate-appearing way in which I could also shed this church-related activity. The goal I had set for myself, totally unknown to Florence, seemed to have generated within me a poisonous fog that was smothering all desire to be involved in personal, evangelistic witnessing of any kind, and I felt neither an inclination nor an ability to reverse the process. I felt that I could not turn back from the course I had started out on, even if I would.

On Monday night of the following week, I started my second week of part-time cab driving with a badly missed item of equipment back in my possession—my wrist watch. The honest gas station attendant in calumet City, Illinois, who might have kept both my watch and the check I had sent him, had returned it to me, securely packaged, in the mail. And that week I began keeping my eyes open for a suitable location where I could start the business operation that was gradually pushing my job in the Highway Department into a second-place status in my mind, in terms of both interest and economic potential. But strangely, in that second week, I found my first customer before I yet had anything to sell or a suitable place to conduct the transaction. It happened on Wednesday night that week, the night I would have been in attendance at Gilead Baptist Church in Charlotte, had I heeded the solemn warning of Pastor Calvin Savage.

I was parked at one of the downtown cab stands by an all-night restaurant, drinking coffee, when I got a call from the dispatcher to pick up a fare at the Hofbrau. This was a tavern just two blocks away, around the corner on the wide avenue that was the main street of downtown Lansing. The name of the place had been made familiar to most residents of the city, even those who didn't patronize it, by a killing that had occurred on the sidewalk in front of the place several years before. A jealous husband had found his wife inside with another man and started a fight with the rival for his wife's affections. When the two of them had been put out, the shooting had followed.

I pulled up in front of the Hofbrau, left the engine idling in neutral, got out and walked into the tavern. In accordance with company instructions, I had my cab driver's cap on with the insignia of Courteous Cab clearly visible on the front. The place was crowded. The air was blue with cigarette smoke, and a babble of voices underscored the music that blared from the jukebox, making the place a seething pot of confused sounds. After standing just inside the door for a moment, since no one approached me, I stepped over to the bar and spoke to the bartender.

"Know who called a cab?"

The bartender was shaking his head negatively when a woman's voice answered from the end of the bar.

"I did."

Surprised that she had heard me speak to the bartender, I looked in the direction of the voice and saw a stoutish, grandmotherly woman with gray hair, holding up her hand to attract my attention. I walked to where she sat beside a male companion.

"Be right out, soon as I finish this drink," she said, holding up a beer glass about one-third full

Since that much could be disposed of in two swallows, I reasoned, I told the lady I would be waiting outside, preferring the fresh air to the noise and smells of the tavern. Standing on the sidewalk, keeping an eye on the cab, I was conscious of a man who came out the door immediately after me, and who had paused on the opposite side of the front entrance, several feet away from me. He lit up a cigar, inhaled, then spoke to me as he blew a cloud of smoke into the air.

"This is a Hell of a town for excitement, ain't it?"

"I don't know," I responded, glancing at him, "I guess it depends on what kind of excitement you're looking for."

He was at least four inches shorter than me, stocky, with a dark complexion and a decidedly prominent nose.

"I mean women, man," he continued. "Hell, you can't find a broad in this town that isn't attached to somebody. Either she's somebody's sister or somebody's wife or somebody's mother. I nearly got my ass thrown in jail the last time I was here for shacking up with somebody else's wife, and I'll be damned if I'm going to try that again right away; not in this town, at least. Hell, I can't even show my face down at the hotel where they found us."

I listened to his tirade, like a fisherman sitting on a riverbank, too busy thinking about something else to notice that a fish was nibbling at his baited hook. I was preoccupied and getting increasingly impatient at the delayed appearance of the woman inside who had ordered the cab. The seconds ticking away were losing me money.

"I guess there's only one thing to do," I suggested, some basic chord in my nature sympathetically touched by his frustrated need.

"What's that?"

"Get married," I counseled idly.

"Shit!" he spat contemptuously, flicking the ashes from his cigar off onto the sidewalk. "I've seen too damn many marriages go to Hell to take a chance on it myself. Besides, who wants to go to bed with the same woman every night for the rest of his life? Not me! I like variety."

I felt that behind his expressed contempt for marriage and a monogamous alliance to last for life, was still a need and a longing that was not being filled, and which he would perhaps not admit even to himself.

"Where are all the wild women in this damn town, anyway?" he asked, breaking into my speculative appraisal of him.

He eyed me inquisitively, rolling the cigar to the opposite corner of his mouth as he spoke. The interrogating gleam in his eye suggested that he suspected me, as a cab driver, of having some hidden, inside information on this subject. Then abruptly, like a drowsy fisherman startled by a sudden tug on his line to the realization that there is a fish biting at his bait, it suddenly dawned on me that I was speaking to my first potential customer in the new business sideline for which I had been laying a foundation.

"I don't know," I answered, groping for some way to arouse and hold his interest, "maybe we'll have to import some from Detroit or Chicago."

He stood there, sucking on his cigar, frustrated with a hunger inside him which he had no way of satisfying. The minutes I had stood waiting for my grandmotherly fare inside the tavern were forgotten as I sought some way of latching onto this man who could be a stepping stone in my climb to success, and holding him until I could lay my hands on the commodity he would be willing to buy at a good price.

"You're staying in Lansing?" I asked.

"Hell, no, just here on business for a couple of days."

"When do you expect to be back again?"

"Next month, probably; why?"

"Maybe by that time," I said, "I'll be able to locate a wild woman for you if there are any around these parts."

"Yeah?" he asked, with a surge of interest, eying me appraisingly, "do you think you can line up something for me by then?"

"I'll do my best," I assured him.

I pulled a small notebook from my inside coat pocket and wrote down my name and the phone number of the Courteous Cab company, tore out the sheet and handed it to him.

"Next time you're back in town," I said, as he took the slip of paper and looked at it, "call this number and ask for me. You can only get me on Monday, Wednesday, or Friday after six. Maybe by then we'll have something you'd be interested in."

"Okay, Garfield," he grinned, removing the cigar from his mouth with one hand and sticking the slip of paper into his shirt pocket with the other. "I'll be giving you a call next month when I'm back in town. You line me up something good and I'll really make it worth your while."

With a wave of his cigar, he started to walk away.

"Hey, just a minute," I called, remembering an important item of information I had forgotten to elicit from him.

He stopped and turned around, facing me.

"How will I know it's you when you call; I mean, what's your name?"

"Oh, yeah," he grinned knowingly. "Why, Hell yes, I guess you want to be sure you're not talking to some cop on the vice squad, hunh? My name's Solomon Weinberger. My friends call me Sol, and I'll consider you one of my friends, Garfield, if you can help me out with this little problem."

"Okay, Mr. Weinberger, I'll be hearing from you sometime next month. Hope I can give you some good news by then."

With a hand-salute gesture, like a general dismissing a buck private, he turned and walked away. And abruptly, I was aware that I had been standing on the sidewalk in front of the Hofbrau perhaps fifteen minutes, waiting for the grandmother inside to finish her drink. I stepped back into the noisy, smoke-filled tavern to the woman who had called a cab, still sitting at the bar, leaning on the shoulder of the man beside her.

"Excuse me, ma'am," I butted in, "I've been waiting fifteen minutes for you and I can't wait any longer."

"Go ahead," she said, "I changed my mind."

With no further word of apology for having kept me waiting, she waved me away. I could have made a scene and insisted on her paying the minimum charge, a procedure recommended by the cab company in such cases, but I felt that the unpleasantness such an attempt might create in the crowded bar wasn't worth it. Besides, I felt that I had already been partially compensated for the trip because I had gotten my first potential customer for the emerging business while waiting outside. The trip had not been a total loss.

Eventually, I reflected as I left the bar, this particular trip might even prove to have been the most profitable one I had made since I began driving a cab. Even a reprimand from the dispatcher that if the same thing happened again, the minimum fare would be coming out of my own pocket, didn't greatly disturb me. For I was already thinking ahead to the next necessary step in the blossoming business sideline; the location of a female attractive enough and willing to go into business with me. Two weeks later, I met her. She was this side of middle age, brunette, bitter, and beaten by life on the night I found her.

It was in the north end of town on one of the long Friday night shifts that I met Madge. It was in the section of the city probably best known for the eruption of trouble, as far as the police department was concerned. In a two-block radius from the intersection of Grand River and Turner Streets, there were a cluster of bars intermixed with cheap restaurants, a hotel, and several second-hand stores. The sidewalks and streets always seemed dirty and littered; the buildings were dilapidated, as if ready to collapse from old age. It was a small Skid Row neighborhood, without even the single redeeming feature of Skid Row areas in larger cities—a Rescue Mission, offering hope and help to the down and out. It was generally in the bars where trouble erupted: the Grenadier, which, in addition to liquor, offered dancing as an added source of sexual aggravation; the Mustang, the Northtown, and several others. The drunken fights that began inside the bars frequently culminated in stabbings or shootings outside.

It was to the Northtown bar in this area that I received a call to pick up a fare on Friday night, after I had been working about four hours. I pulled into an empty parking space in front of the bar and, leaving the engine idling, walked into the bar. As soon as I stepped inside the door, a man sitting at a table with a woman whose back was turned to me, signaled me. The place was small and not too noisy at the moment, so I could hear as he called to me across the intervening distance of the barroom.

"We'll be right out in just a minute."

I nodded, and stepped back outside to wait. In such a neighborhood, with a coin changer on the front seat, I didn't feel safe leaving the cab unattended. Several minutes later the door opened, and the man who had signaled me came out, bearing up the woman on one side, and the bartender on the other side, helping to hold her up. She was evidently quite drunk, but she didn't think so. As they got out onto the sidewalk, she pushed against the bartender. Standing by the cab, holding the door open, I watched the pathetic episode.

"Get your damn filthy hands off me. I can walk by myself," she shouted angrily.

The bartender stepped back away from her, looked at me, and shrugged his shoulders. I returned his visual message, and he turned to go back into the bar. I stood by as the woman's drinking companion helped her into the cab, and I shut the door.

"See that she gets home okay, will you?" the man asked. "She's had a little too much to drink."

"I sure will," I assured him.

As he returned to the bar and I walked around to the other side of the cab and got in, I couldn't help wondering what his relationship to the woman might be, since he wasn't concerned enough about her to take her home and hadn't even offered to pay her cab fare.

"I hope I never see that creep again," the woman in the back seat said heatedly, as I turned back in my seat to ask her destination.

"Sounds like you don't like him."

"I wouldn't care if he dropped dead."

"Where to, Miss?" I asked.

"Alpha Street, right across from the Yankee Cone Shop."

I relayed my destination to the dispatcher, hung up the radio mike, pulled down the meter flag, and pulled away from the curb.

"Hey," said my passenger, as I approached a traffic light a block away, "you got a light?"

"Sure."

Conveniently, the traffic light turned red. I retrieved a book of matches, carried for the benefit of passengers, from my pocket, struck one into flame and held it out to the end of her cigarette as she leaned forward. In the flare of the match light, her features, framed by brunette hair that was wavy but in slight disarray, appeared clear cut and attractive, although her lipstick was smeared.

"Thanks," she said, blowing out a cloud of smoke with the word.

"You're welcome," I returned, as I replaced the book matches in my pocket, and then swung around the corner as the light changed to green.

"Hey, I like you, cab driver," she said, with that uninhibited yielding to first impulses that are typical of those under the influence of alcohol.

Then she followed the compliment with an explanation that robbed it of some of its ego-tickling value.

"I guess I'd like anybody, though, after spending the evening with that bump on the log I was with. Can you imagine it? We sat there for nearly three hours, just looking at each other, and I'll bet he didn't say half a dozen words all that time. I was so bored. I could have killed the guy."

"Why go out with somebody you don't like?" I asked.

"Hell, it was a blind date. I didn't know what I was getting into. I just sat there and drank beer and looked at the people around me, and all I could think of was how many unhappy people there are in the world."

I was silenced by her words, feeling suddenly oppressed by the thought of the world's misery that her words had conjured up. And with no further comment from me, she, too, fell silent, and I heard only the sound of her heavy breathing when I stopped at a stop sign. I drove on in the flow of southbound traffic on one of Lansing's major north-south arteries, painfully conscious of the fact that I was not only doing nothing to alleviate the suffering and sorrow in the world, but that I was pursuing a course that might eventually add to the sum total of grief and heartbreak in the world, if it ever came to light. And yet, I felt as powerless to alter the course I was following as I was to change the world.

257

Finally, at the address she had given me, I got out and walked around to the other side of the cab next to the curb to open the door for my passenger.

"Here we are, Miss," I announced, opening the back door.

There was no response from my passenger. With her head laid back against the seat cushion, it was obvious that she was asleep. As I looked at her, I felt pity for her because her desperate search for a few hours of happiness this evening had ended in such miserable failure; aware, also, that in her drunkenness, she was no more or less happy than I was in a state of sobriety. I saw her as a symbol of multitudes, trying so hard to find happiness, and failing miserably in the attempt. Then I reached down and laid a hand upon her knee, shaking her gently. Her body stirred but she didn't wake up. I put a hand on her shoulder, then, and shook more vigorously.

"Hey, you're home!" I called loudly, as I shook her again.

The combination of noise and movement finally aroused her and she sat up. She looked at me as if confused as to who I was.

"What did you say?" she asked groggily.

"You're home," I repeated.

This time the message got through to her befogged mind. "Oh!"

She reached for the back of the front seat to pull herself forward and over to the side of the cab where I stood holding the door open. Cautiously, she let one foot down to the curb, like a hesitant swimmer testing the water for temperature before diving in. Then, with her purse slung over one arm by a strap, and grasping both sides of the doorway for support, she stepped down with the other foot and stood there a moment, swaying. I stood close by, waiting to catch her if she should start to fall. She took one step forward, stumbled, nearly fell, but regained her balance. I was not eager to provoke the same kind of reaction the bartender had caused when he had tried to help her get to the cab.

"Maybe you'd better hang onto me," I suggested, stepping up beside her and offering her my arm.

"Thanks," she said, "maybe I better."

Then, hanging tightly onto my arm, we walked up the sidewalk to the front steps of the screened-in porch on a modest, white-and-green one-story bungalow. Slowly, and with determined effort, clinging to me, she mounted the steps. Inside the screened porch, I waited by the front door while she searched in her purse for the key.

"Hey," she exclaimed, as she extracted a jangling key ring from her purse, "you gotta' come in and have a cup of coffee with me. How about it?"

The unexpected show of hospitality touched several responsive chords within me simultaneously. It was nearing ten o'clock, and I had put in four hours of the long, eight-hour Friday night shift. It was time for a break. But more than this, in the wake of the evidently good impression I had made on her, in the back of my mind was stirring the possibility that this might be the very woman I was looking for with whom to launch the business venture for which I already had the first potential customer.

"Be glad to," I said, "if it's okay with the boss. I'll have to call in on the radio and see."

"Why don't you go ahead and call your boss," she suggested, brightening perceptibly, "and I'll go in and make some coffee."

"Good enough," I agreed, but lingered a moment before going back to the cab to make sure she could unlock the door.

With the key in her hand, she made several attempts to get it into the keyhole, without success.

"Would you unlock the door, please?" she finally asked, holding the keyring out to me. "The damn keyhole keeps moving on me."

"Be glad to," I said, taking the keyring.

Then it suddenly occurred to me, as I turned the key in the lock, that there might be hidden danger on the other side of the door, which my passenger, in an alcoholic daze, might have forgotten.

"By the way," I said, straightening up and facing her with

one hand still on the key in the lock, "are you sure it won't disturb anybody if I come in?"

"Don't worry," she assured me, "I haven't got any husband. Got rid of him nine years ago, and good riddance."

"Okay," I said, greatly relieved, "you make the coffee and I'll call the boss."

As she took the keyring back, stepped into the darkened house and switched on a lamp near the door, I turned and hurried back to the cab, pulled it into the driveway beside the house, and called the dispatcher. Fortunately, there was no need for a cab in the south end of town at the moment, and he gave me permission to take time out for lunch. But rather than admitting that I had been invited in for coffee by a female fare I had picked up at the Northtown Bar, I told him I'd be at the Yankee Cone Shop restaurant, just across the street. As I shut off the ignition, the cab dome light, and the two-way radio, I was aware that I was taking a chance of arousing the ire of my employer. If a call came through for a cab in my part of town and the dispatcher called the restaurant where I was supposed to be and didn't find me there, I'd be in trouble. But, nothing ventured, nothing gained, I philosophized, locked the darkened cab and mounted the short flight of steps to the front porch. I knocked softly on the door before pushing it open.

"Come on back here in the kitchen," came the female voice from a lighted room at the back of the house, along with the aroma of freshly brewed coffee.

I made my way through the well-kept living room and a moment later, was sitting in the clean, compact, cheerful kitchen, across the table from the woman I had picked up at the Northtown Bar. Instrumental music from a stereo in the living room spilled around us. The hot coffee revived and sobered her somewhat. As she talked about herself, I learned something else about her that convinced me that she might be more than willing to consider a change of employment.

She told me how she was working on the assembly line in the same automobile factory where I had worked for nine months some years before. I remembered it, with renewed revulsion, as the hardest, noisiest, dirtiest job I had ever held down. It was a rough job for a man, let alone for a woman like the disillusioned divorcee who sat across from me.

Having just spent three brutally boring hours with someone who apparently had not been interested in listening to her troubles, or who hadn't responded in a sympathetic way, it had dammed up within her a flood of small talk about problems and frustrations and unfulfilled desires that came pouring out of her as I listened.

And as I sat across from her at the table, sipping coffee, looking interested, I was thinking of the best way to invite her to become involved in the business venture I had been planning. I had appraised her as not being troubled with any moral or religious scruples, or she would not have gone out on a blind date and gotten drunk, and would not have invited me into her home for coffee and conversation. I couldn't help but believe that she would be interested in a job that would be far more pleasant than her dirty, hard job on the assembly line of a factory, and still get paid far more than she was presently earning. So before leaving her house, nearly an hour later, I started laying the groundwork for acquainting her with the opportunities and advantages to be gained from becoming a business partner with me.

"What are you doing next Saturday night?" I asked, preparing to leave.

"Nothing," she said, leaning against the doorway by the open front door as I stood facing her on the enclosed porch.

I had decided that an evening of wining and dining would be the best psychological preparation for broaching such a proposal to her, and it couldn't be in Lansing, where I would run the risk of being seen by someone who knew me, and might relay the gossip report back to Florence. It had to be someplace out of town that might spark her interest in going. The one place that had come to my mind was the city of Detroit, a city of nearly a million people, with all the entertainment attractions of a big city, and that was a safe distance from Lansing; nearly a hundred miles.

"How would you like to take a little trip with me down to Detroit, and see what's going on down there?"

"Detroit?" she squealed in delight. "Hey, that sounds wonderful. I used to live in Detroit."

"No kidding?" It was my turn to be surprised.

"Sure," she continued, effervescently. "Man, it would be great to go out on the town for a night and see all the old places. What time do you want to leave?"

She caught me off guard. I hadn't been prepared for such a spontaneous and enthusiastic acceptance of my proposal.

"I can't say exactly right now, but . . ."

"Why don't you call me when you know for sure and let me know?"

"Good. I'll do that. Is your number in the phone book?"

I suddenly realized that I didn't even know her name yet.

"The only Madge Marlow on Alpha Street that's listed."

"When is the best time to call you?"

"From four o'clock on," she said, her face bright at the prospect of the trip to Detroit, "but don't call before six because I usually sleep for a couple of hours as soon as I get home. Working on the assembly line is no picnic, I'll tell you."

"I know how it is," I empathized. "I've worked on the assembly line myself and about a year of it was all I could take. I had to get out. That's why I was wondering if you might be interested in a job that's only half as much work as the one you've got, will eventually pay twice as much as you're making now, and might be a lot more fun than working on the assembly line for the rest of your life."

"Hey, show me where I can find a job like that," she exclaimed, her face brightening with interest, "and I'll kiss that assembly line job goodbye so fast it will make your head swim. I'd do anything to get off that assembly line."

"Anything?"

"Anything!" she repeated with emphasis. "And I mean anything. Nothing could be worse than that damn job. So where is this fantastic job, anyway?"

Encouraged by a response that implied acceptance of the

proposal I was going to put before her, I did not think it wise to blurt out what I had in mind on such short acquaintance and in such a setting.

"Oh, it's a little business operation I'm going to be starting, maybe within another month."

"What kind of business have you got in mind?"

Seizing on her evident interest as an added inducement to motivate her to follow through on her promise to accompany me to Detroit the following weekend, I deferred an explicit answer.

"I'll give you the details on our trip to Detroit. I can't take time to tell you about it now or I might get in trouble with the boss."

"Well, whatever it is, it couldn't be worse than the ass-breaking job I've got now, so it's got to be something better. I can't wait to hear more about it. It sounds like it's going to be an exciting trip to Detroit," she squealed in child-like anticipation.

"I'm sure it will be, Madge," I assured her. "I'll call and let you know what time we'll be leaving."

While the proposed trip had the appearance to her of being primarily a pleasure excursion, I saw it as a necessary business investment, on which I had a reasonable expectation of reaping ample profits eventually. As I turned to leave, it was not until I had opened the door of the screened-in porch and was on the first step, that she remembered something essential that I had forgotten in the arrangements.

"Hey!" she called, in evident distress.

I turned back to face her, holding the screen door open.

"How will I know it's you when you call?" she asked, "I don't even know your name."

On the top step I wavered a moment in alarmed indecision. If I gave her my real name, it might lead to repercussions that could get back to Florence. And if I dreamed up a fictitious name on the spur of the moment to hide my real identity, she might try to call me at the cab company, only to discover that I had given her a phony name. I would have to take a chance, as I had already taken a chance in telling the dispatcher I would be at the Yankee Cone Shop for supper during the time I was building my relationship with Madge over coffee in her kitchen.

"Garfield Roby," I said, taking the plunge.

"Well, Garfield," she mused dreamily, "what I know of you already is nice enough that I'd like to know more."

"Thanks," I returned, the duplicity in my motive a condemning contrast to her sincerity. "I think you're pretty nice yourself."

"If you think flattery will get you anyplace with me," she intoned softly, "you're absolutely right."

I simulated a smile in response to the genuine one that softened the hard lines of her pretty face. Behind her frank admission, there was an evident hunger to be appreciated, to be praised, to be loved. She had mistaken my show of interest in her for one of personal concern, when it was really only a calculated move to further a budding business that might lead me to the kind of success that had so far eluded me in life.

"I've got to go now," I said, closing the screen door quietly behind me, "but I'll be calling you next week."

"Good night, Garfield."

Her voice trailed after me as I hurried down the walk to the cab, apprehensive that the dispatcher might have tried to reach me at the Yankee Cone Shop. In the cab, I backed out of the drive and drove a block before stopping to call the dispatcher for an expected bawling out. To my relief, he had not tried to get me during the hour I had spent with Madge at her home. But he was irritated at my having taken so long, supposedly for supper. But I didn't mind the lecture, nor the three hours of driving still ahead of me. These minor irritants were more than compensated for in my mind by the fact that I was making progress in my plans to establish a branch of the world's oldest profession in the capital city of Lansing. Unknown to her, Madge Marlow, an attractive, lonely divorcee, was to become a stepping stone on my stairway to success. That expectation neutralized the pain of my belated realization that I had forgotten to collect the four dollar and eighty-five-cent cab fare from Madge that her trip from the Northtown Bar cost. Her fare would have to come out of my own pocket when I turned in my earnings later that night. I was confident that I would be adequately reimbursed the following month by Solomon Weinberger, when I introduced him to Madge, who would by then be working in partnership with me.

I waited until Thursday of the following week to break the fictitious and unpleasant news to Florence that the boss at Courteous Cab had asked me to drive a cab on Saturday night of that week. Circumstances had conspired to give me factual justification for the fiction. There was to be a home football game at Michigan State University that Saturday and, with a great influx of out-of-town visitors and alumni, extra drivers would be needed. I further embellished the lie to include a supposed request from my cab company boss that I stay on the job until late Sunday morning to handle the people who relied on cabs to get them to and from church on Sunday morning. Florence sighed and reiterated her vehement displeasure at having me gone another night in addition to the three I would already have put in, but she grudgingly accepted it. So with the necessary arrangements made at home to account for my absence that coming Saturday night, I called Madge the following Friday night while I was on standby call at the Greyhound bus station.

"Hello?"

"Madge?" I asked, having never heard her voice over the phone before.

"Yes. Who's this?"

"This is Garfield Roby."

"Who?"

I repeated my name with a sinking feeling that in her inebriated state when I had picked her up at the Northtown Bar the preceding Friday night, she had forgotten our conversation and proposed date.

"I'm the driver from Courteous Cab who . . ."

"Oh, you must have the wrong number," she broke in, "I didn't call a cab."

"I know that. I'm the driver who brought you home last Friday night. You asked me in for coffee, and we . . ."

"Oh, Garfield Roby, I'm sorry. I remember you now. Your name just slipped away from me. I don't think things were registering too good with me that night."

"Did you forget the date we made for Saturday night?"

My fingers squeezed the telephone receiver tightly as I faced the possibility of her having forgotten this essential date as completely as she had forgotten my name, and of having to start from scratch again in building a bridge of rapport with her.

"To go to Detroit?" she asked exuberantly, dispelling my fear. "Of course not! I've been waiting to hear from you all week."

"It's still a date, then?"

"Sure, it's a date," she rejoined emphatically, "unless you want to break it."

"Certainly not. How about my picking you up about five tomorrow night?"

"I'll be ready," she promised gaily. "What do you want me to wear?"

"Whatever suits you will suit me," I said, "because I think you'd look great even dressed in a barrel."

"You better be careful with that flattery," she warned, in mock seriousness, "because that stuff goes right to my head."

"I'll be very careful what I say, then," I returned, matching her simulated gravity, "and I'll see you tomorrow about five."

"Okay. G'bye now, Garfield."

"Bye."

I hung up the telephone receiver and emitted a sigh of pleasure and relief. Things were progressing smoothly toward the end I had begun working toward during the five weeks I had been driving a cab. And that night, I didn't mind so much that business was slack and tips were few and far between. For I could foresee the day not far distant, when the sideline business I was going to launch from my cab would bring me a bigger income than that of my job in the Highway Department, plus the added meager income from driving a cab. I envisioned a coming day when I would have to quit both jobs to handle the growing volume of business that I had begun to see as a full-time vocation as a salesman of sexual satisfaction to lust-hungry men.

On the following day, Saturday, I left the Berlincourt farm at four in the afternoon, as far as Florence and her mother knew, to drive a cab in Lansing all night and up until late Sunday morning. Unknown to Florence, I had borrowed one hundred dollars from the credit union to finance the anticipated expenses of the trip to Detroit to wine and dine and entertain my first new employee in the budding business venture. The loan would be repaid with minimal payroll deductions about which Florence would know nothing. In the face of Florence's fears about financial capsize when the baby was born, I had justified the loan to myself as a necessary business investment, in the same way that many men begin a legitimate business venture on borrowed money.

As I drove toward Charlotte, the gently falling rain that began to splatter against the windshield did not dampen my expectations for the evening. I even thought the falling rain would enhance the trip to Detroit as Madge and I would sit together, warm and dry inside the car, listening to romantic music as we traveled. In Charlotte, I stopped at the only drug store to call Madge and make sure she would be ready to go when I got to Lansing in another twenty minutes.

"Hello?" Madge's voice came over the wire, expectantly.

"Hi, Madge. This is Garfield. I was just getting ready to leave and pick you up. Thought I'd let you know so you'd have plenty of time to get ready."

"You're not still thinking of going to Detroit, are you?" Her voice sounded incredulous.

"Sure, why not?" I asked, as a muted clap of thunder penetrated the enclosed phone booth.

"Oh, hon," she exclaimed in distress, "it wouldn't be any fun in the rain. Why don't we go someplace closer to home tonight?"

Her question struck straight at the core of what I had

planned for that evening. To go out with Madge someplace closer to Lansing would thwart that plan. It would add the risk of being seen by someone from either Lansing or Charlotte, who might relay the information to Florence or, even worse, perhaps, to someone who knew me in the Highway Department. I could imagine being confronted in the hallway of the Gray building, or in the cafeteria during lunch or coffee break.

"Hey, Garfield, who was that woman I saw you with Saturday night? It didn't look like your wife."

These very practical reasons for not being seen with Madge in the Lansing area were reinforced by a streak of masculine pride. I didn't want to appear to be the kind of man whose mind could be changed so easily after having firmly made it up.

"Nope," I answered, "I've got my mind set on going to Detroit tonight, Madge."

I waited hopefully for her to capitulate, but she didn't.

"Gee, I wish it hadn't rained," she lamented, with genuine regret in her voice. "I'd have loved to go with you, but maybe some other time; a night when it isn't raining?"

"Sure," I answered, the resignation I felt probably evident in my tone, "some other time."

"Be sure and call me again," she urged, "and if you change your mind about going to Detroit tonight, give me a ring, and we can still make a night of it; okay?"

"Yes. I'll call you if I change my mind, Madge," I promised, knowing as I spoke the words that I would not take up her offer to go somewhere closer to home. There was too great a risk; a risk I couldn't tell her about.

"Don't forget. G'bye now, Garfield."

"Goodbye, Madge."

I hung up the receiver, scooped up the change I had laid out on the shelf under the pay phone and pushed open the folding door of the phone booth. I stepped back into the sights, sounds and smells of a small-town drugstore. I stood there, just outside the phone booth, leaning lightly against the glass top of the candy counter, trying to regain my mental balance after the shock of this sudden and unexpected reversal of my plans. Absent mindedly, I picked up a penny lollipop from a box on the counter and twirled the cellophane-wrapped sucker in my fingers as I surveyed the length of the drug store and its varied activities. I looked about me, not seeing critically, but blankly, groping for some new center of reference, some motivation for taking the next step, not knowing what to do.

At the soda fountain, two teenage boys joked with the schoolgirl clerk, feeling perhaps for the first time the strange new magnetism of sexual desire, but too self-conscious and embarrassed to say or do anything about it. On the opposite side of the store, a harried-looking elderly woman studied the selection of special-occasion greeting cards, facing a need to express regret at someone's death, or happiness at somebody's marriage, or delight at the birth of a child. At the back of the drugstore, a bespectacled, baldheaded pharmacist in a white smock punched and pecked out a prescription label on an ancient typewriter, one key at a time, while in front of the counter, a lean, poorly dressed man in working clothes waited nervously, as if his wife were slowly dying in pain while the druggist slowly pecked out the doctor's instructions for using the prescription, unconcerned about the present pain or imminent death of the one for whom the medicine was intended.

So my plans have been changed, I thought. So what? Everyone's plans are changed. This was the normal course of life. Standing there, I found some alleviation of my mood of discouragement in the thought that my plans for Madge were not necessarily canceled out completely; just postponed. She had sounded genuinely eager to try the same proposed out-of-town trip on another occasion when it wasn't raining.

But what could I do, where could I go, to occupy myself until late the following morning? Florence would doubtless react with suspicion if I were to return home and tell her that I was not needed as a driver after all, after the urgency with which I had represented the need of my services that night by the cab company. She would wonder why they hadn't called me to let me know I wasn't needed before driving all the way into Lansing to find out. Then I thought of my first potential customer for the new business venture, Solomon Weinberger. If I was not able to arrange for the kind of sexual satisfaction he was seeking by the time he returned to Lansing the following month, he might get disgusted and not bother to contact me again.

Then, the deadline date when my first potential customer was due to return to Lansing, and my compulsion to get on with the business venture I had been working toward, gave rise to an idea. It might be profitable for me to follow through on my plan to go to Detroit, even though alone. I could combine whatever pleasures I might find along the way with some calculated business research on how the world's oldest profession was handled in the big city of Detroit. Perhaps, I speculated, I might even encounter a woman to replace Madge as an initial business partner; a woman who might be willing to relocate to Lansing and open shop in a city where competition, as far as I knew, was practically non-existent. The thought of contacting Roseanne, in Calumet City, whose phone number I carried in my wallet, as a possible replacement for Madge, passed through my mind. But I rejected it as premature. I could not hope to interest her in relocating to Lansing until I had a going business that was capable of paying her a salary adequate to compensate for leaving the job she had at the Tropicana as a drink-hustling stripper.

As the final outcome of my several moments of deliberation and reflection, compulsion and imagination had converted the negative development of Madge's change of mind into a positive opportunity.

I laid down the penny lollipop in the box from which I had picked it up, turned up the collar of my raincoat and stepped out into the rain. I got into the car and headed toward Lansing, the first lap of the nearly hundred-mile trip, in a southeasterly direction to Detroit. Thirty minutes later, I was driving through the traffic bottleneck of the island-divided avenue in East Lansing, running between the city of East Lansing on one side and the campus of Michigan State University on the other.

It was a concrete boundary line dividing the two worlds of a commercial-residential small town and the intellectual metropolis of a great university.

Passing by the university buildings on one side, I gave a passing backward thought to my student days there as I had looked forward to preparing for the ministry as my life work. And I thought of the thousands of restless male students who, in spite of alleged immorality on college campuses, were doubtless often frustrated in their attempts to find satisfactory outlets for their pent-up sexual energies.

"I'll be back, fellows," I said, half aloud, casting a glance in the direction of the men's dormitories as I passed them on the east end of the campus, "and if you've got the price, I'll have what you want—solid sexual satisfaction."

As I left East Lansing and the university campus behind, and the boulevard widened out into four lanes, the misty rain seemed to solidify and become slanting sheets of water hurled against the windshield with increasing violence, as though God, or one of His angelic subordinates, were trying to turn me back. The rain had, indeed, had the effect of squelching Madge's interest in making the trip, only because her superficial goal of having fun was one that could be easily diverted by fluctuations in the weather. But the rain had no power to diminish the dark determination that had come to dominate my life in a few short weeks—to achieve the success which had previously eluded me in godly and legitimate endeavors, as a super salesman of sexual services to lust-hungry men.

The more violently the rain was hurled against the windshield, the further I depressed the gas pedal in my determination not to be stopped, or even slowed down, in pursuit of my goal. I pushed against the gas pedal until the speedometer needle moved slowly from fifty, to fifty-five, to sixty, and to sixty-five, a dangerous speed on the slippery highway, and drove on toward the city of Detroit, the destination that the rain had not been able to wash out of my self-determined scheme to achieve success.

CHAPTER 8

⇒ In his classic novel of the French Revolution, *Les Miserables*, Victor Hugo proposed that Napoleon was thwarted in his dream of ruling Europe, at the Battle of Waterloo, not because of the superior military strength or strategy of the Duke of Wellington and the English army, but because God was against him. Hugo believed that God intervened to foil the little Corsican's ambitions, not by any display of supernatural power, but by simply causing it to rain, a certain amount, at a certain time, at a certain place. Hugo asserted that because of the rain that fell the night before the Battle of Waterloo, the subsequently softened ground prevented Napoleon from getting his heavy artillery weapons on the field early in the day. Had he been able to do so, the French novelist was convinced, Napoleon's forces would have won the decisive Battle of Waterloo before the English reinforcements could have arrived on the scene.

While it will continue to be a debatable question as to which side God may have favored, if any, in the decisive military battles of history, there is no disputing the fact that weather conditions have at times spelled the difference between victory and defeat. The history of nations, and of individuals, has been drastically altered, for better or for worse, by heat and cold, wind and sun, snow and rain. And I will never know, in this life, whether it was by the direct intervention of God that a gentle, autumnal rain began to fall in the city of Lansing,

Michigan, U.S.A. on a Saturday afternoon, the first week in November; the Saturday I had planned to make a trip to the city of Detroit, unknown to Florence, my wife.

It may have "happened" that the course I was pursuing collided with the impersonal operation of laws of nature which God had set in motion at the beginning of Creation. But it is a fact that the rain which fell late that afternoon had the effect of altering my life as profoundly as the rain that fell before the Battle of Waterloo changed the personal destiny of Napoleon and the subsequent history of Europe.

For it was only because of the rain that began to fall as I left the Berlincourt farm in Charlotte that afternoon, that Madge, the middle-aged but attractive divorcee, whom I had planned to woo into a partnership in prostitution, did not accompany me on that trip to Detroit, whereon she might well have yielded to my inducements. And had I not been alone on that sordidly conceived trip to Detroit that rainy Saturday night in November, I might never have met someone else, a someone else destined to exert a profound influence on the course of my life.

Arriving in downtown Detroit at seven o'clock in the still down-pouring rain, I turned into the Greyhound bus station in the downtown area and drove up the inclined ramp to the rooftop parking facility. As part of my business research project that had motivated the trip, I had decided to rely on taxicabs to get me around the city. On the first floor of the huge bus terminal, which occupied an entire city block, I stepped into the cafeteria to wash away some of the weariness of the long trip with a sandwich and coffee, and to wait a while for the rain to abate. At a table next to the floor-to-ceiling windows that looked out on the street, I watched people hurrying past, protected somewhat from the rain by the roof that extended out from the bus terminal and over the curb.

On the street, next to the curb, taxicabs were lined up bumper to bumper the whole length of the block. Each one would move ahead every few seconds as the cab at the head of the line was occupied by passengers leaving the bus terminal.

Watching the movement of people on the sidewalk outside and in the cafeteria inside, I felt an outreaching desire to somehow enter into and be a part of every life I saw, but from which I was shut out; only a spectator, not a participant. The resolve that had motivated me back in Charlotte to make this trip useful to the business venture I had conceived as a ladder to success had diminished somewhat during the long, lonely drive. Deeper, more basic feelings had gained the ascendency within me.

I felt lonely, defeated and discouraged. I hungered for companionship, especially the kindred company of an attractive, desirable woman; a kind of closeness that I had not known with Florence since the announcement of her pregnancy seven months before. And sitting there, watching the human scene on the rain-riven street beyond the plate-glass windows, I wondered if one of the drivers in the block-long string of taxicabs, waiting in the rain for their next fare, could do more than provide me with some basic business know-how as links to the world's oldest profession. I wondered if one of them could also help me find fulfillment for my deeply felt personal need of that moment.

I got up from my table by the window with the intention of finding out. I pushed through the glass doors that led out onto the street and approached the first cab in the line. Through the rolled-down window on the driver's side, I could see that the driver was an older man. Gray hairs showed beneath the rim of his driver's cap. As I approached his cab, he reached behind and opened the back door for me. Inside, he turned back to face me with a friendly, inquiring gaze. The gold-rimmed glasses he wore gave him a professional look, as if he should have been a doctor or dentist rather than a cab driver.

"Where to?" he asked.

"I don't know," I said, "you got any suggestions?"

"Depends on what you want," he grinned, showing no sign of being irritated that I was wasting several seconds of his time in not giving an immediate destination.

With some vestige of the same youthful embarrassment I

had experienced years before on the occasion of my first ado-
lescent purchase of a girlie magazine at the drugstore, I groped
for the right words that could express a need I had never
broached to a man, especially a total stranger, before.

"I'm a stranger in town," I confided. "Do you know where
I might be able to locate some, uh . . . female companionship
for the evening?"

The words were out, and they had not sounded as obscene
and shocking as I had thought they would. Then I held my
breath, waiting for an outraged response from the driver, who
might be moral and respectable and even a church goer, insulted that anyone would suppose he might be party to such an
immoral proposition. Instead, he gave me only a sympathetic,
understanding grin as he answered.

"I don't know myself, but I know a guy who can tell you."

"Who's that?"

He glanced at his watch. It was about 7:30.

"Yeah, Harry ought to be in now," he mused, as if to himself, then looked back at me. "Know where the Book Show Bar
is?"

"No, never been there." I had never been to any bar in the
city of Detroit.

"It's right across from the Book-Cadillac Hotel on
Washington, you know where that is . . . Hell, it's only about
six blocks from here; want me to take you there?"

"I guess you better. I didn't bring an umbrella with me."

He pulled away from the bus station and threaded his
way swiftly through the maze of one-way streets in the downtown area, cutting across Woodward, swinging around the
Grand Circus Park, then left onto Washington Boulevard. We
drove past the illuminated splendor of the Book-Cadillac, then
swung left onto Grand River, to stop just around the corner in
front of the Book Show Bar, just across the street from the
mammoth, luxury hotel in the heart of downtown Detroit.

"Now, Gar," he said, having learned my name and home
town en route, "you just go in the Book Show Bar there and ask
for Harry. I know Harry can fix you up with something good."

"How much do I owe you?" I asked.

"A dollar and a quarter."

I was surprised that he tacked on no fee for the inside information he had given me. While I dug out the fare, he supplied a little background about Harry.

"Harry's a great guy; you'll like him. He used to be in vaudeville. Been M.C. in some of the best night spots in Detroit. But he's not in the spotlight anymore. Just kind of faded out of the picture. Still a swell guy, though."

I handed the driver his fare, plus a dollar tip.

"Thanks, and good luck," he said, as I got out of the cab and slammed the door shut behind me.

He pulled away from the curb and out into the traffic as I walked toward the Book Bar. The rain had changed from a downpour to a fine, misty spray that struck my face with an invigorating sting. A red neon sign in the curtained window read "Book Show Bar," and cast a red reflection on the shiny surface of the rain-washed sidewalk.

Just inside the dimly lit bar, a man of about fifty, several inches taller than myself, balding and somewhat paunchy, neatly dressed in a dark business suit, stuck out his hand to me.

"Good evening," he said, with the friendly familiarity of a man accustomed to meeting the public.

I thought immediately that this must be Harry, but didn't ask him. I wasn't yet psychologically prepared to broach the subject that had brought me here.

"Hi," I answered.

"Hope you enjoy your visit here," he said, "and if there's anything I can do for you, let me know."

"Thanks," I said, and stepped on past him to the coat check room, where an attractive brunette smiled, took my raincoat and gave me a check.

The Book Show Bar was narrow and long. It was just wide enough to accommodate the bar, which ran half the length of the room on one side, with one row of tables down the other side and a roomy aisle in between. I sat down at one of the booths and a moment later, a blonde bar girl in a crisp, black uniform came to take my order.

"What will it be?" she smiled.

I drew upon the supply of esoteric knowledge I had picked up at the Gorgeous Girlie Show Bar in Calumet City weeks before.

"Blatz."

I had guessed right. She smiled and whirled away. As I waited, I noted that against the far wall, beyond where the bar ended, was a circular stage that extended out from the wall to provide for the floor show that gave the management the right to call the place a "show" bar. Then the waitress was back with a bottle of Blatz beer.

"That will be one dollar."

As I fished a dollar out of my wallet, I asked the bar girl a question.

"Where can I find Harry?"

"He's sitting at the bar by the door," she said, pointing to the friendly welcomer who had met me at the door when I came in. "Did you want to speak to him?"

"I'd like to, if he's got a minute."

"I'll tell him you'd like to see him."

And after our business transaction was finished, I saw her walk to the front of the bar and deliver my message. As she leaned over Harry's shoulder, he turned his head and looked in my direction. With only a dozen people scattered through the bar, he had no difficulty spotting me. Harry excused himself from the company of the man he had been talking with at the bar, slipped off his bar stool and walked back toward my table.

"You want to see me?" he asked genially.

He was chewing gum, and in the dim light, he looked a little like Bob Hope, with a few years added.

"Yeah, can you sit down for a minute?"

He pulled out a chair and sat down, facing me across the table.

"Can I buy you a drink?" I asked, seeking to make a favorable impression.

"No, thanks. I've got one at the bar I haven't finished yet. What's on your mind?"

"My name's Garfield Roby," I said, thrusting my hand out as if I were greeting a stranger at the Gilead Baptist Church in Charlotte.

Harry shook my hand for the second time that evening.

"Glad to know you," he said, then waited expectantly for me to broach what was on my mind.

I picked up the three-quarters filled glass of beer and studied the foam that bubbled on the surface as I searched for the right words that did not seem to come any more easily just because I had first spoken them a few moments before to a friendly cab driver. I referred to the cab driver himself, who had told me his name was "Jack," as an opening wedge.

"Jack, the cab driver, told me you would be a good man to see to . . . uh . . . locate some . . . uh, female companionship for the evening."

The difficult words were finally out. Had the bar not been so dimly lit, Harry might have detected a flush of embarrassment reddening my cheeks. I expected either laughter or a lecture from Harry, but I got neither. The subject I had broached seemed as commonplace and worthy of serious consideration as topics like the weather, sports, or the stock market.

"What's the matter with Jack?" Harry asked, in evident surprise. "Hasn't he got any girls on the string?"

"I don't know."

I lifted the glass of beer to my lips and took a sip for lack of anything further to say, surprised at the implication that Jack, the cab driver, might have had connections in this line which he had chosen not to divulge to me for some unknown reason. Harry was silent a moment. He cupped his hands together, like a monk in meditation, then tapped his fingers together nervously, as if uncertain as to how to respond to my request.

"Where you from, Garfield?" he asked abruptly, eyeing me.

"Lansing."

"You in business up there?"

"I work in the Highway Department."

The information produced an unexpected response from Harry. He mentioned the name of a man very high up in the Highway Department, close to the Highway Commissioner, and asked if I knew him.

"I've heard his name," I acknowledged, "but I haven't run into him personally."

"What hotel you staying at?"

"I'm not staying overnight, Harry. I'm just in town for an evening of relaxation. I'm going back to Lansing later tonight."

"Got any identification with you, Garfield?"

I pulled out my wallet and extracted my driver's license and several credit cards and handed them to Harry. As he proceeded to examining my credentials, some corner of my mind that still retained an objective interest in furthering the business research I had come to Detroit for, impressed me that what Harry was doing would also have to be part of any similarly successful operation back in Lansing. I would have to screen any male client whom I might direct to Madge or her replacement, to be sure that he was not an undercover agent for the police vice squad, bent on entrapping me and whoever might be working for me. Harry returned my I.D. cards to me, apparently satisfied that I was who I had claimed to be.

"I'll tell you what," he said, as I returned my credentials to my wallet and he glanced at his watch, "it's a little early right now. But if you want to drop back about nine o'clock, I might be able to do something for you."

I didn't feel like sitting in the Book Bar that long.

"I think I'll go out and stretch my legs a little," I said, as we both got up from the table. "Then I'll drop back."

"Okay, Garfield, I'll be looking for you," he grinned.

Harry returned to his companion at the bar as I retrieved my raincoat and hat from the hat-check girl and stepped back out onto the sidewalk. There, I made a pleasant discovery. The fine, misty rain that had been falling when I had first stepped into the Book Bar had ceased altogether. The cool, rain-washed air was a refreshing change from the stuffy interior of the bar. As I set out on a leisurely walking tour of the downtown area to kill time until Harry could connect me with some "female companionship," the street lights, lighted shop windows and headlights of passing cars, reflected on the rain-slicked streets and sidewalks, creating a realistic replica of the watery street canals of Venice.

Several blocks from the Book Bar, on busy Cadillac Square, I came to the light-emblazed marquee of the Gayety Burlesque Theatre. With a newly acquired business motivation that was attuned to all the refinements and variations of sexual stimulation for financial gain, I paused to scrutinize the array of enlarged photographs of the scantily clad and seductively posed exotic dancers who were the lesser stars of the live stage show inside. A life-size poster in the center of the display advertised the attributes of a ravishing redhead named June Harlowe, billed as the feature attraction.

Studying the voluptuous, semi-clothed figure of the star stripper of the show, I was tempted to enter the theatre and partake of a visual appetizer for the real, live encounter that Harry had promised to arrange for me later that evening. But then a bitter memory from several months before checked the rising impulse within me. The bold, lustful display of professional pulchritude adorning the swinging doors of the Gayety reminded me of a honky-tonk bar in calumet City, Illinois weeks before. I recalled how I had been left feeling thwarted, cheated, with an aroused appetite that had not been satisfied. I did not want another such experience that would culminate only in frustration.

For in addition to an easily aroused capacity for sexual response, such as a talented strip teaser could initiate, there was within me, at the moment, a deeper, less easily understood hunger for a personal and intimate contact with a real, live woman which no amount of voyeuristic viewing from a distance could satisfy. I turned away from the Gayety and its photographic panorama of feminine pulchritude and walked on.

As I started to walk back in the direction of the Book Bar, I approached a cab parked next to the curb, as close to the pedestrian crosswalk as possible. The driver, short, heavy set, middle aged, and with the visor of his cap pulled down low over horn-rimmed glasses, stood on the sidewalk leaning against the front fender of his cab, arms folded like an Indian chief, an unlit cigar clenched between his teeth. He gave me an appraising look as I came to the crosswalk, intending to cross the street, and I felt as if I were being scrutinized by a shrewd judge of human nature.

"I see you don't care much for burlesque," he commented, having evidently seen me pause in front of the Gayety to survey the display.

"Nope; not tonight."

I paused by his cab, feeling somewhat of a fraternal kinship with another man who drove a taxi, even as I was supposed to be doing in Lansing at that very moment.

"Well, I guess burlesque is alright," he said, shrugging his shoulders and removing the cigar from his mouth to wave it in an arc to express his indifference, "but it's not like the real thing, where you can touch it as well as look at it."

"You're right," I agreed, sensing that he was leading up to something that might have a bearing on my reason for being in Detroit, "but the real thing is hard to find sometimes."

"Nah," he replied disdainfully, nodding away my rebuttal as trivial as he replaced the cigar in his mouth, "not if you know who to see."

"Who's a good man to see?"

"You're looking at him," he announced proudly, a knowing grin spreading across his face. Then, waving me into his cab, "get inside and we'll talk it over."

The urgency of getting back to the Book Bar to keep my appointment with Harry was suddenly diminished by an interesting possibility inherent in his invitation. Here was the opportunity I had hoped for, to learn more about how a cab driver in Detroit handled the same kind of operation I would soon be launching in Lansing. The driver stepped toward the rear of his cab, opened the door for me, and I got inside. As I got in, it struck me as unusual that the cab company name emblazoned on the door was located in Canada; or perhaps not so unusual, since Canada was only ten minutes away from downtown Detroit through the automobile tunnel under the Detroit river. My speculations continued as I settled in the roomy back seat. The driver closed the door and then walked around the outside of the cab and got in the driver's seat, closing the door behind him. He twisted around to face me.

"What's your name?" he asked.

I was tempted for a moment to give a fictitious name, not knowing what might lie ahead, but remembering Harry and the identification he had required, I decided that in this particular situation, honesty might indeed be the best policy.

"Garfield Roby."

"Mine's Goldie," he said, sticking out his hand. "Glad to know you, Garfield."

I couldn't help voicing my surprise as I shook his hand with characteristic Baptist vigor.

"Goldie? That's an unusual name."

"Just a nickname," he explained. "My name's really Ed, but the other fellows call me Goldie 'cause I got so many gold fillings in my teeth. I could show you, but I don't think you're interested."

"I guess that's the safest place to carry gold these days," I observed.

"You can say that again. Driving a cab is risky business these days. We had a cab driver get shot here in Detroit just last week; did'ja read about it in the paper?"

"No, I missed that."

"Some guy tried to hold him up, and he resisted. Stupid jerk, anyway. Man, if some young punk tries to hold me up, he can have my money. It's not worth dying for."

With that brief exchange, the incidental preliminary conversation gave way to the more important business for which he had invited me to step into his cab.

282

"Well, let's get down to business, Garfield. You tell me what you want and I'll take you there."

He stretched out both hands, as though measuring the length of a fish he had caught, to indicate the variety that was available.

"Just say the word—redhead, blonde, brunette, black, white, any color, any shape. Whatever you want, I can get for you."

He looked back at me expectantly, like a waiter in a restaurant, waiting for me to read off my culinary preferences from a menu. The very possibility of such a wide selection of choices temporarily immobilized my decision-making capacity. I had no criteria for expressing a preference. In the ensuing moment of indecision, Goldie offered a helpful suggestion.

"What did you think of the feature attraction at the Gayety tonight—June Harlowe?"

"She looked alright," I murmured approvingly, recalling the seductive shape of the voluptuous redhead who had been billed as the star exotic dancer of the show.

"I can take you to a girl that's a spitting image of her," he breathed, as excited as if he were offering to take me to a hidden gold mine. "No kidding, she could be June Harlowe's twin sister."

"Sounds interesting," I assented, feeling already aroused at the prospect of touching a real, live duplicate of the sensual exotic, whose life-size poster had attracted my eye beneath the blazing lights of the Gayety marquee.

"Okay," he grinned, "it's just fifteen minutes from here."

He turned back and switched on the ignition, and it suddenly struck me that this was too simple, too easy. He didn't even know who or what I was, apart from the name I had given him. Evidently, the same thought struck him at the same time. With one hand on the steering wheel, he twisted back in his seat to face me again.

"Say, Garfield, you aren't with the vice squad, are you?"

There was a hint of panic in his tone, knowing that he had already placed himself in possible jeopardy of a pandering charge if I were, indeed, a plainclothes policeman. I almost laughed out loud at the incongruous question, but putting my hand to my mouth quickly, I converted the sound that had come rattling up in my throat into a cough. Certainly he should have known that if I was a member of the Detroit police vice squad, out rounding up pimps and prostitutes, I would not admit it to a suspect.

"No, I'm not with the vice squad, Goldie."

His formerly affable manner became suddenly more business-like, as he realized that in his enthusiasm for selling the product he had to offer, he had rushed ahead without taking the necessary precautions to learn whom he was dealing with. He reached down beside himself and picked up a clipboard off the seat. On it was a blank sheet of paper. He handed it back to me along with a ballpoint pen.

"Write your name on there, will you, Garfield?"

I complied, wondering at the value of this strange ritual, and handed it back to him.

"Now can I see your driver's license, Garfield?"

When I extracted the license from my wallet and handed it to him, he compared my signature on the paper with the one on the license. It was an extra precaution Harry hadn't taken when he had given me a screening interview at the Book Show Bar.

"You're from Lansing, huh, Garfield?" he asked, returning my driver's license. "How long you in Detroit for?"

"Just for tonight," I told him, as I returned the license to my wallet and stuck it back in my hip pocket.

"Just come down for a night on the town, huh?"

"You might say that."

"Well, this will be a night you won't forget, Garfield," he assured me as he pulled the cab away from the curb and swung left onto Cadillac Square.

Fifteen minutes later, we were in the sixteen hundred block of Cass Avenue, which ran parallel to the main street of Woodward through the heart of the downtown business district. On Cass, Goldie pulled over to the curb. Across the street was a seedy-looking hotel, flanked on either side by run-down looking business places that were closed—a dry-cleaning store, a small grocery store, and a restaurant.

"Here we are," Goldie announced exuberantly.

I stepped out onto the sidewalk as he got out and came around the cab. He had stopped in front of a four-story, brick apartment building that was set back from the street about twenty feet with buildings on either side. On the sidewalk, Goldie faced me to give me the necessary instructions for gaining admittance to the apartment building.

"Just go in the front door, Garfield, and push the buzzer for apartment number sixteen. Carole will ring a buzzer for the inside door. When you hear it, open the door, and take the elevator to the fourth floor. Her apartment's the third one on the right after you get off the elevator. Boy, believe me, you'll think you're seeing June Harlowe in person when Carole opens the door."

The analytical part of my mind that was taking note of the mechanics of this business operation for transferring to Lansing was impressed with the security arrangements that allowed the woman inside to open the door to a male client who had already been screened for possible police connections. There was one other specific and necessary item of information that hadn't been discussed en route to the place.

"Is there a kind of . . . uh . . . a standard fee for things like this, Goldie?" I asked.

"Twenty dollars is the minimum, Garfield," he answered, as matter-of-factly as if he were quoting the price of bread or potatoes. "That's what it is all over town right now. Of course, if you want a party or something special, why, it's more. But that's for you to work out with the girl."

"I see," I said, relieved that there would not have to be any embarrassing discussion or argument about the monetary value for the satisfaction I was shortly going to be seeking. "And how much do I owe you?"

"The cab fare is a dollar seventy-five, Garfield, and I usually get a ten-dollar fee for bringing you here."

As I pulled several bills from my wallet, I recalled how I had been duped in the Gorgeous Girlie Show Bar in Calumet City, and had been promised something that had not been produced. I had no assurance that in going inside the apartment building and pushing the buzzer for apartment sixteen, that there was a redhead named Carole who looked like June Harlowe, and who would answer.

"How about coming in with me, Goldie," I suggested, fingering the bills, "just so I don't get lost, or maybe get the wrong apartment."

My fears of fraud were immediately dispelled by the easygoing willingness with which Goldie acceded to my request.

"Sure, be glad to. But let's finish our business first."

I gave him a ten and a five and took my change.

"Now before I take you in, Garfield," he said, stuffing my money into his pocket, "just let me shut off the engine and lock the cab."

I stood waiting while he took those precautionary measures against theft or vandalism, and a moment later he was back beside me on the sidewalk.

"Now follow me, Garfield," he instructed, starting up the walk that led to the apartment building. "I'll take you right to your dream woman's door."

I followed Goldie up a short flight of concrete steps and through a pair of heavy glass doors at the top. Then up another short flight of steps, we stopped before another glass door in a vestibule with a row of apartment number doorbells next to the door that was obviously locked. I watched as he confidently depressed the button labeled Apartment 16, then followed him swiftly up another short flight of steps as a buzzer sounded and he opened another glass door. Then I stepped with him onto the small elevator, and soon stepped out onto the carpeted fourth floor. He led me down the hallway to the apartment he had described and applied the brass door knocker lightly. A moment later, the door was swung open. At sight of the woman who stood in the open doorway, I stood staring upward in confused astonishment.

"Hi, Carole!" exuded Goldie, with a grin, then motioning to me with his hand. "I brought you a friend. This is Garfield Roby from Lansing."

Before either of us could speak a word, the cab driver continued like a salesman with a memorized sales pitch.

"What did I tell you, Garfield," he gloated triumphantly, eyeing me, "could she double for June Harlow, or couldn't she?"

"No doubt about it," I conceded, keeping the consternation I felt out of my voice.

The woman who stood in the light of the open-doored apartment, dressed in high-heeled slippers and a shortie gold-brocaded bed jacket that came to mid-thigh did, indeed, bear a striking resemblance to the exotic dancer whose almost life-size poster I had scrutinized admiringly outside the Gayety Burlesque Theatre. But there was one vital measurement of the star of the show that had not been depicted accurately in the poster. The woman who stood smiling in the doorway in front of me appeared to be at least seven or eight inches taller than I. The top of my head came to her shoulder. Both the woman and Goldie looked at me as I stood there silently.

"What's the matter, boy?" Goldie asked, slapping me on the back like a fraternal lodge brother, "speechless, huh?"

"Kind of," I muttered, wondering how I could extricate myself from this hopelessly embarrassing situation.

To even think of an erotic encounter with a woman this much taller than myself, no matter how attractive she was, seemed out of the question. It brought immediately to my mind remembered photos of pint-size Hollywood movie star, Mickey Rooney, alongside some of the wives he had successively married, some of them a foot or more taller than he was. I could recall how such photos had always struck me as a ridiculous, and inescapably comic, marital situation.

"Why don't you come on in, honey?" the tall, shapely redhead urged, not grasping the reason for my evident state of shock.

"Yeah," commented Goldie, slapping me on the back, "you two don't need me around."

Then he turned away and started walking down the hall toward the elevator.

"Have yourself a good time, Garfield," he called over his shoulder, and disappeared from sight around the corner.

"Come on in, honey," the woman urged again, as I heard the elevator door slam behind Goldie. "Uh, what did you say your name was again?"

"Garfield," I said, stepping into the roomy, well-furnished apartment as she closed the door behind me.

The sound of the closing door contributed to my trapped feeling. Only a temperamental tendency to avoid hurting another person's feelings, if I could, had prevented me from blurting out in the hallway the reaction that I had experienced at my first glimpse of Carole. Added to this was a natural reluctance to broach the subject of my personal psycho-sexual reactions to a woman who was a total stranger. And something else about her bothered me even as she asked for my coat. The outfit she was wearing was too obviously designed to accommodate as many male customers as possible with a minimum of time spent in disrobing. It did not look as if she had any clothes on under the satin, thigh-length bed jacket. For her, it would simply be a matter of loosening several buttons and lying down on the bed. This, too, had the effect of inhibiting whatever erotic desires I had brought with me to her door. As she stood behind me and put her hands on the lapels of my raincoat to pull it down off my shoulders, a clock facing me on the wall suggested a way of escape from the impossible situation. It read twenty minutes past eight.

"Is that clock right?" I gasped in simulated shock, as I pulled away from her grasp and cast a hurried glance at my own wrist watch so that she could not see it.

"Sure, honey," she replied, "why, what's the matter?"

I turned around to face her.

"My watch must have stopped and I didn't know it," I said, thinking a phrase at a time ahead as I improvised an excuse to depart abruptly. "I thought it was only twenty after seven."

"What's the difference, honey?"

"I was going to meet a buddy of mine downtown at the Book Show Bar at eight o'clock," I said, juggling my appointment time with Harry to meet the need of the moment. "I'm twenty minutes late already. I'd better get going."

I started toward the door.

"You can use the phone and call and tell him you'll be a few minutes late," she suggested.

I turned, my hand on the doorknob.

"He's the kind of guy that wouldn't wait very long. I'll be lucky if he's still there when I get there."

Then to add to an appearance of genuineness to my unexpectedly hasty departure before transacting the business I had supposedly come there for, I made a suggestion.

"I'll call you later this evening, Carole."

Discomfited, she stepped over to the table where the telephone was, extracted a card and pencil from a drawer and wrote down her phone number. She brought it to me as I stood by the door and handed it to me.

"Thanks; I'll be calling you later," I reassured her, but with no intention of doing it, and pulled the door open.

As I started down the hallway, I turned back for a parting wave. She stood in the open doorway regarding me with suspicion, as if she thought I was retreating with undue haste for some reason other than the spurious one I had manufactured on the spur of the moment. I hurried on down the hall and heard her apartment door close behind me. With a sigh of relief, I left the apartment building, stepped back onto the sidewalk, then walked a block over to Woodward, thinking cabs might be more plentiful there.

For twenty minutes, getting damp in the rainy mist, I vainly tried to flag down cabs filled with passengers that passed me by. Finally, an empty one pulled over to the curb, driven by an older man with a tense, harried expression.

As I rode back downtown, along the wide avenue filled

with pleasure seekers, I began kicking myself mentally for not having stuck with my appointment with Harry instead of having been diverted by Goldie, the cab driver who had picked me up at the Gayety. The man had been too sexually obtuse, too insensitive to take into account that the match he had arranged was like pairing a pygmy with an Amazon. It was the kind of blunder I would not make with clients in Lansing. Back downtown, I walked back into the Book Show Bar fifteen minutes past the time Harry had asked me to return. He was sitting at his usual spot, just inside the front door; this time alone. He swung around on his bar stool as I entered, recognizing me immediately.

"I see you got back," he grinned.

"Hope I'm not too late."

"Nope," he assured me, "business is just getting started for the night. I'll finish my drink and then see what I can do for you. Why don't you grab a table and I'll be with you in a few minutes."

I sat down at one of the few empty tables left along the wall. More people had come in since the first time I had entered an hour and a half earlier, swelling the volume of talk and laughter mingled with the tinkle of glasses. From the waitress who immediately appeared, I ordered the necessary minimum bottle of beer to pay for occupying a table while I waited for Harry. As I sat in the semi-darkness of the bar, slowly sipping my beer, a solitary surveyor of the animated scenes of action surrounding me, the lights came on over the circular stage halfway down the length of the bar. A four-man combo took up their instruments and began with the introductory strains of an old, familiar pop song. Then, a willowy, buxom brunette stepped to the front of the stage, spotlighted in a form-fitting black sheath evening gown. She began to sing in a voice that was soft and mellow, with a sexy huskiness.

"When I fall in love . . . it will be forever . . . or I'll never fall in love."

They were sad words, plaintive words, I mused, as I sat there alone, listening and watching. They were words that expressed the belief that there was such a thing as a love between a man and woman that would not change or fade with the passing years. And in spite of bitter experiences to the contrary, the heart continued to yearn for a love such as this, else such a song would never have been written and would have no power to touch the hearts of those who listened.

"When I fall in love . . . it will be forever . . ." the refrain was repeated.

I wondered if I had ever used the word "forever" to Florence before or after our marriage. And I could not help reflecting upon the mystery of why I was there, sitting alone, listening to the melancholy words that seemed to be expressive of some hidden hunger within my own heart. Why was I here, a hundred miles away from the woman I had married in the expectation of finding in her all that I had looked for and longed for in a woman's love? Even in the midst of a planned venture that was a denial of love—the intended merchandising of sexual gratification as a cash-and-carry commodity—there was something in my nature that responded to the seemingly unrealistic pledge being sung by the vocalist, never to fall in love unless it was "forever." My reverie was interrupted then as Harry slid his slightly bulging midriff into a chair across from me.

"I think I've got something you'll like," he said, pulling out a pack of cigarettes and lighting one. "Her name is Diane. I was just talking to her on the phone. She's real nice looking, got her own apartment. If you want to go over right now, I'll call her and tell her you're coming."

"I'd just like to ask you one question, Harry," I said, still tasting the embarrassment and total loss of time and money that I had just been through with Carole, the spitting image of exotic dancer June Harlowe. "Do you know about how tall she is?"

"Diane? I'd say she's about five feet five, probably a little shorter than you. Why?"

"It's just that some of these showgirl types that are six feet tall and over kind of inhibit me, that's all."

Harry blew a cloud of smoke ceilingward and proceeded to give me directions for getting to Diane's apartment.

"You take the Lodge expressway to Montrose," he began, flicking the ash from his cigarette, and ending up with an address, "5720 Boston Boulevard, Apartment Number Four."

I fished in my pocket for a five-dollar bill, folded it into the palm of my right hand, then extended it to Harry for a farewell handshake.

"Thanks a lot Harry," I said, transferring the five to the cupped palm of his hand as I shook it.

He smiled as he felt the tangible evidence of my appreciation and stuck it into his pocket without looking at it. It occurred to me as I got up from the table that Harry might be accustomed to getting bigger tips than mine for his unusual customer service, but I had to start thinking of economy.

"That's alright," he beamed, "glad I could be of help. I'll call Diane and tell her you're coming right over."

"Okay; thanks again, Harry."

He waved and walked to the back of the bar to call Diane as I got my hat and coat from the check room. The cab fare to get to Diane's apartment would have been astronomical, so I began a brisk walk to the Greyhound Bus station, about six blocks away, to get my car. Minutes later, I was caught up in the fast-paced traffic on the Lodge expressway, skirting the downtown area. It was nearly twenty-five minutes later that I found the address Harry had given me and pulled into a most-ly empty parking lot behind the apartment building.

In a small vestibule inside the front door, I ran my finger down the row of doorbells for individual apartments until I came to number four, and pushed the button. It was close enough to the outside lobby door that I could hear the bell ringing in the apartment. A moment later, the buzzer sounded and I pushed open the inner locked door and stepped inside onto plush carpeting. Looking down the hallway, I saw a door open, and a slim, dark-haired girl in a white silk blouse and black, skin-tight leotards appeared in the partially open door-way, smiling.

"Hi," she called softly, evidently certain that I was the expected arrival whom Harry had called her about.

I waved to her, mounted a short flight of steps, and walked down the corridor toward her. She opened the door wider to admit me and then closed it as I stepped into the apartment. I heard a lock snap into place as the door closed. As I stepped back against the wall of the vestibule to let her pass by me and lead the way, I saw that Harry had not misled me in describing Diane's physical endowments. She was just a trifle shorter than myself, and her face and form were such as would excite almost any man. Her artfully applied makeup was subdued, not gaudy, just enough to enhance her natural beauty. I followed her into a living room that was cozy in size and expensively as well as tastefully furnished.

"I'll take your coat," she said demurely.

I slipped off my raincoat and handed it to her, savoring her grace of movement as she carefully draped it over the back of an overstuffed chair in a corner of the room. Soft music flowed through the apartment from some hidden source, and there was a pleasant scent of gardenias in the air.

"Sit down," she invited, motioning to the love seat sofa on one side of the room. "I'll get you something to drink."

I sat down and surveyed the room and its contents while she disappeared into the adjoining kitchenette.

"Sorry," she called out a moment later, "but I don't seem to have anything except Coke; is that alright?"

"My favorite beverage," I answered.

A moment later she reappeared, her high-heeled steps accompanied by the tinkle of ice cubes in the tall glass of Coke that she carried. She set it down on the coffee table in front of me and sat down on the sofa beside me.

"You're lucky," she smiled. "That was the last one left in the refrigerator."

"I'll be glad to share it with you," I offered, holding it out to her.

"No, thanks, I really wouldn't care for any."

As I lifted the glass of Coke to my lips, she pulled a flat, embossed silver box of cigarettes from the shelf under the coffee table, opened the box and held it out to me.

"Cigarette?"

"No, thanks. I don't smoke."

"No bad habits?" she asked, as she closed the box and tapped her cigarette on the lid before laying the box back down on the coffee table.

"Oh, I have some," I admitted suddenly, painfully aware that the attractive girl who sat close to me was representative of one of the worst of my bad habits. "It's just that smoking isn't one of them."

"I wish I could stop," she sighed, then lit up, inhaled and blew out a cloud of smoke, "but I guess the reason I don't is that I really don't want to quit bad enough. I enjoy it too much. Why make yourself miserable by denying yourself something you enjoy so much?"

"I guess you're right," I said, just to be agreeable, knowing that there were sound arguments and manifold evidences that could be brought out in opposition to the philosophy of hedonism which she had voiced.

But I hadn't come there for a philosophical debate, so instead of answering further, I idly rotated the glass in my hand, causing the ice cubes to tinkle against the sides of the glass.

"May I ask what the pin is that you're wearing?" she inquired, looking at me obliquely, cigarette poised between her fingers in a graceful pose, suggestive of a detail-disciplined Geisha girl of the Orient.

"What pin?" I asked, puzzled.

"That pin on your coat lapel," she replied, pointing at it with the tip of her cigarette.

I looked down at my coat lapel, to be as suddenly humiliated as if I had been stripped of my clothes on a busy, public street, revealing some distinctive birth mark which I had wanted to keep hidden. I was wearing my best suit, the one I ordinarily wore only to church on Sunday. I had neglected to remove the silver emblem of the "Cross and Crown" attendance contest that had been initiated at Gilead Baptist Church several months before to induce more faithful attendance on the part of young people. The pin identified me as a professing, church-going Christian. I suddenly felt like Peter, who had denied knowing Christ with his words. I was denying Him by my actions, in the sordid setting of that very moment. I found myself unable to repeat the facetious explanation of the symbol which I had given in church, aimed at provoking laughter from the young people. "This means," I had said of the cross running diagonally through a crown, "that if you cross me, I'll crown you."

To Diane, the dark-haired, play-for-pay girl who sat beside me, I answered soberly, with a tinge of guilty reluctance. "This means that if I'm willing to bear a cross in this life, I'll wear a crown in the next."

Without turning my head to look at her, I could see, out of the corner of my eye, that she was regarding me with an expression that was both quizzical and amused.

"That's kind of hard to do, isn't it?" she asked quietly.

"Yes, it's pretty rough at times," I conceded, and not wanting to pursue the uncomfortable subject any further, I switched the conversation to another channel.

"Where's the music coming from?" I asked.

"That radio on the shelf."

She pointed to a recessed bookshelf filled with a number of volumes, with a small radio tucked between two sections on one shelf. I got up for a closer look. It was emitting such an excellent, full-bodied tone in the symphonic string music that was coming from the speaker, that I could hardly believe it was coming from such a small radio cabinet.

"It's an import from Japan," she explained, as I examined it. "A friend of mine gave it to me. It's very expensive."

I surmised silently that the friend had probably gotten something from Diane in return for his expensive gift. The thought brought to my mind an unpleasant aspect of the transaction I was facing. Turning and walking back to the sofa, I reached into my coat pocket and drew out two ten-dollar bills

295

on the strength of the counsel I had gotten earlier from Goldie, the cab driver, that twenty dollars was the minimum for such a commodity all over town.

"By the way," I said casually, depositing the two ten-dollar bills in her lap as I turned and sat down on the sofa beside her again, "I found a couple of pieces of paper lying in the hallway when I came in, so I picked them up, thinking you might have a wastebasket. I didn't want to leave the place looking cluttered up."

She smiled at my unique way of broaching the business part of our contract, and snuffed out her cigarette.

"You understand that twenty is the minimum, of course?"

"I kind of gathered that from talking with different people."

"If you'd like me to invite a girl friend over," she began, "it would cost a little more, maybe thirty-five or forty."

"I think," I replied gently, "I had better settle for the minimum service."

"Okay," she said with a practiced, professional smile and a shrug of her shoulders as she stood up.

Since it was now clearly established that I was only in the market for the economy-priced sexual encounter, she was not going to waste any more precious time on preliminaries.

"Let's go into the bedroom and get undressed," she invited sweetly, stepping around the coffee table to lead the way.

I followed her down a short, carpeted hallway past an open door that led into a tile bath and on into the bedroom. The furnishings were clean and neat, but simple. Just a large double bed, a vanity, and two chairs, one in each corner.

"You can lay your clothes on that chair," she instructed, pointing to the one nearest me. "I've got to go to the bathroom a minute. I'll be right back."

I sat down on the chair near the bed and began to unlace my shoes, in a growing fever of anticipation at the prospect of slaking a basic human appetite that had not been satisfied in months, dating from the time of Florence's angry announcement of her unexpected, unwanted pregnancy. By the time I had stripped to my briefs, Diane was back. Sitting on the edge of the bed, I watched avidly as she began to undress, in a private version of the strip-tease show I had passed up at the Gayety. She pulled the gleaming, white satin blouse over her head, dropped it on the opposite chair from the one that held my clothes, then slid the leotards down over her hips in smooth, proficient movements. She exhibited as little show of self-consciousness at my presence as if she had been disrobing at the YWCA to take a swim. Then, stepping up in front of me and turning her back to me, dressed only in bra and bikini brief panties, she made an unexpected but titillating request.

"Would you unhook my bra, please, hon?"

"Be glad to," I responded, standing to my feet beside the bed, close behind her.

Aware that her request might simply be one of her often-used techniques to arouse sexual desire in a male client and then satisfy it as soon as possible, I nevertheless felt an intended thrill of expectation as I unfastened the hooks of her brassiere. As she turned to face me, she pulled the straps of the bra down from her shoulders and draped it over the back of the chair behind her, giving me time to be aroused by the sight of her firm, full breasts.

Then I impulsively did something that, for me, was an instinctive part of the natural foreplay in an intimate relationship between a man and a woman as a passionate prelude to a sexual encounter. I took her in my arms and drew her close to me, excited by the contact of my bare skin against the resilient fullness of her breasts. But as I moved my head closer to her upturned face, intending to kiss her, she guessed my intention and abruptly turned her head away. Puzzled by her inexplicable action, I drew back my head, but continued holding her in a loose embrace.

"You can kiss me anywhere except on the lips," she said quietly. "I don't allow any man to kiss me there."

I let my arms fall back to my sides and stood there staring at her in stunned speechlessness. Her unexpected action and incredible word of explanation had affected me psychologically like an abrupt slap in the face. I had been pushed rudely away in a totally unforeseeable show of aversion by the woman with whom I had been on the verge of consummating sexual union. The kiss that I had been about to bestow had been one of tenderness; in it had been a movement of the soul as much as the body; it had contained elements that were emotional and spiritual as well as physical. To reject this outward show of my inner feelings was the same as rejecting me.

She stood before me, regarding me with a look that seemed to be a mixture of amusement and cool, clinical curiosity as the spark of sexual desire that she had fanned into flame within me was put out as suddenly as an ignited match would be extinguished by a bucket of water thrown over it. I was no longer physically or emotionally able to conclude a sexual union; neither did I desire it any longer with this professionally seductive woman who, in spite of her learned techniques of sexual arousal, had rejected me as a person. Fortunately then, the sound of the doorbell spared me the painful necessity of trying to explain my reaction to her refusal to let me kiss her on the lips.

"Who in the Devil can that be?" she queried petulantly, turning away from me and reaching for a silk dressing gown on the chair behind her.

As she hurried out of the bedroom to answer the doorbell, I walked around to the other side of the bed and picked up my clothes from the chair. As I was dressing, I could hear Diane talking with someone in the hall whom she had evidently admitted through the locked outer door. I was able to hear only her concluding remark plainly.

"Why don't you come back in about ten minutes?"

I gathered that there was another impatient customer awaiting admittance on her doorstep who would not be offended by her peculiar idiosyncrasy of refusing to be kissed on the lips. I was almost completely dressed by the time she returned to the bedroom.

"You don't have to go yet," she said, standing in the bedroom doorway.

"I guess there's no reason to stay any longer," I replied, pulling on a shoe and bending down to tie it.

"Not if you've got what you came here for."

"No, I didn't," I replied, standing up, "but I guess you haven't got what I want, at least not to sell."

"What are you looking for?"

"Love," I responded instantaneously, looking her directly in the eye.

My answer, as I uttered it, was as much a surprise to me as it may have been to her. It might not even have risen to the surface of my mind from some subterranean depth within me had her probing question not drawn it upward out of me.

"You sure came to the wrong place for that," she chided.

Then there was another interruption in the personal kind of exchange between a man and a woman that was supposed to be private and intimate. The telephone in her bedroom rang.

"Excuse me," she said stepping past me to reach the phone on a stand beside the bed.

I finished knotting my necktie as she answered the phone.

"Hello? Oh, hello, Harry. Yeah, your friend got here all right. He's just leaving."

From the way she described me to Harry as "your friend," it made me feel as if the only reason I had been admitted to her apartment was because Harry had felt sorry for me and had talked her into seeing me. Perhaps, I reflected she is accustomed to clients from a higher income bracket whose investments in sexual pleasure far exceeded the minimum charge of twenty dollars that she had collected from me. The conversation with Harry concluded as she answered an evident inquiry from him.

"Yeah, they just got here before you called. I told them to wait across the street and come back in ten minutes. Yeah, okay, I'll call you later, Harry. Bye."

As she hung up the phone, I walked out of the bedroom into the living room and picked up my coat.

"What you need is a good affair," she prescribed, watching me as I donned my raincoat.

She followed me to the door.

"Do you want my phone number?" she asked.

"I don't think so; thanks anyway." I answered as I opened the door.

I stepped out into the hall and threw a parting word of farewell over my shoulder, without looking back at her.

"Been nice knowing you," I said, without conviction.

"Goodbye," came her voice, as I walked down the hallway.

I didn't turn back to answer, and heard the door click shut behind her.

As I got into my car and drove back downtown, my emotions were a mixture of sexual frustration and anger at myself. I felt that I should have taken by force what she had refused to give willingly, her lips as well as the rest of her body. At the very least, I argued with myself, I should have demanded a partial refund. I hadn't done so because I had felt an aversion to haggling over the price of the unsatisfying service I had received, especially in such a highly charged emotional situation. It was another case of a fraudulent label having been put on the sexual package I was buying, as had happened weeks before at the Gorgeous Girlie Show Bar in Calumet City, Illinois.

As I maneuvered my way through the fast expressway traffic, the thought also crossed my mind that had the episode with Diane followed through to its natural culmination of satisfaction, without her bizarre refusal to be kissed on the lips, she was the kind of woman I would have tried to induce to relocate to Lansing to work in partnership with me. She had possessed the youthfulness, the physical sex appeal, the intelligence and the erotic skills that would have qualified her for the role to a surpassing degree. But a slap in the face, even if only psychological rather than physical, was no inducement to cause me to think of setting up business with the one who had administered the slap.

En route back downtown, passed by one car after another, driven by people with purpose or destination in mind, the rain began falling again. The whish-whish of the windshield wipers that danced back and forth before my eyes in unison like twin ballerinas did nothing to allay the loneliness that I felt as I followed the four-lane thoroughfare back to the downtown area. It was nearing eleven o'clock when I turned off the exit ramp that led into Jefferson Avenue. Traffic was lighter than it had been earlier in the evening. I had been in Detroit three hours since my arrival, and the few things I had learned about how the world's oldest profession was handled in the big city seemed like very inadequate compensation for the frustrations I had encountered in seeking an outlet for my own aroused sexual appetite.

At Jefferson and Woodward I had to stop for a traffic light. Waiting, I glanced to my right across the Detroit River and saw the lights of Windsor, Canada. On my left, towering up out of sight, was the newest modern office building in downtown Detroit, the Consolidated Gas Building, famous for two things; the statue of a nude woman in the fountain plaza in front of the building, and the Top of the Flame dining room on the 20th floor. Up there was light and music, exquisite food, low-keyed laughter and people looking out and down over the rest of the city from a privileged perspective that only wealth could gain.

As I turned left on Woodward, the city's main downtown traffic artery, I glanced at the massive twenty-foot high bronze figure of a man, sitting with legs folded, in front of the City-County Building. Although I could not see it through the rain, I knew that engraved on the curved concrete wall behind the statue that represented the Spirit of Detroit was a verse from the Bible. It was a verse familiar to me, from the New Testament book of Second Corinthians.

"Now the Lord is that Spirit, and where the Spirit of the Lord is, there is liberty."

The verse, remembered in passing, came to me as a Divinely uttered commentary on my own condition at the moment. I did not have liberty. I was in bondage, driven by two seemingly contradictory objectives; to achieve a slimy success as a self-coronated prince of prostitution to compensate for my previous failures in legitimate endeavors, and to find something that had not been clearly identified in my own mind until I had voiced it to Diane, the call girl, a few minutes before; an elusive, intangible, mysterious force, or experience, or attraction, called "love." No, I did not have liberty, which suggested to me, disturbingly, that the Spirit of the Lord was not involved in my desperate search for two equally elusive entities, success and love. Yet, realizing that, I could not turn back and return to the city of Charlotte; to Florence, my wife; to the unborn child I had fathered; to my stifling routine as a clerk in the state Highway Department. I was too bound, driven, obsessed by unslaked cravings that were physical, emotional, and spiritual.

As I stopped at another traffic light on Woodward Avenue in downtown Detroit, out of the corner of my eye on my right I was aware of a woman walking on the sidewalk in the downpouring rain with no umbrella or raincoat, trying to shield herself with a folded newspaper held over her head. As a purely chivalrous impulse to offer her a ride arose within me, another car pulled up alongside between my car and the curb. I watched as the solitary male driver leaned over to roll down a window and call something to the woman. Perhaps it was an offer of a ride, or some offending obscenity. The woman paused for a moment to listen, then threw one hand down to her side in a disgusted gesture of dismissal of his offer, whatever it had been; sincere or salacious. Perhaps, I thought, that man, too, is seeking the same kind of satisfaction that I had been seeking, with no more success than I had found.

Yes, it was a frustrating, miserable pursuit, I thought, as I turned right off Woodward at the next corner, looking for love and success late at night in the rain-deserted streets of a big city. If I had been unable to find a satisfactory substitute for the real thing with either of the two prostitutes whose individual peculiarities had turned me off, where else could I look?

This was the question on my mind as I pulled into a parking space across the street from the Greyhound bus terminal, where my big-city explorations had begun earlier in the evening. I had neither the money nor the inclination to waste in repeating the strategy I had started on several hours before, asking a taxi driver to guide me to the person and place where my ill-understood but compelling hunger could be satisfied.

With the engine shut off, I sat there in the car across from the lighted, people-silhouetted windows of the Greyhound cafeteria from where I had set out earlier, seeking something to fill a void within me, as well as doing some business research along the way, only to find emptiness. Then, strangely, as it had happened several months before in the Tropicana Cabaret of Calumet City, Illinois, a fragment of almost-forgotten information from the past came to my mind to point me in a new direction.

Several years before, I had read a newspaper story about a woman who had been arrested for "soliciting" on the floor of a ballroom in Detroit, this being the legal term for a prostitute seeking to induce a man to purchase her sexual services. The back-page filler story had lodged in my memory, perhaps, because it had raised questions in my mind but had provided no answers. I had visualized the "ballroom" mentioned in the news account as a place of public entertainment where couples went together for an evening of dancing, either sweethearts, husbands and wives, or clandestine lovers. In such a setting, the story had sparked in my mind a dramatic scenario of a prostitute approaching a couple who were dancing, or sitting one out, and making a blatant overture to the man.

"How would you like to leave this woman you're with, sir, and come to my place and go to bed with me, for a nominal fee?"

Such a scene was impossible, I had realized. Yet, if a scene similar to this had not actually occurred, what had happened that had warranted a newspaper story? Because the unlikely scene which the story had projected in my mind was so bizarre, I had also remembered the name of the ballroom associated with it—the Artison.

Feeling a strange compulsion to unravel the mystery and perhaps, in the process, find a woman to replace Madge in my budding business enterprise, as well as find an enigmatic personal satisfaction I was seeking, the next logical step seemed to be to go into the Greyhound terminal across the street and see if I could find the Artison Ballroom in a phone directory.

I got out of the car and dashed across the street in the pouring rain. In the huge terminal, sparsely peopled with haggard-looking passengers waiting for buses, I went to the row of public phone booths along one wall and began thumbing through the yellow pages of the mammoth phone directory. I was pleasantly surprised to find not only the Artison Ballroom listed, but several others as well, all conveniently near on Woodward Avenue. In addition to the Artison, there were three other ballrooms listed, all in a five-block stretch of Woodward. There were also the Trees, the Moulin Rouge, and the Hollywood. And all advertised one exciting feature not usually connected with a ballroom: "dancing partners available." In such a setting, I began to understand how solicitation for prostitution could be carried out.

I looked up the phone number of the Artison and dialed it. As the phone rang several times and there was no answer, hope began to fade within me. I had struck another dead end in my vain search for the elusive twin entities of success and love. I was about ready to hang up when the phone stopped ringing and a female voice answered.

"Artison."

"Is this the Artison Ballroom?"

"Yes."

"Are you still open?"

"We're open until two."

I almost gasped in unbelief. This was such a radical departure from my own long-established life style.

I could hardly believe it. It seemed incredible that people would stay up dancing until two in the morning. Excited, I sought more information.

"I'm from out of town. I just saw your number in the

phone book, and it mentioned partners available. How does that work?"

"We have about a dozen girls who work here as dance instructors. You buy ten tickets for $1.50. That entitles you to ask any girl to dance with you."

It was my first inkling that a unique form of entertainment known as "taxi dancing," which I had read about as flourishing in New York City, was also carried on in Detroit. I couldn't help wondering if the other three ballrooms on Woodward operated in the same way.

"I noticed there are several other ballrooms in the same neighborhood," I continued, intent on getting all the information I could in an easy, inexpensive way rather than by a possibly embarrassing trial-and-error search. "Are they all the same kind of . . . uh, . . . setup?"

"Yes, they are," she replied tartly, evidently irritated at being asked for information about competitors.

"And do they all stay open until two in the morning?"

I had exhausted her patience with that question. She had wasted all the time she intended on someone who might not even turn out to be a cash customer.

"You'll have to call them and find out!" Bang!

The receiver was slammed down at the other end. The rude termination of our telephone conversation, even though warranted, perhaps, by my extended interrogation, produced in me a reaction of aversion toward the Artison. I decided at that moment, that since the other three ballrooms had the same service to offer, I would try one of them instead. As I made my way to the terminal cafeteria through the cavernosus, high-ceilinged terminal where a motley and sizeable collection of travelers stood, sat, or lounged, waiting for buses, I understood how easily solicitation for prostitution could be carried on behind such a legitimate facade. When I had first read the newspaper item several years before, I had thought the "ballroom" named in the article was a public one where couples came to dance, and I had wondered how a woman could solicit male customers in such a setting. But it appeared that the Artison and the other "ballrooms" on Woodward, specialized in providing female dancing partners for an exclusively male clientele.

In the Greyhound cafeteria, a bowl of chili and a cup of coffee to wash away some of my physical and emotional weariness was enhanced by the awareness that I had more than two hours ahead of me in which to explore the unknown erotic environment of the ballrooms on Woodward Avenue, only fifteen minutes away by car. Then, back in the car, with the windshield wipers swish-swishing rhythmically to the beat of the rain upon the roof of the car, I drove back to Woodward Avenue. On Woodward, I commenced another mile of a puzzling pilgrimage, the underlying purpose of which I did not fully understand.

On the surface, as far as my rational faculties could determine, I had come to Detroit primarily to acquire a practical working knowledge of the business of prostitution that I could apply back in Lansing, and perhaps a female business partner to replace Madge, who had been temporarily diverted by the rain. But as I drove north on Woodward in the rain, on the wide, pedestrian-emptied concourse that led through Detroit's downtown shopping and theatre section, all the mental observations I had made about Harry and Goldie, Carole and Diane, had been pushed into the background of my mind. The furtherance of that illegal business venture which had been conceived in Calumet City, Illinois, several months before had been subordinated to something else that was driving me on through the rain-washed late-night hours in the city of Detroit while most of its nearly million inhabitants slept.

The frank and disturbing question of Diane, the dark-haired call girl, came back to me.

"What are you looking for?"

"Love," I had answered spontaneously, without thought or premeditation.

But I was no longer sure what I meant by the word. Had it been only lust, a physical appetite that was driving me, why had I not following through on the opportunity to release that restless physical energy with Diane? If it was only lust, I mused, it had to have the appearance of love, or it was not acceptable to me. Perhaps that was what had suddenly and completely quenched the desire I had felt toward Diane. Her strange peccadillo of being willing to yield èvery part of her body to me except her lips meant to me that she was not giving herself to me; only parts of her body, selling the temporary use of select parts of her anatomy. The essence of love was the act of self-giving. It was an act that could not be induced for a gift of money. It had to be a natural and spontaneous response of one personality toward another. And why was it, I wondered, as I drove down the wide, rain-riven street, that I had turned away from the one place in the world where I should expect to find love; from Florence, my wife? The unanswerable questions that coursed through my mind as I drove north along the deserted boulevard only added to the weariness I felt; a compound of physical tiredness from hours of driving, and the emotional frustration of the buffeting experiences I had been through since arriving in Detroit.

The disturbing questions were then temporarily erased from my mind as I saw just ahead and across the street a lighted marquee over the sidewalk with the word, "Artison" in neon lights. Still feeling the sting of the receiver that had been slammed down in my ear by the woman who had answered the phone there, I cruised slowly past, looking for the other ballrooms in that area. I passed by the Trees Dance Studio, the Moulin Rouge, and finally stopped across the street from the Hollywood Ballroom. Perhaps I decided on trying the Hollywood first because the name was a familiar, household word; it was synonymous with the glamour and romance of the film industry. I was drawn, too, by the huge sign on top of the two-story, brick building housing the dance hall, which advertised "50 Dancing Partners." A parking place was the next problem. Three blocks away, on a side street, I found one.

Finally, on the sidewalk in front of the Hollywood Ballroom, rain-damp and a little winded by my brisk walk from the side-street parking place, I paused to regain my breath. Standing beneath the marquee that extended out over the sidewalk, I looked through the swinging, glass-paneled door that led inside, curious for a glimpse of what was within. All I could see was a red-carpeted stairway leading up. Music from the second-floor ballroom spilled out around me over a loudspeaker above the double doors. The sound of rain falling on the marquee was drowned out by the lyrics of a male vocalist, singing words that struck a strangely responsive chord within me.

"A man once said . . . That love is a treasure . . . How true his words, how true . . . The man who said . . . That love is a treasure . . . He knew, how well he knew."

Driven by a confused compulsion to find that treasure called "love" that the male vocalist was singing about, I turned into the street-level entrance of the second-floor Hollywood Ballroom.

CHAPTER 9

⟹ Like an explorer stepping into a strange, new world, with no inkling of what might lie ahead of him in the way of peril or pleasure, I pushed my way carefully through the red, swinging, glass-paneled doors. But once inside, on the first step of the wide, red-carpeted stairway leading upward, I halted, suddenly remembering a humiliating episode from earlier in the evening. I pulled back the raincoat that covered the lapels of my suit coat to see it still gleaming there—the Cross and Crown bronze emblem that had evoked a probing question from Diane, the call girl. I unpinned it and slipped it into my pocket. I wanted no repetition of that awkward, painful moment I had experienced in her apartment. Then I continued on up the stairway, with the music from the ballroom above me growing louder with each step.

"I see your face . . . And there I find my fortune . . . No kingdom filled with gold . . . Could be so rare . . . When we embrace, and you kiss me . . . Oh, my darling, each kiss is like a jewel beyond compare . . ."

On a landing at the top of the stairway, I stepped through a curtained entrance. Immediately on my left was a small room with a metal grillwork across the front in which a middle-aged woman sat, obviously to collect the required admission fee. She had on too much make-up and her auburn hair was pulled back into a tight bun on her neck, reminding me more of an old-fashioned school teacher I had once had, than the doorkeeper in a nocturnal palace of pleasure.

"How much?" I asked.

"Ten tickets for a dollar fifty."

I laid two dollars on the counter, and she handed me a strip of tickets and my change. Then I went on into the dimly lit interior of the Hollywood Ballroom. Adjacent to the cashier's cage was a coat-check room, where I checked my somewhat soaked raincoat. I paused for a drink of water at a fountain by the wall, then leaned against the wall to survey the setup as a first-time visitor to the night-time world of taxi-dancing.

The dance floor, which was spacious, with only half a dozen couples dancing at the moment, was separated from the long lounge area where I stood by a brass, waist-high railing. Over the center of the dance floor, a gargantuan disc, containing multicolored circular panes of glass, rotated continuously, casting a constantly changing pattern of colored light upon the dancers and the floor. The music, which I had first heard spilling out onto the street with an irresistible drawing power, was from 45 rpm records, amplified over the loudspeakers to the volume of a live dance band.

As I leaned against the wall in the semi-gloom, I watched the dancers on the floor, swaying to the music, feeling apprehensive about attempting something that I hadn't done since I was a worldly senior in high school years before. What I saw assured me that I should be able to equal, if not outdo, some of the men on the dance floor. While one couple was moving with the liquid fluidity of proficient dancers, most were just holding their female partners close and shuffling around the perimeter of the floor. One man was obviously not even in step with the music, and in the darkness of a far corner of the dance floor, one couple seemed not to be moving at all, just standing still and embracing. Watching the unmoving couple brought back to my mind the news item that had drawn me here, showing how easily solicitation for prostitution could be employed by the females hired as dance hostesses to dance with any man who came in off the street as I had, although this sordid inducement had been subordinated to a deeper personal need. As I had told Diane, the call girl, I was looking for "love," not just a practicing or potential prostitute who would be willing to relocate to Lansing and become my business partner in launching a "sex for sale" business sideline there.

With a renewed hope that I might find in this unlikely place the "love" I was looking for, in addition to a slimy form of success as a self-coronated prince of prostitution, and reassured by what I saw, that I could function on the dance floor with at least as much ability as those I saw, I turned my attention to the selection of dance partners available. I did so with an ego-boosting confidence born of the assurance that no matter which one I asked to dance with me, none could or would reject me. My display of tickets would guarantee a yielding to my request or run the risk of a reprimand from the management.

I looked down the extended length of the semi-darkened lounge area. Along the brass railing that separated the dancers from the lounge area were strung out several sofas and lounge chairs for the use of the female partners who were available, for a price, to dance with any male, such as myself, who came in off the street. Across a wide aisle from these comfortable easy chairs, along the wall that opened into the rest rooms, was a line of less comfortable straight-backed chairs for the male clients, several of whom were sitting and watching the dancers, perhaps trying to work up the necessary courage to approach one of the available dance partners and ask her to dance.

At the moment, with perhaps half a dozen of the hostesses on the dance floor, and several at the refreshment stand, there were only six girls sitting strung out along the railing, available as dance partners. There was nowhere near the fifty dance partners advertised on the outside of the building housing the ballroom. I restrained an irritated impulse to complain to the management about fraudulent advertising, but shrugged it off philosophically. Perhaps, I speculated, there had been as many as fifty dancing partners available during the ballroom's heyday during World War II, when Detroit was the arsenal of democracy and may have unloosed on the place a flood of defense factory workers and servicemen coming into the place nightly in search of female companionship. But something else also immediately quashed any rising impulse of irritation that there were not more dancing partners to choose from than the twelve or fifteen presently on the premises.

Of the six girls sitting strung out along the railing, one caught my eye and kindled my interest. Five of the girls, in a variety of sizes and shapes, sat bunched together, talking and smoking to alleviate their boredom while waiting for some timid male to step away from the shadows on the wall and ask one of them to dance. But the one who had caught my attention sat apart from the others, her seeming aloofness from them conveying to me an impression that she was out of place here, even as much as I was.

She was probably five-feet-two inches tall, blonde hair piled up high on top of her head with a pony tail behind, and wearing a simply cut, black taffeta dress with flared skirt, and matching black, high-heeled shoes. She sat gracefully erect, looking straight ahead, reminding me of a queen sitting upon her throne. As I stood in the shadows by the wall fifteen feet away and looked at her, I could not shake off the impression that she was not waiting for just another customer. She was waiting for something important to happen in her life or for someone long expected to appear. I wanted to ask her to dance with me, yet I hesitated. It had been so many years since I had been on a dance floor that I did not want to foist my first, awkward stumbling off onto her. So I approached a buxom brunette in a green, too-tight jersey dress, who sat on the outside of the five who were bunched together gossiping. She looked up as I approached.

"Are you available?" I asked.

"Sure am," she answered, putting on a smile as she got up, "that's what I'm getting paid for."

I followed her onto the dance floor, having been made unmistakably aware that what she was doing was being done only because it was her job. I stood with her a moment on the dance floor, as one record ended and another began. Fortunately, it was slow enough to accommodate the basic dance steps I had learned years before. I said nothing for the first few moments, concentrating on moving my feet in time with the music. An instinctive sense of rhythm helped me. After a few stumbling steps, kicking her toes and bumping her knees, I began to move with more assurance.

"I haven't danced for a long time," I apologized. "I almost forgot how."

"You're doing better than some of the schnooks that come in here," she said, looking at me. "I think some of 'em have never been on a dance floor before in their lives."

After a few more moments, in which I noted that each new record selection, which used up one of my strips of tickets, only lasted from two to three minutes, I was pleased to find that I could maneuver my partner in a wide, circular pattern around the perimeter of the dance floor without stepping on her toes. Free of the need to concentrate on the movement of my feet, I broached the question that had been poised in my mind since I had begun dancing.

"Do you happen to know the blonde young lady in the black dress?"

"Her name's Colette, and all I know about her is what some of the fellows I've danced with have told me. They all call her 'Miss Frigidaire.' She looks like a hot number, but she doesn't warm up to anybody, and believe me, some of the fellows have tried every trick they know. I heard one guy even offered her a hundred bucks to spend the night with him, and she turned him down cold. Can you imagine it?"

The amazement in her tone implied that had she been made the same offer, she would not have turned it down. As we continued to move around the floor, I stole furtive glances in the direction of the blonde girl in the black dress who sat alone, hoping that someone else would not come along and ask her to dance before I could get back to her. And after ten minutes of growing confidence in my rapidly revived ability to keep step with the music without treading on my partner's toes, I handed the strip of tickets to the woman I had danced with. Later, at the end of the evening, I assumed she would turn in the tickets for a cash commission. While she returned to her seat in the lounge area, rejoining the other girls, I walked over to the ticket cage and bought another strip of ten tickets. With the tickets in my coat pocket, I turned back to the lounge area, quietly elated to see that Colette was still sitting alone, even though three of the five other girls were now out on the dance floor. As I walked toward her, I derived no feeling of confidence from the tickets in my pocket. I didn't want to buy her time and company. I did not go to her with an attitude, or expectation, of demanding that she fulfill her obligation to dance with me just because I had bought some tickets, and she was an employee there, and I was a customer. I paused in front of her to bend down slightly from the waist like a courtier bowing before royalty.

"Would you care to dance?" I asked.

My tone was personal rather than possessive. My voice and manner of approach were intended to convey my recognition of her sovereign right as an individual to decline my invitation if she found anything about me to be personally objectionable. I had interrupted what must have been a pensive mood or melancholy reverie. A look of pleased surprise tugged the corners of her lips upwards, like a hint of sunshine ready to break through the clouds of hidden concern that had drawn the lines of her face into a serious expression. The green eyes that I looked into, gold flecked and artistically enhanced with eye shadow, were not opaque, but transparent. They were, in that first moment of visual contact, windows through which I looked to see a hidden world within her that exerted a magnetic pull upon something deep within me.

"I'd love to," she smiled, rising.

I followed her onto the dance floor, where she turned to face me. I took her right hand in mine, extended out, and put my left hand around her slender waist. I did not have to draw her to me. She stepped into my encircling embrace. The top of her head was level with my eyes. She nestled her head against my shoulder as we began to dance, and the scented, fine spun gold of her softly waving hair brushed my cheek. For several minutes, I was tense and self-conscious of the movements of my feet, fearful lest I step on one of her delicate, high-heeled slippers, so dangerously close to my thick-soled, wingtip brogans. But after a few moments of moving in time with the music, and not stepping on her toes or bumping her knees, as I had initially with my first partner, I could relax and begin to experience a fluid merging with the music and the woman whose graceful movements so skillfully mirrored my own.

"What's your name?" I asked, not wanting her to know that I had already learned her name from the first girl I had danced with.

"Colette."

"That's French, isn't it?"

"Wee, wee, monsieur."

At her answer, we both laughed, even though it was nothing really funny.

"You've just exhausted my French vocabulary," I continued, as we circled the floor slowly. "I hope you can speak English fluently."

"I've gotten along alright so far," she smiled, looking into my eyes. "And what's your name?"

"Garfield Roby."

It was strange, I reflected, as I told her my name, that I had felt no hesitation, no apprehension about giving her my full name as I had in some of my earlier contacts that evening.

"How do you like your job?" I asked.

"I hate it!" she replied, and both her reply and the vehemence with which she uttered it surprised me. "I'd much rather be doing what I used to do—modeling."

"Why aren't you doing it, then, if you dislike this job so much?"

"Too many photographers got the idea that my body belonged to them just because I posed for them."

As we moved around the floor in an easy-going, two-step

pattern, which was all that I was sure of, I pondered the unpleasant situations that must have given rise to the sentiment she had just expressed.

"You can't sell yourself," I mused aloud, distilling a universal principle of human experience from my encounter with Diane, the call girl earlier in the evening. "You can only give yourself away."

Colette drew her head back and looked at me in evident surprise.

"Where did you learn that?"

"In the school of hard knocks," I smiled.

The record to which we had been dancing came to an end, reminding me that I was supposed to be paying for the pleasure I was finding by handing Colette one of the tickets in my pocket each time a record came to an end. To reinforce the pleasant illusion that I had harbored from the beginning, that dancing with Colette was a mutually voluntary arrangement rather than an enforceable business contract, I reached into my pocket and handed the whole strip of ten tickets to her.

"Since I'm not very good at arithmetic," I said, "why don't you let me know when these are used up. I wouldn't want to cheat you out of any of your hard-earned commission."

"Thank you," she smiled, obviously pleased that I had decided to use all the tickets with her, thereby boosting her pay for that evening's work.

As she folded the tickets and stuck them into a concealed pocket on the side of her dress, and while we waited for the next music selection to start, I drew a handkerchief from my pocket to wipe the perspiration that had gathered on my forehead. Along with the rainfall had come a rising humidity and an unseasonably high temperature for the month of November, one of the many freakish weather variations typical of Michigan.

"It is warm tonight, isn't it?" she observed sympathetically.

Her eyes and tone of voice registered pity for the male of the species standing before her, wearing a suit coat and necktie, while she was lightly dressed in a flimsy, low-cut, black dress that looked as light as nothing.

"Maybe it's just because I have to work so hard to keep from stepping on your toes," I said.

"You're doing a good job," she smiled, stepping back into my arms as the music started. "You haven't stepped on them once yet."

"Let me know if I do," I suggested, "and I'll give you a quarter each time. How's that?"

"I'm afraid I won't make much money that way," she laughed, and it seemed to me that her laughter was the sweetest sound I had ever heard.

It was perhaps forty minutes later, as the music of another record ended, and I released Colette, but stood facing her, that she glanced at her watch and made a disturbing announcement.

"Oh, oh, it's time for me to leave you for . . ."

"It's not closing time, is it?" I broke in, alarmed.

"Oh, no," she smiled, "it's not one o'clock yet. We're open for another hour. But you'll have to excuse me for about fifteen minutes. I have a special number to do."

"A special number?"

"I'm going to sing a song up on the stage. Every night one of us girls has to go up on the stage and do a special number; kind of an extra to attract customers, you know. You can go over and sit down and listen to me if you want to. But I have to go to the rest room now and change."

As she turned away, I walked beside her across the dance floor where other couples were dancing again, to the lounge area behind the separating railing.

"You will dance with me some more afterwards, won't you?" I asked, worried, as she pushed open the door of the ladies' rest room.

"Certainly!" she assured me with a smile, "we haven't used up all the tickets you gave me yet."

Relieved, I found an empty chair against the wall and sat down, facing the ballroom floor and the stage, to wait expectantly for Colette's "special number." It was no more than five minutes later that she reappeared, stepping through the rest room door. She saw me, smiled, and waved, as I stared in wide-eyed wonder at the transformation she had wrought in such a few short minutes.

In an impressive demonstration of wardrobe wizardry, she had changed the atmosphere of a rainy November night into a balmy summer evening. Her simply cut, black taffeta frock had been changed to a sparkling white, knee-length dress with a bouffant skirt that rustled as she stepped onto the dance floor. On her head was a broad-brimmed hat, and tilted across one shoulder was a lace-trimmed parasol such as aristocratic ladies in the Old South once carried to shield them from the sun. I watched, enchanted, as she stepped briskly and gracefully across the dance floor area and mounted the steps of the stage that was inset into the wall, and which, in better days, had probably been occupied by a live band for dancing.

The half dozen couples on the dance floor paused as the music stopped and a spotlight illuminated Colette. Then her voice, silken soft, vibrant and throaty, came over the microphone in front of her that was mounted on a floor stand.

"I'd like to sing an old favorite that I'm sure most of you know. It's called 'Fascination,' and I'd like to dedicate it to all lovers here tonight."

There were scattered hand claps from some of the couples on the dance floor and from those on the sidelines. Then the music of the well-known pop song filled the dance hall, and Colette began to sing.

The half dozen couples on the floor continued dancing, preoccupied, perhaps, with each other, while Colette and her enchanting voice were pushed into the background of their awareness. But for me, sitting in the semi-darkness on the sidelines, enthralled by her lilting voice, smitten by her spotlighted beauty, the familiar music and long-forgotten words were as if I were hearing them for the first time; as if they were being sung by Colette just to me and just for me.

It was fascination, I know,
And it might have ended right there at the start;
Just a passing glance,
Just a brief romance,
And I would have gone on my way, empty hearted.

It was fascination, I know,
Seeing you alone, with the moonlight above,
Then I touched your hand, and when I kissed you,
Fascination turned into love.

As she repeated the chorus in a lilting, silvery soprano voice that seemed equal to anything I had ever heard on records, I felt as if Colette were singing them to me alone. But her captivating and professional performance also evoked sudden questions in my mind. With such beauty and talent, why wasn't she on television or in films or on records? What was she doing in a place like this, wasting such talents as a poorly paid taxi dancer? The questions remained in my mind as I listened to her repeat the final stanza. Then, too soon, her inspired performance was over. As the music ended and the spotlight went off, she came down from the stage, balancing the parasol gracefully on one shoulder, to a smattering of applause, including my own, and some exuberant wolf whistles from some of the male clients.

"See you in a few minutes," she smiled, passing me en route to the ladies' room to change.

Ten minutes later she reappeared, dressed again as bewitchingly as when I had first seen her and, together, we walked out onto the dance floor.

"How did you like my number?" Colette asked, as she stepped into my embrace and we began moving again to the music.

"Fantastic! You were beautiful. With all your talent, how come you aren't on records as a vocalist instead of working at a job you despise?"

"I almost was . . . once," she replied wistfully.

"What happened?" I asked, sensing some tragic thwarting of natural talents comparable to that which had happened in my own life.

"I'd rather not talk about if, if you don't mind."

I glanced briefly into her eyes and saw pain mirrored there which forbade me from probing further. Then she returned her head to my shoulder as we merged our movements with the music of an appropriately seasonal ballad that I recognized, "September in the Rain."

"Do you know the words of the song they're playing?" I asked.

"Just a few phrases here and there," Colette replied, drawing her head back to look at me. "Why?"

"Would you sing what you know for me, and just hum the rest?"

"If you don't mind if I make a change in the title. After all, it's November, not September."

"I'm sure any changes you make in the wording will be an improvement."

She smiled her appreciation of the compliment and, when the refrain began again, she sang as we danced.

The leaves of brown,

Came tumbling down, remember?

That November, in the rain . . .

As Colette continued singing softly, here and there a phrase she knew, and humming the rest as we danced, I closed my eyes and succumbed to a state of mind, the preliminary symptoms of which are almost identical with those of love, a state called "infatuation."

It was a growing, enveloping encirclement of my mind and heart and senses that was pushing out of my mind and interest the sordid business research venture that had been my principal motive in coming to Detroit that evening.

When the record ended, and there was a momentary lull before the next record began, we stood facing each other on the dance floor.

"That was beautiful, Colette." I applauded her singing with both my hands and eyes. "I hope you enjoyed singing as much as I enjoyed listening."

"I do love to sing, especially for someone who appreciates it."

Facing each other, inches apart, the depths to which she had stirred me was expressed in a comment that surprised me as well as her.

"I've been looking all over Detroit for you, Colette," I said soberly, looking into her eyes.

"How could you?" she laughed, "you didn't even know I was here."

"If I had," I answered seriously, "I would have come here first instead of looking in other places."

She smiled with both her eyes and her lips. It was far different from the smile I had seen on the face of Diane, the call girl. That smile had been only on the surface, skin deep, an acquired business asset, nothing more. Colette's smile was a transparent one, through which some of the hidden sunlight within the depths of her personality shone through, warm and life-giving. And as the music started again, and she stepped back into my arms, I discovered that I was finding in this woman who was dancing with me more of what I had really been deeply hungering for, for a far lesser price than what I had gotten from Diane, the professional play-for-pay girl. My contact with Diane had been almost wholly physical. There had been no release, no meeting and merging of our separate personalities. Even though our bodies had touched in the intimacy of erotic foreplay, we had not really touched each other. This woman who was dancing with me was somehow giving herself to me, in the few words we had exchanged, in her smiles, in the song she had sung. And holding Colette in a light embrace as we danced, although both fully clothed, was a more exciting and fulfilling experience than had been the naked skin-to-skin contact with Diane.

As we continued circling the spacious, color-splashed

dance floor, almost as if we were alone, since there were only two or three other couples dancing, the woman in my arms suddenly seemed so much a beautiful child that I wanted to pick her up and carry her through the trials and troubles of this world, adoring, protecting her. But no sooner had I spread the wings of imagination to follow the unfolding of this fantasy, than they were clipped by a recollection from the realm of reality. I was a married man, and a contemptibly deceitful and unfaithful husband at that, indulging in illicit fantasies while I held another woman in my arms, while a hundred miles away, my wife, bearing the growing life which I had implanted within her womb, endured the loneliness of the night alone. And if, in the darkness, she reached out for the comfort of a husband who was not there, she doubtless would turn for comfort to the erroneous belief that out of love for her, the missing husband was spending the night at work, driving a taxicab in a nearby city to help meet the added expense of the coming baby. And I was more than an unfaithful husband, I reflected, as we danced in silent synchronization with the music, I was also a disobedient child of God, reveling the night away in one of the Devil's chief palaces of pleasure for the ungodly, the dance hall. And out of the unspoken bitterness of my own meditation, I spoke a question into the air.

"How would you like to dance with me on streets of gold?"

Colette looked up at me, and the movement of taking her head from my shoulder caused me to look down into her eyes. There was a sudden frown of puzzlement crossing her face at my unexpected question, so unrelated to anything that had been said between us up until that time. And if she was startled by my question, I was equally stunned by her reply.

"I would," she answered, the seriousness of her answer evident in both her eyes and tone of voice, "but not this kind of dancing."

She must have seen the questioning look on my face, but she offered no more by way of explanation. The music ended, and we stood close together, as we had been when we were dancing, without breaking apart.

"I'm afraid you've used up all the tickets you gave me," said Colette gently, sounding reluctant to insert a commercial reminder into the intimacy of a growing personal rapport, "so if you want to dance with me anymore, I guess you'll have to . . ."

"I'll be right back," I said, stepping back from her. "You stay right here and don't dance with anyone else, okay?"

"I'll wait right here," she promised, obviously as pleased as I was at the prospect of continuing to dance with me.

I hurried over to the ticket cage, bought ten dollars' worth of tickets, returned to Colette and handed them to her.

"If you dance with me until closing time," she protested, slipping them into a pocket of her dress, "you won't use up all these tickets."

"Keep them anyway, Colette," I brushed aside her considerate objection, "you deserve a bonus for taking the risk of getting your toes stepped on by a lousy dancer like me."

"I think you're a good dancer," she objected, as the music started and she stepped back into my arms again.

"Thank you. This comes as news to me."

"You're easy to dance with," she added, "compared to some of the fellows who come in here. It's really restful to dance with you. If all my customers were as good, this job wouldn't be so bad."

She rested her head on my shoulder again, in a position that had become as familiar as though it belonged there. I lost count of the number of times one music selection ended, a momentary pause as we stood close facing each other, and then began to dance again. Not until I recognized a familiar selection being played did I have any inkling of how swiftly time had flown since I had begun to dance with Colette. The words drifted through my mind from having heard them years before, as the familiar strains of music flowed around us.

Good-night, angel, till we meet tomorrow . . . Good night, angel . . . parting is such sorrow.

"Is this the last number?" I asked, alarmed that the short hour of enchantment I had spent with her was about to end so soon.

"I'm afraid it is," she answered, looking up at me.

"Can I take you home, Colette?" I pleaded hopefully, wanting to know her better, desperate to prolong the rare enjoyment I had found in her company.

"We aren't allowed to leave with our customers," she answered with evident sincerity. "I'm sorry."

In the few moments that were left to dance with her while the final music selection drew to its inevitable close, I pondered silently whether this was really a strictly enforced ruling of the management, or whether it was just a polite subterfuge for avoiding a climax to the evening, which had no appeal for her.

"I could wait outside for you," I suggested, "then no one would see you leave with me."

"I'm afraid not," she declined trying to soften the effects of her refusal with a smile.

But I was not to be put off so easily. "I promise I'll take you straight home," I assured her, with all the earnestness I could convey in tone and glance. "No delays, no detours."

"All right," she finally capitulated with a sigh, "since you promise to take me straight home. There's a drugstore on Woodward, just a block from the Hollywood. You can wait for me there. It takes me about fifteen minutes to cash in my tickets."

"See you there in fifteen minutes," I said, and turned away to retrieve my coat and hat from the check room.

On the street, it was raining as hard as it had been when I had arrived at the Hollywood more than two and a half hours earlier. Colette hadn't said which direction on Woodward from the Hollywood was located the drugstore where I was to wait for her. Looking down the wide, deserted, rain-washed avenue to the right, I saw a drugstore on the corner of the next block. But looking to the left, I saw another one at the end of the block in which the ballroom was situated. To avoid the risk of waiting in the wrong drugstore and missing her, I decided to wait in the doorway of a closed restaurant next to the ballroom entrance. Ten minutes later she appeared, smiling when she saw me. I stepped up beside her and she took my proffered arm, a vital safety precaution as she tried to hurry on the rain-slicked sidewalk in high heels.

"The car's down this way," I said, and started walking south on Woodward, Colette's arm lightly linked through mine.

As we crossed a side street, the water was so deep along the curb that I knew her feet would be soaking wet by the time we reached the car. Approaching one of the drug stores she had mentioned, I made a gallant proposal.

"How would you like to wait in this drugstore while I bring the car here, instead of getting all wet walking to it?"

"Thank you for being so thoughtful," she smiled, responding to my gentle pressure on her arm as I guided her toward the entrance to the drug store.

I walked inside with her and sat down at the soda fountain long enough to pay for the vanilla milk shake she ordered, then left, promising to be back with the car within ten minutes.

I hurried the three blocks to where the car was parked. As I tried to find my back to Woodward, in an unfamiliar city, through a maze of one-way streets and "no left turn" signs, I finally got back to the drug store, having taken a good ten minutes to do so. I double parked and, leaving the engine running, hurried into the drug store to get Colette. The stool at the soda fountain where she had been sitting when I left was now empty. I looked around the drug store, but she was nowhere in sight. I hurried back outside, looked up and down Woodward Avenue, but there was no trace of her figure hurrying away in the distance. She had vanished as swiftly and surely as a mirage of water before a thirst-crazed desert wanderer.

I walked slowly back to the car, no longer caring if a police car came along to give me a ticket for double parking. So quickly the little world of warmth and happiness that I had found had burst like a bubble. The world I inhabited was again what it had been before I had climbed the red-carpeted steps of the Hollywood Ballroom; the world of a cold, lonely and miserable night, with emptiness, weariness and disappointment inside and a cold, uncaring, sleeping city on the outside. I turned on the windshield wipers and drove south on Woodward to get to the Ford expressway that would take me back to the world I had fled; back to the world of a pregnant wife whom I would now have to face with a lie on my lips; back to a life of hidden hunger and lonely fantasies.

As I drove through the deserted, rain-riven streets of the great sleeping metropolis, as it neared three o'clock in the morning, a phrase from "The Hound of Heaven," by English poet Francis Thompson, echoed through the lonely reaches of my mind.

"Naught shelters thee, that will not shelter Me."

Later, on the expressway, facing the long, lonely miles that lay ahead of me on my way back to Charlotte, I turned back for warmth and comfort to those magic moments, that swiftly fleeting hour of enchantment when I had danced with a woman who had seemed to be all that I had never found in a woman before, not even the woman I had married and who was now bearing my child.

As I thought back to the moment when Colette had fled from the drugstore where she had promised to wait for me, perhaps in a taxi or with some girl friend who worked at the Hollywood and who had a car, I couldn't feel bitterly toward her. I tried to place myself in her situation. While I knew the sincerity of my intentions, she could not have known what was in my heart. She would have had no way of knowing but what I might have intended to drive her forcibly to some secluded place and rape her, a plan that had doubtless crossed the minds of some of her less gentle male customers before. So as I drove homeward through the dark, lonely hours of early morning, with the cars that passed being few and far between, I found a glow in reliving those moments when I had danced with Colette; when I had heard the music of her speaking and singing, and several times the rippling cascade of her laughter.

I wondered again about the strange contradictions in her personality that were hinted at in what she had said and in what one of her co-workers had said about her—a woman who didn't warm up to the men she danced with, and yet had seemed so wonderfully warm toward me, in smiles and conversations, and in the way she had rested her head on my shoulder as we danced. A woman who hated her job as a taxi-dancer, and yet had turned down the offer of a hundred dollars to go out with a customer. And I wondered again what might lie behind the enigmatic answer she had given me when I had asked her if she'd like to dance on streets of gold.

"Not this kind of dancing."

Did her response indicate religious convictions, that she thought the kind of dancing she did for a living was somehow incompatible with the golden streets of Heaven, even as I had been taught in the churches I had attended through the years of growing up? And if she thought there was something wrong with that kind of dancing, why was she doing it?

Strangely missing from my reflections about the evening behind me as I drove were the pointers I had picked up about the planned business venture in Lansing, which had been the principal motive for the trip to Detroit in the first place. It had been completely pushed out of my mind by a woman about whom I knew little more than her first name; a woman whom I might never have met had it not been for the rain that had begun to fall late in the afternoon of the preceding day, and was still falling. It was ironic, I thought, as the windshield wipers cleared an arc of visibility through which I could see the highway ahead of me, that the rain that had deterred Madge, the divorcee, from accompanying me on the trip, had also provided the means of flight for Colette from the drug store where she had promised to wait while I went to get the car. But in spite of having run out on me and reneging on her promise to let me take her home, I felt no ill will toward her; only a desire and determination to see her again.

The lingering influence of Colette pursued me, unnoticed by Florence or her mother the following Sunday afternoon, as they sat at a table polishing Hilda's special-occasion silverware. Retrieving from the front parlor the bowling bag that contained a concertina I had once used at missions, jails, and street meetings in Chicago, I paused in the large doorway that led into the kitchen.

"Flo, I'm going upstairs and practice with the concertina for a little while."

It was Hilda who protested with solicitous concern rather than Florence.

"Mercy, Garfield," she remonstrated, looking up from her work, "how can you move your fingers up in that cold room? I should think they'd freeze up."

"I don't want to drive you and Florence out of the house," I explained. "When I'm trying to learn a new song, it sounds pretty awful at first."

"Why, that doesn't matter, Garfield. I don't mind hearing it, and I'm sure Florence doesn't mind. But you suit yourself."

Florence remained glumly noncommittal, still smoldering with resentment over the part-time taxi-driving job, as I turned away to carry out my expressed intention. I couldn't divulge to Hilda and Florence the real reason I wanted to practice in private. So I continued on upstairs, closing both the stairway door and the upstairs bedroom door behind me. Alone in the huge, unheated bedroom, I set the bowling ball bag down on the big, double bed, removed the concertina, and stepped over by the double front windows that looked down on the front yard and the blacktop highway that ran in front of the house. But as I expanded the bellows to their full length and looked out the windows, I didn't really see the stately oak trees in the front yard, whose branches, with a few autumn-colored leaves still clinging, touched the roof.

Instead, in my mind's eye, I saw a vision of summertime loveliness. I saw a woman standing upon a ballroom stage, dressed in a shimmering white frock, wearing a broad-brimmed hat and carrying a lace-trimmed parasol; a woman with incredibly white skin, blonde hair, and green eyes; whose voice, when she sang, was like warm, liquid silver being poured out with an amazing capacity to heal wounds of the mind and heart and spirit. I saw a mysterious, enchanting, singing taxi dancer at the Hollywood Ballroom in Detroit, named Colette.

And downstairs, Florence and Hilda would have been shocked and scandalized if they could have heard me as I began to softly sing aloud the melody that my fumbling fingers sought out on the concertina.

"It was fascination, I know . . ."

The impact which Colette had made upon me, and the strength of my desire to see her again, were further evidenced by the preparation I began to make for a return encounter. The following week, I enrolled at a private dance studio to take some dancing lessons. The second-floor studio was conveniently located a block from the Courteous Cab garage, so that it was not out of my way when I left the Highway Department to go to the cab-driving job. On the three nights I drove a cab, the half-hour lessons were sandwiched in between the time I left the Highway Department at five, and started on the cab-driving job at six. After two weeks of the crash dancing course in ballroom dancing, I was ready to return to Detroit, hopeful that my newly acquired proficiency in dancing would make a favorable impression on Colette.

But I could not face Florence again and repeat the fiction that I was again needed on a Saturday night by the cab company. To get back to Detroit and see Colette again, I begged off working from the cab company boss on Friday night, the longest, busiest night of the week. So on a Friday night, the second week after I had first met Colette, while Florence was on her way home to Charlotte with the car-pool riders, thinking that I was on my way to the cab company to work all night, I started for Detroit. Unlike the first night I had driven to Detroit two weeks before in the rain, at a recklessly furious speed, I drove this time at a more leisurely rate since I didn't expect the ballroom to be open until at least nine o'clock. And when I arrived in Detroit, I felt no impulse to seek out sexual stimulation in any of its varied forms in downtown Detroit. For I had come this time primarily to see one person. The hunger that I felt to see Colette again was not lust; that I knew. The delight I had found in her company had stemmed, not from a contact of body with body, which had been slight, but, rather, from a touching of personalities, of mind, and spirit, and soul.

When I finally arrived at the Hollywood Ballroom in Detroit that Friday night, it was nearing ten o'clock. Unreasonably, I felt a little hurt to find Colette already dancing with another customer. I sat down on one of the straight-backed chairs in the shadows along the wall, to wait for her to finish. It was fifteen minutes before her customer released her, and then, after walking to the cashier's cage with him to get additional tickets which he bought and handed to her, she went to the ladies' room. I patiently waited another fifteen minutes for her to reappear and take her place on one of the lounge sofas along the brass rail, indicating that she was again available as a dance partner.

As I sat looking at her, separated by a distance of about ten feet, I was quick to notice that both her dress and hairdo were dramatically different from the first time I had seen her two weeks before. Instead of the simple, black taffeta dress with flaring skirt that she had worn then, tonight she wore a green sheath gown with a satin sheen, with diaphanous balloon sleeves that covered her arms, and with lace ruffles around the edge of her skirt. The high-heeled slippers she wore were gleaming gold, bringing to mind the story of Cinderella and her golden slippers. And tonight, her hair, instead of being upswept and gathered behind in a pony tail, was loose, and framed her delicately chiseled features and amazingly white skin in soft waves of gold that fell to her shoulders.

As I waited and watched, while other male clients picked the partner of their choice from the eight or ten girls strung out along the brass railing, I wondered how I would start a conversation with the woman who had run out on her promise to let me take her home two weeks before. I didn't want to embarrass her or startle her with a brusque demand for either explanation or apology. After a few moments of silent, diplomatic deliberation on the subject, I decided to leave the initiative with her. If she felt the need to hide behind a pretense of not remembering me at all, I would let her do so, until and if she felt free to volunteer an explanation of her own. I walked over to where she sat, somewhat apart from the other girls, and stopped in front of her, bowing slightly from the waist as I had the first night we had met.

"Would you care to dance?"

There was no mention of my name, no sudden look of apprehension at being confronted by the customer she had run out on. The gracious response and the smile were as charming to me as they had been the first night.

"Certainly," she smiled, getting up.

With a confidence and sense of assurance that I hadn't possessed the first night I had asked her to dance, resulting from my two weeks of dancing lessons, we began to move easily with the music. After several moments of a smooth, silent circling of the dance floor, maneuvering around a dozen other couples on the dance floor, she asked a question.

"Haven't I danced with you before?"

Had she really completely forgotten fleeing in the rain that night two weeks before, leaving me to come back to the drug store and find her gone? Had it meant that little to her?

"Yes, Colette, you've danced with me before."

Perhaps the hurt that I felt was evident in my tone of rebuke.

"You know my name," she added, looking at me searchingly, and with apparent surprise, "but I'm afraid I've forgotten yours."

"Garfield Roby."

I looked away from her as I spoke, wondering if the attraction that I had felt toward this woman had been all on my side, with none on her side.

"That does sound familiar."

And then she settled closer in my arms. Perhaps the dancing lessons I had taken had imparted to her a sense of proficiency on my part that induced her to relax in my embrace. Perhaps, too, I thought, she remembers more than she has been willing to admit. But it didn't matter for very long, as to how much she had remembered about me, or how much she had forgotten. All that mattered was that she was there in my embrace again, close to me, her head on my shoulder, the fragrant scent of her softly cascading hair in my nostrils. I closed my eyes as we danced, and the fantasy that had enveloped me when I had first held her on the dance floor, two weeks before, stole back around me; a projected vision of a life shared with the exquisite creature whose movements were melted into my own by the music that flowed around us and into us.

Although I knew little more about her than her first name, the woman whom I held in my arms seemed to possess the mystery, the allure, the grace of movement, the beauty of form, the warm, outgoing personality, that held out a promise of fulfilling all of my needs and desires in a woman; needs and desires that I hadn't known existed within me until she had brought them to the surface of my conscious mind. Whether the dancing lessons I had taken had impressed her favorably or not, I couldn't tell. But it was evident that something had impressed her. Perhaps it was a gesture of mine. When sitting out a fast rock number later in the evening, she mentioned a draft along the floor that was making her feet cold. I had gotten up, went to the refreshment stand at the rear, and gotten a pot of tea with a cup and brought it back to her. But before pouring the tea into the cup that she held, I set the pot of tea on the floor by her feet. Then, slipping off one of her high-heeled, golden slippers at a time, I had let the steam from the hot tea water warm her feet. Her peal of appreciative laughter at my originality was reward enough for my effort. And then, as she sat close beside me, sipping the tea, I asked a question I had asked her two weeks before.

"Can I take you home tonight, Colette, if I drive you straight home?"

There had still been no mention of what had happened the first night we had met, in response to the same proposal. But at least this time there was no stalling, no attempted evasion, no protest that it was against the rules.

"Of course," she smiled. "By two o'clock, I'm tired enough to appreciate a ride home."

But if she now trusted me enough to drive her home, her trust did not extend beyond her doorstep. She immediately qualified her acceptance of my offer to drive her home, with a barrier that would forestall any possible complications beyond her threshold.

"I'm afraid I won't be able to invite you in, though," she added plaintively, as if genuinely sorry. "The landlady is quite fussy about having men come into the apartment, especially after two o'clock in the morning."

The claim sounded legitimate, and I accepted it as such.

"I understand," I said, thankful for just the privilege of taking her home from the ballroom. "I'll say goodnight at your doorstep and be on my way."

"Will you be staying here until two?" she asked, "or will you be back later."

I looked at my watch, the watch that brought back sad and newly repugnant scenes from Calumet City, Illinois. It was ten minutes to midnight. I had danced with Colette for almost an hour since arriving. It would be both expensive and perhaps unfair to attempt to monopolize her time for the next two hours.

"I'll be back at two," I said, and, remembering her counsel of two weeks before that it was against the rules for her to leave with a customer, I added, "I'll wait for you downstairs."

She smiled her appreciation, and got up to return to the lounge chairs across the wide aisle where the other girls sat, indicating that she was again available as a dancing partner. I returned the teapot and cup to the refreshment stand and retrieved my coat from the check room. As I prepared to leave, I saw that Colette was already dancing with another man. It didn't bother me. I knew that she was dancing with him for the sake of a paycheck. But she would be leaving with me later, not because she would get paid for it, but because she had evidently discovered some quality in me that was appealing. I walked out and down the red-carpeted stairs, wrapped in the quiet enjoyment that this assumption spun around me.

After lingering over a spaghetti dinner at a restaurant on Woodward that kept late hours, where the music on the juke box included old-time popular favorites like "Dancing in the Dark" and classical numbers like Stravinsky's "Ritual Fire Dance," I returned to the Hollywood at a quarter of two, to wait on the street by the ground-level entrance for Colette to appear. It was the third week in November, and tonight there was no rain to aid her in reneging on her promise to let me take her home. Christmas decorations on the lamp posts along Woodward and in the store windows, as well as the chill wind that swept down the wide thoroughfare, heralded the arrival of the Christmas season in the big city.

By the time Colette appeared at ten minutes after two, I was thoroughly chilled from waiting on the sidewalk. I was glad to get into the sheltering warmth of the car, parked a block away.

"Now I'll take you straight home," I said, turning to her on the seat, the engine idling, "but you'll have to tell me where it is."

"You don't have to take me straight home," she smiled, obviously pleased that I was proving to be a man of my word, "if you'd like to drive around a little, it's alright."

Quietly exhilarated at the trust she had placed in me, although I was still a virtual stranger to her, I swung left onto Woodward and started driving south, with no particular destination in mind. For the moment, just to extend for a brief time the pleasure of her company was enough. And with this evidence of her confidence in me, I felt it safe to ask the question that had been buzzing like an unwelcome fly around the back of my mind all evening.

"May I ask a personal question, Colette?" I began cautiously.

"My name isn't really Colette, she answered, the first of a series of surprising revelations about herself, "It's Corrine. I just adopted the name of Colette to help keep wolves off my track, and there are plenty of them who show up at the Hollywood."

I couldn't help turning my head to glance at her, prompted by a mixture of surprise and delight that she had voluntarily confided in me.

"I'm trusting you to keep my secret," she said. "Even the boss doesn't know my real name."

"You can be sure I won't tell a soul."

"Now, what was the question you wanted to ask me?"

"Did you forget, Colette . . . I'm sorry, I mean, Corrine, did you forget that when I danced with you for the first time two weeks ago, you agreed to let me take you home? Then, when I went to get the car and left you in a drugstore because it was raining so hard, when I came back to get you, you were gone?"

"No, I didn't forget," she said, a half smile on her face as I glanced at her, "I just thought that since you didn't say anything about it, I wouldn't either."

"But why did you leave? Did you think you couldn't trust me?"

"Not so much that," she answered meditatively, "it was just that I didn't want you to think I go out with just anybody the first time I meet them. Besides, I thought that if you really wanted to see me, you'd be back. And I was right, wasn't I?"

"Yes," I answered quietly, holding back the flood of words that would have given her some indication of how much I had wanted to see her again, "you were right."

"Corrine," I said aloud.

"What?"

"I was just saying the name . . . Corrine . . . it's beautiful; much better than Colette."

"Thank you," she answered. "I'm sorry I forgot your name, but I didn't forget the question you asked me. That's one reason I hoped you'd come back. I wanted to ask you about it."

"Which question? It seems like I asked you so many on that first night we met."

I was sure I knew which question she meant, because her own cryptic reply to that question had lingered so unforgettably in my own mind.

"The one where you asked me, 'How would you like to dance on streets of gold?' I don't know how many times I've thought of that since you asked me. I couldn't get it out of my mind. I've been asking myself ever since then, 'What in the world did he mean?'"

"And I haven't forgotten your answer."

As we drove down the broad, emptied, winter-chilled street, with now and then a car passing, the stops for traffic lights didn't break the continuity of companionship that flowed around us in the car.

"You did mean Heaven when you said 'streets of gold,' didn't you?" she continued. "That's the only place I've heard of where there will be streets of gold."

"Yes, that's what I meant, Corrine."

Perhaps there was a pensive note in my voice as I recalled the particular frame of mind, of guilt and self-condemnation, out of which I had asked that question. And thinking ahead, anticipating the question she would ask next, I tried to devise some evasion that would spare me telling her my position in life; a married man whose wife was expecting a first child, a delinquent Christian, the mental context of self-reproach out of which my unusual question had been conceived. And in an effort to avoid the probing queries about my background that she might ask, I directed one to her.

"What did you mean," I asked, "by saying that you wouldn't like to do the kind of dancing we were doing on the golden streets of Heaven?"

"Because I don't think they'll be doing that kind of dancing there. If the church thinks it's evil in this life, then it certainly wouldn't be done in Heaven."

"Which church is that?" I asked, aware that most fundamentalist Protestant churches regarded social dancing as evil, including the Gilead Baptist Church in Charlotte, where I was an increasingly absentee member.

"Seventh Day Adventist," she answered, "the remnant church. The only one that keeps all of the Ten Commandments, not just some of them. That's another reason I'm working at the ballroom under an assumed name. If the people in the church knew I was working there, they'd really be shocked."

I felt a mild irritation at the spiritual smugness inherent in the description of her denomination as "the only one that keeps all of the Ten Commandments." In the school where I had started to prepare for the ministry, the church in which Corrine had so proudly boasted membership had been designated as a "cult." One of my textbooks had charged this particular denomination with perverting some of the cardinal doctrines of Christianity as derived from the pages of Scripture. But I had felt at the time, and still did, that the doctrinal peculiarities were minor, rather than major. At any rate, I felt no desire to get into an involved theological discussion. I wanted to know the woman who sat beside be better. It was enough for the moment, and it was a source of great comfort to me that, in spite of doctrinal differences, she, too, had an expectation for the future that included a Heaven with streets of gold.

"Well," I said, shifting gears as a traffic light changed, "it's not so important as to whether there will be that kind of dancing in Heaven or not. The important thing is getting there."

"That's right," she conceded, "we've got to be ready when Jesus comes. That's why I feel bad about working last night."

"What do you mean by that?"

I was both puzzled and a little abashed that she could be anything but pleased that she had been there at the Hollywood when I had returned to see her, especially after having been given a brush-off two weeks before.

"For one thing, I was working on the Sabbath. It started last night at sundown, you know. That was breaking the

Fourth Commandment. And if Jesus had come last night and found me working in that place, I don't know whether he would have taken me to Heaven or not."

I didn't feel like challenging what I thought were erroneous convictions in an attempt to comfort her, and so I drove on in silence. She continued, voicing a rationalization for her misdemeanor in working the night before.

"I wouldn't have worked last night if it wasn't that the rent is due tomorrow. Maybe the Lord will understand."

"I'm sure He will."

I was thankful that behind her rigid concept of a rules and regulations kind of Christianity, there was room for a merciful and understanding God who would accept from His creatures a level of performance that was short of perfection. And I wondered if perhaps God, in mercy toward me, had permitted her to act in violation of her own church-taught precepts, so that she might be there at the Hollywood when I arrived. I shuddered to think of the possibility of having made the long trip with such high hopes of seeing her again and not finding her at the Hollywood when I arrived.

I was not aware of how far we had driven until a lull in our conversation allowed a glance at the surroundings. The stores and buildings had thinned out considerably, indicating that we were nearing the outskirts of the city. Ahead on the right, I saw a neon sign that said, "Eat," a place that was evidently open all night.

"Are you hungry, Corrine?" I asked, slowing down as we approached the place.

"I could sure use a hamburger and a milk shake," she responded eagerly. "I usually have something to eat downtown before I go home."

The parking places for the entire block in front of the restaurant were filled, so I turned left into the driveway of a closed gas station across the street.

"I'll bet you'd like a vanilla milk shake," I said, opening the door to get out.

"How did you know? Vanilla's my favorite."

"That's what you ordered when I left you in the drug store the first night we met, remember?"

"That's right; I did. I forgot. I'm sorry."

Her tone of regret convinced me that she must, indeed, have felt some reluctance over having fled the drugstore that night in the rain, and that she had done so only for the sound and sensible reasons she had given me.

"Better lock the doors on your side," I cautioned, as I got out of the car.

"Thank you for thinking of it," she smiled, and moved to comply with my suggestion as I turned away from the car to cross the street to the crowded restaurant.

It was fifteen minutes before I returned to the car with the take-out lunch. For myself, I had gotten an order of toast and coffee.

"It's a good thing we didn't go inside," I said, getting back into the front seat and closing the door. "The place is really jammed. It would have taken an hour just to get waited on."

I opened the sack and handed Corrine her hamburger and milk shake. The steam from my coffee formed a cloud on the windshield as the pleasant aroma from our early morning snack filled the car.

"I see you're a bowler," Corrine ventured, in one of the conversational interludes between bites of food.

"Once in a while. How did you guess?"

"I saw the bowling ball on the floor in the back seat."

I was suddenly glad that her observation reminded me of a little surprise I had planned for her but had forgotten until that moment.

"That's not a bowling ball," I replied.

"It isn't? What is it, then, or shouldn't I ask?"

"It's quite alright to ask," I said, setting my coffee cup and unfinished toast on the dashboard, "but it might be better to show you than to tell you."

I reached behind my seat, grabbed the handle of the bowling bag, and carefully lifted it up onto my lap. I unzipped the brown canvas bag as Corrine looked on with curiosity, and pulled out the octagon-shaped musical instrument, smaller than a dinner plate in diameter, about ten inches long when compressed, but expandable to three times that length when used.

"What is it?" Corrine asked, mystified.

"It's a concertina," I explained, putting the empty case onto the back seat. "I use it at jail services sometimes to drown out my bad singing."

I released the snaps that held the bellows contracted, expanded the concertina to its full length, and squeezed it in and out randomly to give her an idea of the sound.

"It's like a little accordion, isn't it?" Corrine asked, excited.

"Just about, but it doesn't have quite as much volume."

"Would you play something for me?" she pleaded. "I've never heard one of those."

"On one condition."

"What's that?"

"If you'll sing what I play."

"If it's a song I know, I'll be glad to."

"There's only one problem," I said, compressing the bellows. "I'm afraid there isn't enough room to play here in the car. But if you want to roll your window down, I can step outside to your side of the car and play it. I guess we can stand five minutes without freezing."

"Sure, that's a good idea," she agreed happily.

I got out of the car with the concertina and walked around to her side of the car. I stood close to the car, facing her through the open window as I expanded the bellows of the concertina, feeling reasonably safe on the street with a crowded all-night restaurant just across the way.

"Remember this song?" I asked, as I began to finger the keys and move the bellows in and out to the familiar strains of "Fascination."

"Of course, I remember," she smiled through the open car window, obviously pleased at my choice. "That was the special number I did at the Hollywood the first night we met. I'll be glad to sing it."

340

I began again and, after improvising a brief introduction, Corrine began singing through the open window, looking at me as I faced her, playing the concertina.

In the predawn stillness of the street, with only an occasional passing car to interrupt, and away from the distortion of the loudspeakers at the Hollywood Ballroom, Corrine's voice seemed even more beautiful and delicately distinct; more mellow and, strangely, more deeply moving than the first night I had heard her sing. And the final words, as she sang this time for my ears alone, seemed excitingly closer to being reality than when I had first heard her sing them at the Hollywood.

"It was fascination, I know . . . Seeing you alone, with the moonlight above . . . Then I touched your hand, and when I kissed you . . . Fascination turned into love."

Looking into Corrine's eyes as she sang the final words, I could not help thinking that they applied to us. For, although we had not yet kissed each other on the lips, we had surely kissed each other with our eyes, and perhaps in our thoughts.

Then, abruptly, I was startled by a wholly unexpected sound from the street behind me. It was a vigorous, enthusiastic clapping of a single pair of hands. I whirled around to face the street, tucking the concertina protectively under one arm as I did. There, stepping unsteadily toward me, was a middle-aged man, neatly dressed, wearing a fedora hat and a trench coat, but with the flushed face and bulbous nose of an obvious alcoholic.

"Hey, folks, zat was beautiful," he said, in a slurred voice as he staggered toward me.

One hand was held out toward me as he approached, in which I could see one or more dollar bills tightly clenched.

"Here, man," he said, holding the money toward me, as Corrine looked on apprehensively through the open window, "put this in the collection plate for me."

"Thank you, sir," I said, realizing that he had misinterpreted our performance, "but I wasn't doing this to collect money."

"Ain'tchu in the Salvation Army?" he asked.

"No, I'm afraid not. We're traveling on the same road, but we're not part of that organization."

Disconcerted that he had misjudged my motive and message in the song he had evidently heard us sing, his former friendliness turned to hostility.

"Well, goddam, man, if you ain't the Salvation Army," he said, sticking the crumpled dollar bills back into his coat pocket, "you must be either drunk or crazy, singing on the street at three o'clock in the morning."

He turned and staggered away down the street. Relieved that the episode was ended, I turned to face Corrine.

"Thank God he didn't cause any trouble," she sighed.

"Well, at least he knew a beautiful voice when he heard one."

"I'll bet he stopped because of your concertina," Corrine demurred modestly. "He probably never saw or heard anything like that before. I know I haven't, and you play it really well."

Corrine rolled up her window as I walked around to the other side of the car and got in. The weather was too chilly to endure more than the one song I had played for her and, besides, I was not prepared to cope with any more strangers on the street who might stop to applaud or heckle.

"That was fun," Corrine smiled, genuinely pleased, as I replaced the concertina in the bowling ball case and returned it to the back seat. "I hope we can do it again somewhere else, and maybe not so early in the morning."

"Maybe the Lord sent that man along to emphasize a point I made the first night we met," I said, looking into her eyes as she finished her milk shake.

"What's that?"

"I said that with a beautiful voice like you have, Corrine, I don't know why you're working at a job you hate. You could be a success on records, either sacred or popular."

"I have done some singing for charity groups around Detroit," she admitted pensively, averting my gaze. "Seven years ago, I sang for a whole week at the Masonic Temple downtown for meetings our church put on. One night there were six thousand people there."

Then, remembering how my initial query about this area of her life had been turned away the first night we met, I pressed her no further about the matter.

But as we finished our post-midnight snack before leaving the scene, I could not help suspecting that there must be some hidden tragedy in the life of one who could sing so beautifully, yet held a job she despised and had to keep hidden from the church of which she was a member.

By the time we finished our interrupted snack, a growing sense of drowsiness impelled me to look at my watch. It was ten minutes to four. I was not accustomed to being up all night, as Corrine appeared to be, even with my Friday night taxi driving that lasted until two in the morning. And at the moment, the long, hundred-mile drive home to Charlotte still ahead of me seemed beyond my depleted reservoir of strength.

"I guess I'd better start thinking about getting you home, and then myself," I said, as I turned on the ignition and the headlights.

"To get me home," Corrine said, as I pulled out onto Woodward Avenue again, "just drive straight back the way we came until we pass the Hollywood. I live only eight blocks from there. But where is home for you?"

If I had told her where I lived at our first meeting, she had evidently forgotten about it, and so had I.

"Home for me," I replied, instinctively avoiding any mention of Charlotte, "is about a hundred miles from here, in Lansing."

When we reached Corrine's apartment on Second Street, just off Cass, twenty minutes later, she had a suggestion motivated by a growing concern for my welfare.

"Would you like to come in and lie down on the sofa for a little while before you start home? I wouldn't want you to go to sleep on the way home and have an accident."

"The way I feel," I answered gratefully, "I can't turn down an offer like that."

The protest she had voiced at the start of the evening about a fussy landlady who did not tolerate early morning male visitors, was forgotten. Or else her concern for my safety had come to outweigh her fears of offending the landlady. On the porch of the Cromwell Apartments, not very far from the vast Masonic Temple where Corrine had sung as a soloist before a great crowd of people, I stood beside her as she unlocked the front door that led into a vestibule. Then I followed her down a short carpeted hallway to a first-floor apartment at the back of the building. She opened the apartment door and invited me into a spacious, two-room apartment; a living room with a combination sofa and pull-away bed, and a large kitchen. It was evident from a sweeping survey of the apartment that Corrine, in addition to other obvious talents, was an immaculate housekeeper.

"Why don't you make yourself comfortable," she invited, after hanging our coats in a closet by the door, "and I'll make some tea before you rest."

I sat down on the comfortable sofa as Corrine stepped through a swinging door that led into the kitchen. Sitting there, I scanned, with interest and affection, the furnishings of someone who had come to mean so much to me in such a short time. Against one wall was a small desk, and on it, a bright blue feather-plume pen and a book. An end table beside the sofa held a feminine, lace-trimmed lamp and several magazines. Across the room, between the double windows, was a record cabinet containing a portable record player and a pile of LP albums. The walls were tastefully decorated with landscape scenes; a forest and sea, and snow-capped mountains.

Five minutes later, Corrine called me into the cheerfully appointed and spotless kitchen where we had tea and cookies in intimate closeness at a small table. Then, too weary from the lateness of the hour to converse at length, I followed Corrine back into the living room. After removing only my shoes, coat, and necktie, I laid down on the sofa and Corrine covered me with a blanket. Then she retired to the kitchen with a book, the door shut between us.

A short time later, when I was awakened by her gentle shaking of my shoulder and her voice calling my name, dawn was streaking through the living room windows. And minutes later, after splashing the sleep out of my eyes with cold water, I slipped into the coat that she held for me and prepared to take leave of her. Standing in the open doorway of her apartment, facing her, I reached out for her hand—not for a physical embrace, not for a kiss, just for a final squeeze of her hand.

"It's been wonderful being with you, Corrine," I said, looking deep into her eyes, which looked so bright and alert while mine felt so sleep-bleared.

In the few short hours we had been together, I felt that I had come to know this woman as well as I could have if I had known her for years. Perhaps she, too, had come to have something of that same feeling toward me. Only that could explain our final exchange of words.

"When will I be seeing you again, Garfield?" she smiled, probably anticipating another meeting within several days or a week at the most.

But between the hidden variables of which Corrine knew nothing—Florence's advanced state of pregnancy, the fluctuations of business at the cab company, and my depleted finances, I could not look ahead in that moment and name a date with certainty.

"I'm not sure, Corrine. I guess we'll have to leave that up to the Lord."

A frown of bewilderment chased the smile from her face. I saw the question on her face and in her eyes that I could not answer in that moment. With a final, quick squeeze of her hand, I walked away from her, sensing a sudden need for urgency in getting away before she could voice the question I knew she was thinking as to why I could not name a definite time when I would be coming back to see her. But when I reached the jog in the hallway that, after turning, would hide me from her sight, I turned back for a final look at her. The lamplight behind her made gleaming highlights on her golden hair. There was a half-smile of benediction and unexpressed longing on her face, and the endlessness of Eternity in her eyes. And then I spoke words that arose spontaneously in my heart, not planned or premeditated. They were words that bore a surface similarity, yet in content were worlds apart from the words I had spoken weeks before to a bar girl named Kim, in a honky-tonk strip bar in Calumet City, Illinois. The exact words I had never thought of speaking to any woman before, for the depth of feeling that prompted them, I had never felt for any woman before.

"I love you, in the Lord, Corrine."

She could not have been more startled by my unexpected declaration than I was totally overwhelmed by her immediate response.

"I love you, in the Lord, Garfield."

I turned and hurried on down the hallway then, clutching her words to me like a destitute vagrant who had just found a priceless cache of jewels, desperately racing away from the scene lest someone call him back and demand their return to the rightful owner. The outside apartment door locked behind me, and I hurried down the steps in the first light of a cold November morning. And as I left Detroit behind, although my body was weary, there was within me a silent geyser of happiness that gave me strength. I had no need to turn on the car radio, for my heart was singing.

It was nearing seven o'clock when I finally arrived at the Berlincourt farm in Charlotte. Florence and her mother were already up, getting started on the weekly ritual of the Saturday washing. Understandably miffed at my lateness in getting home, Florence nevertheless accepted my fabricated story that because of a shortage of cab drivers the preceding night, the manager had asked me to stay on until the regular day-shift drivers checked in. Then I retired to the upstairs bedroom and slept until noon.

Strangely, although this newborn attachment to Corrine had been expressed to her as I left her, in the language of religious devotion, it did nothing to rekindle my declining interest in some of the activities I had been involved in at Gilead

Baptist Church, such as the regular Sunday afternoon service at the county jail in Charlotte. Alone in the big farmhouse while Florence and her mother were gone for a short time on a shopping trip in Charlotte, I called Dave Brown, my youthful assistant during the preceding year at young people's meetings, and asked him to assume responsibility for the jail service. My plea was that the part-time taxi-driving job was taking too much of my time and strength, and that it was a temporary arrangement until after the baby was born. Then, I told him, Florence would be returning to her job with the state and I could quit the taxi-driving job. Dave was willing and able to take over the responsibility, leaving me with no further obligations to take me back to Gilead Baptist Church.

The influence of the woman whom I had known so briefly, but so deeply, in a few stolen hours we had shared, pursued me into the following week, exerting a pervasive effect upon not only the minor problems in my life, but on the major issues as well. It had a shattering impact upon the illicit, neurotic business venture that had been the motivation for that initial trip to Detroit on the night I had first met Corrine—the salacious scheme of achieving success by becoming a self-coronated prince of prostitution.

On the first day of the following work week when I went back to my job in the Highway Department, I used my lunch hour to return to the library the books I had checked out several weeks before, dealing with prostitution. I had no more need of them, nor interest in them. Nor was there any longer left within me any intention of putting to use what little practical knowledge I had gleaned from their pages, supplemented by the experiences I had gone through in Detroit before meeting Corrine. And the final death stroke to that mad endeavor was delivered on Wednesday night of that same week.

I was on a trip in the cab, taking two elderly, garrulous ladies from the south end of town to a large, downtown church for a Bohemian supper. While they were supplying me with unsought details about the menu and the after-dinner speaker, the backseat dialogue was interrupted by a call from the dispatcher.

"Eight two."

I snatched the microphone of the two-way radio from its cradle with my right hand while guiding the steering wheel with my left, and spoke my cab number into the mike. The dispatcher's voice came back with a startling message.

"Eight two, I've got a phone number you're supposed to call as soon as you get a chance. Call in when you're green and I'll give it to you."

Panic suddenly flooded through me as I thought of Florence and the baby that was due the following month. The something she feared might happen some night while I was miles away driving a cab must have happened. I spoke into the cab mike, not waiting for an opening, the desperation I felt doubtless evident in my voice.

"Is it about my wife?"

The dispatcher's voice came back sounding irritated at my taking up precious radio time for further details. He didn't know that my wife was pregnant.

"I don't know. It was a man who called. He didn't say it was an emergency."

Relief swept over me. Even if it were some doctor, or some male neighbor who lived near the Berlincourt farm, if it was an emergency, he would have said so.

"Thank you," I spoke into the mike, terminated the exchange with the dispatcher, and hung up the mike on its dashboard hook.

"I hope nothing's wrong," came the querulous voice of one of the ladies in the back seat.

"No, I guess not. I thought my wife might be trying to get me. She's expecting a baby next month. But I guess it's nothing urgent, or whoever called would have said so."

The disclosure elicited a gush of questions and comments.

"When is the baby expected? I'll bet you're hoping for a boy. Do you have other children? Babies are sweet. I think they're adorable."

The geyser of talk about babies lasted until we reached our destination, a sprawling religious complex, one of the largest and oldest churches in downtown Lansing. I double parked in front of the church, held the door open for my passengers to climb out, and gave them change. Then I slipped back into the front seat to call the dispatcher.

"Eight two."

I waited for the dispatcher's acknowledgment that he had heard my call. It came back immediately, and I continued.

"Eight two, green at Central Methodist Church. You've got a phone number for me to call."

"Here it is," came the dispatcher's voice. "That's Ivanhoe 48755. You're supposed to ask for Solomon Weinberger. Want to repeat that back to me?"

I repeated the information back.

"Right," clipped the dispatcher, "call in after you make your call."

Ambivalent and powerful emotions flooded through me in the wake of the unexpected information I had received. There was, first of all, a great wave of relief that swept over me, to know that Florence was not having trouble, no danger of a miscarriage as she had feared might happen. But the name of the man who had called for me, Solomon Weinberger, which had been almost completely pushed from my mind since meeting Corrine, evoked a response of guilt and shame as I remembered the circumstances of our first meeting more than a month before at the Hofbrau tavern. I felt almost like a criminal, who, after serving time in prison, being released and going straight, is brought face to face with an accomplice in his past crimes.

For it was Solomon Weinberger, loitering near the doorway of the Hofbrau where I waited for a cab fare inside, who had clearly identified himself as my first potential client in the salacious sideline of prostitution for which I had been then laying the foundation. It had been his lust-laden appetite for extramarital sex that I had promised to be able to satisfy when he returned to Lansing on business a month later; the urgent deadline that had impelled me to travel to Detroit on that rainy November night that had resulted in my meeting with Corrine. In a way, I owed him a debt of gratitude which I knew he wouldn't appreciate if I tried to express it, because it was my meeting with Corrine that had really caused me to renege on the promise of sexual satisfaction that I had held out to him.

I sat there in the cab, in front of the towering stone edifice of the ancient church, deliberating. My initial impulse was not to return the man's call at all. But if I didn't, he would probably call the dispatcher again, and the dispatcher would call me, irritated at having had to call me twice for a personal call. But besides this, I also felt a need to make a clean, decisive break with this part of an almost criminal interlude in my life, to put it finally and forever behind me. Then, noting the dearth of traffic on the wide expanse of Capitol Avenue, where I was double parked, and remembering that just inside the front door of the church was a telephone, I got out of the cab and hurried into the church.

Inside the deserted church foyer, with the sounds and smells of a Bohemian supper wafting up from the basement, I dialed the number, thinking it was probably a local hotel where the man was staying. Above a hubbub of voices in the background, and a blaring juke box, a gruff male voice answered.

"Hofbrau."

It was the downtown tavern where I had first met Solomon Weinberger, and where I had entered into a voluntary business understanding with him.

"A Solomon Weinberger asked me to call this number," I said, "is he there?"

"Who?"

The name was obviously unfamiliar to the bartender or he was having difficulty hearing me with all the noise surrounding him.

"Solomon Weinberger!" I almost shouted into the phone.

"Just a minute," came the perturbed reply, "I'll see if he's here."

I heard him call the name, pause, then call it again much louder. Evidently the second call got a response.

"Here he comes."

A moment later, another male voice spoke into the phone, one that sounded vaguely familiar.

"Hello. This is Solomon Weinberger."

"Mr. Weinberger, this is Garfield Roby, Courteous Cab Company. I was told to call you at this number."

"Oh, yeah, Garfield!"

There was a jubilance and a note of recognition in his voice, as if he were speaking to an old, long-lost friend.

"Remember me?" he continued. "I talked with you at the Hofbrau about six weeks ago. I didn't get back in town as soon as I told you I would, but here I am. You said you might have a strange piece lined up for me when I came back to town."

A shiver of revulsion swept through me at this crude reminder of what we had discussed. It was strange that I felt offended at the man's coarse language and that, looking back, the episode that had occurred upon a downtown sidewalk nearly two months before now seemed as unreal as the ghostly mists of an early summer morning. In the ensuing pause, he must have thought that I had completely forgotten the prospect I had held out to him at the time, of helping him to secure the kind of sexual gratification he had been searching for then, and was still seeking.

"Hey, what's the matter? You didn't forget me and the little talk we had, did you? I told you I'd make it worth your while."

"I'm afraid I almost did."

"Well, what's the scoop?" he demanded impatiently. "Any luck in locating a broad for me?"

The reaction, both strong and strange, which his words produced, held me back from an immediate reply. In our first meeting, he had used the same term, "broad," to describe the kind of woman he was looking for, and it had not bothered me then. Now it did. The feeling I had come to have for Corrine seemed, in that moment, to have extended outwardly to all other women as well. Corrine had become more to me than just a person in her own right; she had also become a representative woman. To call any woman a "broad," a thing to be used with contempt or unconcern as a means of sexual gratification, was also to call Corrine a "broad." It seemed akin to blasphemy. But mixed with my strange, new reaction of offense to the disparaging term, was also a feeling of pity for the man I was talking to. For I was aware that I had found something in Corrine that this man had obviously never found in a woman, and perhaps never would. And I pitied him for that.

"I'm sorry, Mr. Weinberger," I finally said, "I'm afraid I won't be able to help you out after all."

"Well, I don't give up easily when I want something real bad, Garfield. I'll be back in town after the first of the year. Think you could find something for me by then?"

"I'm afraid I won't be able to help you at all, Mr. Weinberger, not after the first of the year or ever. A week after I talked with you, I met an angel of God who . . ."

"Boy, do you know what you sound like?" he broke in abruptly, with a voice that was angry.

"No, Mr. Weinberger," I said, somewhat saddened by his evident antagonism at my trying to relay to him something precious and beautiful that had come into my life since I had met him, "what do I sound like?"

"You sound just like one of these religious nuts that I've run into before. You better see a head shrink before you go off the deep end. Well, I won't bother you anymore. So long, boy."

The background bedlam of the Hofbrau bar and the husky, belligerent voice of Solomon Weinberger were suddenly cut off as if someone with a knife had cut the connecting telephone cable. I hung up the receiver slowly, sadly. And as I walked out of the church and back to my cab, I was impressed with a vivid, new awareness of what I had been delivered from through my meeting with Corrine. I sat in the cab a moment as occasional passing cars veered around me, momentarily spellbound by the awareness of the deep change that had been wrought within me; of the complete turnabout that had happened in the course I had been pursuing several short months before. It seemed, in that moment of retrospect, as if I had been a leper on my way to a colony of other lepers, to live out a life of continuing moral disintegration. But midway, the boat on which I was being transported to an isolated leper's island had turned around and had taken me back, cleansed and healed of my defilement, to live a normal, healthy life, surrounded by the joys, the satisfactions, and happiness from which the leper, in previous ages, had been completely and permanently separated.

Sitting there, while cars and pedestrians passed by unnoticed, I was unable to pick up the radio microphone and call the dispatcher to let him know I was available again. I was mesmerized by the clear vision of the ultimate destination from which I had been turned back through my meeting with Corrine. And a haunting question emerged in my mind. What if it had not rained that Saturday night in November when I had first gone to Detroit? What if it had not rained, and Madge, the cab fare divorcee, had accompanied me and succumbed to my persuasion to become a business partner in the prostitution sideline I was on the way to establishing? If it had not rained, and she had accompanied me, I would never have met Corrine, and would doubtless have continued on the despicable, downward course of moral and spiritual degeneration that I had been following.

With the green lights blinking on the roof of my cab, I breathed a prayer of thanks to God for the way in which my carefully laid plans of several months before had been so radically disrupted. It seemed, in that moment of backward-looking insight, as if the mad scheme to become a practitioner in the world's oldest profession had grown within me, not only because of the failures I had experienced in my vocational endeavors, but also because there had been a vacuum at the center of my life; an inner emptiness that could only be filled by a woman's love, a kind of love that could draw forth from within me a corresponding and complete love for her. For when I had met Corrine, that desperate and diabolical plan had been pushed out of my mind and heart by her, and she had filled that empty place with herself.

In that moment, I became convinced that, whatever other results might have followed from the rain that fell on that Saturday night in November, one purpose that must have been included in the mind and heart of God, perhaps even the primary purpose, was to turn me back from the course I had been following before I met Corrine. A relevant phrase from the Sermon on the Mount came to me.

"He sendeth rain on the just and on the unjust."

"Thank you, Lord," I breathed aloud, with eyes closed and face uplifted, "for sending the rain that led me to Corrine."

Then I reached for the radio microphone.

"Eight two, green at Central Methodist Church."

On the following night, Thursday, one of the nights I didn't drive a cab, I sat alone, following supper, in the spacious living room of the Berlincourt farm, listening to some sacred instrumentals on the record player. In the kitchen, Florence was laboriously and dutifully helping her mother with the supper dishes. As I pondered again the profound influence that Corrine had begun to exert upon my life, I was thinking of the question she had asked me just before I left her apartment in Detroit, as dawn was beginning to streak the eastern sky.

"When will I be seeing you again, Garfield?"

As I was attempting to reach a decision as to which would be the better choice; to tell Florence that I had to drive a cab on Saturday night again, or to try to get a Friday night off from the manager of the cab company, so that I could go down to Detroit and see Corrine again, Florence walked into the living room where I sat. She walked past me to replace on a shelf against the wall, a decorative, hand-painted plate that she had taken to the kitchen for washing. As she walked past me, affording a profile view of her ever-expanding midriff, I was shocked at the sight. Perhaps it was only because in recent weeks I had not been paying careful attention to the gradual swell of her abdomen as the baby grew within her. She had reached the eighth month of pregnancy. It was the time of the final weeks of pregnancy that, in previous generations, had impelled expectant mothers, imbued with a Victorian modesty, to stay cloistered at home to avoid offending the public scrutiny of their appearance.

As Florence turned to go back into the kitchen, a dishcloth that she had absent mindedly carried with her slipped from her fingers and fell to the floor. Without thinking, she started to bend down from the waist to retrieve it, but she could not push her hand any further down toward the floor than her knees. The expansion of her pregnancy was like a barrel attached to her waist. As I made a move to get up and pick up the washcloth for her, she moved as quickly to show that in spite of the physical handicap, she could still perform the necessary household chores that fell to her. She bent down in the only way she could, bending her knees and squatting down, back straight, the girth of her belly settling in her lap. I settled back on the sofa, rebuffed by her spirit of independence in my attempt to be helpful.

"It must be nice to be a man," she said, repeating a complaint I had heard numerous times before during the months of her enlarging pregnancy, "just sit around and listen to music while I have to carry this weight around. I'll sure be glad when it's over."

She made her way back into the kitchen, not guessing the effect that the simple episode had made upon me. Her plainly displayed condition brought home to my mind something that had not entered my thoughts in recent weeks; that the expected arrival of the child that had swelled her form into such an ungainly shape was but five weeks away, providing the doctor's prediction was correct. If the doctor was wrong, as doctors sometimes were, it could happen sooner. And there was also the possibility, remote, perhaps, but still not to be discounted completely, of something going wrong. A fall on the sometimes slippery porch steps, or on the highly polished floors where Florence worked. Either could precipitate a miscarriage. I remembered the moment of panic the night before, when I had thought the dispatcher's instruction to call a phone number had meant that Florence was in trouble.

This remembered episode, and Florence's condition as it had just been forcibly impressed upon my mind, seemed to relay to me an unwanted, unwelcome answer to the question I had been pondering before she walked into the room; the question that Corrine had asked me a week before.

"When will I be seeing you again, Garfield?"

If something should happen to Florence or to the expected child on a Friday or Saturday night when I was supposed to be driving a cab in Lansing, but was actually a hundred miles away in Detroit with Corrine, I would never be able to forgive myself. And as I thought of the agony that would overwhelm Florence if she should call the cab company in such an event, only to be told that I was not driving a cab, and that neither the dispatcher, nor the manager, nor any of the other drivers knew my whereabouts, the answer to Corrine's plaintive, parting question was clear. I could not risk going to Detroit again to see Corrine until after the expected child was born. And that might be as late as the end of the first month of the new year, January, the month in which the baby was expected to arrive.

I walked over to one of the living room windows, out of sight of Florence and her mother in the kitchen, and pulled back the lace curtain. It was a bleak prospect that met my eyes and that dawned in my mind. Outside, the ground was hard and frozen, the trees were stripped of all their foliage, and the early evening sky was overcast. Dark-edged, snow-burdened clouds were being pushed heavily across the sombre, gray sky by a chill wind that whipped the leafless branches, as if with a vicious intention of breaking them off. And within me, the prospect was equally dreary. It would probably be five or six weeks before I could risk going to Detroit to see Corrine again. Christmas would come and go, and New Year's Eve as well. The new year would already be old before I could see her again.

As I looked out upon the barren landscape, huge, lazy

flakes of snow, the first of winter, came drifting down; sometimes swirled about by intermittent gusts of wind, sometimes descending undisturbed in their descent, like mythical fairies clinging to miniature, white umbrellas. I wondered as I watched, if, a hundred miles away in Detroit, Corrine was perhaps looking out a window, seeing the same snowflakes with some of the same adoring wonder that I had always felt at the annual, but ever-new spectacle of winter's first snow. And at that moment, just thinking of her, alone, made the intervening weeks that I would have to wait before seeing her again, seem almost like forever.

But the painful prospect was softened somewhat by the knowledge that I had something to comfort me during the long wait; Corrine's last words to me; words that had already had a profound effect upon me; words that could not fail ultimately to have an unforeseeable effect upon Florence and upon the child yet to be born. I turned those wondrous words over again in my mind as I stood there in front of the window, watching the snow come down. They were words that seemed to me more many splendored than the snowflakes falling from Heaven.

"I love you, in the Lord, Garfield."

I had to hear those words again, spilling like liquid music from Corrine's lips, after the child in Florence's belly was born.

CHAPTER 10

⇒ The birth of a child, viewed by a philosopher on a mountain top, may appear to be a wondrous and awesome event. Exceeding in significance the mystery of a mighty oak tree growing from an acorn, is the spectacle of a Moses, a Michelangelo, an Einstein, or a Lincoln, all springing from the same unimpressive source—a helpless, illiterate, unthinking bundle of uncontrolled appetites and bodily members—a baby. But any philosopher, whether formally educated or self-schooled, if he is married and has impregnated the woman to whom he is married, must leave his speculating and come down from his mountain top to be involved in the actual experience of a child being born. And in the valley of experience, to be personally caught up in the birth of a child is something far different than mountain-top reflections about it.

In the teeming valley of everyday living, with its many pressures and perplexities and problems that demand an immediate response without time for a leisurely appraisal, the wonder of the birth of a child may be eclipsed by worry; the hints of future glory may be overshadowed by harbingers of grief; the mystery may be temporarily swallowed up in misery. For at different times and in varying situations, the birth of a child has not always brought joy. It has also turned the paradise of secret lovers into purgatory; has ruined reputations; has incited clans to blood feuds; and has expelled sons or daughters from the home of outraged parents. The same

358

event has been known to cause both dancing in the streets and weeping in secret chambers; open joy and hidden heartbreak.

These opposing reactions attending the birth of a particular child have flowed from the pivotal question as to whether the child who was born, whether to high station or low, to the poor or to the rich, to the educated or to the illiterate, was wanted or unwanted. For the child who is born into the world unwanted, the world may often become a place of torment, as with a young boy who, at the age of 12, won the dubious distinction of becoming the youngest drug addict in the city of New York, to die from an overdose of heroin. Or he may grow up with a hidden resentment at being unwanted to become another Richard Speck, with the tattoo "Born to raise Hell" on his arm; driven by an inner anger that culminated in the motiveless murder of seven student nurses in the city of Chicago. Woe to the child who is born into the world unwanted, and woe to the world into which an unwanted child is born!

The particular child, with its unknown potential for good or evil, mediocrity or greatness, that, in the closing days of the ninth month of Florence's pregnancy had pushed her belly to its maximum perimeter of unsightly expansion, was wanted; but not, perhaps, for the reasons that would have a beneficial effect upon the child. With Florence, the only reasons I had heard her explicitly voice for wanting the child to be born was to be rid of the physical discomfort involved in carrying the weight of the unborn child around with her everywhere she went. She may have had other reasons, but she had kept them hidden from me. And my primary reason for wanting the baby to be born was one that showed me ill prepared to become a father. I wanted the child to be born so that, without a troubled conscience about Florence having some pregnancy mishap, I could secretly fly back to Detroit to see Corrine again. It was a desire that had grown stronger and more compelling through the weeks that I had not seen her, while waiting for the baby to be born. So while I wanted the child to be born for a selfish, even despicable reason, I did not particularly want the strain of attendant inconveniences that most fathers go through before and after the birth of a child, such as having needed hours of sleep and rest interrupted.

It was just as dawn was streaking the eastern sky, on a show-flurried, fourteen-above-zero Sunday morning, in the third week of January, that I was jolted out of a sound sleep by Florence.

"Gar! Gar, wake up!"

I heard my name being called at the same time I felt Florence's hand shaking my shoulder, catapulting me into a groggy state of premature wakefulness.

"What's the matter?" I asked, sitting upright in bed, dazed.

"I think it's finally time, thank God," she breathed, sitting up in bed beside me, supporting herself on her hands. "I didn't want to wake you up until I was sure, but I've had three labor pains in the last hour. They must have been about twenty minutes apart."

"Have I got time to shave?" I asked, as I got out of the warm bed into the frigid bedroom and threw on a bathrobe.

I turned on a table lamp in the corner to see Florence struggling to get to her feet over the side of the bed, pushing the immense girth of her belly in front of her.

"I'm sure you have. The doctor said the labor pains might last for two or three hours before the baby is due. It's just that we ought to get dressed and be ready. It takes me so long to do anything. I'm glad I've got my bag all packed."

I hurried down the cold stairway, my slippers slip-slopping on the steps, having no exalted thoughts about the mystery or wonder or significance pertaining to the birth of a child; only a mild feeling of annoyance that it couldn't be arranged to happen during decent hours, after people were up and awake.

An hour later, I stood by the living room door with Florence's small suitcase, ready to leave for the hospital. Hilda stood by in a flannel housecoat, her gray hair disheveled, empathetic concern etched on her face for the daughter who was about to go through, for the first time, the same painful ordeal that she had been through on four successive occasions years before.

"I just know everything's going to be alright, Florence," she said, giving her daughter a motherly hug by the door, "and Garfield, if there's anything I can do, you just call me. I'm going to stay home from church this morning, so if you need me for anything, you just call and I'll be right down there; that is, if the old Chevy isn't frozen up."

"Good grief, Mom," Florence protested, turning to her mother, "you don't need to stay home from church. There wouldn't be anything you could do if you were there, so why don't you just . . ."

She broke off in the middle of the sentence and an expression that denoted an approaching crisis spread over her face.

"Oh, oh," she said, pressing the palms of her hands cautiously against her abdomen as I opened the door, "I'd better wait a minute. I feel another one coming."

"Here, Florence," ordered her mother, with the authority derived from personal experience, "you sit down here in the rocking chair."

Hilda stepped over and swung the chair around so that it faced Florence, who lowered herself slowly and awkwardly into it. Then Hilda and I stood by in helpless, uncomfortable silence, as Florence clenched her teeth to keep from crying and gripped the arms of the rocking chair as the wave of pain swept over her. In seconds, it was over.

"Boy, the way that one felt" she gasped, starting to get up, "I might have the baby before we get to the hospital. We'd better get going."

I held the door open for Florence and, with the small suitcase in one hand, helped to guide her down the concrete steps with the other hand, then over the ruts in the frozen, snow-flecked ground to the car. As we backed out of the driveway, Hilda braved the freezing weather in her bathrobe for a final, motherly wave from the porch. And twenty minutes later, Florence was secure and comfortable in the high, tight-sheet-ed bed on the second-floor maternity ward of the Hayes-Green-Beach hospital in downtown Charlotte. The hospital was a modern, two-story, brick, 100-bed facility, adequate for the needs of a small town, barring an epidemic of some kind.

In one of the pre-delivery waiting rooms, I stood beside Florence's bed, the sheet stretched over her abdomen looking like a small Eskimo igloo. It was only five minutes after Florence had gotten settled in bed that another of the labor contractions heralded its approach.

"Can I hold your hand, Gar?" she gasped, the words forced from between her teeth by the pushing wave of pain. "It's easier when there's something to hang onto."

On the solid wood headstead of the hospital bed, there was no bar or projection for her to grasp. I extended my right hand to her and she gripped it with her left hand like a drowning person hanging to a life raft before the onslaught of an approaching, high-crested wave. As she squeezed my hand with her left hand, her right hand clutched the corner of her pillow and compressed it into a crumpled wad. At the same time, she exerted the same kind of pressure on my hand. She turned her face away from me on the pillow while the full fury of the pain-wave swept through her. I gritted my own teeth to keep from crying out, and resisted with difficulty the sudden impulse to jerk my hand away from her painfully constricting grip. I held back the involuntary bodily reactions that erupted within me, for her pain was greater than mine. Seconds later, as the pain subsided and Florence relaxed her grip on my hand, I doubted in that moment if I could have picked up anything with it had the need arose. My hand was temporarily paralyzed. She turned her face back toward me, an apologetic expression on it.

"I hope I didn't squeeze too hard."

"Not at all, Florence."

I gave her a grin I didn't feel, my hand hanging limply beside me as the blood rushed back into the fingers with a tingle of pain. Then the nurse walked in, curls as red as her lipstick pushing out from under her starched cap, eyes peer-

ing at Florence from behind her glasses with clinical coolness.

"Had another one yet?" she asked brightly, as she laid a
hand on Florence's forehead, where beads of perspiration had
gathered.

"Just before you walked in."

"How long has it been since the last one?"

"I had one just before I left home, and it took about twenty-five minutes after that to get down here and check in."

"Twenty," I corrected.

"Do either of you have a watch?" asked the nurse, as she
pulled open a drawer in Florence's bedside stand and pulled
out a pad of paper and a pencil.

"I do," I said.

"You can help your wife, Mr. Roby, and me, too," she said,
handing the pad of paper and pencil to me, "if you'll keep
track of the time between contractions and jot it down. When
they start coming five minutes apart, then we'll know it's
about time for the baby to come out."

"How long will that be?" Florence asked.

"When did you start having contractions, Mrs. Roby?"

"Five o'clock this morning."

"And it's seven fifteen now," said the nurse, looking at her
watch, "probably about nine o'clock or not long after that, the
baby should be ready to come out."

"Two more hours of this?" Florence groaned.

"It might even be longer," warned the nurse. "It takes anywhere from three to five hours of labor, or an average of one
hundred and thirty-five contractions for the baby to come
out."

The nurse stood looking down at Florence, seemingly as
unaffected by her prediction of continuing pain as if she had
just informed her what hours the hospital snack bar would be
open.

"Well, if I get through this," Florence grimaced, shifting
her body in a vain attempt to find a comfortable position, "I
bet I'll never go through it again."

"Every mother says that the first time," responded the nurse jovially, turning to go, "but after the baby's out and you hold it in your arms, you'll want another one, probably as many as you can have."

"Some women must be crazy," Florence muttered, unconvinced, "if they want to go through this more than once."

"It's a good thing some of them are, then," laughed the nurse from the doorway, "or you and I and your husband might not be here now."

She whirled away, leaving me standing by Florence's bed holding the pad and pencil, feeling not quite so useless as I had before. So I stood by Florence's bedside, drawn into the physical anguish of childbirth in a practical way, as a recorder of the gradually decreasing time intervals between her contractions. After the first bone-crushing grip around my fingers, I asked Florence to grip my wrist instead. Each time, as the contractions ceased and her grip upon my wrist relaxed, it left the white imprint of her fingers for a few seconds afterwards until the blood rushed back into the surface tissues from which it had been forced by her grip. The accumulating perspiration on her forehead gradually reduced to limpness the curls which she had carefully set in her hair the night before, and the roots of her brunette hair glistened with the sweat of her effort.

As I stood there, shifting my gaze alternately from her face to the hands of my watch, I understood why the time of extended and periodic spasms of pain that she was going through was called "labor." It was if she were standing alone on an ocean shore, waist high in the water as waves rushed in, buffeting her, knocking her down, to recede briefly while she got up again, then came rushing back upon her with renewed fury. Further up the shore, I stood and watched, a silent spectator. The column of figures on the pad I held in my hand grew longer as the time difference between the spasms of labor pain dwindled with aggravating slowness, from twenty minutes to eighteen, to sixteen, thirteen, eleven . . .

As a new seizure began less than ten minutes from the

preceding one, and Florence twisted on the bed and turned her head away from me, I sensed the cry that came pushing against her clenched teeth, but which she bravely held back. And I was impressed with the manifest unfairness of the arrangement; that in the circumstances leading to the birth of a child, the man got most of the pleasure, while the woman got all of the pain. But as a surge of mingled pity and indignation welled up within me, I heard the echo of a voice from the dawn of human history come reverberating down the corridor of the centuries to fill the room where I stood with Florence. It was the voice of the Lord God in the Garden of Eden, speaking to Eve, the first woman.

"I will greatly multiply thy sorrow and thy conception; in sorrow thou shalt bring forth children . . ."

I was witnessing, helpless to reverse or undo it, part of the legacy of pain that Eve had bequeathed to all her daughters as a result of her disobedience.

Then, as Florence began to relax again, releasing her desperate hold upon my wrist, the nurse stuck her head through the door.

"How are we coming?"

"About ten minutes apart now," I said, making a note of the last contraction.

"Good," she beamed, "it won't be much longer."

"I hope not," Florence sighed, weakened by the struggle, with some of the resilience gone from her voice.

As the nurse left, Florence looked up at me, able in the intervals of rest between contractions to think, not of herself, but of me.

"Gar," she pleaded, pushing a sweat-dampened lock of hair back from her forehead, "you don't have to stay here. I'm sure it isn't a pleasant experience for you. If you want to go downstairs and wait, you can. Just leave me your watch, and I can write down the time as well as you can. It'll give me something to do and keep my mind occupied."

"You're sure you wouldn't rather have me stay?"

"No," she repeated vigorously, "I'd rather have you wait

downstairs in the lobby. It's enough to know that you're here. I can have the nurse page you if I really need you for anything."

I handed the pad and pencil to her, then slipped the expandable metal watch band down over my wrist to give to her. As I gave her the watch, scenes from the summer before in Calumet City, Illinois, in which the watch had played a key part, flashed across my mind.

I was thankful in that moment that Florence had known nothing of my real, hidden purpose for having pawned it at a gas station there on the way back home after driving her brother to Chicago to catch his plane. As she took it from my hand and slipped it on her own wrist, I shuddered inwardly at what her reaction would have been if she had known about that enigmatic episode. She would have doubtless dropped the watch with revulsion as an unclean thing, infected with some loathsome, communicable disease. She might even have hurled the watch back at me angrily, ordering me to leave the hospital room to endure the ordeal of childbirth alone; crushed in spirit by the agonizing knowledge that the very man who had implanted the seed of new life within her had so basely betrayed her trust. But if I felt no more self-condemnation than I did at the memory, as I turned away from her to leave the room, perhaps it was because the shameful episode seemed as though it had happened so long ago that it was part of my distant childhood rather than an event that had happened less than six months before.

"Gar." Her voice pursued me as I started to walk away from the bed.

I paused and looked back at her.

"Thanks for being here, and for being so willing to help," she said, her eyes misty with gratitude, "I really appreciate it."

I stepped back over to the side of her bed, bent down and planted a light, reassuring kiss on her cheek, then turned to leave the room.

"Maybe after the baby's born," her voice followed after me, "you'll kiss me again like I was your wife instead of a sister."

Suppressing the sigh that arose from within me as I felt the burden of need contained in her rebuke, I stepped back to the bed, bent down again and placed a kiss full on her lips.

"Is that better?" I asked.

"Much better," she half smiled, then reached for my hand.

"It seems like we've gotten kind of far apart since I got pregnant, Gar," she continued, holding my hand in both of hers. "I hope we'll be closer again after the baby's born."

"I'm sure we will be, Florence," I said, looking down at her.

My glance ricocheted off the hungry appeal in her eyes and turned for escape to the flower design on the lace curtains at the far side of the room. Then I engaged her gaze again, just long enough to deliver a few words that I improvised in an attempt to hide the truth behind a veneer of banter.

"After all, you'll have to admit that it's been pretty hard to get close to you at all lately, with your stomach sticking out the way it has been."

She laughed. "I guess that has made it kind of difficult."

On my way out of the room, I paused in the doorway and looked back to see her regarding me with an expression in which her laughter at my quip had given way to skepticism. My cleverness had not convinced her that after the baby was born we would be any closer together. A simple declaration that I still loved her would have sufficed to meet her need of the moment, but I could no longer speak the words that had once fallen so readily from my lips.

"Be sure and have me paged if you want me," I instructed her.

"I will."

As I stepped out of the room and walked down the gleaming, antiseptic-smelling hallway to go to the first-floor waiting room, I felt, for the most irrational of reasons, a strange twinge of guilt. I felt that I had been momentarily unfaithful to Corrine in planting a kiss upon the lips of Florence, my wife. But I consoled myself with the thought that what I had done had been an act of mercy, like giving an anesthetic to a patient in pain, about to undergo surgery.

In the waiting room, I joined three other people already there; an elderly couple, and a young man, dark-haired, tieless, his gray slacks wrinkled as if he had slept in them. Then, putting on my reading glasses, I picked up from the seat beside me the already wrinkled Sunday edition of the daily newspaper of Michigan's capital city.

I sought to anesthetize my awareness of the slow, dragging passage of time while Florence suffered through labor pains on the floor above by surveying the parade of current developments in the larger world beyond the hospital walls.

The front page headline on the paper thundered an ominous prophecy: "Russians Foresee Inevitability of H-Bomb Warfare." I lowered the newspaper a moment to stare unseeingly at the far wall of the waiting room. It was not a comforting prospect that the child I had fathered, and was about to be born, would be stepping into this kind of a world where a war, far more horrible than the two preceding World Wars, seemed inevitable.

Disturbed, I continued a restless perusal of the paper. I read that President Dwight Eisenhower, beginning his fourth and final year in the White House, with access to intelligence information on which the front-page was based, had nevertheless not abandoned the achievement of peace as an attainable goal. Having concluded a triumphant goodwill tour of Europe, Asia, and Africa, he was making plans to visit Latin American countries and Japan, after a scheduled visit with Soviet Premier Khrushchev. And although it was only January, the political jockeying for the presidential election in November was being given generous newspaper coverage. Pollsters were predicting that Vice President Richard Nixon would get the Republican nomination for president. Mention was made also of several Democratic challengers to Nixon, including a then obscure U.S. Senator from Massachusetts named John F. Kennedy.

"Mr. Garfield Roby."

The sound of my name booming from the hospital intercom loudspeaker jolted me into dropping the newspaper. I jumped up from my chair and hurried toward the elevator even as additional instructions were repeated over the loud-speaker.

"Mr. Garfield Roby, please come to O.B."

On the second floor, the head nurse gave me the news. "They just took your wife into the delivery room, Mr. Roby. She should be out with your new baby in about fifteen minutes."

"Can I wait here?"

"Certainly. There's a small room down the hall just for expectant fathers where you can sit down."

I turned away from her chart-filled desk to wander down the wide, polished hallway, and paused in front of the huge glass window that provided a clear view of the nursery. Only two of the dozen cribs were occupied by newborn babies. One was sleeping peacefully, while the other was crying with mouth opened wide in spasms of infant fury that shook its body. Happily, the room was soundproof, and I could not hear the infant's crying in full force. I watched as a nurse, immaculate in white starched uniform, busied herself with bottles of formula preparation, seemingly oblivious of the crying infant. I might have mentally charged her with malfeasance of duty had I not read or heard somewhere that it was essential for their lung expansion that newborn babies be allowed to cry.

As I stood there in front of the nursery window, while the sounds of hospital routine surrounded me—soft-soled nurses hurrying back and forth on their necessary errands, sporadic calls over the intercom requesting some doctor—I was momentarily distracted from my role as an expectant father, and from the painful ordeal that Florence was going through at that moment. The source of distraction was the unheard cry of protest that was contorting the face of the crying infant behind the soundproof window.

This was probably how I had come into the world, I mused, howling in protest, some thirty-six years before. And so had every other member of the human race who had sprung from the line of Adam, come wailing into the world.

And how many, I wondered, had grown up to endure some of the same vicissitudes that had befallen the Biblical patriarch, Job; to be driven to the same desperate state of mind that he had been pushed to, cursing the day that he had been born into such a world of inexplicable suffering, unmitigated evil, and inevitable death. Standing there before the plate-glass window of the nursery, I was impelled to look back on the world into which I had grown from infancy to youth. In spite of the pinch of poverty, my brother and sister and I had been loved by our parents, who had provided security and physical comfort.

But that world, I saw in retrospect, had been like the eggshell world into which a baby chicken is born. A day had come when its tissue-thin walls had been broken into by the impact of the larger world outside. For me, my childhood world had been shattered by shock waves of the Japanese attack on Pearl Harbor, catapulting America into the inferno of World War II. Intimidated by the bugle blast of American military might, I had been pushed out into that larger, and, in many ways, more terrifying world.

And after coming face to face with the violence, the corruption, the injustice, the sorrow, the shame, the suffering, the pain, and the death, which filled this larger world, I had been driven to make a profound choice. I would have to do either what I could to change that world into which I had been cast, or I wanted to leave it. I could not accept it as it was. That had been the idealistic resolve that had strengthened me to defy military authority and refuse to bear arms, after my request for transfer to non-combatant duty had been denied. Instead of destroying lives on a foreign battlefield, I had resolved to set out upon a dedicated search to find the cause and cure of war.

And my search, I reflected, as I stood in front of the nursery window watching but not seeing the activities within, had indeed culminated in success some months after a military court-martial board had sentenced me to five years' imprisonment for insubordination. For I was still convinced that I had, indeed, discovered the cause and cure of war, as well as the solution for all other personal and social evils, in the experience of religious conversion that I had undergone while in military confinement. But my efforts to apply that discovery in the world had been interrupted by the conflicting cross currents of legitimate and sinful inclinations that had emerged within me like a maelstrom in the hidden depths of my own being.

I was like a scientist who had discovered a serum that could cure a lethal plague that was sweeping the world, but whose labors to mass produce and dispense the serum had been brought to a standstill by the unfortunate fact that he, himself, had become infected with the deadly malady which he had been trying to cure in others.

In that moment of retrospective waiting, in a small-town hospital, I could feel an outreach of human sympathy for the anguish of heart and mind out of which Karl Marx, poring over endless pages of history in the London library, had voiced the fierce but misguided premise of the Communist Manifesto.

"Philosophers have described the world; it is time to change the world."

My solitary efforts to change the world had come to naught, while the movement that Marx had set in motion was continuing to reap an ever-expanding harvest of horror on a global scale.

"Mr. Roby!"

The authoritative masculine voice at my elbow broke into the flow of my far-ranging thoughts, like the suddenly closed sluice gates of a dam, closing to arrest the flow of a great river. I turned to look into the smiling face of Doctor Larson, whom Florence had been visiting during her pregnancy. His dark hair was still covered by a white surgical cap.

"Congratulations, Mr. Roby!" he grinned, extending his right hand, "you've got a strong, healthy son."

I grasped his hand, trying to relay my sense of appreciation for his part in Florence's hour of crisis by the fervency of my grip.

"How's Florence?" I asked.

371

"It was hard for her," he said, hinting that what had happened in the delivery room had been more of an ordeal for Florence than it was for most women. "Your wife's a little older than most women are when they have their first baby."

There was an unintended rebuke to me in his disclosure. Had it not been for me and my fruitless search for the right vocational niche in society, the baby might have been born in the first year of our marriage rather than the fifth, perhaps sparing Florence some of the physical pain she had gone through during childbirth.

"She'll be alright," he assured me, noting the concern that his remark had produced, "but I would suggest you wait a couple or three hours before seeing your wife. She needs the rest after what she's been through. You can see the baby, though. They'll be bringing them both out in a minute."

"Thanks, doctor."

With a comradely squeeze of my arm, he whirled away and hurried down the hallway in the opposite direction from the delivery room. Several minutes later, as I waited before the nursery window watching the double swinging doors that led into the delivery room, they were pushed open and the stretcher on which Florence lay, silent and still, was pushed through the doors. It was a shock to see the sheet that covered her no longer bulging with the unsightly hill of flesh that had been there before. I was glad for her that the burden of that awkward and uncomfortable weight had finally been removed from her. Then, as one nurse maneuvered the stretcher on which Florence was lying into a room at the end of the hall, another nurse came walking briskly down the hall toward me, bearing a small, blanketed bundle in her arms.

"Mr. Roby?"

"Yes, that's me."

"Here's your son."

There was a gleam of maternal excitement in her eyes, evoked, perhaps, by the anticipation of a similar experience still future for her. I looked down into the tiny, wrinkled, red face of the human being whose destiny would be profoundly affected through the formative years of his life by my actions, and felt a heavy weight of responsibility settle down over me. I hid it behind a "proud father" grin.

"He doesn't seem to be too impressed about being here," I observed, as the nurse stood close beside me, cradling him in her arms.

"Oh, he will as soon as he starts to find out what it's all about. I'll tell you how much he weighs in about five minutes. His name's Paul, isn't it?"

"Right."

She hurried on into the nursery with Paul Roby, fifteen minutes old. I stood before the window and watched as my son was bathed, weighed, dressed in a white kimono, and placed in a crib. A moment later, the nurse returned to report the quantitative statistics that always seemed to be supremely important to hospital staffs, to parents and grandparents.

"Upon his arrival in this world," announced the nurse happily, "Paul Roby weighed seven pounds, four ounces, is approximately eighteen inches long, and is a very healthy baby."

I thanked her for the information, and she hurried away. I lingered in front of the plate-glass window and watched while my son's spasm of crying ended and his form quieted into sleep, like the other two babies in the nursery. Then I left the hospital to drive back to the Berlincourt farm and report the news to Hilda. After eating a light lunch with her in a house that seemed quiet and empty with Florence gone, I drove Hilda back to the hospital for her first eager look at her newest grandson.

As Hilda and I stood together, looking through the nursery window, the living God spoke to my heart and mind in a more eloquent and forceful way than He had been able to speak to me through previous weeks of preaching, patiently listened to in church. Almost oblivious of Hilda's murmured exclamations of pleasure and admiration, the sight of my newborn son was used by the Spirit of God to bring before my mind's eye another cradle scene from the past; the setting of the Incarnation. This, I suddenly realized, was what Jesus Christ had looked like when He had been born into this world—the world that He had made, but which knew Him not.

As I watched the nurse pick up Paul from the position in which he had been lying on his back, to turn him over onto his stomach, the word "incredible" flashed through my mind at this living illustration of Bible truth; that the God who upheld all things by the word of his power, and by whom all things were made and held together, had voluntarily made Himself so weak for my sake, and for the sake of every other person in the world, that He could not even turn over in bed; could not perform the elemental tasks of feeding Himself, of changing His own raiment. What incredible humility, I thought, what love and what character revealed in a God who would stoop so low for the sake of sinful man.

And as I thought of the respects in which my infant son was like the Babe of Bethlehem, I was also aware of other details in which the circumstances of their births were radically different. This son of mine had been born in a place of immaculate, germ-free cleanliness and warmth, with skilled attendants to provide every comfort and protection that modern medical science could provide. But that Babe, the infant who was God incarnate, had come into the world in the smelly and unsanitary setting of a stable. No wonder, I reflected, that most of the world could not and would not believe the angelic announcement that had heralded His birth . . . "unto you is born this day in the city of David, a Savior which is Christ the Lord." To the natural mind, it was indeed too incredible to be true. Only the experienced miracle of conversion, putting a man in vital and personal touch with the living God, could enable and incline the human mind to accept the greater miracle of the Incarnation.

"Well, what do you think of your new son, Garfield?" Hilda broke into my thoughts.

"Incredible!" I murmured, not turning my head to look at her, my mind still looking beyond my infant son to the circumstances of the birth of the Son of God.

"I guess you're right about that," she agreed, oblivious of my inner vision that had elicited the sense of wonder expressed in my answer. "A baby is an amazing thing, when you stop to think about it. Doesn't the Bible say something about us being wonderfully made?"

"It's in Psalm 139," I answered, as the mountaintop sense of inner illumination faded. "David said, 'I will praise thee, for I am fearfully and wonderfully made.'"

We left then, to return later in the afternoon to visit Florence. The baby was with her, cradled in her arms when we stepped into the room. As I looked at her, it was obvious that at that moment, Florence felt nothing of that heavy weight that had descended on me earlier, in the hallway outside the nursery window, as I had realized that responsibility for this single human life had fallen upon our shoulders. Her face, as she looked down at the small bundle of blanketed life in her arms, shone with a radiance that I had never seen there, unless it had been on the day we had stood together before the altar in the church where we were married. I stood by the bed and looked on as Florence and her mother were caught up in music that I could not hear, the melody of motherhood. I remembered what Jesus had said; that when a child is born, a woman forgets the anguish of birth for joy that a child is born into the world. Then Florence became aware that I was standing there.

"Here, Gar," she said, lifting the baby toward me, "hold your son for a few minutes."

I took the doll-size living being from her arms, without the blanket. Holding him in my arms, I could feel the contours and movements of the small body through the thin cotton gown. I looked down at the eyes that were mere slits of reflected light, eyes that could not see nor recognize the face that looked down on him. As I took one of the miniature hands between my thumb and forefinger of one hand to feel it, it seemed unbelievable that such weak, innocent hands could ever grow up to be like those I had seen in a newspaper ad that morning, manacled with handcuffs. But I knew that without the right quality and quantity of love, sacrifice, attention, guidance, discipline and prayer from his parents, it could happen. Suddenly I was aware of Hilda, standing by the foot of the bed looking on. She, too, had almost as vital an interest in this child as I did, or Florence; a tie of physical kinship to him.

"Would you like to hold him, Hilda?" I asked, turning to her.

"Certainly, I'd like to hold my new grandson," she asserted emphatically, as if insulted that I would even have to ask such a question.

She took the baby carefully and rocked him back and forth in her arms.

"You look to me like a very sweet little boy, Paul Roby," she cooed, lifting his face up close to her own.

"That's probably what my mother said about me when I was born, Hilda," I said, "but look how I turned out."

Hilda leaped to my defense at the self-disparaging remark that had been intended humorously.

"I don't know about that, Garfield," she shot back, "I think you turned out all right. I think you're a very fine son-in-law. If your son grows up to be like his dad, why, I think he'll do all right."

Perhaps you wouldn't say that, Hilda, I thought to myself, turning my gaze from the commendatory twinkle in her eyes, *if you knew all there was to know about me.*

Florence said nothing about entertaining a hope that the son she had brought into the world might grow up to emulate his father. After several more minutes of grandmothering Paul, Hilda handed him carefully back to Florence for a final time of holding him close to her before the nurse came to take him back to the nursery.

"Now you know how much weight I had to carry around the last three weeks," Florence said, looking up at me as she cuddled the baby, "but it was worth it."

It was evident that this child would not want for attention and love from either his mother or grandmother. Moments later, the nurse came to get the baby, and, shortly thereafter,

Hilda and I left to let Florence get more much-needed rest. It was three days later that Florence was allowed to bring the baby home, evoking a torrent of surprised comment from Hilda.

"My land," she exclaimed, as Florence stepped ahead of me with the baby into the Berlincourt living room, "these doctors sure do things different nowadays. It used to be that a woman had to stay at the hospital two or three weeks after she had a baby. Now they send them home after two or three days."

After the first week of washing diapers, mixing formula, and being awakened two or three times every night, Florence's enthusiasm over the new baby had not appreciably diminished. She adjusted to the changes in our daily routine that were necessitated by the arrival of the baby without murmuring, such as the change in our sleeping quarters. It was too cold in the unheated upstairs bedroom for the baby, so Florence and I had to move downstairs and take over the bedroom that Brady, her brother, had occupied before he went to California. But for me, after a week of being awakened several times a night, to lie there and listen to the crying of my infant son until Florence could get a bottle warmed, some of the wonder that the first glimpse of the baby in the hospital had aroused within me began to fade.

And with the major crisis of childbirth behind for Florence, the desire to return to Detroit and see Corrine grew stronger within me. But I knew of only one way I could have a legitimate excuse for being gone from home long enough to drive to Detroit and back without arousing questions and suspicious in Florence's mind. I would have to take up again the part-time job of driving a taxi that I had temporarily resigned before the baby was born, at Florence's insistent pleading. At least, I would have to lead Florence to believe I was taking it up again. Sitting at the supper table one night, the second week after the baby was born, I fabricated a story to test Florence's reaction to a proposed resumption of the part-time cab-driving job.

"The manager at Courteous Cab called me today," I announced casually, "to ask when I'd be coming back to work."

In a sudden show of agitation, Florence's coffee cup clattered to its saucer, almost slipping out of her fingers.

"Going back to work? I hope you told him 'never'!"

Desperation suddenly knotted my insides. The part-time taxi-driving job was my lifeline to Corrine. Without that, I could not possibly be gone from home long enough to go to Detroit and see her. I picked up a slice of bread that I didn't want and buttered it, just to have something to do to help me sound casual in answering and to avoid Florence's belligerent stare. I could feel Hilda's eyes on me also, sensing, perhaps, the makings of a minor argument that could develop into a major domestic discord.

"I told him I'd talk to you about it and call him back tomorrow."

"Well, you can call him tomorrow and tell him you're not coming back to work," she bristled. "I've had enough of you're being gone three nights a week, including all night on Friday. Even if nothing did go wrong in having the baby, I still didn't like it."

There was a moment of uncomfortable silence at the table as I quietly pushed into my mouth food that had lost its savor. Hilda picked at her food silently, restrained from speaking, perhaps, by a feeling that it was a matter on which she had no right to express an opinion. Then, realizing, perhaps, that she might have sounded too domineering in so forcefully instructing me what to do about the cab-driving job, Florence continued in a tone that was more pleading than demanding.

"Just give me two or three more weeks to be home with the baby, Gar, then I'll go back to work. We haven't gone too far in the hole yet since I've been off work."

"That's because we haven't got the big bills yet," I said, trying to put up a gentle but determined fight to resume the cab-driving job.

"What big bills?"

"There are going to be expenses at the hospital that the insurance won't cover. Then the doctor's bills for office calls and circumcising the baby. Then we'll have the winter taxes to pay on the house in Charlotte this month, besides the car license."

"I don't care, Gar," she continued, while Hilda sat between us in sympathetic silence. "I'd rather try to get by on just your paycheck until I go back to work. I'll even start checking the paper for a babysitter tomorrow."

"Why, Florence," Hilda broke in indignantly, "I'll be more than glad to take care of the little tyke whenever you want to go back to work. And you won't have to pay out money for a baby sitter, either. Mercy, you and Garfield have helped me so much by being here, I just owe you an awful lot."

"There!" Florence beamed triumphantly, "it's all settled. Where could I get a better baby sitter than my own Mom?"

Florence leaned over and put an arm around her mother's shoulder, drawing her head over to plant a kiss on her cheek.

"Thanks, Mom, for offering," she said, with evident gratitude.

Then Florence's sensitivity about finances and her solicitude for her mother prompted an additional comment.

"But you're not going to do it for nothing, Mom. I'm going to pay you just what I would a regular baby sitter."

While Hilda argued that she wanted no payment for taking care of her new grandchild, and Florence just as emphatically opposed her position, I sat silently making a show of finishing the food on my plate, temporarily ignored by Florence and her mother as if I were not there. As I glanced out the window at the barren, snow-covered landscape, I felt as if I were on a ship that was carrying me away from Corrine. She was standing on the shore watching with wondering eyes as the distance between us widened. There was pain and perplexity in her eyes, for I could not call out across the widening rift of water an explanation or a single, parting endearment. Had I seen Corrine for the last time, without even having said goodbye to her? Perhaps something of the sombre thoughts that were flying through my mind was etched on my face as I stared absently out the kitchen window beside the table.

"But maybe you'd rather be gone three nights a week than to be home with me and the baby. Is that it, Gar?"

Florence's words had been cast in the form of a question, but in the tone of her voice there was an accusation born of suspicion.

"No," I sighed, trying to manufacture the semblance of a smile, "I just wanted to help out as much as I could, that's all."

"If you really want to be helpful, you can stay home nights with the baby and me. Besides, I can't see where you came out ahead for all the time you did drive a cab. I never saw any of the money."

"It went into bills—tires for the car, for one thing," I reminded her.

I was thankful that the sound of crying from the back bedroom spared me any further interrogation as to what I had done with the extra money I had earned driving a cab.

"Oh, oh, he's awake," said Florence, pushing her chair back from the table.

She jumped up and headed for the refrigerator to get out a bottle of the ready-mixed formula that she kept made up ahead. While Florence took care of the baby, I retired to the spacious living room in the front of the house, to sit alone on the sofa and listen to words that were echoing softly in my mind, like the mystic call of the sea coming to a land-bound mariner.

"I love you, in the Lord, Garfield."

Would I ever hear those words again from the lips of Corrine? At the moment, with the shift in Florence's concern from keeping a balanced budget to having me stay home nights, I had little justification for insisting on continuing with the cab-driving job. If I did insist, it could lead to the sullen silence of a cold war in the home, or might erupt into a heated explosion of angry words and actions. I did not want to bring down such a storm upon the innocent head of my infant son, less than two weeks old. Yet, without the necessary ruse of the part-time job as a smoke screen to hide the real reason for extended absences from home, how and when would I ever get down to Detroit to see Corrine again?

To think of Corrine coming to Lansing to see me was out of the question. I was sure that she would be willing to do it, but I dared not ask her. There would be too great a risk of being seen by someone who knew me, a report that might eventually get back to Florence on the gossip grapevine. But there was another equally hazardous risk that made any thought of Corrine coming to Lansing unthinkable. Corrine's curiosity would certainly be aroused as to the need for the secretive precautions I would have to take in arranging clandestine meetings with her. She would soon suspect what I had kept back from her at our first and second meetings—that I was married. I felt sure that had she known this about me at our first meeting in the Hollywood Ballroom, I never would have been given the precious privilege of taking her home from the ballroom the second time I saw her. There never would have been the long, intimate drive to the outskirts of Detroit; having a carry-out snack at three in the morning; playing the concertina on the street, accompanying Corrine as she sang "Fascination." I never would have been invited into her apartment, in violation of her landlady's wishes, for a much-needed hour of rest before the long drive back to Lansing.

And if she had known I was married, she might never have spoken those incredible words that I still cherished in my memory like priceless jewels.

"I love you, in the Lord, Garfield."

If she had known, not only that I was married, but that I was an expectant father as well, she would never have asked that parting question that still haunted my waking thoughts and stirred up restless desires to return to her.

"When will I be seeing you again, Garfield?"

I was certain that, if Corrine had known this truth, the brief but magic moments of enchantment we had shared would never have come to pass. And I was equally certain that if she were to discover the truth about my situation now, then all that I strangely hoped still might be between us could and would never come to pass. My solitary reflections, sitting alone in the living room, came to this unhappy conclusion. I was shut up, for the present, to waiting and hoping for some unforeseeable way to open which would enable me to get back to Detroit to see Corrine again face to face. And astonishingly, that unexpected way was opened on the following Saturday of that week, in a letter that was delivered to the Berlincourt farm.

Alone in the big, empty farmhouse, with Florence and her mother gone into town on a shopping trip with the baby, I sat on the living room sofa to scan several pieces of mail that had been delivered that day. Two were bills, which I quickly set aside. Then, from a business-size envelope addressed to Florence and me, I pulled out a folder printed on glossy, high-quality paper. On the cover was a striking black-and-white pen drawing of a young man bent down on one knee, fitting a shoe to the foot of a man seated above him. Above the illustration was the arresting caption, "The Shoe Clerk Who Made History." My interest was immediately aroused. Poignant memories of bygone times, places, and people from the city of Chicago were evoked as I read the script beneath the arresting illustration.

In the back room of a Boston shoe store, a Sunday School teacher who came to call on his pupil, the shoe clerk, stayed to pray with him. In that private prayer meeting, a new life was born. Dwight L. Moody, the young shoe clerk, became a new creature in Christ Jesus. In the weeks following Moody's conversion, God's Word took on new meaning for him. He saw in its pages the only solution for all of the soul-sickness of mankind. And in his heart he knew that God had chosen him to be a channel through whom that message could be carried to lost and dying men. Impelled by the conviction that only God's Word could meet man's needs, Moody went forth from that shoe store to evangelize hundreds of thousands around the world. History will long remember him as a man with a message from God

Under the impact of the final words of the brief biographical sketch of D. L. Moody, I laid the folder down on the sofa beside me, thankful that I was alone in the huge, empty farmhouse. "A man with a message from God." That was what I had once been, following my conversion in military service during the closing days of World War II. But soon thereafter, unlike Moody, I had encountered the acerbic, anti-Christian writings of "the great agnostic," Robert G. Ingersoll, a contemporary of Abraham Lincoln, who had dealt a devastating blow to my newfound religious faith that had left me reeling between doubt and despair for several years following. Then there had been a push toward the recovery of my faith in the living God and His Word, through the Moral Re-Armament movement that had brought to Lansing its dynamic call to live by four moral standards distilled form the Sermon on the Mount: absolute honesty, absolute purity, absolute unselfishness, and absolute love. Their impact had kindled the dream and desire of preparing for the ministry as my life work. This had been followed by my marriage to Florence as a needed helpmate in carrying out that dream. Then, with Florence, I had gone to Chicago to enroll in the school for pastors and missionaries that had been founded by Dwight L. Moody; there to have my dream shattered upon the rocks of sexual excesses that I had not been able to entirely subjugate, even with a wife beside me.

And after this brief backward look, I picked up the folder again. It announced the annual mid-winter retreat called "Founder's Week" that had become a tradition at Moody. It was a week during which all student classes were canceled so that students could attend the meetings that had been designed as a time of spiritual revival and refreshment; not only for students, but for faculty members, returning alumni, and friends of the school as well. It was intended to deepen the commitment on the part of the students, friends and supporters to the basic purpose for which the school had been established—to carry out the Scriptural commission engraved on the corner-stone of the arch that led into Institute Square from LaSalle Street: "Go ye into all the world, and preach the Gospel to every creature."

As I studied the program of events for the Founder's Week Conference, scheduled to start a week later on the first of February, a mood of spiritual nostalgia enveloped me, evoking a backward-looking hunger to be again the man of God, like Moody, that I had aspired to be when I had entered Moody as an older student. And then, that backward look stimulated the recollection of a looseleaf binder full of typewritten letters that I had written to my invalid mother, enabling her, although confined to a wheel chair with multiple sclerosis, to share adventures and newly gained insights on the streets of Chicago. My mother had saved the letters and returned them to me when we moved back to Lansing. I remembered that they were upstairs in one of the boxes of belongings we had brought to the farm but had never unpacked. I went upstairs to the frigid bedroom and ransacked several boxes until I found the loose-leaf binder containing the letters I had written. Then I took it back downstairs, sat down again on the sofa, and opened the binder of letters. I turned to the first letter I had written to my mother from Chicago, dated five years before.

"The two weeks I've been here," began the letter, "have caused me to feel a genuine gratitude to God, and to the human instrument which he used to found this school. It was in 1880 that D. L. Moody knelt on a then vacant lot where Institute buildings now stand and asked God to establish there a training school for Christian laymen. From all over the United States, Canada, Mexico, Holland, Germany, the Philippine Islands, Korea, Japan, and Australia, I have been privileged to enter into a rich, rewarding relationship with people who have consecrated their lives to the Lord's service; young men and women just out of high school, as well as those approaching middle age, who have been arrested and turned around by God's hand after having long followed other self-willed vocations."

With the last word of that first, glowing letter, I was transferred from Chicago back to Charlotte; from the spiritual battlefields on the streets of a great city, to the quiet, deserted living room of the Berlincourt farm. As I sat on the sofa, looking out the window at the winter landscape, the open notebook spread open on my lap, some of the experiences that I had just relived in the reading of that first letter seemed to have happened not merely five years ago, but five thousand years ago. And the person about whom I had been reading was not me, but a total stranger, as distant and as dead as St. Francis of Assisi or Martin Luther.

Yet, I read on, thumbing through the letters, perhaps, because the life that was described in those letters seemed to be a life of purpose and conflict and drama. It was a stark and total contrast to the life I was presently living and had been living since leaving Chicago—a lower echelon clerk in the State Highway Department, dealing not with needy people, but filing papers and making Xerox copies and coloring in geometric shapes on highway road plans. I read on through letters that recounted experiences in meeting people on the streets, at missions, and in jails, mingled with profiles of other students at Moody whose lives had become vitally connected to my own.

One of them, who loomed up from the page before me like a genie from a bottle, standing out like a skyscraper towering above lesser buildings, was Jerry Lewis. At the age of forty, he had left New York City to come to Moody and prepare for the ministry. I didn't have to read the descriptive words on the page before me to visualize Jerry, slightly taller and heavier than I, his Jewish face etched with the chronic woebegone expression of a St. Bernard dog, a legacy of the life he had lived before coming to Moody. I could still remember the highlights of the testimony he had given in a Chicago Skid Row mission one night.

He had been living high and fast in New York City. He had been living dangerously, too, as a highly paid dope smuggler for then underworld czar, Lucky Luciano. Then Jerry had been apprehended by police on one of his drug-smuggling trips in and out of the country, and had been thrown into jail in New York City to await trial. When a kindly, visiting grandmother had given him a Bible, he had spit on it, then kicked it into a corner of his jail cell. Later, out of sheer boredom, he had picked it up and started reading. It resulted in his conversion, followed by a suspended prison sentence and the radical change in his life, from smuggling narcotics to preparations to preach the Gospel.

I paged my way through the rest of the letters to the end of the looseleaf binder. My vicarious sense of exaltation over what I had read was canceled out and overwhelmed by my keen awareness of what I had omitted in the letters to my mother; my silent, solitary battle to bring my sexual proclivities into subjugation. This was the battle that too many times had ended in defeat, resulting in my decision to leave Moody and abandon my hope of entering the ministry. And no one had known the reason I had abandoned that high endeavor; not my mother, or Florence, or any of the deans or counselors or fellow students at Moody.

With the notebook of letters closed on my lap, I sat there on the sofa, studying the design of the carpet on the floor without seeing it, as spiritual longings for the life I had abandoned crowded in upon me. I felt the stirring of a genuine hunger to return to my spiritual alma mater, the school that D. L. Moody had founded in the heart of Chicago. But along with a hunger to return to the scenes where I had begun to prepare for the ministry, was a reluctance to see the faces of former classmates; those who had gone on to graduate from Moody and become pastors and missionaries after I had quit Moody and had left Chicago in defeat. I shrank from the prospect of encountering former classmates, some of whom would surely be there. There would be the inevitable questions about what I had been doing since leaving Moody. And in reply, I would have to conceal, behind lying evasions, the truth that was too sordid to confess. Never could I speak to anyone there of the incredible turn my life had taken since leaving Moody. Never could I tell former classmates or teachers about the failure-fostered vocational choice I had made in a honky-tonk bar in Calumet City, Illinois, the year before; nor of how it had culminated in my meeting with a religious-minded taxi dancer named Corrine, who shared my expectation of one day walking on Heavenly streets of gold.

Then, as the thought of Corrine, who had been for a time pushed from my mind by the scenes I had been reliving at Moody, returned to my mind, it suddenly dawned on me like sunrise dispelling the darkness, that the Founder's Week announcement that had come in the mail could provide the very opportunity I had been desperately hoping for to see Corrine again. For if Florence would consent to my being gone several days for a very worthy purpose, to attend Founder's Week meetings in Chicago, I could use one of those days to stop in Detroit on my return trip to see Corrine. For I was sure that, as much as she might enjoy it, Florence would not even consider accompanying me. She would not want to take Paul on such a long trip in mid winter; neither would she want to burden her mother by leaving him with her for several days and nights.

I carried the notebook of letters back upstairs, marveling at the Providential way in which my former tie to Moody had opened this opportunity to see Corrine again without inciting a verbal battle with Florence over resuming the cab-driving job. Even though I felt that I would have to slink unobtrusively in and out of whatever meetings I might attend, careful to avoid anyone who might know me and ask the inevitable questions about my spiritual health and progress since leaving Moody, it was a risk I was willing to take for the sake of seeing Corrine again soon.

That evening, while the baby was asleep in the back bedroom and Hilda was studying her Sunday school lesson for the morrow, I broached the idea to Florence as she sat with me in the front room. She was sitting at the piano, playing some of the familiar hymns that she knew by heart.

"While you were gone today," I said, as she turned one ear

to me while continuing to stroke the keys, "I was reading some of the letters I wrote to Mother while we were at Moody."

"Too bad you decided to quit. That's something I could never figure out."

"I've been thinking about going back to . . ."

Her hands struck the keys in an abrupt cacophony of discord as she twisted around on the piano bench to face me, interrupting what I was about to say.

"What!" she exclaimed incredulously. "Are you kidding? You're thinking about going back to Moody?"

"I meant just for some of the meetings of Founder's week. A folder about it came in the mail today. It starts Monday and runs for a week. I thought it would be good for me to go down for maybe the last day or two of meetings."

"That's different," she said, obviously relieved, facing me from the piano bench. "I'd like to go myself, but I wouldn't think of taking the baby on a long trip like that, and I wouldn't want to leave him with Mom for that long. It would be too much for her."

I sat on the sofa across from her, waiting patiently for an expression of approval from her as to my going alone. I didn't want to risk hardening her opposition to the proposal by pushing it too quickly and too aggressively.

"When would you want to go?" Her question was a happy herald of forthcoming approval.

"I could leave on Thursday afternoon, be there in Chicago Friday and Saturday, and start back on Saturday night or Sunday morning. I could probably stay overnight at Sophie's mission, so the only expense would be gas and maybe something to eat on the way."

"Well, I wouldn't mind your being gone for that," she said, turning back to the keyboard, "half as much as I've minded your being gone on that taxi-driving job, I'll tell you that. That was really bugging me. But if you've got the money to get down there and back, it's alright with me."

Florence resumed playing the piano, the matter settled. As I sat there on the sofa behind her, I could not help the spontaneous expression of thanks that rocketed skyward from within me, certain that Heavenly influences had intervened to grant this deep desire of my heart. As Florence continued playing, unmindful of the happiness that her approval had produced, I sat there, hearing the music she was playing, but not listening; reveling silently in the expectation that I would be seeing Corrine again, face to face, by the end of the following week.

On the first day of the following week, from work, I placed a long distance phone call to the little Gospel Mission on Western Avenue in Chicago where Florence and I had spent many a Sunday afternoon when living in Chicago, with a happy handful of other Christians, for a message from the Word of God by a layman or visiting pastor, then afterwards a warm, informal fellowship meal prepared by Sophie in her apartment behind the Mission.

"I'll be glad to put you up, Brother Roby," came her happy, Polish accent over the wire from Chicago, "for two or three nights, or as long as you want to stay."

I hung up, elated at moving one step closer to my eventual reunion with Corrine. And that same day, during lunch hour, I hurried downtown on another important mission having to do with Corrine—to pick out a belated birthday gift and card to send to her. The date of her birthday, January the 7th, was one of the little tidbits of information I had gleaned from the brief exchanges of our two previous encounters. I had postponed sending her anything, hoping that it would be possible to see her in person to celebrate the occasion. And I had not wanted to write to her without being able to name the date when I would be returning to see her again.

In a downtown greeting card store, I picked out a beautiful card that I was sure would arouse Corrine's admiration; a glittery winter wonderland scene of a scarfed and gloved and booted couple walking down a snow-drifted country road. Then, hurrying down the wind-chilled main street of the downtown shopping area, wondering what to get Corrine for a suitable birthday gift, I passed a record shop whose window answered my question. "Christmas LP albums, one-third off," proclaimed a sign in the window. I stopped in front of the store, remembering a complaint that Corrine had voiced on my last visit before Christmas. She didn't have a single LP album of Christmas music to play on her stereo at home. What if Christmas was past? There were others coming.

Inside the record store, I picked a double record album that had all the old Christmas carols, as well as contemporary songs about Christmas, done by a list of musical celebrities in the fields of both sacred and secular music. The store packed it in a sturdy mailing carton, and on my way back to the Gray building, I stopped at the post office and mailed it to Corrine.

Later that afternoon, in the cafeteria during coffee break, I added a brief personal message to the endearing sentiments of the birthday card. In it, I told Corrine of the combination Christmas-birthday gift I was sending separately. I told her about the spiritual retreat I was planning to attend in Chicago, including the name and address of the Mission where I would be staying one or two nights; and best of all, that I would be stopping off to see her on Saturday night of that week on my return trip from Chicago.

On the LP album of Christmas music that I had already mailed, I had used the return address of the record shop where I had bought it. For Corrine's birthday card, which I mailed later that same day, I put no return address. For even though I had told her I would be seeing her at the end of the week, if she knew my home address, she might impulsively send a "thank you" note, which would be like a lighted stick of dynamite if delivered to the door of the Berlincourt farm.

So on Thursday of that week, I left work at noon and started out alone on the pilgrimage of two hundred and fifty miles to my spiritual alma mater in Chicago as the necessary roundabout route that would take me back to Detroit on my return trip to see Corrine again.

CHAPTER 11

⇒ It was 5:30 when I reached the outskirts of Chicago, and an hour later when I pulled over to the curb a block away from the little Mission on Western Avenue where I would be staying for two nights. I got out, locked the car, and, carrying the small suitcase I had brought along, walked back toward the Mission past ancient apartment houses and shabby-looking stores and taverns.

I paused in front of the familiar brick two-story apartment building, flanked on one side by a tavern and on the other by a grocery store, both of which advertised beer and liquor. The Mission, whose store-window front provided the only evidence of a religious function inside, was still the same as it had been when I was a student at Moody, preparing for the ministry as my life vocation. There was still the huge pulpit Bible, opened to the Gospel of John, third chapter and sixteenth verse.

"For God so loved the world that He gave His only begotten Son, that whosoever believeth in Him should not perish, but have everlasting life."

Behind the open Bible was a painting of Jesus as the Good Shepherd, holding a lamb, with other sheep following Him. Drapes hid the interior of the Mission, securing privacy for those gathered within from the stares of passers-by who might be only curious, rather than concerned. There were still the printed placards surrounding the Bible, indicating the multilingual neighborhood to which the Mission sought to minister under Sophie's supervision; English language services Wednesday night; German on Tuesday night; Polish on Thursday and Saturday nights and on Sunday afternoon at 3:00. "Everybody welcome," announced another placard, "come and leave your burdens here."

I walked around to the side door that led into Sophie's apartment behind the Mission, and knocked. Within several minutes, I heard an inside door open and approaching footsteps. Then the curtain on the glass panel of the door was pulled back, and Sophie's face beamed through it in happy recognition. Bespectacled, and still able to see after what she described as a "miraculous" recovery from cataracts on both eyes, her blackish-brown hair drawn tight in an old-fashioned braid around her head, and her sharply pointed nose reminding me, as it always had, of Pinnochio, the wooden puppet that came to life.

"Brother Roby!" she exclaimed jubilantly as she opened the door wide, "the Lord bless thee and come in. Didn't you bring your wife?"

"No," I explained, stepping through the door and closing it behind me, "she didn't want to leave the baby with her mother to take care of, and he's a little young to be taking such a long trip in this kind of weather."

Sophie already knew about the baby from an announcement Florence had sent. I followed her up the short flight of steps that led into her apartment, answering her queries about Florence and the baby. In her apartment, I renewed my acquaintance with Sister Kosloski, the frail, stoop-shouldered Polish grandmother who occupied one of the second-floor apartments, and who had been a helper to Sophie in maintaining the Mission. She expressed her delight at seeing me again, less by her limited English vocabulary than by squeezing one of my hands in both of hers, while her eyes shed a bright light of welcome and a smile turned her face into a thousand happy wrinkles.

Then, standing in the kitchen, pungent with the smell of

Sophie's mouth-watering shish kabobs, Sophie called to someone in the living room. A solidly built Spanish-looking man
with bronzed complexion and black hair and a friendly smile
appeared in the doorway that led from the kitchen into the living room.

"Brother Roby," Sophie introduced, "this is Frank Vera."

As I extended my hand to shake his, I could feel without
looking down that where the first finger of his right hand
should have been, there was only a stump of flesh. I suppressed an impulse, springing from morbid curiosity, to look
down at the disfigured hand that I had just grasped.

"Brother Vera just got saved at the Mission two months
ago; isn't that right, Brother Vera?" Sophie announced proudly.

"That's right, Sophie, and I thank the Lord for it. I don't
know where I'd be tonight if it wasn't for the Mission here."

"You can give Brother Roby your testimony later, Frank,"
Sophie cut in. "He's probably hungry, and supper's ready, so
why don't we sit down and eat."

Before supper was finished, there was an interruption
while Sister Kosloski, with a jangle of keys, went out to unlock
the front door of the Mission and turn on the lights for the
meeting scheduled to start at 7:30.

"Aren't we going in for the meeting?" I asked, a little surprised that Sophie made no mention of quickly terminating
our supper.

"I don't think it would do you or Brother Frank here any
good," she laughed. "Everything's in Polish. They sing in
Polish, they pray in Polish, and they preach in Polish. And the
Bible says God is not the author of confusion. Sister Kosloski
can stay for the service. She understands Polish better than
English. You and I and Frank can stay here and have our own
meeting in a language you can both understand."

In the course of the supper-table conversation, I had ventured the question of whether Sophie and Frank might both
like to tell about their conversion experience on a small tape
recorder I had packed in my suitcase especially for that pur-

pose. My plan to stop off in Detroit on the way home had given rise to a guilty compulsion to take back to Florence some concrete evidence of the fact that I had really been in Chicago during the time I was gone. To take such a tape back with me for Florence to hear would also serve as a compensatory surprise gift to make up to her for not having come along on the trip. So after the supper table was cleared away, I set up the tape recorder and we sat around the kitchen table for a private testimony meeting. I sat back and listened as Sophie spoke into the microphone in front of her, details about herself that had not even been divulged during the two years that Florence and I had made regular Sunday afternoon visits there for spirited, spiritual fellowship and good Polish cooking.

Sophie, I learned as I listened, at the age of forty-seven, had come from New York City as a widow, with enough money from her husband's insurance to make a down payment on the brick apartment building which at that time had a small grocery store in the front part. She had planned to finish paying for the property by rental income and her work as a skilled seamstress, working in her own home.

"I was raised a Catholic," she said, getting into the religious climax of her story. "You should have seen my apartment then. I had statues all over the place; Mary, the saints, candles, incense. I'm telling you, it was just like a church except there weren't any pews for people to sit on."

Sophie related how her fervent Catholicism had first been bombarded by a plumber whom she had called to repair a broken water pipe. He had bluntly raised a question as to whether Sophie was not violating the second of the Ten Commandments, which prohibited the making or setting up of images of any kind. Her initial reaction of wrath had prompted her to tell the plumber never to come back again. But complications developed with the repaired water pipe, and the same plumber had to be recalled to finish what he had started, or she would lose a good deal of money. Additional calls by the plumber, who brought additional Scripture references to her, brought conviction and conversion to Sophie; not just conversion from Catholicism to Protestantism, but from religion to Christ. It was after that, and as a result, that the grocery store had been turned into a Mission, giving Sophie an opportunity to convey her discovery to others in the neighborhood. All this had happened ten years before Florence and I had made our first visit there.

Then I turned the tape over to the other side and listened while Frank Vera recorded something of his own life prior to his conversion at the Mission. I was amazed to learn that Frank had been a professional musician, a trumpeter who, at one time, had played with some big-name dance bands—Harry James and Tommy Dorsey, among others. But he had lost the first finger of his right hand in an accident, and it had brought to an end his career as a musician. But he knew nothing else to do for a livelihood. Music had been his life. To forget what he had lost, and the seemingly useless years that lay ahead of him, he had turned to alcohol. And alcohol had robbed him first of his home, then of his wife, then of one menial job after another. And finally, without job or home or money, drunk on the last money he had possessed, he had stumbled into the Mission one night just to get off the street and sit down and rest for a few minutes. Frank's concluding words touched my heart.

"And so I can honestly say that it's a good thing I lost this finger," he said, holding up the truncated hand across the table for emphasis, "because if I hadn't, I might never have turned to the Lord."

I shut off the tape recorder. With the meeting in the Mission over by then, Sister Kosloski returned. Then we gathered in Sophie's living room to read from the Bible and do something that I hadn't done for a long time. I got down on my knees with the others to pray. But even in my praying that made mention of Florence and the baby back in Charlotte, of Sophie and the work of the Mission, and the others kneeling there in the room, there was one matter of deep concern to me that was held back; a name that was on my mind and heart but was not uttered by my lips—Corrine.

A short time later, after a final cup of convivial tea and a piece of Sophie's homemade sponge cake, I went upstairs to occupy a small spare room of Sister Kosloski's apartment. Alone in the darkness, I laid awake for a while, thrilled anew with recalling the wonderful way in which the living God had intervened in the lives of Sophie and Frank. Their testimonies had brought back to my remembrance in a vivid way the times and the places in the past in which God had also worked in my life. It was a brief hour of spiritual splendor when my failures were forgotten, and grief was swallowed up in gladness at the remembered ways in which God had touched my own life and, through me, the lives of at least a few other people. But my final thought before drifting off to sleep was that in two more nights I would be seeing Corrine again; would be looking into her eyes again, hearing her voice again, feeling her head on my shoulder again as we danced the way we had the first night we met.

At seven o'clock the following Friday night, one night closer to seeing Corrine again, I sat in the slowly filling block-long amphitheatre of historic Moody Church on Chicago's near north side. "Ever welcome are the stranger and the poor," read a plaque on the church near the front doors. The meeting at Moody Church was the final, climactic gathering for Founder's Week. During the day there had been messages and workshops, film showings and alumni reunions. In the evening, each day of Founder's Week activities, there was an evening service at the huge church, a fifteen-minute walk from the solid square block of modern, concrete buildings that made up the campus of Moody Bible Institute on the corner of Chicago Avenue and LaSalle Street, near downtown Chicago.

As I sat almost alone in a block of still-vacant seats in the left front section of the church, shadowed by the balcony that stretched back like an elongated horse shoe along the sides and around the back of the vast church, broken fragments of the day I had spent passed through my mind again. I remembered lingering on the sidewalk of LaSalle Street in front of Crowell Hall, by the archway that led into the courtyard-like arena surrounded on all sides by Institute buildings, impressed anew with the uniqueness of this place that had been raised up in the midst of a mighty metropolis where the primary pursuits were business, pleasure, and crime. I remembered feeling as small and insignificant as Moses must have felt in the presence of the burning bush, as I realized that this towering complex of buildings had once been a vacant, weed-covered lot where D. L. Moody had knelt and prayed. His faith had spawned a multimillion-dollar institution that had sent thousands of students out with a message of hope into every corner of the world, and into the streets, the missions, the jails, the hospitals and homes of Chicago as well.

I remembered how I, too, had come to this place, fired with the high resolve to give myself to carrying out "the great commission." But I had run aground, spiritually shipwrecked, even before sailing from port for distant fields of spiritual conquest. And now I had returned, my heart again hungry for the things of God, turned back, through my meeting with Corrine, from a diabolical course leading to disaster. And so I had slipped in and out of the meetings at the Institute during the day, arriving late and leaving early; trying to be as unobtrusive as a secret agent. Wraith-like, I had left the Institute grounds during the dangerous hour of lunch time for a solitary walk by the nearby Oak Street beach. A midwinter thaw in the weather had produced a clear sky and a warm sun that brought a comforting preview of spring. I had walked there, listening and watching, as the white-capped waves of Lake Michigan had broken over the curving shoreline, reliving some of the restful, meditative hours I had spent there as a former student at Moody.

But all the things that had happened in recent weeks since my first meeting with Corrine—the living re-enactment of the Incarnation of Christ unfolded before my eyes in the birth of my own son, the report I had heard the preceding night at Sophie's of what God had done in her life and in Frank Vera's life and the events of the day that lay behind me—all had the effect of preparing my mind and heart for the hour ahead of me, sitting alone at Moody Church on the final night of Founder's Week. For as the farmer breaks up the hard soil before attempting to plant his seed, so does God permit and initiate certain circumstances in the lives of individuals before sending someone to plant the living seed of His Word in their hearts.

And as He had brought things into my life to prepare me for that hour, so, too, He had prepared a man to bring me a personal message from Him. This is frequently God's way, as demonstrated again and again upon the pages of Scripture. Sometimes God speaks directly to a man, by vision or by the written Word. And sometimes He sends a man with a message. He sent the prophet Nathan to relay to David His reaction to David's hitherto hidden sins of adultery and murder. He sent the prophet Samuel with a message of rebuke and warning of impending judgment to King Saul because of Saul's disobedience in failing to destroy a heathen tribe that had plagued Israel. He sent an obscure disciple named Ananias with instructions to be relayed to the blinded Saul of Tarsus, helpless in Damascus where he had gone to bind and persecute Christians. He sent Peter to the Roman centurion, Cornelius, and He sent Philip to the Ethiopian eunuch as he rode home from Jerusalem in his chariot, pondering a Scripture which he could not understand. And for me, that night, He had sent an obedient servant of His all the way from Omaha, Nebraska to deliver a message to me in the city of Chicago.

All that I knew about the man who was to mount the pulpit at Moody Church that night before an audience of five to six thousand people, was what I had read in the program I had been given when I entered. I knew only that his name was R. R. Brown, and that he was the pastor of the Omaha Gospel Tabernacle in Omaha, Nebraska. I supposed only that he had come to Chicago to preach to the great throng of people who would fill Moody Church that evening for the final service of the week. I had no inkling that I was to be singled out for a special message from the living God. Neither did the man from Omaha, for he knew neither my name nor anything of the circumstances of my life. And after the preliminaries, the congregational hymns that were sung, a solo, and several selections by the Moody Chorale, he got up to preach.

He began with a brief but fervent prayer that seemed to break a hole through the vast vaulted roof of the church, opening a skyway straight up to the throne of God, from whence would shortly come pouring down the living words of the living God. Then he announced the portion of Scripture on which he would be preaching.

"I will be speaking this evening from the first chapter of the last book in the Bible, the book of Revelation, verses ten through seventeen."

In the ensuing pause, there was a rustle of turning pages as Bibles were opened by practically everyone in attendance in the great enclosure. It sounded for a moment as if a thousand pigeons had been turned loose in the church and were perched on the balcony railing, ruffling their feathers. In my own Bible, I followed along, as the pastor from Nebraska read aloud.

"I was in the spirit on the Lord's Day, and heard behind me a great voice, as of a trumpet, saying, I am Alpha and Omega, the first and the last; and, What thou seest, write in a book . . ."

The following verses that were read aloud from the pulpit were a word picture of Jesus Christ as He appeared to the apostle John, after His resurrection, while John was an exile of Rome on the island of Patmos, off the coast of Greece. It was not the same Jesus of Nazareth whom John had walked and talked with, his divinity hidden beneath a human form; with a face that could be streaked with sweat; feet that could get dusty and bruised from walking the roads of Judea and Galilee; with flesh that could bleed from thorns and a Roman soldier's scourge, and from nails driven into hands and feet. No, the being whom John saw and described was Jesus Christ in his glorified state, somewhat as he had appeared in the transfiguration that Peter and James and John had witnessed during his earthly sojourn. Now, his hair was seen to be white as snow, his feet like unto fine brass as if they burned in a furnace, his voice as the sound of many waters, and his eyes as a flame of fire. The preacher read the verses describing the Apostle John's reaction to this awesome sight, falling at the feet of Christ as if dead, and concluded with the words of the risen Christ to John.

"Fear not, I am the first and the last. I am he that liveth and was dead, and behold, I am alive forevermore, Amen, and have the keys of Hell and of death."

Then, with the Scripture reading finished, like the rest of the vast assembly, I relaxed in my seat, the Bible open in my lap, expecting only to be comforted and inspired by an exposition of the passage that had just been read aloud.

"The book of Revelation," began the preacher, looking out over the vast throng waiting expectantly before him, "begins with the most marvelous post-resurrection portrait of the Lord Jesus Christ to be found anywhere; it beggars description. I have stayed in its presence by the hour. I think what we need to have brought back to the Church in this hour is a new vision of the Lord Jesus Christ, a consciousness of this glorious Person. I feel we are Romanizing Protestantism, preaching a church-consciousness instead of a Christ-consciousness, and we are majoring in confessing instead of repentance. We need not only to confess with the lips but to surrender with the heart, the things that plague our lives. This is the hour when we need to hear. God is trying to get our attention, but we do not listen. How many of us have heard the voice of God? How many have heard the voice of God with respect to a life of victory and freedom from the enslavement of self and to sin? We need once more, not the imposition of a set of rules, but rather, a revelation of this glorious One who is capable of enabling young and old to live triumphantly, victoriously, joyfully, fruitfully, and creatively as the Son of God."

With that introduction, the preacher went back to the passage of Scripture that he had read, to extract from it a sequence of action verbs what would bear up the remainder of his message. They were the key words that depicted the reactions of the Apostle John upon seeing the glorified Christ ... "I heard ... I turned ... I saw ... I fell at His feet."

As the preacher's message unfolded, it was obvious that his barbed words were aimed primarily at lukewarm, back-slidden, lackadaisical Christians. And I was in that category. The evident aim of his message was to produce in the hearts of his hearers the same kind of reaction to the vision of the glorified Christ that John had exhibited; to fall at the feet of Jesus Christ in contrition, repentance, surrender; to yield the life anew to Him who had bought it by his own blood. Then, in the amazing, supernatural way never understood by worldly reporters who might attend such a meeting to write a news story about it, the one message going forth from the speaker was personalized and custom fitted to the specific needs of a multitude of different individuals in that great congregation.

The speaker did not know my name nor my circumstances nor what it was in my life that was making me less a Christian than I should be. But as he spoke, his words had the effect of making me painfully aware of sin in my life in one particular area. And at the conclusion of the message, when the preacher invited Christians to come forward in an outward show of their inner convictions, people began going forward to the altar from all over the great auditorium; quietly, without noise or hysteria, although here and there was the sound of muffled crying. They came forward from the main floor and the balcony. In that action of walking humbly to the front of the church, before a multitude of witnesses, they were each surrendering something that had been holding them back from being the kind of loving, holy, radiant Christians that they knew they were meant to be. As many different kinds of particular sins were being surrendered and confessed as there were people leaving their seats; grudges held too long, offenses unforgiven, trusts betrayed, obligations shirked, stealing, lying, cheating, slandering, sins of the flesh and of the spirit.

I wanted to move forward, too. But in that moment, as I sat and watched, God impressed it upon my heart that He wanted a different kind of response from me. He wanted from me not a public show of repentance, but a private evidence of it. He wanted me to go not forward in the church, but back to the little Mission where I was to spend the night, to write a letter to Corrine. It was to be a letter in which I would confess the truth that I had kept from her since the first night we had met—that I was married. And I realized in that moment of awareness of what God wanted me to do, that the disclosure would undoubtedly mean the end of my budding relationship to Corrine. To tell her the truth about myself would be the same as telling her goodbye.

I remained sitting quietly, sadly, after the closing congregational hymn was finished; after those who had gone forward had been taken into a counseling room behind the pulpit platform. No one had seen me make a move to go forward. No casual observer could have guessed that I had been affected in any way by the message that had been preached there that evening. But as I left the slowly emptying church that night, my heart warmed and revived as it had not been for many months. I, too, was on my way to an altar known only to God, where, in repentance and brokenness of heart, I could be reconciled to Him from whom I had grown increasingly estranged in the months since I had left Moody in solitary, secretive defeat.

At the Mission that night, I sat alone at a small writing desk in the little room that had been provided for me, a blanket thrown around my shoulders for warmth, groping for the starting place in the letter I had to write to Corrine. Impelling me to write was a love toward Corrine that had been enriched, expanded, and purified by an influx of love from God that poured out through me as a living channel to surround her. It was a love that had its source, not in myself alone, but in Him as well. For in that moment, I was aware that He loved Corrine with a love that was higher, deeper, and more pure, more unchanging, than my own. And so, a love that was both divine and human in origin, like a master symphony conductor, rapped its baton before the lifeless congerie of words stored in my mind, and they began to flow freely from the tip of my pen onto the white sheet of paper on the desk before me, bypassing my thinking, analytical mind, and flowing directly from my heart through my fingers and onto the paper.

I began with the most commonplace of subjects, the weather, but only that I might use it as a physical illustration of a spiritual reality. On the way home from Moody Church, it had begun raining, bringing back to me a vivid recollection of the first night I had met Corrine; the night she had fled from the drugstore where she had promised to wait while I went to get the car.

"Dear Corrine," I began.

The movement of the pen upon the paper, as I spelled out her name, was as if I had caressed her with my hand.

"Heaven is weeping over Chicago tonight," I wrote, "not only literally, but spiritually. Not only is it raining outside like the first night we met, but I cannot help but believe that if there is joy in the presence of the angels of God over one sinner who repents, as Jesus said, then there must be tears shed by the angels over the many who have not repented. At the final meeting of Founder's Week, here in Chicago, I saw evidence that God had touched many hearts, my own included. And if rain, like that which is now falling from heaven, falls from my eyes as I write this letter, it will be because this, my first letter to you, may also be my last."

I had to pause to wipe my eyes, even as Abraham may have done many times on his way to the place where God had commanded him to give up his only and well-beloved son, Isaac, as a human sacrifice. And then the words flowed from my heart, through my fingers as the pen moved, filling page after page, as I tried to pour out something of what Corrine had come to mean to me in the short time I had known her, so briefly, but so deeply. Perhaps I continued writing at such great length because I was trying to postpone the confession that I felt I had to make, and which was the primary reason for writing the letter. But at last, after having stopped several times to wipe tears from my eyes, emotionally spent and spiritually exhausted, I finally wrote the words that I had kept back from Corrine since the first night we met; the words now confessed with sorrow, "alas, I am married." And following this confession, my final words.

"It is finished."

I meant that the long, long, tear-stained letter was finished, but something more also. For I had a feeling as I quoted from Scripture the same words that Jesus had spoken from the cross before He died, that God was now applying these same words to our relationship. "It is finished." Yet, in spite of the Spirit-impressed feeling of finality with which I had written the closing words of the letter, I still felt a heavy-hearted compulsion to follow through on my original plan—to stop off in Detroit on my way home to Lansing. The document I had written meant too much to me, and it would probably mean too much to Corrine, to entrust to the U. S. mail. I had to deliver it to Corrine in person, in what I was certain would be a final, face-to-face encounter with her.

As I left Chicago on Saturday afternoon, to drive the nearly three hundred miles to Detroit before going back home to Charlotte, I felt inwardly cleansed, purged. I was on a mission to terminate by telling the truth something God had impressed me to end. But when I arrived in Detroit, about eight o'clock that night, I was weary from the long drive. And within me was a growing reluctance to give to Corrine the lengthy letter I had written into the early hours of that morning in Chicago, words that I was certain would sever our relationship, finally and completely.

At the Hollywood, by ten o'clock, I bought tickets, went in, and checked my coat. Corrine was there, overjoyed to see me again.

"Welcome back, darling," she smiled, and took my hand happily as we walked onto the dance floor.

But after a few superficial remarks about having had a pleasant trip from Chicago, I fell into a brooding silence. I was thinking, as I held Corrine close and moved with her while the music melted us into a unity, that this would be the last time I would see her; the last time I would hear her voice, look into her eyes, hold her in my arms. The very prospect paralyzed my ability to think, to speak. It caused me to attempt to hide with a veneer of empty words the heavy-hearted task that God had laid upon me in Chicago. I had planned to give Corrine the letter in my inside coat pocket on the dance floor and then leave immediately. Now, when the moment I had planned for had arrived, I found that I couldn't make the move required to carry out the plan.

"Why so quiet, Garfield?" Corrine finally asked, as we circled the dance floor, maneuvering around other couples.

The words of reply that came to my mind almost instantly were doubtless prompted by the Spirit of God.

"The Lord may not give me permission to see you again." But I didn't speak the words aloud. I couldn't.

"I'll tell you later," I answered soberly, avoiding her gaze.

"Can you wait until two and take me home?" she asked.

Concern was etched on her face as to what it was that I was keeping back from her. Her suggestion gave me a chance to postpone the delivery of the written message I had been appointed to give to her, and I seized it, like a drowning seaman clinging to a piece of wreckage to prolong his life a little longer.

"Yes. I'll come back for you at two."

After finishing the last dance for the amount of tickets I had bought, we left the floor hand in hand, something that the other girls who worked there had probably never seen her do with a customer. She walked beside me to the coat-check room.

"You aren't leaving now, are you?" I asked in surprise as Corrine stepped past the coat-check counter as if to get her own coat.

"No," she smiled mysteriously, "I've just got something I want to give you before I forget it."

While Corrine stepped back to the rear of the coat room, the hat-check girl got my coat and handed it to me. When Corrine rejoined me a moment later, I had my coat on, ready to leave. In her hand she carried a manila envelope. Then she drew me gently by the sleeve away from the coat-check counter to the semi-privacy of the foyer just inside the double swinging doors that led out to the stairway exit.

"Here's a little surprise I made for you," she said, holding the envelope out to me. "I was going to give it to you for Christmas, but you didn't show up so I saved it for you."

It would have been the opportune moment to reach into my inside coat pocket and extract the bulky letter and hand it to her and then flee, but I didn't.

"It isn't a Christmas present exactly," she said as I took the envelope from her hand, "but I thought you'd like it."

Without a hint as to what was inside, I knew it would be of inestimable value to me just because it would express something of Corrine and her feeling for me.

"Thank you," I said.

I was unable to look into her eyes at length, overwhelmed with the thought that this was the last time I would be doing so.

I turned away from her then, leaving her standing there watching after me, hurried past the cashier's cage, through the swinging double doors, swiftly down the red-carpeted flight of steps and out onto the cold, sparsely peopled sidewalk. A short time later, in a little all-night restaurant on Woodward, near the City-County building, I sat at the long lunch counter having coffee and toast. As I sat there, I pulled from my pocket the oversized manila envelope that Corrine had given me and opened it. I pulled out a sheet of paper that was folded over to hide and protect what was inside.

It was breathtakingly beautiful, five inches across, so intricately cut in a web of delicate, connecting links, forming a precise geometrical design, that I sat there marveling that human hands could create such beauty with such simple raw materials. It was a giant, religiously realistic replica of a snowflake. I thought, as I gazed at it admiringly, that it must surely equal the beauty of enlarged photographs of actual snowflakes that I had seen in books. And it spoke to me at once, not only of the God who was the originator of snowflakes, millions falling to the ground, and each one different; it spoke so eloquently also of the sensitivity to beauty of the woman who had made it.

I looked at it wonderingly for a long, long moment, then reverently placed it back into its protective sheet of folded paper and, after replacing it in the manila envelope, slipped it back into the side pocket of my suit coat.

And at two o'clock in the morning, I returned to the Hollywood Ballroom to pick up Corrine, who was still "Colette" to the management and clientele and other girls who worked at the Hollywood. It was a few minutes later that I pulled over to the curb in front of the Cromwell Apartments on Second Street, near the Masonic auditorium where Corrine had once sung before a great crowd of people. Leaving the engine idling, I reached into my inside coat pocket and pulled out the letter that I should have given her on the dance floor. The delay in doing what I was supposed to do had only increased my physical weariness and weakened my resolution to do what God had impressed upon my heart to do in Chicago the night before.

"My, what a long letter," Corrine exclaimed, as she took the bulky, sealed envelope.

Then came an unexpected complication.

"Garfield, would you read it to me?" she asked in a pleading tone.

I found myself unable to refuse her request. I took it back from her hand and opened the sealed flap. My own handwriting was large enough so that I needed no glasses to read aloud what I had written, in the illumination from the street light that spilled into the front seat of the car. With the engine idling and heater turned on low, I began to read the letter to Corrine, pausing at intervals where tears had come to my eyes, to prevent the same thing from happening again in Corrine's presence. And finally, I came to the final words of the last page of the letter, containing the bitter truth that I had hidden from Corrine since the first night we met.

"Alas, I am married. It is finished."

I handed the letter back to Corrine, waiting for her response to my dismal disclosure.

"I thought you might be married," she said, in a tone of subdued sadness.

I looked at her, startled. She was looking ahead down the empty street, perhaps reluctant to look into the eyes of a man who had held back this essential truth from her.

"What made you think so?" I was shocked that she had even entertained such a suspicion and yet had said nothing about it to me.

"Because when I asked you when you'd be coming back, you were so uncertain," she answered, still looking straight ahead, "and you didn't offer any explanation as to why you couldn't tell me when you'd be coming back. I've danced with a lot of men since I've been working at the Hollywood, Garfield. I can usually tell when a man is married and is trying to hide it."

I sat slumped forward with my arms circling the steering wheel for support. I stared ahead down the street at the traffic light, which kept changing although there was no traffic, abashed by the knowledge that she had suspected my subterfuge but had said nothing about it.

"But I've got a confession to make to you, too, Garfield."

I turned to look at her and her eyes met mine as she spoke.

"I'm married, too."

I stared at her in astonished speechlessness. She must have sensed the sudden questions that began to race through my mind at this unexpected revelation. Why did she have the job she did, dancing with strange men every night, if she was married? Why had she invited me into her apartment, running the risk of encountering an outraged husband? And where was her husband, and what kind of man was he? Her answer came without my having to give utterance to the questions that had exploded in my mind.

"We're separated. My husband lives just across the Detroit River, in Canada."

My first reaction, after the initial shock subsided, was one

408

of comfort, knowing that we were both in the same boat, both married but evidently unhappily married. The realization sparked a sudden surge of hope within me that was at complete variance with the purpose of the letter I had just read to her, and its closing words of Spirit-impressed finality: "It is finished."

Perhaps, I hopefully speculated, since we were both married, Corrine would have no objection to our continuing to see each other. Perhaps such a relationship would not seem as morally objectionable to her as it might have been if she were single and I were married. Yes, these thoughts leaped through my mind, in spite of the fact that God had impressed it upon my heart in Chicago that my relationship to Corrine was to be terminated. But my eagerness to betray the task God had given me to do was dashed to pieces by Corrine's next words, carefully and deliberately voiced.

"Since we're both married, Garfield, and I want to do what's right, I think we had better not see each other any more."

I was suddenly humiliated. The task that God had given me to do, since I had been so reluctant in carrying it out, had been given to another—to Corrine. It was she to whom it was given to speak the words that were to bring our short but wonderful relationship to an end.

"Would you like to come in and rest a while before you drive home?" she asked quietly.

Since we must part, according to the Spirit-impressed decree of God, and Corrine's expressed will as well, to delay would only prolong and intensify the agony. Better a quick severance, if it must be, than a lingering, tearing farewell.

"No, thank you, Corrine," I said, savoring her name as I spoke it for the last time, "I think I'd better get going."

I got out of the car and walked slowly around to the other side to open the door for her. Then I walked beside her silently toward the apartment building entrance, her high heels staccato sharp on the silent street. I walked up the short flight of steps beside her and, on the top step, we turned to face each other. I took one of her gloved hands in mine while, with the other hand, she clutched the thick white envelope containing the letter I had written. I looked into her eyes for the last time, then bent my head down to place a gentle and chaste kiss upon her lips. She did not turn her face away, perhaps as certain as I that this, our first kiss was also to be our last one.

"Goodbye, Corrine," I said, and gave her hand a final squeeze.

Then I turned and walked down the steps as her answering "goodbye" trailed after me. I heard the front door of the apartment building open and close as I got into the car. And before I drove away, I looked up to see her standing inside the glass door, the curtain pulled back, her face pinched and sad in the light from the street lamp. She waved as I started to pull away from the curb. I returned her wave and drove empty-hearted down an empty street.

As I drove north on Grand River, out of Detroit, I could hardly convince myself that a relationship between a man and a woman that had brought so much warmth and happiness in so short a time should end so abruptly, with such finality, leaving me with no tangible evidence of its birth and brief blossoming, except an exquisite but lifeless paper snowflake hidden in my pocket. And as I left Detroit behind, the miles that lay ahead of me before I would reach Charlotte seemed longer and lonelier than they had ever seemed before.

In Chicago, there had been a blending of joy in the bitter wine of renunciation that I had drunk from a cup of God's making as I had sat late into the night writing the letter that I knew would mean saying goodbye to Corrine. It was an unavoidable part of being a Christian. "If any man will come after me," Jesus had said, "let him deny himself, and take up his cross daily, and follow me." But now, driving homeward alone, I tasted only the bitter sense of loss in this life-giving relationship that had been ended. Like the children of Israel, after their deliverance from the land of Egypt by the hand of Moses, I wanted to turn back. But I could not. It was Corrine, as well as God, who had decided that we should not meet again.

A cold, grey February dawn was lightening the landscape when I finally pulled into the gravel drive of the Berlincourt farm. The huge farmhouse loomed dark and silent. Everyone was still asleep. With the headlights and engine turned off, I remained sitting behind the steering wheel, too physically weary and emotionally spent to get out of the car. I had left the farm on a Thursday morning and now it was Sunday morning. How much had happened in those three days! I had left with a hidden song in my heart, looking forward to seeing Corrine again. I had returned, crushed in spirit by the certainty that I would and should never see her again. I had started out for Chicago and Founder's Week with spiritual hunger and a hope of being strengthened for the role of a father that had fallen heavily upon me. I had returned with a single act of obedience to God to my credit; the writing of the farewell letter to Corrine. But it had left me deprived of the new source of joy and revived spiritual concern that Corrine's influence had evoked within me.

It occurred to me as I sat there, dumbly immobilized by the sequence of recent events, that had I been able to foresee the outcome of my return visit to my spiritual alma mater, Moody Bible Institute, I probably would not have had the courage to go. With these melancholy thoughts weighing me down, I pushed my way wearily up the frozen, rutted incline that led to the farmhouse.

I made my way quietly through the empty, darkened living room and kitchen to the back bedroom. To Florence, who had been alerted to my arrival by the sound of the car, I whispered my intention of going upstairs to our former bedroom where I could sleep undisturbed by the baby's crying and by the preparations of Florence's mother getting up to go to church.

"I'm glad you got home safely," she whispered, so as not to awaken the baby. "You probably won't feel like going to church, will you?"

"Probably not," I answered, but for reasons totally unknown to Florence.

I removed my shoes and padded from the bedroom and up the stairs to the second-floor bedroom. Then I slept, except for several fits of momentary wakefulness, until two in the afternoon. Lying awake, as my eyes wandered aimlessly over the interior of the large bedroom, I saw the coat that I had taken off and draped carelessly over the back of a chair. Sticking up conspicuously out of a side pocket was the manila envelope containing the paper snowflake Corrine had given to me. Quickly, I got out of bed, fearful that Florence might come upstairs at any moment, retrieved the incriminating envelope and buried it hastily under a box of books in the corner of the room. As I returned to bed, relieved that the telltale envelope was safely hidden, I was suddenly aware that it was a good thing I had not slept downstairs with Florence and the baby. Florence, getting up to feed the baby, or to have breakfast with her mother, would surely have seen the envelope and, with natural curiosity, would have asked me about it.

As I lay in bed, still weary in spite of my long sleep, It occurred to me that the paper snowflake was a dangerous souvenir to have in the house. But it was too precious a memento of Corrine to throw away or destroy. It was all that I had that could still speak to me of her in a visible, tangible, touchable way. Would she, I wondered, equally cherish the long letter I had left with her, telling all that she had come to mean to me in the short time I had known her? And I wondered about the LP album of Christmas music that I had mailed to her for a combination Christmas and birthday gift before going to Chicago. She had said nothing about receiving it and, preoccupied with the sad certainty that it was to be our last encounter, it had not entered my mind to ask about it. Perhaps, I speculated, it had gotten lost in the mail; another intervention of God to rebuke a relationship that had been conceived in the soil of deception.

During the passage of a long, lonely weekend, I decided upon the only safe place to keep the precious and beautiful snowflake souvenir of the unforgettable few hours I had shared with Corrine. I took it to work with me the following Monday, hidden away in my brief case. At work, I attached it carefully with Scotch tape to the window by my desk. I deliberately placed it below the level of my desk, where it could not be seen by others, to arouse questions or comments about it, but where it was easily visible to me as I sat at my desk. I did not dream, during the days of that first week that God had put Corrine out of my life, with her concurrence, that the solitary paper snowflake, which was my only legacy of having known her, was to be swelled by other, even more priceless tokens, to be delivered to the very door of the Berlincourt farm.

It was on Thursday night of that first week after I had said goodbye to Corrine, that I arrived home from work and stepped through the door to the usual smells and sights. Hilda was in the kitchen putting the final touches on supper. Florence was sitting in the rocking chair in the dining room, holding the bottle that Paul was sucking. Draping my topcoat over the nearest chair, I stepped over beside Florence to look down at the sight of my son, Paul Roby, now four weeks old. Enfolded in a warm blanket, gently rocked back and forth, the warm milk assuaging his hunger, his eyes were starting to close in sleep.

"Isn't he sweet?" Florence murmured, looking not at me but down at the small bundle of life for which she had gone through the valley of pain. "He'll be asleep in another minute."

"If he's sweet, it's only because some of your sweetness has rubbed off on him," I said, aware that Florence needed and was deserving of some expressions of praise for what she had been through in bringing Paul into the world.

Unimpressed by my compliment, perhaps guessing that it was superficial, Florence suddenly remembered something that seemed of greater importance at the moment.

"Oh, Gar, there's a package came in the mail for you today. It's from Sophie. It's on the table in the front room"

Curious as to what Sophie could have mailed to me from

Chicago, in a package, the week after my fateful overnight stay at her Mission, I walked into the front room and saw it lying on an end table by the window. I picked up the flat, rectangular package, wrapped none too neatly in brown wrapping paper and tied with string. With my back to Florence, I opened the package. As the folds of the paper were pulled back, and I saw what was inside, I remembered the soiled shirt I had absent mindedly left behind at Sophie's during my two-night stay there for Founder's Week. But as I pulled the paper wrapping back further, I could see that the shirt was no longer dirty and wrinkled. Sophie had washed and ironed it, and had even starched the collar.

But then, pulling the paper away from the collar, I saw something else that caused my heart to almost stop beating. Tucked inside the shirt was a bulky letter addressed to me at the Mission in unfamiliar handwriting. But in the upper left-hand corner, the name of the sender crackled through my mind like a thunderclap of impending doom . . . Corrine! As I stared at the name, frozen into the immobility of fear, I was smitten by the sudden certainty that God had chosen the living room of the Berlincourt farm to expose the deception I had practiced upon Florence since before the baby was born. Panic stricken, I glanced over my shoulder to see if Florence was looking at me; if the damning evidence had already been seen. Her eyes were fixed intently on the baby in her arms. Quickly, desperately, with my back still turned toward her, I snatched the letter out of the starch-stiffened circle of the shirt collar and thrust it into my inside coat pocket.

"What's in the package?" Florence asked.

As I turned to face her, the incriminating letter safely hidden away in my coat pocket, she looked up at me.

"I left a dirty shirt behind when I was there for Founder's Week," I said, holding it up for her inspection, trembling inwardly at how close Florence had come to finding out about something that no longer mattered because it was finished.

"Wasn't she sweet to wash and iron it?" Florence exclaimed. "She's a real jewel."

"Yes," I agreed, passing in front of her, the baby asleep in her lap, "she's a real jewel. I'll take the shirt upstairs and keep it for a special occasion."

As I opened the door to the enclosed stairway that led to the second-floor bedroom, Hilda's voice came from the kitchen.

"Supper will be ready in about ten minutes, Garfield, so don't stay up there too long."

"I won't," I promised, closing the door behind me.

Upstairs, with the bedroom door closed behind me, I set the shirt down on a dresser and lifted my eyes Heavenward, convinced that God must have had a hand in this unexpected and mysterious development. I walked over to a window and pulled the dangerous letter out of my inside coat pocket. When I had mentioned, in the birthday card to Corrine, the address of the Mission where I would be staying in Chicago for two nights, it had never entered my mind that she might send a letter to that address, especially since she knew I would be seeing her in person at the end of that week. I looked at the postmark to see when it had been mailed. It had been mailed in Detroit on February 3rd, the day before I had left for Chicago. Four days later, when I had left Chicago, the letter Corrine had sent to me had still not arrived at the Mission.

I sat down on the edge of the bed by the window, trying to understand what Providential circumstances had been juggled by the intervening hand of God. Had the mail been held up between Detroit and Chicago? What had Sophie thought when she had received a letter addressed to me from a woman whose name did not have the prefix of "Mrs." on the return address? And what if I had not left a soiled shirt behind at the mission, in which Sophie could forward Corrine's letter to me in a concealing and innocent-looking cloak so as not to arouse Florence's suspicions and questions.

As I examined the letter, looking for clues, trying to imagine what Sophie must have thought when she found it in her mailbox after I had left, I noticed one detail for which I was thankful. On the back side of the envelope, Corrine had thought of a final postscript to add after she had evidently sealed the letter before mailing it. On the flap was evidence that she had received the Christmas-birthday present I had mailed to her before setting out for Chicago.

"How I thank God," she had written on the back side of the envelope, "for the gift of my new LP album of beautiful Christmas music."

The message was followed by a Scripture reference, Philippians 1:3. With the letter still unopened in my hand, I got up quickly and stepped to the dresser to open the Bible that was there to look up the reference. It was a touching message, coming to me from Corrine by way of the pages of God's Word.

"I thank my God upon every remembrance of you."

Still holding the letter in my hand, I walked back to the window to stand looking upward into the sky through the winter-stripped branches of the giant oak three that grew beside the house. I did not have to open the letter and read the contents to discern a reason as to why God might have prevented it from being delivered to me while I was in Chicago. It might well have affected me to the point of either not writing, or not delivering the letter that I had written to Corrine from there, under the impress of the Spirit of God. For even at that very moment, just the brief, touching message I had read on the outside flap of the envelope had created within me an impulse to respond by flying back to Corrine as soon as I could.

And perhaps, I reflected, Sophie's heart had been touched, as had mine, by the poignant message on the back side of the envelope. Perhaps Sophie had concluded, on the basis of these words and the Scripture verse following them, that this must have been a Christian friendship, above reproach or suspicion, and that it was none of her business to speculate or entertain suspicions about it. Perhaps the injunction of Scripture that a Christian was to be "wise as a serpent and harmless as a dove" had prompted Sophie to send the letter tucked inside the shirt, trusting the Lord to handle it from there.

Then, sitting down again on the bed in the presence of this

mystery, another question beset my mind and held me back from opening it. What had restrained Florence from opening the package? She knew Sophie as well as I did. Why hadn't curiosity impelled her to open the package and find the letter inside? But finally, in the wake of the troubled questions that had flooded through my mind, hunger for the contents of the first and last letter I might ever receive from Corrine pushed aside the unanswered questions that had overwhelmed me.

I carefully tore off one end of the long, white business envelope and pulled out three handwritten pages. I laid the envelope on the bed beside me and opened the folded pages reverently. And there, looking up at me from a brilliant color photograph, was Corrine. It was a Corrine I had not yet seen, in the bright afternoon sunlight of spring or summer, standing before the white, ornately engraved door of an obviously wealthy home, perhaps part of her hidden past. She was dressed in a billowing flare of blue ruffles and high-heeled slippers. Her blonde hair curled and waved in a golden glory of lights and shadows. "Blue Angel" was the descriptive title that leaped into my mind as I drank in the beauty of face and form before me.

Then I looked away from her photograph, feeling the pain of knowing that I could not yield to the magnetic pull which her likeness, smiling up at me from the photograph, exerted. Having this photo of her in my possession would not make it easier to hold to the purpose which God had impressed upon my heart in Chicago. Sadly, I placed the snapshot of Corrine on the envelope beside me to read the letter. Would they contain words that would only bring more pain, knowing that I could no longer respond to them; knowing that Corrine's words and likeness had come to me as if from someone already in the grave, placed out of my reach by God as surely as if dead?

Suddenly, at the sound of the downstairs stairway door being opened, I jumped up from the edge of the bed, lifting up the mattress and throwing all the pieces of incriminating evidence under it, and let it flop back down in place.

"Garfield!" I heard Hilda call up the stairway, "supper's on the table."

"Be right down," I called.

I stood by the bed until I heard the downstairs door close, then lifted the mattress and retrieved the scattered and priceless items I had hastily thrown there. I took one last, long look at the photograph of Corrine, then, slipping it back into the envelope along with the unread pages of her letter, I hid the envelope in the bottom of the same box of books where I had hidden the paper snowflake a week before.

With the explosive evidence hidden, I lingered a moment longer before the window, trying to fathom the mystery. I couldn't shake off the conviction that God had shaped this development, and it was not difficult to decide whose benefit had been uppermost in His plans. He, the holy One of Israel, was surely not one to become a collaborator in protecting me from the deserved exposure of the sinful sequence of actions in recent months that had eventually led to my meeting with Corrine. It must have been, I was forced to admit, to protect Florence, the innocent one, from the cruel discovery, even if belatedly, of her husband's attachment to another woman. For even though that attachment had now been brought to an end, the discovery that it had even existed for several months during her pregnancy could have had a shattering effect upon Florence. It could even have communicated to our infant son some harmful repercussions relayed through her.

I concluded that if God had intervened at this time, in this unusual way, it must have been primarily out of concern for Florence and our infant son, rather than to spare me the deserved pain of exposure. And yet, I could not at the same time believe that God was completely ignoring me and the deep, hidden need that had drawn me into this secretive situation. I believed that there must still be some measure of mercy in His heart for me also, disobedient child though I was. Perhaps, I mused, standing by the window, the mysterious chain of circumstances that had brought Corrine's letter to me, even passing through Florence's hands without her knowing it, was a reward that He had engineered as a result of my feeble act of obedience in writing the letter to Corrine containing the truth that had resulted in terminating my relationship with her.

My obedience had been reluctant and incomplete; but perhaps it had not been overlooked or despised by Him who took note of the fall of a sparrow, and who knew the number of hairs upon the head of each of His children. But whatever God's purpose had been in the strange chain of events, I was thankful that the marital mischief in my life had been kept hidden from Florence. I dropped to my knees by the side of the bed.

"Thank you, Father," I breathed aloud, looking Heavenward.

Then I got to my feet quickly and hurried downstairs to the supper that was waiting.

The following day, hidden in an inside coat pocket, I took to work the letter from Corrine, saving it to read at the office where I could do so without fear of discovery. Alone at my desk during lunch hour that day, I read the words that Corrine had written. They were an echo of my own in the long letter I had written to her in Chicago. She had found in me something that had touched her as deeply as she had touched me. Then, I hid the priceless letter in a bottom drawer of my desk and, donning overcoat and hat, went for a walk on the winter-chilled downtown sidewalks, to be alone with the thoughts that Corrine's letter and her photo had aroused.

In the days that followed, my lunch hour at work became a special time of day; a time spent in gazing at the bewitching loveliness of the one whom God had placed out of reach for me; of reading again the words of the first and last letter she would ever write to me. Enraptured by the smiling face that I would see no more in the flesh, captivated by the words of her letter that I read and reread, my heart touched anew each time I looked at the paper snowflake on the window by my desk, I responded to Corrine in the only way that was open to me. I poured out my response to her in words committed to paper;

words that she would never see, yet words that were drawn out of me as the sea water is pulled upward to form clouds by the sun.

They were the kind of words that I had not written in years. For the touch of Corrine seemed to have resurrected a part of me that I thought had been left forever behind with the long-ago years of my impulsive and idealistic youth. It was a part of me that responded to her in the language of the aspiring poet. The words that I began to write were formed as an oyster spins a pearl, out of its own living secretions, as the inmost part of my being reached out to Corrine in thought and desire and cherished memory.

> I saw a strange, new star one night;
> Its burning beauty, clear and bright,
> Engulfed my soul in fire.
> "You're mine," I whispered Heavenward,
> And reached for it, but Heaven heard,
> And drew it ever higher.
>
> Now, beyond my reach it shines,
> Though still within my view;
> And that sky-jewel that cannot be mine,
> That star I lost, was you.

I soon discovered that the hardest part of the day was quitting time. For when I got home, shut up to an indoor existence in the winter cold, I was not able to sit down in privacy and continue pouring out in a flow of words what I had found so briefly in Corrine. But just as a surging river that may be damned up by natural or man-made barriers may sometimes carve a new channel to continue its progress, so I was impelled to take up at home a kind of research that was a safer way of continuing to reach out to Corrine in thought and feeling and written word. From forgotten notebooks that had been long stored in cardboard boxes and carried from place to place in the moves I had made before meeting and marrying Florence, I turned to words that I had written more than a decade before; words akin to those that Corrine had called forth from deep within me, and expressed only after we had parted. They were words that had been called into existence by a girl whom I had kissed goodbye at a train station in Lansing, to embark upon military service in the closing days of World War II.

When I had left her, she had worn a diamond engagement ring upon her finger, a dream of happiness that had turned to dust at the touch of the war that engulfed us. I recalled the letter I had written to her from Camp Hale, Colorado, after months of anguish and soul searching, in which I disclosed that I had laid down my arms as a conscientious objector, and had been court martialed and sentenced to a dishonorable discharge and five years' imprisonment. Her response to my announcement had been quick and cutting. I could still remember the essence and almost the exact words of her outraged reaction. They coursed through my mind with some of the same searing contempt and condemnation that I had felt years before when I had first read them.

"Now that I know you're the kind of man who wouldn't fight to keep the Japs from coming over here and raping me, your mother and sister, I never want to see you again. I couldn't possibly love such a man. If you want your engagement ring back, you can come and get it. You'll find it at the bottom of the Grand River, where I threw it when I got your letter. Goodbye, and good riddance."

At that moment, looking back from a perspective of fifteen years' distance, I could see one effect of her violent rupture of our engagement that had been hidden from me at the time. That part of my nature that she had awakened, and had responded to in the language of a poet to a woman's touch, had ceased to speak within me. Yet, as I turned the pages and read the poems that had been written years before and totally forgotten, they did not bring back to my mind some dimly remembered face or scene from the distant past; they brought before my mind the face, the form, the voice, the name, of Corrine.

Hidden from the inquisitive eyes
Of men, a strange world mysteriously exists;
Except for you, no mortal eyes
Have pierced its impenetrable mists.

For it lies deep within my heart
Where eternal fogs protectingly surround it;
I thought it safe from the probing eyes
Of humans, yet, how easily you found it . . .

As I read the long-forgotten words, life seemed to begin flowing through them. For they seemed suddenly to convey as perfect an expression as I could wish for the feelings, the desires, that were alive in my heart for Corrine. Then it came to me, with the force of a revelation, as if from God, that these words had been written, kept through the intervening years, to enable me to say to her, not to any other before her, all that she had come to mean to me.

At that moment of insightful realization, sitting alone on the front room sofa with the notebook of poems on my lap, because these words now represented something within me that was alive, precious, vital and beautiful, they became living words. After all the years of lying in literary limbo, I now saw a new beauty in the words; not simply because I had written them long ago, but because they seemed to capture something of the beauty of my embryonic relationship to Corrine, even though it had been terminated. And there abruptly emerged within me a spontaneous desire, probably one that is universally felt whenever a mortal stumbles upon something exceedingly beautiful, whether a sunset, a song, a sonnet, a bird, or a flower; the impulse to shout out to the world, "Come and see what I have found!" And I thought it sad, in that moment, that the beauty that I had found in my brief knowing of Corrine, and as it seemed wonderfully expressed in the words I had written long ago, could not in some way be shared with the world.

It was not because the words I had written could lay claim

to literary excellence. They would never rank with the odes and sonnets of Shelley or Shakespeare or Poe, for they were rather ordinary words. Their chief value lay in the extraordinary reality to which they pointed so graphically. For it was not the words, in themselves, that struck me as being so praiseworthy; it was what I had found in Corrine that was so wonderful. That was what I wanted to shout to the world, and what if the words of that shout were only common words? The world, I reflected, had not been electrified by the eloquence or literary brilliance of the man who had discovered gold in California in the early history of America. His words may have been crude and unpolished, but they succeeded in drawing attention to the fact that he had discovered gold! This was the important thing.

And I had discovered gold of a different sort; a kind that the world needed more desperately, perhaps, than the glittering, metallic kind; the gold of true love between a man and a woman. The world should know that if one man and one woman could find such love, then others could also. And why not? I speculated. Why could not these words, that seemed to describe so vividly what I had found in Corrine, be woven onto an LP record album, with music backgrounds and sound effects, to be sent out into the world; bringing hope or inspiration or blessing to any who would listen, and learn that the love between a man and a woman could be a thing of such exquisite beauty?

With the notebook of poems lying open on my lap, forgotten for the moment, while the sounds of conversation between Florence and her mother came from the kitchen, I sat entranced by a vision of creating something of beauty that would go out into the highways and byways of life as a living demonstration of a love between one man and one woman that was a thing of surpassing beauty. Spellbound by the possibilities for good in such a venture, I was carried away on a tide of emotion to the conclusion that surely God would sanction the help of Corrine in carrying out such an idealistic venture. There could surely be nothing sinful about laboring together to create something beautiful that could be an inspiration and a blessing to others.

I went to bed that night with the glowing vision of building with Corrine something of beauty that would bless the world. It filled me with an excited anticipation of achievement that seemed to render me invulnerable to the interludes of irritation I had previously felt at being awakened at midnight and at four in the morning by the baby's cry for a bottle and a change of diapers. And at work the next day, during lunch hour, seated at my desk, where occasional glances at the paper snowflake on the window nearby could inspire me, I wrote a letter to Corrine. The impression that God had laid upon my heart in Chicago three weeks before, that the long, tear-stained letter I had written to Corrine was to be my last and final communication with her, was pushed from my memory by the emotionally clouded rationalization that surely God would approve a continued relationship, not as incipient lovers, but as co-creators of something beautiful that might bring a blessing to multitudes, and would acknowledge Him as its source.

Dear Corrine, I wrote.

Three weeks ago when I brought to you a letter written in Chicago, telling you that I was married, you expressed the judgment that we should not see each other again. But since that time I have not been able to convince myself that our meeting was accidental. I believe that it was somehow arranged by God to further His purpose in either your life, or mine, or perhaps in both of our lives. Is it possible that having met and come to know each other for such a little time, it is necessary to say goodbye, when I still see a wonderful possibility that we might be of mutual joy and blessing to one another? At least, I am certain that you can be that to me.

Perhaps the key to our having been brought together is to be found in something that came to me just last night. It is this. Although in coming to know you, Corrine, I have been stirred by a desire to write, as I had not been for nearly seventeen years, I had written a number of poems before that time and kept them.

Last night, as I was reading over some of those words written so long ago, they seemed to come alive, because of you, and glow with a beauty they never had before. And a possibility occurred to me of putting those poems on a record with fitting musical backgrounds and sound effects. You could, without doubt, be of great help in bringing this lately born desire of my heart to completion. It would be a matter of working together to create something of beauty that might bring comfort, gladness, and hope to many lonely hearts. And if successful on the record market, it would bring a share of the monetary rewards to you.

I am somewhat familiar with the ways of weaving music and sound effects into a dramatic presentation, and believe that, with your help, something of real beauty and benefit to others could be produced. Perhaps as much as technical assistance, you could provide a more needed element, the inspiration to push the project through to completion. I doubt if I could or would do it alone. I am quite certain that without your help, Corrine, these poems shall be put back into the mausoleum of forgetfulness where they had lain for so long, until my meeting with you caused me once again to bring them forth. For it was my meeting with you that brought back to life the man who wrote them. The love that brought these words to birth was rekindled in my heart again through you.

I have not forgotten that we both are married, Corrine; that we both have bound ourselves by the laws which God has given us in regard to marriage. And yet, I believe, that without breaking the laws of either God or man, we can be co-workers together in this venture to produce and bring to broken, lonely hearts something of beauty that will bring blessing and hope and understanding to those upon whose ears and hearts these words and music may one day fall.

Eternally yours, in Him,
Garfield.

At the close of the letter, I gave my address in the Highway Department as one to which Corrine could write in reply to my proposal. Her reply was relayed to me in the middle of the following week, along with a frown and a word of rebuke from the office manager.

"Gar, we'd rather not have employees get personal mail at the office. That's a policy that applies to everybody."

I took the long business envelope from his hand, bearing the now-familiar scrawl, embellished with artistic flourishes across the front. The joy at hearing from Corrine canceled out the irritation I had felt at the scolding I had gotten about receiving personal mail. But as the office manager walked away, a feeling of indignation erupted within me as I discovered that the letter, although addressed to me by name, had been opened. Had someone read it, I wondered, far enough to see that it was not official Highway business, or, perhaps further, out of curiosity? My momentary anger at this seeming invasion of my privacy, even though by a state employee, was washed away by the opening words of Corrine's letter.

Dear Garfield. I was very glad to hear from you, and will be happy to be of any help that I can in the project you described.

Later that afternoon, alone in the cafeteria for coffee break, I reread her letter again with growing wonder, happily amazed that my letter had changed Corrine's mind about continuing to see each other. Pondering this reversal of her decision, I did not think she had changed her mind simply because she was the kind of person who could be easily persuaded to abandon moral scruples that were derived from deeply rooted religious convictions. Neither could I attribute her change of mind to any mesmeric powers of persuasion on my part. I suspected that she had changed her mind primarily because there must be within her something of the same hunger that was in my own heart; the hunger, the yearning, the need, to love and be loved; a hunger which I innocently believed could be satisfied with a purely spiritual and Platonic relationship. "In the Lord."

But to carry out this creative venture in which I had sought and secured Corrine's promise of assistance, I would have to devise a legitimate appearing reason for being gone from home long enough for periodic trips to Detroit and back.